The Guardian of Threshold

A NOVEL BY A.A. VOLTS

WAVE PUBLISHING COMPANY
KISSIMMEE, FL, 34759

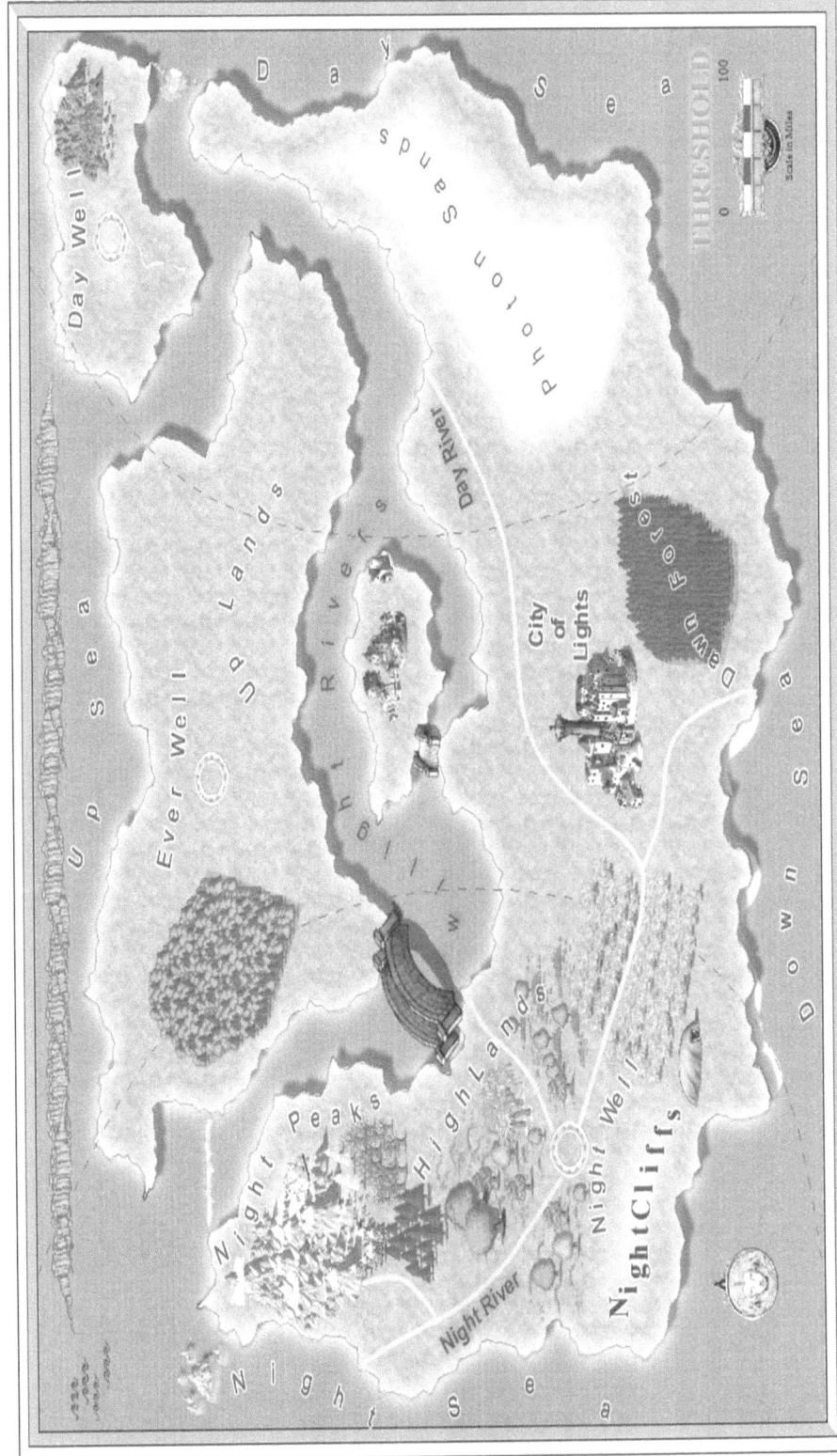

COPYRIGHT

Published by

Wave Publishing Company

For Information, contact: Books@AAVolts.com

Author Blog: www.AAVolts.com
Facebook.com/TheGuardianOfThreshold
Twitter.com/ThresholdSeries

DEDICATION

I want to dedicate this book to my beautiful family: without their support, this book wouldn't exist. Special thanks to my wife Rachael—her love, care, and support were instrumental in bringing this work to life. Honey, I love you with all my heart and soul. I'm looking forward to growing old by your side.

I also want to dedicate this book to the woman who dedicated her life to me: my mother. She's the best mother and role model I could ever wish for. Mom, thanks for being so wonderful and for always supporting me.

And to my son, Gabriel, I hope this book inspires you and keeps your love for reading alive. I'm extremely proud of you and always will be. I know you're capable of great feats, and the world expects no less from you. The sky is not the limit—there's no limit, and the possibilities are infinite and unimaginable.

I also want to dedicate this book to all those who may feel hopeless and discouraged, just know that there's more to life than meets the eye.

"The world is my country, all mankind are my brethren and to do good is my religion."—*Thomas Paine*

Excerpt from *Dweller on the Threshold*
Dweller on the Threshold is the second book of the *Threshold Series*.

It is said that everything in the universe has a purpose, a natural order of things that must be preserved at *all* cost. But not everyone has heard the saying. When Mark ventured into Threshold he had no idea of the consequences

Please see the end of this book for a sample chapter of book two of the *Threshold Series*.

Excerpt from *I Am Goblin*
I Am Goblin is the first book of my new middle-grade *I Am Chronicles*.

The streets of Boston are full of history, but few people know that a secret society of monstrous creatures thrives among us. Clash Goldblood is one such being, cursed to live his life as a ten-year-old boy. But, if you were to pass him by, you would never guess.

In his quest to take back what's rightfully his—The Prudential Building, Clash is determined to shatter the veil of secrecy that has held the city together for centuries.

Embark on the adventure of a lifetime with Clash and his friends as they attempt to retake Mr. Moneybags's empire.

Contents

CHAPTER ONE

Flight Test

"This is four-three-four-zero-seven requesting permission to taxi, straight-out departure," I said into the headset.

"Roger, four-zero-seven, hold short," replied the ground operator with a thick Boston accent.

It had taken me hours of flying and several written exams just to get this far. Now all I needed to earn my private pilot's license was a solo flight and my upcoming seventeenth birthday.

For my final test, I would have to take off from Hanscom Field in Bedford, Massachusetts, which was the closest airport to Stoneham, my hometown, and then fly over downtown Boston, return to Hanscom Field, and hopefully finish with a perfect landing.

I rubbed my eyes trying to keep them open. Although they were normally big, bright, and brown, I doubted they looked like that now. I hadn't slept well for the past three nights, thanks to those damn nightmares again.

The fleeting thought that maybe I shouldn't fly crossed my mind, yet I decided to get it over and done with. *That way, I wouldn't have to hear my father complain that I never finished anything,* I told myself. Sure, I quit piano, but who could stand Ms. Toepkey's ruler smackings every time they messed up? Karate could've been fun, but my teacher was no Mr. Miyagi. Football was the worst—being around those obnoxious jocks just made me sick, especially since I wasn't what anyone would call popular material. Besides, those things always felt more like chores than a half-decent pastime.

A faint thunderclap in the distance called my attention back to reality. If I wanted to complete my test today, I didn't have time to waste; a storm was on the way. Part of me wanted to postpone my test, but at the same time I felt… silly for even thinking about it. Besides, a little excitement wouldn't hurt—or so I thought.

As I waited for a reply from the ground operator, I had the strange sensation that someone or something was watching me. I even thought I heard it whisper my name. I tried to concentrate on the task at hand, but I couldn't shake the dreadful feeling that crept into the cockpit. At the same time, it had grown so cold inside that my hands trembled and my cracked lips burned. Fortunately the headset kept my ears somewhat warm.

"Four-zero-seven," the ground operator said loudly, almost making me jump out of my seat, "yah cleared to taxi, runway eleven."

Relieved, I acknowledged my clearance and applied ten percent throttle. I took comfort knowing that soon the engine would be warm enough to turn on the heater.

As the airplane rolled across the cold taxiway, I struggled with the rudder controls. The Cessna zigged, then zagged because I was unable to keep the centerline, well… centered. No biggie though, the rudder controls always took some getting used to.

Although my hands were extremely cold, they started to sweat. I still had time to back out, but I wasn't going to give up that easily.

"Four-zero-seven," I said as I arrived at the end of the taxiway, "holding short on runway eleven."

"Four-zero-seven, contact Hanscom Tower at one-one-eight-point-five."

I fumbled with the controls on the radio and entered the new frequency. Switching radio frequencies brought me some reassurance because Guiles, my instructor, was sitting somewhere up in the tower, ready, willing, and able to help if needed.

"Hanscom Tower," I said, "four-three-four-zero-seven, holding short on runway eleven, straight-out departure, VFR."

"Four-zero-seven, Visual Flight Rules departure approved," the traffic controller said, thankfully without an accent. "Hold short, runway eleven."

"Roger," I quickly said, trying to sound confident.

"Mark," Guiles said, "are you ready?"

"Yes, I am," I lied.

"Then just relax and have a great flight. I'll see you when you land," Guiles said, sounding almost... dare I say it? Proud.

"Four-zero-seven, you're clear for takeoff, runway eleven. Straight-out departure approved, good flight."

"Roger, cleared for takeoff," I repeated as required. I thrust the throttle forward, and the Cessna slid effortlessly into position at the center of the runway.

"Here goes nothing," I said before taking my foot off the brakes and opening the throttle all the way.

No matter how many times I take off, the symptoms are always the same. Right after applying full throttle, my body slams against the seat, and butterflies do a number in my stomach.

When I reached 65 knots, I slowly pulled the yoke toward me, and the Cessna gently lifted off the ground. As the airplane climbed toward my assigned altitude, it bounced when I encountered minor turbulence. Flying in a small airplane is much different than flying on a commercial jetliner. On the commercial planes, there are gentle ups and downs, but on a small craft such as the Cessna, they feel like the sudden drops of a roller coaster. The falling sensation took a bit of getting used to.

Outside, a few trees stubbornly still displayed their fall colors even though it was already winter. That's when I remembered what my instructor used to tell me: "Pay attention to traffic, not the wonders of nature while you're piloting." It was hard for me to ignore such wonders, because that was when I felt closest to my mom. Often when I was flying, I wondered how a person could cease to exist after death. My dad's insistence that after death there was nothing didn't make mourning my mother any easier. How could I believe that and cope? Contrary to my atheist upbringing, I tried to convince myself there had to be something after death… surely anything had to be better than nothing at all.

Time passed quickly, as it usually did when I flew. By the time I reached Boston, I was halfway through my test. Boston was gorgeous as usual. As I flew over the Charles River, I saw dozens of people exercising by the bank, despite the cold. Harvard looked too small for a school of such status. I wondered if I would ever be good enough for it.

"Four-zero-seven, do you read?" asked the tower controller.

"Roger," I said.

"Four-zero-seven," said the radio controller after a pause, "it seems that the storm got here much sooner than anticipated. Visibility and weather conditions are deteriorating fast. Turn around immediately and head back. Expect heavy turbulence."

"Roger, turning back now," I said, thinking there would finally be some excitement. Heavy turbulence? I failed to see how it was possible. The sky was still blue as far as I could see, and the sun was shining brightly. It wasn't until I finished executing the steep twenty-degree turn that I realized what he meant.

I stared perplexed as the sky turned from a baby blue color to a bruised purple. Even before my compass pointed toward the correct heading, the heavy turbulence started. I tightened my seatbelt. Seconds later, I was thrown violently around.

The day seemed to turn to night, but the clouds weren't the worst part. I was more concerned with the mysterious haze that accompanied the storm. With such limited visibility, it was hard not to lose my sense of direction.

As I flew into the storm, the faint hint of sun slowly disappeared behind me as if being swallowed by the thick clouds and dense haze. I no longer knew which way was up or down.

I stopped looking outside the windshield and focused all my attention on the altimeter. I used the horizon indicator and the compass as my guides. Although I didn't have any lessons on instrument flying, I knew just enough so I wouldn't completely lose my bearings, thanks to some flight simulator practice on the computer.

I must have been about five miles from the airport when I heard Guiles's voice on the radio. "Mark, pay close attention," he said, "this isn't going to be an easy landing, and you don't have enough fuel to go elsewhere. You'll have to execute a crosswind landing. Remember? We talked about them."

"Yes, I remember," I lied. I vaguely remembered making a few attempts at it in the simulator—none of which ended well—but I decided to keep that to myself. There was no need to worry Guiles even further.

"It's not hard," said Guiles, probably just to reassure me. "All you have to do is maintain a higher RPM than usual and apply full rudder just before you touch down."

Crosswind landings were challenging in any circumstance. Add poor visibility on top of my inexperience, and it was a recipe for disaster.

I did my best to align the Cessna with the runway. At first I thought I had it. I was wrong; as I got closer I could see that the airplane was off target by about two hundred feet. Visibility was so poor that it was hard to know for sure.

I was so shocked that I almost forgot to apply full throttle, retract the flaps, and pull back on the elevator controls in order to avoid hitting a parked plane at the end of the runway. Once back in the air, I came around for another try. Unfortunately, the visibility just kept getting worse. It seemed the longer I circled the airport, the worse my situation became.

I decided that once I had located the runway, I would give myself some extra time and space to properly align the Cessna. After a few minutes and a few precisely timed sharp turns at the command of the tower operator, I was finally able to find the runway. So I flew about six miles past the airport, fighting rain, haze, and violent winds as I climbed to fifteen hundred feet. I didn't know if it was going to make a difference, but it was worth a shot.

My second approach was even worse than the first. The winds were stronger. The haze was blinding, and my fuel was getting very low. I should have landed in Boston while the winds were calm. Why didn't I think of that earlier?

I was beginning to lose hope. Who was I kidding? I wasn't going to land. I wish I could say that I thought about my father and friends when I stumbled upon the realization that I might die. But I didn't: all I could think about was my mother. If I died, would I see her? Or would I sink into a world of nothingness?

Again, I suddenly felt an evil presence sitting next to me, mocking me, savoring my fate. But I told myself it was the stress getting the best of me.

I made two more approach attempts, but neither was even close. I started to doubt there was any chance I'd get out of this unscathed.

As I circled the airport for my fifth and probably last try, I heard the brief crackling of the radio and then Guiles's voice through the tight headset. "Mark, you're running on fumes. You need to put that bird down…" He said something else too, but I couldn't hear it over the deafening thunder that cut the transmission short. Flashes of light bathed the Cessna; one came close to hitting it. I hated lightning—I always have and probably always will.

"Roger," I said while I checked the fuel gauge.

In the heat of the moment, I missed what probably was my last chance to land. The weather still gave no sign of improving. I climbed to a safe altitude and turned around quickly. *Maybe if I'm really lucky, I'll get another shot*, I thought.

I was about to take a left turn toward Hanscom Field when the engine started to skip and rattle. A jolt of desperation shot through me. I felt the blood drain from my legs. Strangely enough, I found some comfort knowing it would be a quick death. I wouldn't have to wait much longer to find out what lingered beyond death.

"Mayday, my engine is out! Mayday, mayday!" I said over the radio, losing the last bit of self-control I still had. Immediately, the airplane began to lose speed. I was forced to tip the elevator control forward in an effort to retain some speed. In an aircraft, speed equals lift, and lift was what I desperately needed.

The sudden silence in the cockpit was disconcerting and surreal. All I could hear were raindrops smashing against the windshield. Then even that stopped. I stared at the motionless propeller and felt powerless, much like the airplane. I kept picturing it crashing into trees, tearing itself and me apart bit by bit. I pictured my limbs being ripped from my body, my bones breaking as the plane slammed into the ground. Maybe I wouldn't feel any pain. Maybe there was a limit to how much pain a person could suffer before the brain shut down. I hoped so.

"Mayday! Mayday!" I said as I passed the one-thousand-foot mark, heading toward zero on the altimeter needles.

"Remember to pull up just before you hit the ground, try to find a clearing or something," said Guiles.

Hit the ground? It took a while for those words to sink in. If there was a clearing, I sure as hell couldn't see it. At five hundred feet, the alarms in the cockpit began driving me insane. I quickly looked for the reset button to shut them off. That's when I noticed a clear path through the fog, seemingly made for the sole purpose of guiding me. Out of options and with the ground quickly approaching, I followed the whole through the fog. That's when I saw the next best thing to a runway. I-95 was right below me, looking smooth as a rug.

"I-95! I can see I-95!" I said, almost crying.

I lowered the flaps all the way, double-checked and retightened my seatbelt until my ribs hurt, and just like that I was ready for a bumpy emergency landing on the interstate.

"I'm landing on I-95," I said. At least Guiles would know where to send the rescue crew. At that very moment, I imagined dedicated men and women getting the call. I could picture them hurrying to my aid, expecting the worst.

Time seemed to completely stop as I glided toward the interstate. It was as though everything had come to a halt… the wind, the lightning, the rain; even the fog seemed to dissipate. The airplane silently glided as though guided by an invisible hand. Then, in a matter of milliseconds, I lived through all my sixteen years. I relived every argument, every joy, even every tear and smile, as if my memories were the only luggage I would take with me into whatever came next.

My training finally kicked in. I had to avoid landing anywhere near people or buildings. In the back of my mind, I could almost hear Guiles's voice saying, "Not near the Burlington Mall."

As long as I stayed on the interstate, the mall would be safe.

As I lined up with the interstate—which was fairly empty for two o'clock on a Thursday afternoon—I did my best to keep the airplane centered over the pavement. Luckily, this particular stretch of the interstate was fairly straight.

Somewhere below me there was the Burlington Mall, where hundreds if not thousands of unsuspecting people shopped, getting ready for Christmas. The poor weather conditions prevented me from pinpointing the mall's exact location. Unfortunately, the interstate was my only viable option. Landing in the woods was out of the question—that tended to be rather fatal. Not that crashing into solid asphalt was any prettier, but at least I'd have a chance.

"How are you doing?" Guiles asked as I tried to keep calm.

"I guess… I'm okay."

"You can do this." His confidence was infectious.

As I got closer to the ground, I tried to restart the engine one more time, but it was useless. I can't say I was surprised. I was about to make an emergency landing, and there was nothing I could do to avoid it.

My only consolation was the prospect of maybe seeing my mother again.

"Oh God, here we go!" I said, even though I was raised an atheist. There I was flying… no, I was falling at 85 mph, with nothing more than a few feet separating me from death.

My heart pounded like it was trying to burst out of my chest. My hands burned. Sweat dripped from my forehead despite the cold, and my body shook uncontrollably.

Silence was suddenly broken as chaos blared into life. I heard brakes screeching as motorists stopped violently when they realized I was about to land this beast of a plane right in front of them. The cars ahead of me swerved into the median as I fell the final few feet toward the pavement.

CHAPTER TWO
From Bad to Worse

As a sudden warmth flooded my body, I managed to straighten the airplane just before it hit the interstate by applying all the left rudder I could at the last moment.

I was astonished at how well I was doing. It was as if I'd made an emergency landing before. The Cessna gently touched the wet asphalt. Honestly, it was the smoothest touchdown I had ever performed, almost like it wasn't me flying. Then finally I understood: it wasn't me. I wouldn't have been able to pull that off. I had help, from whom I didn't know.

As my mind raced to figure out what had just happened, I forcefully and stupidly applied full brakes. Almost immediately, smoke started coming out of the landing gear as if it was on fire. The whole plane skidded sideways and came to a sudden stop on the grass median, narrowly missing a few cars.

When I came about, I was in shock and unable to move… I had pulled it off. But that wasn't me. They were my hands, but I wasn't controlling them. The part where I pushed hard on the brakes, that was me. But, not the rest. I wanted to think that somehow my mother helped me, but I discounted the thought as wishful thinking.

After a minute or so, I finally felt safe enough to move. I pushed the radio button and said, "I made it! I'm in the median, but I made it."

"Are you all right?" asked Guiles and the tower operator, almost at the same time.

"I think I am. I just have a bump on my head," I said as something warm oozed down my forehead. I ran my finger along my scalp to see the extent of the damage: blood dripped down my forehead, but the cut appeared minor. I wiped my bloody fingers on my pants and looked around to make sure that I and everyone else around me were in one piece.

"Mark, hang on, emergency services are on their way!" Guiles said. I could hear his sigh of relief over the radio.

I unbuckled my seatbelt and opened the passenger door, since my door was blocked by the median. The Cessna's left wing almost touched the grass, but aside from some worn tires and a badly bent propeller, the airplane seemed to be in fairly good shape. I wish my head had been so lucky.

When I stumbled outside, I noticed that traffic had come to a halt on both sides of the highway. Some motorists had come out of their cars to see if I was okay. Some seemed thrilled, while others appeared upset and looked at me with accusing eyes. I could almost hear their thoughts. *How do I dare mess up their afternoon commute?*

My whole life, I'd never seen so much action in one place. The sound of sirens filled the air. I could see an army of EMTs, police cars, and fire trucks making their way toward me in the distance. They used the median, the interstate shoulder, and any other openings they could to get to me. Scattered emergency lights decorated both the northbound and southbound lanes.

"Are you all right?" asked the first police officer on the scene.

"I'm... okay," I said, still shaking and bleeding.

Emergency vehicles and news vans quickly surrounded the place. There were even a couple helicopters circling above. One was from the police department, and the other was from a local TV station.

"What's your name?" the officer asked politely as she opened her first aid kit and examined my wound.

"Mark," I said. "Mark Anthony Ryser."

"Mark! Were you flying that airplane? Is there anyone else?" she asked, looking at the plane.

"No, there isn't anyone else. I ran out of fuel and had to make an emergency landing," I said, afraid I would be in trouble.

"Well, nice landing," she said and smiled, much to my surprise.

"So... I'm not in trouble?"

"Not that I know of. I'm sure the FAA will eventually have some questions for you. They're the ones who investigate this sort of thing," she said casually. "Now, Mark, I need to inform your parents. What's your mom's number?"

"My mom's dead," I said as she cleaned the wound on my forehead and placed a bandage over it.

"I'm sorry. Who's responsible for you?" she asked politely.

"My dad," I said reluctantly. I could only imagine the kind of trouble I would be in after he found out.

"We need to contact him. Can you call him?" She took out her notepad and started to take notes.

I reached for my cell phone in my left pocket, but when I was just about to dial my dad's number, the phone rang in my hands.

"Dad?" I asked, surprised. "I need to tell you something—"

"Are you okay? I'm watching you on the news right now!" he said. I'd never heard my dad sound so worried before.

"Yes, thank God. I'm fine, but the police need to talk to you." I was tempted to just pass the phone to the officer, afraid of what he would say to me.

"I'm glad you're all right. Don't worry... everything will be fine. Please put the officer on."

"Sure."

Soon I was completely surrounded by police, paramedics, and firefighters. Everyone seemed to be excited or at least amused by all the action. Against my wishes, the paramedics loaded me into the back of the ambulance to take me to the Lahey Clinic Medical Center emergency room. The ambulance took off, driving through the grass to avoid the traffic congestion I had created.

When we arrived at the hospital, my dad was already outside waiting for the ambulance. He must have been in the area because there was no way he could've made it there that quick. I think he was still on the phone with the police officer. He only hung up when the paramedics unloaded me from the ambulance.

"Are you okay?" he asked when he saw me being carried into the hospital.

"I'm fine, Dad. I guess they need to check me out just in case," I said to calm him down.

By the time I arrived in the hospital, the paramedics had already started an IV and some medication. Even though I felt fairly fine, they told me not to move around much. It wasn't long before a doctor came in to examine me. He introduced himself as Dr. Raymond. I tried to explain that I was fine, but it was useless. He ordered blood work, MRIs, and x-rays.

After a couple hours of waiting around, I saw Dr. Raymond again. He walked in, chart in hand, sporting a bright smile.

"I have good news and bad news," he said. "Which one do you want first?"

"I'll take the good news."

"Well, you're fine, and you can go home as soon as we finish processing your discharge papers."

"What's the bad news?"

"Bad news is that there's an army of reporters waiting outside to hear from you. They aren't sure if you're a hero or a villain."

"Do I have to talk to them?"

"You don't have to. Besides, I wouldn't worry too much about what they think. Anyone who can land an airplane on the interstate is a hero in my book. Best of luck to you."

After a painful injection in my butt of all places and a couple of signatures, the doctor discharged me. Apparently, the injection was for pain. I was just grateful that the cut on my forehead didn't require any stitches.

We managed to escape most of the reporters by leaving through a staff door. Unfortunately, we left the hospital just in time for the rush hour. Traffic was the worst I'd ever seen, and it was entirely my fault. It was the first time I'd gotten stuck in a traffic jam that I had caused.

My dad turned on the radio. I was glad at least it filled the void and awkwardness in the air.

"Your afternoon commute is bound to be a mess. Heavy traffic remains on both lanes of I-95 around the Burlington Mall exit because of an unusual crash. An airplane had to perform an emergency landing right on the interstate. It's still unclear how long the cleanup will take," said the traffic report.

"That's what I call an attention-getter," my dad remarked.

I was so caught up in my own thoughts that I didn't reply.

As we passed the scene of the crash, the airplane was still in the same spot, surrounded by a bunch of guys wearing black jackets, backpacks, and baseball caps. They were examining every inch of it and jotting down notes.

"They must be from the FAA," my dad said as we drove slowly by.

I turned my face the other way and pretended not to pay any attention. I didn't feel like talking about it. Not to mention that I was afraid the FAA guys would want to talk to me. I still hoped for a peaceful end to an otherwise hectic and emotionally charged day.

We ordered pizza on the way. We were both exhausted, and honestly, neither one of us was what anyone would call a great cook.

I headed upstairs and jumped in the shower. I had every reason to be happy, but I wasn't. On the contrary, I felt even more depressed. It's true that I was alive and well, but my mother wasn't. She died all those years ago, and it was my fault. It wasn't her time. Unable to hold all the emotions in any longer, I just stood under the water and cried. The water was so hot it burned my skin, but the physical pain eased my emotional pain, so I didn't bother to turn it off. When I couldn't take any more, I shut the water off just in time to hear the delivery guy ring the doorbell.

I rushed downstairs and grabbed a couple of slices of the extra cheese pizza and went back up to my room to watch some TV while I ate.

I had almost forgotten about the events of the day when the eleven o'clock news started.

"Breaking news: an amazing emergency landing was performed by the sixteen-year-old Mark Anthony Ryser after he ran out of fuel."

The news anchor then proceeded to show footage from the helicopter.

I watched myself stumble out of the airplane and glance around, looking dazed and confused. My forehead was bleeding worse than I remembered. I gazed in awe as I almost fell but barely caught myself. I saw the Burlington police officer park her patrol car as she rushed over to help me. She sat me on the grass, and in no time at all, she had assessed the situation and opened her first aid kit while checking my limbs and head. She flashed a flashlight in my eyes, which I didn't remember. Come to think of it, she did a lot of things that I didn't remember. I guess I was truly in shock.

The news cut to someone reporting live from the scene of the accident.

"Good evening. For many of us, this was a day to remember during this holiday shopping season. After all, it's not every day we see an airplane land on the interstate. Luckily, no one was seriously hurt."

"Is it true that he was just a kid?" the news anchor asked. "Here at the station, we heard that he's just sixteen."

"That's right, Phillip. Sixteen-year-old Mark was performing his first solo flight when the weather suddenly took a turn for the worse. After several failed attempts to land at Hanscom field, the young pilot ran out of fuel and had to land on the interstate."

"Wow, this is just amazing. This kid is a hero."

"Well, that's debatable. He could have hit the Burlington Mall. One little miscalculation on his part and hundreds might have been hurt," said the reporter in the field.

I really didn't like that guy. I wondered what he would have said if he knew I hadn't done any calculations at all; there weren't any to do.

"I personally think he's a hero. I can't imagine being sixteen and having to perform an emergency landing on the busiest New England interstate," the news anchor said in my defense. I was so tired that I couldn't even appreciate the fact that he was trying to help me, so I changed the channel to Comedy Central to see if I could relax a bit and fall asleep.

Maybe I should skip school tomorrow, I thought. *I'm sure all anybody will want to talk about is my emergency landing. I will probably have to explain it a million times to Jonas, but at least him I can stand.*

I ended up spending most of my Friday sitting in front of the computer in my pajamas playing video games; I couldn't bear the thought of going to school.

It was almost four o'clock when the doorbell rang. I was so distracted that I failed to realize Jonas would definitely be stopping by after school, and I was sure Carla, his twin sister, would be with him. I couldn't afford to let her see me in my pajamas, so I dressed as quickly as I could while my father kept yelling at me to answer the door.

"Hey," I said, almost out of breath.

"Are you okay?" Carla asked. "We heard what happened."

"I'm fine."

"How did it happen?" asked Carla, looking concerned.

"Well, the storm took me by surprise, it came out of nowhere, and I couldn't see the runway."

"Oh my God, that's insane," said Carla, looking at my forehead.

"You could have been killed," said Jonas. "Were you scared?"

"Yes, very scared. I thought it was the end."

"The school was filled with insane stories about your emergency landing," Jonas said.

"What do you mean?"

"Some people said you were so high you couldn't find the runway, while others think you're a legend for being able to land like that," said Carla. "You know how people exaggerate."

"One thing is for sure," said Jonas, "you're sort of a celebrity. Are you going out to dinner with us tonight?"

"No thanks, not tonight. I think I'll just veg out and play video games or something."

"I'll be online later if you want to play," said Jonas.

After I gave them countless assurances that I was all right and explained the whole ordeal in great detail, they finally seemed satisfied and left.

On Monday, I was late for the school bus as usual, but at least I didn't have to bang on the doors for Gus to open them. I guess he felt bad for me. As soon as I stepped into the bus, silence fell. I took the first free seat I could find. The bus was about to start moving when we heard a loud bang on the door. I was pleasantly surprised to see Carla with her beautiful brown hair and innocent face entering the bus. Behind her was Jonas, with his round face and somewhat large and clumsy body, climbing the stairs.

I moved aside, hoping Carla would sit next to me, but she chose the seat right behind me instead. Jonas threw his backpack on the empty seat next to Carla and made himself comfortable by my side.

"Good morning," Carla said, smiling.

"Hey, nice to see you guys."

"We figured you might need some company just in case anyone wants to be funny or mess with you," said Jonas, looking tired. He wasn't used to being up this early because his mother drove him and Carla to school every morning on the way to work. They had insisted several times that I ride to school with them, but I chose not to. Just seeing their mother made me miss mine even more.

In school, everyone seemed to be staring at me, but few dared to ask for details. My teachers were especially nice during the beginning of the week, but that quickly faded, and before I knew it everything was back to normal.

***

Friday, 18th of December

It happened again last night: it was the same nightmare I'd been having night after night after my mother died, but since last week's accident, they had become stronger and more frequent, haunting me constantly.

The nightmares usually featured the same diabolical figure, but last night it was different. This time, it talked to me while it chased me around that damp cave.

The figure taunted me. I think it wanted me to face it. I was afraid the nightmares were here to stay. I could still see that ungodly place whenever I blinked, down to the smallest gory detail. I could still smell the fetid and rotten air of that cave. And although I couldn't see them, I was certain putrid corpses lay hidden under the thick cover of darkness.

How long would I be haunted by these nightmares? I couldn't seem to stop them. Each night, they got worse. After a while, I even started to dream about a disturbing figure staring at me from the foot of the bed as I slept, studying me. As the nights passed, the figure became clearer and even more menacing. Lately, I could sense it near me even when I was awake. For Christ's sake, I could feel it standing next to me in the bathroom, on the bus, in school, and even in the airplane before I had my emergency landing. As if it was waiting for the first opportunity to get me. But when I looked around, there was nothing. Nothing except a sense of dread that evaded any logic and yet seemed to consume any shred of hope.

I thought I was doing a pretty good job at controlling my anger, but lately I'd been… more direct and much less patient with everything and everyone than usual.

I just wished I could get a normal night's sleep like everyone else.

The worst part was that I was clueless about why this was happening. Was I losing it? Maybe I'd already lost it and just didn't know.

There was something strange in the figure's voice—maybe if I were not so scared, I would've investigated it further.

Although my heart pounded, I glanced at the clock. It was four in the morning. The room was still covered in darkness, so for the rest of the night I just lay there in the dark. Too scared to scream, too terrified to even move. My only protection was the thin cotton sheet covering my body. I didn't dare close my eyes except for blinking, and even that I tried to avoid.

I remained frozen in place while the clock crawled toward six o'clock. In a futile effort to distract myself, I counted the remaining minutes and even the seconds. I hoped it would stop me from thinking about the horrific scenes that I'd dreamt.

I was forced to make peace with the fact that I wasn't as brave as I would like to be, I wasn't as grown-up as I thought I was, and I was definitely not as strong as I led the whole world to believe.

I finally fell asleep, only to be awakened a few minutes later by the defiant alarm clock.

Groggy and still shaken, I waited to hear the usual sounds that signaled that my dad was up and about before I dared to leave the safety of my bed.

I changed out of my pajamas, and carefully folded and set them aside to wear one more night. I've always hated to do the laundry, so I tried to use my clothes as long as possible before I washed them.

While I was in the bathroom brushing my teeth and washing my face, I heard my dad's heavy footsteps getting closer to the door.

He knocked with a disturbingly soft knock that seemed like it couldn't possibly have come from his giant hands.

"Are you up already?" he asked, walking in right as I flushed the toilet.

"Morning, Dad," I said, probably sounding crankier than usual and definitely more tired than I intended. Not getting the right amount of sleep all week had taken its toll.

I could see the concern on his face, but he didn't bother questioning me. Knowing him, he probably assumed I was on drugs or something. I didn't mind—after all, we weren't exactly best friends anyway. After my mother's death, a steel wall had been erected between us. Her passing had changed us both and not for the better.

"Make sure you're not late," he said, closing the door. As usual, I didn't care to reply. I was too busy gathering my stuff for yet another excruciating day of high school.

I ran downstairs, skipping every other step to save time. I found my dad standing in the living room fiddling with the TV remote with one hand while holding his morning coffee with the other.

"Later, Dad," I said as I sped past him on my way to catch the disturbingly yellow bus.

"Are you sure you're okay?"

"Yes, I'm fine," I said to put his mind at ease. "I gotta run. I don't want to be late."

CHAPTER THREE
High School

I almost missed the bus. I arrived at the bus stop just as Gus was closing the door. For some unknown reason, he insisted on being early. I missed the bus more times than I could count.

If I hadn't banged on the doors as hard as I could, I don't think he would have reopened them. Thankfully, he did. I couldn't take another day of riding my bike to school and freezing to death. Although I had my driver's license, I lacked a car. If you asked me, I'd say that sixteen is too old to ride the bus or be driven to school. I tried to persuade my dad to loan me his car, but after last week's accident I'd be lucky if he let me ride my bike. I couldn't wait until I got my own car. For some strange reason, I had to wait until my seventeen birthday. I could fly an airplane, but I wasn't allowed to drive a car.

If my dad hadn't been working from home today, I would have skipped school. Unfortunately, my father worked from home on Fridays—one of the perks of the information technology company he worked for. By seven in the morning he'd have gone into his home office, only to come out every once in a while, parading around the house with his Bluetooth headset. I could swear that he spent all day on the phone. It was impossible to talk to him while he had the headset glued to his ear.

I was exhausted on the way to school. Luckily, the number of carless losers was minimal, so I was able to lie down uncomfortably on one of the back seats. I must have fallen asleep because the next thing I knew Gus was nudging my left shoulder hard trying to wake me.

"Get up. I'm running late," he said, even though he wasn't. "If you don't get up, I'll have to get the principal."

"Okay, okay! I'm up," I said, annoyed as I mumbled and cursed under my breath.

As I approached the front of the bus, I realized that Gus had parked the bus much further away than usual.

What I hadn't noticed was that several feet away stood a rather odd and out-of-place white and yellow sign that read "ROAD CLOSED." It was located just before the Stoneham High main building. Nothing exciting ever happened at Stoneham High. I just hoped that we had no school today.

I thought about turning around and heading back home, but a tall figure wearing a dark blue uniform and a fluorescent yellow jacket waved me closer.

"The school is in lockdown," said a Stoneham police officer. His badge said his name was Ryan.

"What happened?" I asked. There were four police cruisers and two fire trucks parked in the school fire lanes; their bright, spinning lights screamed caution.

"Someone called in a bomb threat."

"Should I go home?" I asked hopefully.

"Nothing to worry about, probably just a prank. You wouldn't happen to know anything about that, would you? Your fellow students seem to think that you do," the officer said.

"No, sir." I was about to point out that I had just arrived when the police chief burst out of the building.

"All clear! Let's move out before the press gets here," the chief yelled. "Take down that barricade, Sergeant Ryan. Stoneham doesn't need any more negative publicity."

"Yes, sir," replied Sergeant Ryan without taking his eyes off me. He seemed suspicious. As if the fact that I was the last kid to arrive made me guilty somehow.

"Hey, kid, what are you waiting for? Go to class, you're already late as it is," the chief ordered.

I walked past him without uttering a word. I was afraid that if I did, he too would think I was somehow involved. I was known to be blamed for these sorts of things; maybe it was because I didn't care what other people thought of me so I never even bothered to defend my reputation.

I managed to sneak past the administrative staff, who were busy tending to the firefighters.

Regrettably, my teacher Christi Black, or Mrs. Black as she liked to be called, wasn't busy at all. She usually spent her mornings sitting on her chair either painting or admiring her freshly painted nails. That was exactly what she was doing when I walked in. Some of us suspected she went out every night and wanted to look as spiffy as possible.

The rest of the classroom sat in almost complete silence; if it were not for the occasional scribbling noises of graphite on paper, I would've doubted I was in high school. As always, the room smelled of chalk, which made me sneeze for several minutes before my nostrils got accustomed to it.

"How nice of you to join us," Mrs. Black said sarcastically, attracting a stream of muffled laughs from around the room.

"Good morning," I said, scouting the room in an effort to find the closest seat to Carla. A good ten minutes passed before I could muster enough courage to interrupt Mrs. Black's nail polishing session. As much as I liked not doing any work, I was bored; surely anything had to be better than nothing at all.

"Excuse me, Mrs. Black. What's today's assignment?" Carla gave me a subtle look. Jonas didn't divert his gaze from his English assignment.

"Page eighty-nine, Mr. Ryser," Mrs. Black replied, looking over her glasses, something she did only when she was extremely annoyed.

Although I worked hard to catch up, I left a couple of questions unanswered. I turned in my paper and went straight to French class, which was boring as usual. I still didn't know why I would need to speak French. Sure, I'd probably visit France one day, but I was sure the hotel staff would speak English fluently. Try explaining that to Mrs. Finningan, though.

"As you may have heard, we had an incident this morning…" She paused and looked around as though searching for the person responsible. "Someone called in a fake bomb threat. I don't know who it was, but I'm certain the police will find out. If I were that person, I would turn myself in right away." That's how Mrs. Finningan started her class. Throughout the whole hour, she kept reminding us to rat out the person who called in the bomb threat, as if we knew who it was. We heard it in English, French, Spanish, and even in German. She was determined, I had to give her that much.

On a rather strange and interesting note, during History class, I kept hearing the girls whisper and giggle, but whenever I looked at them, they would blush and turn away.

"See you all later," Wendy said, turning slightly to Jonas and me as we were leaving class, much to my astonishment since she never talked to me.

"That was different. Maybe she's finally falling for me," said Jonas as we navigated the sea of people in the hallways.

We arrived at the science lab just as the class was starting. It would've been another quiet Chemistry class if Jonas hadn't messed up his experiment and filled the whole lab and ground floor with thick black smoke, setting off the fire alarm and triggering pandemonium among the student body in the process.

We were told to evacuate the building and go to the courtyard. Fortunately, the smoke covered the lab so quickly that nobody else saw that Jonas's experiment was the cause of the incident. I dealt uncomfortably with the bumping and grinding as people rushed to be the first to leave the building, probably not because they thought it was on fire, but so they would be the first ones to get to the few remaining cardboard pieces outside to go sledding on the snowy hills.

About three minutes later, the fire trucks arrived at Stoneham High for the second time that morning. By the time the chief gave the all-clear, it was lunchtime.

"I'll get our usual table," said Jonas as he headed for the cafeteria.

"I'll be there in a few," I replied as I went the opposite way toward the restrooms. I'd grown accustomed to always washing my hands before eating. Jonas, on the other hand, thought the practice was a waste of time.

In the restroom, everyone tried to guess who called in the fake bomb threat, but they stopped talking when I entered.

After I was done, I waited patiently outside for Carla to come out of the girls' restroom. We took our time walking carelessly through the grounds, talking about nothing and everything. It was my favorite time of the day. A good ten minutes or so passed before we reached the cafeteria. Jonas was already halfway through his lunch. We talked about the usual stuff, and since nothing ever really happened in Stoneham, the whole school was abuzz about who had called in the fake bomb threat and what had caused the fire alarm to go off. Some people speculated there was a bomb after all and it had detonated, while others thought someone caused the incident so they could play outside in the snow.

"Well, you did it again... you're the lead suspect," said Jonas as he shoved not two, but three whole French fries into his mouth.

"It doesn't surprise me," said Carla. "It seems these people have nothing better to do."

"And what makes you think that Mark didn't do it?" asked Jonas, sporting a quizzical look.

"I didn't!" I said indignantly. "Thanks for the vote of confidence."

"It isn't necessarily a bad thing. You have to admit, being bad and all has its advantages with the ladies," Jonas said with a grin.

"If by 'ladies' you mean white trailer trash with a probation officer," Carla said as she perused the interior of her pink and purple backpack, apparently trying to find something. We laughed as Jonas gathered our used trays.

I hadn't realized that I was spellbound by Carla's beauty until Jonas asked, "Are you guys coming?"

"Yes," I said, snapping out of daze.

We walked to Math class while secretly making fun of the popular kids as we passed them. I could've been popular if I wanted it. All I had to do was hang out with the "right" crowd. The only problem was that I couldn't stand them.

"See you later, Mark," said Carla in her soft and sweet voice. I wouldn't see her again until after school because of our different schedules.

With all the excitement, I almost forgot about the strange and dreadful presence that followed me around. Little did I know that my brief, chaotic peace would soon end.

I arrived on time to Mr. Campbell's Math class and took my usual seat in the darkest and quietest corner of the room. The fluorescent light in the back was burnt out, making it my favorite spot. Some days, I was even able to sneak a snooze or two, depending on how tired I was and how boring the lesson of the day was; today was definitely one of those days.

The class had barely started when I found myself slowly drifting toward an infinite void, only to be brought back violently by the loud and stern voice of Mr. Campbell.

"Wake up, Mark. You're here to learn and not to sleep."

As he spoke, I felt death itself approaching; the dread was unmistakable, invisible, and ever-menacing. I was fed up. I was tired of being followed around. I refused to sit idly by while that thing, whatever it was, made fun of me. Feeling a false sense of security, I got up and said loudly: "What do you want from me?"

"What did you say?" Mr. Campbell asked as the whole class paused to look at me.

"Hmmm… nothing," I said—in vain.

"You just tripled your workload, young man. I suggest you learn some respect," said Mr. Campbell.

Mr. Campbell believed that equations made the most effective detentions, so he walked over and threw about ten sheets of paper on my desk.

"I expect it on my desk before the end of class."

"There's no way I can finish this today!" I said, still sensing the diabolical presence and the same dreadful feeling.

"You'll never finish it if you don't start."

By the end of Mr. Campbell's class, my brain hurt, not to mention my hands and fingers from squeezing the pencil too hard. It took me a while, but I finished it, fifteen minutes late.

That's when I realized it was almost 3:45 p.m. and the last bus had probably already left and I might as well start the walk to my house.

***

As I walked back, the sky grumbled and the cold invaded my being. My backpack provided limited protection, while my shoulders paid a heavy price. My eyes felt tired and sore, but my lungs thrived on the crisp New England winter air.

My week had been long and dreadful. I still couldn't believe that I had missed the bus again. Somehow, I missed it most days of the week.

Overcome with boredom, I walked with my head down, looking at the asphalt as though I was searching for something. Then suddenly out of the corner of my eye, I caught a glimpse of Jonas and Carla's matching sneakers as they quickly caught up to me.

The twins were not only my childhood friends, but also my only friends. They seemed cold, given the shivering noises that Carla made while she adjusted her earmuffs and the frantic motion Jonas did with his hands, rubbing them together trying to warm up.

They carried overstuffed backpacks and seemed to suffer the same pain as I did; yet they didn't seem to care, as though the pain was normal. Perhaps the cold was more of a pressing matter.

"Did you guys miss the bus too?" I asked, surprised.

"No, when I didn't see you in the bus, I decided to wait for you, and Jonas followed."

"Hey!" Jonas said. "I was planning on waiting anyway."

Jonas had barely finished speaking when a rolling thunder announced the imminent arrival of either heavy rain or an ice storm. Overstuffed clouds seemed to cover Stoneham, promising to burst over the small New England town like a water balloon.

When we were about a block away from our street, huge raindrops started to fall, hitting first my backpack and then my face.

As the rain increased, so did our steps. Soon our careless steps turned into an all-out race to see who would be the first to find shelter from the freezing rain—the finish line was the poorly maintained porch of 12 Hersam Street, my Victorian-style house.

I was the first to arrive, probably because I was part of the school track team and in fairly good physical shape; Jonas was second. He crashed into me, using me as a human emergency brake and panting like a wild animal. He was chubby and not a very good runner; he had barely managed to arrive before Carla, who didn't seem to be trying very hard.

Much to my disappointment, Carla didn't use me as a human brake, choosing the cold, hard wall instead.

We stood still for a few seconds to catch our breath. I was amazed by the power of nature as torrents of rain fell with a mysterious raw energy that charged every drop.

"Are we doing anything later on?" I asked, wanting to see Carla again.

"Sure, how does dinner sound?" Carla said, smiling. She had the kind of smile that gave life meaning.

"Where?" asked Jonas before I even had the chance to reply to Carla's question. Jonas always jumped at the opportunity to go out whenever I went—it had something to do with the fact that his parents only allowed him to go out if I went. I kept hoping that one of these days Jonas wouldn't want to go out to dinner so I could tell Carla how I really felt about her. I should have told her during our walk in school, but it didn't seem like the right time or place.

One of these days, I'll have my chance, I thought. *But how is Jonas going to feel about it? He's my best friend. I'm not really sure how he would take it if I got involved with his sister. That's if she even likes me.*

Although the twins were fifteen years old, their parents felt it was safer for them go out with me because I seemed capable of defending myself should the need arise. I guess being over six feet tall had its advantages.

"So where do you guys feel like going?" I asked, only to regret it a split second later.

"Uh, let me think," Jonas said without really meaning it because he immediately added, "what about La Luna's? We always eat there on Fridays."

"That's because you only want to eat there," Carla objected, rolling her beautiful Caribbean blue eyes. "For once, can we please go somewhere else?"

I almost instinctively replied with a resounding, "Yes!" There was something in the way she spoke that drew me closer, something that made me want to agree with her and fulfill her every wish and desire.

"No, we can't! I have a date there," said Jonas. By "date" he meant he would try to hit on Wendy Hartwell—the Stoneham High cheerleader captain who worked at La Luna's as a waitress. Well, "worked" was not really the right word to describe what she did there. Her father owned the place, which was conveniently located right on the busy main street where all the school kids hung out.

Wendy only worked there so she could flirt with all the high school jocks who frequented the joint. I personally had never seen Wendy carry a single tray, plate, or dish. Her favorite, and as far as I could tell only, responsibility was to walk around with her pink feather pen and bedazzled order book, taking customers' orders, flirting, and bossing everyone around, including her father.

"Fine, but you better ask her out already... not that she will accept, but at least then you can move on and we can finally eat at a different restaurant for a change," said Carla.

With a discreet flick of her hair, Carla picked up her pink backpack and ran toward her house across the street.

I must have been staring at her, because next thing I knew, I was getting elbowed in the stomach by Jonas.

"I'll see you later," Jonas said, looking wary.

"Yep, I'll see you," I said as casually as I could. Jonas ran, but he was unable to avoid getting completely soaked by the rainstorm, which seemed to be growing stronger.

A few seconds passed before I realized I was standing alone in the cold, lost in wonderment, thinking about Carla and what I should do with the whole Jonas situation.

How could I tell him? Should I tell him? Maybe I should talk to Carla first... after all, he doesn't need to know, if the feeling isn't mutual, I thought. Since that wasn't something I would be able to solve right then and there, I thought it was best to go inside.

A.A. Volts

My house was simply that: a house. It wasn't a home anymore. Long gone were all the things that made my house a home. My house was condemned to be forever just a house, for it was incomplete, much like a puzzle missing its centerpiece. The bond that held our house and our family together was gone.

CHAPTER FOUR
Memories

As soon as I walked into the foyer, I took off my shoes and kicked them out of the way—I must have been insane when I decided to wear my new Nike sneakers. I don't know why new sneakers always insisted on molding my feet to their exquisite shape, instead of it being the other way around. What was I thinking? Everyone except me knew not to wear new sneakers when they had PE class.

I kicked them so hard that I almost knocked out our old butler, Charles Woody. I gave him that name when we first got him. I was only four at the time. It seemed fitting too, especially because he was made out of wood.

Charles was one of those cheesy wooden child-sized butlers people insisted on using as decoration, a doorstop, or simply as irrefutable proof of their lack of style.

Luckily, old Charles wobbled but didn't fall. I never really liked him. You wouldn't either, if when you were four you had a scary-looking wooden butler whose hard wood eyes seemed to follow you everywhere you went. Not to mention the fact that he was almost twice my size, smelled like cedar, and looked like he belonged in a bad 1950s horror movie.

If he weren't one of my mom's favorite "art" pieces, I would've thrown him in the trash a long time ago. I still remembered how she used to joke that one day she was going to retire old Charles and have him replaced with a real butler. Unfortunately, that day never came.

As I passed near old Charles, I threw my house keys into the crystal bowl that sat on his tray. The keys were already in the air when I remembered what my mom used to say: "Mark! One day you are going to break that bowl. It has survived not one but two world wars, and it would be a shame if it didn't survive you."

As the keys landed in the crystal bowl, it sang a sweet melody that only true Waterford crystal could. They twirled around for a bit before finally settling on the bottom.

There were so many memories packed into my house that every time I opened the door it was like taking a trip into the past. I often wondered why I always remembered the painful memories; after all, there were more beautiful memories—although they seemed so distant that it might as well have been a lifetime ago.

The moment I dreaded had arrived. Every day I fought the same battle, but it never got any easier.

The "Sorrows Hallway" waited for me. Unfortunately, it stood between the stairs and my bedroom, so I didn't have much choice in the matter, especially since my dad wouldn't let me sleep in the living room.

Every day, I sped down the Sorrows Hallway, careful not to catch a glimpse of my happy past. The pictures that hung on the wall cut through my soul every time I walked past them.

I took mere seconds to run the length of the narrow, long hallway, but it felt like hours. I tried to keep my focus on the door handle to avoid looking at the old photographs on the walls, but despite my best effort, I still caught fleeting glimpses of joyful moments frozen forever in time. Those pictures only served to remind me of how much my life had changed.

The first one was my favorite picture of her. I saw myself when I was still small enough to sit in her lap. I was happy as a clam at high water. But, those pictures no longer brought me joy. Instead, they reminded me of how happy I'd been back then. And to think that I hadn't even realized or appreciated that fact until it was too late. So many lost moments that I could never get back.

30

Tomorrow will mark the eleventh anniversary of her passing. I couldn't help it as a single, lonely tear streamed down my face.

If I could remove that day from the calendar, I would. Nobody should ever lose a family member in the month of December. Needless to say, Christmas had stopped being a joyful celebration long ago. She died the day after we had decorated the Christmas tree. She used to love Christmas; she would get all giddy. I could see the spark in her eyes when December came about. She would plan the decorations for days. She had villages, blow-up snowmen, and Santa hats that she used to hang all around the house. And she wasn't content until my dad hung tons of lights outside. Our house was the most decorated house on the block. Some of the neighbors would even complain about the traffic jam we created.

I started to sob as tears began rolling down my face. I forced myself to be strong and wiped them away.

Not a single day passed that I didn't think of her at least four or five times, sometimes more....

She was often the first thought on my mind when I woke up and the last when I went to bed. On some extremely rare days, I would forget about her, only to suddenly remember and feel devastated by guilt, followed by utter sadness.

Will this ever get easier? I wondered, even though I felt it wouldn't.

I was a much different person back then, before the cursed and fatal car accident that ripped my life apart and took the life of my mother.

That sweet and calm five-year-old boy still lived somewhere inside me, lost in a dark corner. I could feel him yearning to get out into the world. Sometimes I felt like I was my own worst enemy.

Yet it scared me to think about what would happen if I found my old self. *Would I be able to survive or even cope?* I wondered as I entered my bedroom, banging the door shut with more force than necessary.

I tossed my heavy backpack onto my bed. Although I felt relieved, my shoulders still hurt.

My eyes burned, and I couldn't stop yawning. My bed seemed so inviting, but I still had to finish my homework. My dad insisted that I do all my homework on the day it was assigned.

Why do teachers like to give exams on Mondays? After all, don't I deserve a couple of days off to help me keep my sanity? That's if I haven't lost it already.

I felt so defiant that if I didn't have another flight test tomorrow morning, I wouldn't finish my homework, but that's what I get for making an eight o'clock appointment. I would've made it for later, but the forecast called for heavy winds and snow beginning early Saturday afternoon. I didn't want a repeat of last week's crash landing, so I figured I'd better make sure the weather was calm this time around.

I figured if I worked hard enough, I might be able to get most, if not all, of my homework done before dinner. Otherwise my Friday night dinner with Jonas and Carla could be in jeopardy.

I had grown accustomed to our Friday night ritual, but it was worth missing for my flight test tomorrow. I'd been looking forward to it all week—I just hoped that I could get a decent night's sleep. I'd practiced all week on the flight simulator because I needed everything to go without a hitch. I loved the adrenaline rush from flying; perhaps it was the sense of freedom, or maybe it was the blissful, temporary amnesia I experienced while flying.

***

Even though I was set on accomplishing as much homework as I could, my eyes were getting heavier, and before I even realized it, they started to close.

I fought it for a few seconds, but ultimately the fatigue won. It wasn't very common for me to get tired this early in the day, but then again, I always felt worn out whenever I was bored. Unfortunately, patience wasn't one of my strong suits.

I'd never taken a nap in the afternoon before, but today was different. My muscles felt weak. I would have paid not to have to move them. I guess all the physical and emotional stress had drained my energy—or perhaps I just wanted to escape real life.

So I finally gave in to the fatigue and pushed the contents of my bed aside and onto the floor. I heard a loud thump as my backpack hit the hardwood floor. I pulled my pillow closer and let gravity do the rest. *Ah, nothing wrong with a little afternoon nap*, I thought as I closed my eyes.

For a few seconds, I lay in my bed with my eyes closed and relaxed as a thick black veil fell over me.

At first I saw nothing out of the ordinary, just blackness, as though I was staring into deep and starless space. It wasn't until a few minutes later, when I was almost asleep, that I saw some strange and brilliant orbs float majestically into my field of vision. At first, they were small and few, but after a few minutes, they grew so intense that I thought fireworks were exploding inside my head.

I didn't know where I was, but I didn't seem to experience the constant rage and sadness that I normally felt. I enjoyed the much-needed relief so much that I decided to go with the flow. After all, moments of tranquility were so rare in my life that I embraced it to the point where I became so relaxed that I forgot I had a body at all. Suddenly, innumerable scintillating flakes charged toward me, and as they hit me, I felt my body vibrate and come alive with a brisk, powerful, and yet painless jolt of electricity. I was paralyzed and unable to scream.

Soon the vibrations became uncontrollable, as if an unprecedented amount of power was coursing through me, and as it did, it overcharged every single cell in my body. I felt my body swaying. I had been drunk once, but this felt much worse. At times it felt like my body was going to hit the ceiling, but I didn't dare open my eyes to check.

Then out of nowhere, I heard a loud boom that shook me to my core. I wondered if I was in any danger or if I was still even alive because my heart felt like it was about to burst—but after a few seconds, I realized I wasn't in any immediate danger. Not knowing what else to do, I decided to relax and go with the flow.

Not five seconds passed before my body started to feel lighter, as though it were suddenly inflated with helium. I was oddly aware of every cell in my body as they tingled and gave me a strange, yet pleasant sensation. At that moment, I felt my body lift up as if gravity had suddenly been turned off. I was floating… I don't mean my physical body, but dare I say it? My spirit.

At first I couldn't see much, yet I knew exactly where everything was. It was a different form of vision, an internal sense, or radar if you will. I could feel my surroundings. I guess it was what I had heard some people call the mind's eye. Best way I can describe it, is that every object seemed to possess its own energy.

I was floating upward when a frightening thought invaded my soul.

Am I dead? I wondered out loud.

Nothing could have prepared me for what was about to happen—the simple act of asking that question caused a jolt of panic to start building inside me. I felt lost and alone as I floated in utter silence; I felt dreadful.

"You don't know what death is!" came a whispered and raspy reply.

I stopped moving immediately. I just floated in place, petrified by the fear as chills overtook my body.

After a good few seconds of silence, I managed to ask, "Who… are you? Why can't I see you?" My head was spinning, making me feel dizzy and sick to my stomach.

If I hadn't experienced so many panic attacks, I would have thought that I was dying (I wasn't totally sure I hadn't), but somehow that voice made death seem warm and even inviting.

"Trust me, you don't want to see me. For the moment, you just have to do what I say," the raspy voice replied.

"Where am—"

"Where you shouldn't be. Do not continue! Turn back now before it's too late."

"What do you mean?" I asked, more scared than curious.

"Consider yourself warned. Don't venture into this realm again!" As soon as it finished speaking, I felt an invisible force push me, sending me tumbling down toward the floor. I was falling at such extreme speed that all I saw were streaks of light as my body fell through the air.

As the ground grew larger, I tried to change course, but all I managed to do was spin out of control. That's when my heart did what I thought was impossible: it sped up even more. As a last resort, I tried to reach for something to grab, but there wasn't anything within reach. So I did the only thing I could: I covered my eyes with both hands so hard that I felt them burn. Yet that didn't bring me any relief, as I could still "see" everything as clear as day.

I thought I was either going to die from the crash or from a heart attack—that is, if I wasn't dead already, which was still a serious possibility.

Just when I thought things couldn't get any worse, the floor of my bedroom opened to reveal an abyss that seemed at least fifteen hundred feet deep. A fall that shouldn't have taken more than a few seconds seemed to last over three minutes—three whole minutes of desperation.

Just as suddenly as it started, it was over. I felt my body hit the ground, but much to my surprise, instead of pain I felt the rather pleasant sensation of a very soft landing. My body bounced up and down on my bed as though I had fallen from a great height. I was alive… confused, but alive nonetheless.

As I lay there, awake and contemplating what had just happened, it occurred to me that I didn't know how to feel about the whole thing.

My heart still raced, my face was still covered in cold sweat, my T-shirt was drenched, and the sheets were soaked.

What was that all about? I thought as my eyes sought out the alarm clock next to my nightstand and I realized it was past five o'clock. I quickly got up to take a cold shower. After all, I still had to find something to wear, something simple and yet classic.

I still felt tired even after taking a shower. Part of me wanted to stay home and finish my homework and relax. But at the same time, I didn't want to miss the opportunity to be around Carla. Whenever I was close to her, I felt the season change to spring. It must have been her natural scent, which could transform my reality in the simple blink of an eye.

***

After I finished showering, I took another look at the clock, which read 5:44 p.m. I was already late and still undecided about what to wear. Pressed for time, I grabbed the first unwrinkled shirt I saw and my new jeans.

I still wasn't sure if I should wear my white or navy blue winter jacket. In the end I opted for the blue one, which seemed less conspicuous. After all, I didn't want to make it too obvious that I liked her.

After putting on some of my dad's cologne, I set my sights for the stairs while avoiding the photographs in the Sorrows Hallway.

I made my way downstairs and found my dad pacing back and forth as he talked to Phil, his partner at work. Much to my dismay, he put Phil on hold and came over to talk to me.

"Hey! Where are you going so fast?" he asked as he took off his Bluetooth headset and held it in his giant hands, which only made his hands look bigger and the headset even smaller.

"Oh, hi, Dad, I gotta run, I'm late for dinner with the… guys."

"I see. Any girls at this dinner?" he asked, although he knew Carla would be there. After all, the three of us had been going out every Friday for the past couple of years. We grew up together, and being neighbors made us inseparable.

"Yes, she will be there, and no, I will not ask her out, Dad," I said as I heard Phil's voice through the tiny wireless headset in my dad's hand asking, "Miles? Are you still there?"

"I'm running late, Dad, but I won't be home too late, I promise," I said, pointing at the headset in his hands. He froze for a second as if he had something else to tell me, but I didn't give him the chance. I closed the door and left.

***

"Hey!" someone said from behind me. I turned around, surprised to see Jonas standing there. I guess I was still jumpy from earlier.

"Are you ready?" said Jonas, sporting his normal contented and careless look. I quickly recovered from the scare he gave me.

"Sure," I said as we both started to walk toward La Luna's. Thankfully, it wasn't very far from where we lived. Although the rain had stopped, the cold seemed to have intensified.

"You're late, and now we're late," said Jonas as we walked briskly uphill toward Main Street.

"Sorry, I fell asleep," I said reluctantly, unsure if I should tell him what had just happened to me. I didn't want him thinking that I was going crazy.

"What happened? Did you fall off the bed and hit your head? Because if that's the reason, I'm sure that's normal, at least for you," said Jonas, unable to contain his laughter.

"Very funny. Seriously though, I had this terrible nightmare. It was… surreal. I think…" I paused, "I think… I died." I finally finished. Having just realized the implications of what I'd said, I had to get more information. There had to be someone in town who could help me.

"You obviously didn't die," said Jonas.

As we got to the corner of Main Street, I turned right while he tried to turn left to go toward the restaurant.

"Where are you going? La Luna is this way," he said as he quickly turned around and started following me.

"Mark? Where are you— I mean, where are we going?" asked Jonas, as I paid no attention to him. I was caught up in my own thoughts.

"Mark Anthony!" said Jonas.

"Yes?"

"Where the hell are we going?"

"I need to stop by the library on the way, there's something I have to do there," I said, only paying the necessary attention to be considered sociable as I gazed into the distance, trying to sort out my options.

What Jonas didn't know was that a window of hope had opened up for me when I uttered the words "I died." He couldn't have known the implications of that, or the possibilities I'd just envisioned. He couldn't have known that it meant I could see my mother again.

If I was right, I would be able to see her every night, and I would once again feel a sense of normalcy. Just the thought of feeling her love and care made me drown in hope and wonderment.

"Carla isn't going to be happy that we're late again, but oh well," said Jonas carelessly. He hated being bossed around by his older sibling; although they were twins, Carla had been born a full two minutes before Jonas, and she never let him forget who was the boss.

"I just hope she doesn't order my food. So, do you care to fill me in on why we're going to the library?" Jonas finally asked.

"It's about what happened to me this afternoon, I need to check on something," I said vaguely.

"Do you mean the dream?"

"It wasn't a dream, it was more like a very real nightmare," I said.

"Then it was a nightmare. But why do you seem to be so... so happy?" said Jonas, looking puzzled.

It was true; I'd been filled with immense joy and happiness, a strange feeling that I hadn't experienced in years. Even the biting cold felt warm and comforting. My hands, which had been freezing just before my epiphany, now felt painlessly numb. At that moment, nothing could hurt me.

"I'm not 100 percent sure yet... promise me you won't laugh?" I asked, having decided to fill him in.

"I can promise that I'll try not to," said Jonas, already laughing.

"This afternoon I took a nap in which I felt my soul lift out of my body and hover in the air. I was certain that I was dead when a strange voice started to talk to me. It was like a warning to stay away from that place. Then I started to fall through the floor, which ended up with me falling into my bed awake," I said.

"So why is that good?" asked Jonas, confused.

"Don't you see it? I was sure that I'd died, yet here I am talking to you. Don't you realize what that means?"

"Huh... it means you're glad you didn't die," said Jonas lightly.

"No! It means there's a small chance I can see my...my mother again; talk to her, maybe even touch her."

"Mark, it was just a dream—no, a nightmare," said Jonas seriously. As delicately as he could, he added, "We all have those once in a while, but it doesn't mean we'll see our dead loved ones again."

"There has to be more to it, I know there is. If that thing hadn't stopped me, I would've found out," I said. "I'm hoping the librarian will know more about it and maybe even recommend me a book or two."

"Okay, my friend, we're almost there," said Jonas, apparently not sure what else to say as we passed the old Stoneham Theatre & Ensemble red brick building, which happened to be located right in the heart of Stoneham.

It was fairly dark already. The signs and theater marquee were brightly lit, giving us a warm yellow glow as we passed underneath.

I could not help but notice the sign on the marquee advertising the next Christmas showing. My mother loved that theater.

***

The ambient light seemed to change as we got closer to the Stoneham Public Library. I looked up, trying to find out why, and that's when I noticed that the streetlights near the library were burnt out, leaving the library illuminated by only shades of red and orange of the winter sky, which served to make the brick building seem sinister.

The library was surrounded by a park filled with trees, some as high as a two-story building, and benches spread throughout the property, all now deserted due to the cold.

"I wonder if they are still open," said Jonas, looking around.

"I hope so," I said, cringing as I looked inside, searching for any signs of life.

I climbed the front steps, skipping every other step in a rush to get in faster.

I grabbed the handle on the door and pulled it as my heart sped up. Much to my relief, the cold metal door clicked open.

We still hadn't seen any signs of life inside, but at least the lights were still on.

As we entered the library we could see the librarian getting ready to close.

"I'm sorry, but we are about to close in less than five minutes," she said as she approached us from the back of the library, carrying a few books.

"We won't be long, we promise," said Jonas quickly.

"Maybe you can help us, I'm looking for books regarding something that happened to me today," I said nervously.

"And what was that?" asked the librarian.

"I had this dream, or nightmare, in which I was floating in the air when some creature talked to me. Are there any books on anything remotely related?" I asked. I was hopeful but also rather embarrassed. There was something about saying it out loud that made it sound unbelievable and even crazy.

"Without doing any research, it's hard to tell. Perhaps books on dream interpretation? I think we have a few of those," she suggested.

"I was looking for something more specific, perhaps more scientific," I replied.

"Sorry, I can't help you off the top of my head. But feel free to look around for a couple of minutes if you like. You'll find dream-related books in the non-fiction section just down the corridor. Just don't take too long," she finished.

Jonas and I proceeded to the darker end of the library, where the lights had already been turned off for the night as we looked for the right section.

After a good minute, we found what seemed to be the correct section.

We started to go through the many titles and authors, but we didn't find anything helpful.

"This isn't what I need," I said, frustrated as time ran short.

"Maybe we have the wrong section," suggested Jonas.

Just as he finished speaking, I saw another librarian walking toward us. I was sure she was going to tell us that we needed to leave.

"Quick question," I said. "I'm looking for books related to floating while sleeping. Do you know of any?"

"Oh dear. I think I know what you mean," she said in very calm and soft voice. "But you're in the wrong section. Follow me." She turned around and took off at a surprisingly fast pace for a woman of her age.

As we followed her to the back of the library, I couldn't help but notice that her outfit seemed strange and outdated. She wore a full-length pinstriped dress with a white Peter Pan collar and a red satin ribbon. *Who still wears those these days?* Also, her face looked so... different and yet familiar.

"Right this way," she said as she briskly navigated through the maze of bookshelves. "Don't you love the smell of old books?"

"Smells like sweet vanilla," I said, surprised I hadn't sneezed yet.

"That's because of the books. They actually smell like a combination of grassy notes with a tang of acids and a hint of vanilla over an underlying mustiness. This unmistakable smell is as much a part of the books as their contents," replied the librarian. She then added, "True story."

She led us deeper into the old and now deserted library. The only source of light was a rather dim yellow light bulb that had been left on.

It seemed that we had passed every subject imaginable before we finally came to a halt in the New Age section, which was located all the way in the back as if hidden in shame.

The old librarian put on a beautiful old Victorian sterling lorgnette—I had never seen one of those before, except on TV. It had an exquisite spring flower motif and an engraved handle with the initials "EB" on it.

Just when I was about to ask the meaning of the engraving, she turned around, and I was able to read her badge: "Mrs. Emerald Barnes—Librarian."

"Where is it now... it should be right... here it is!" she said as she removed the book from a shelf across from me and brought it closer to her face. She blew on the book, and thousands of small dust particles flew off, looking for a place to settle.

"This is it! *A Guide to Astral Projection and Related Techniques,* by Victor Windlow. This should clarify things a bit," she said, handing me the book. I held it as if it contained the secrets of the universe.

"There are many other books on the subject, but this is by far my favorite, and I think you will like it as well," Mrs. Barnes added. "Come back and see me after you have a chance to read it," she said, putting away her lorgnette.

"Astral projection? What exactly is astral projection?" I asked.

"Everything you need to know is in there, but in a nutshell, astral projection is when your body falls asleep and your soul, or spirit separates from your body to explore other realms, primarily the world beyond," Mrs. Barnes said in the most serious tone. "It's simpler than it sounds, really. You see, every being is made of two basic elements, two different building blocks if you will: the material body that we all know and understand, and the spiritual body which is ignored by most, including doctors and scientists."

"When we sleep, the physical body rests, and the astral body gets its exercise. So you see, we all live dual lives, so to speak, one while awake and another while we sleep at night," explained Mrs. Barnes. "We do this every single night. You do it as well. Somehow when you had your astral experience, you were able to trick your consciousness into remaining aware—" She was interrupted by the sound of heels walking toward us.

"Boys? Come on, I need to close, where are you guys?" asked the other librarian.

"We're here!" I said loudly enough so she could hear me.

"How did you know about my dream?" I asked Mrs. Barnes. I didn't remember telling her about it.

"I have to go now; come back and see me when you have read that book. There's much more that I need to tell you," she said, before she disappeared among the bookshelves.

"Oh… there you are! Have you found the book you needed?" asked the other librarian.

I couldn't help but notice that she was dressed differently from Mrs. Barnes, and even more puzzling was the fact that her badge was also different. It read "Jane Olstein—Librarian—Middlesex County Public Library."

"Yes, we have, thank you," I said, dumbfounded.

"Follow me, and I'll check that out for you," said Ms. Jane as she turned, heading toward the front of the library. As we walked behind her, I looked at Jonas. He looked astonished, and for the first time since I'd met him, he was at a loss for words.

"Astral projection huh? Interesting," said Ms. Jane, flipping through pages randomly. "I wouldn't have imagined this was what you were looking for."

"Yes, I didn't know it either; the other librarian helped us find it," I said while she scanned my library card.

"What other librarian?" asked Ms. Jane, surprised.

"The older lady, with white curly hair in a bun and an old-style dress. I believe her name was Mrs. Barnes," I said.

"I'm… the only one… here," stuttered Ms. Jane. "I've been working here for over twenty years. I've been the only librarian for a long time," said Ms. Jane as chills ran down my spine and goose bumps spread over my body.

"But we just talked to her," said Jonas.

"I'm afraid that's… impossible," objected Ms. Jane. "You see, Mrs. Barnes passed away in 1987, back when I first started working here, and how do you even know what she looked like?"

Ms. Jane looked all around as if she were the one who had just seen a ghost. She got so pale she looked more like one than Mrs. Barnes did.

"Would you be a dear and wait for me while I shut off the lights and lock the doors?" said Ms. Jane. Her hand shook as she nervously handed me back the book.

"Sure, no problem," I said, feeling a bit guilty for having caused such a strong reaction in her.

"Okay, I just need to shut off the computers. One second, please," said Ms. Jane, still looking distressed.

We waited for her to shut down the computers and the last of the remaining lights, and then we followed her outside, where she insisted we wait for her to lock the doors.

During our time at the library, the weather outside had grown even colder, something I'd thought impossible.

Ms. Jane opened her rather large red purse and searched desperately for her library keys. Her cheeks were now rosy, having recovered some color.

A few seconds passed before I heard the clinking sounds of keys as she pulled them from the bottom of her purse.

"Okay, have a good night," said Ms. Jane as we all made our way down the stairs to the sidewalk.

She hopped in her yellow Volkswagen Beetle and left Jonas and me there, looking puzzled.

We walked the next two blocks in complete silence. I was concentrating on skimming my newly acquired book while Jonas just walked beside me silently, which was a rarity.

"Let me ask you something," Jonas finally said, not sounding like his usual self. "You're not having a thing with my sister? Are you?"

"Ah? No! I'm not having a thing with your sister. Why do you ask?" I said.

"You two have been acting strange lately," said Jonas, matter-of-factly.

"You know, she'll date someone, sometime," I said, trying to gauge his reaction.

"I feel bad for the poor guy already," said Jonas, cracking his knuckles as if he was trying to convince me of his determination and strength.

It was definitely not the answer that I'd hoped for.

After that, we continued walking toward La Luna's in awkward silence.

***

Before long, we had arrived at La Luna restaurant.

"Carla isn't going to be happy," said Jonas, looking around at the usual places we sat. "There she is!" he said, pointing frantically.

As we walked toward the table, Carla looked at us, seemingly upset. She seemed anxious, but maybe she was just embarrassed to be sitting alone.

"Where have you guys been?" she asked impatiently when she saw us. "I've been sitting here for over half an hour, looking as though I was stood up, just waiting—"

"Mark had to make a quick stop at the library and I had to go with him," said Jonas, as if I had forced him.

"Nice try, but the library closes at six, and it's now 6:25," said Carla, looking at her watch. "For all I know, you guys stopped at the video game store. Again."

"It's true! We went to the library and saw a spirit," said Jonas, taking Carla and me by surprise.

"Right," said Carla, opening the menu.

"He's not lying," I said as I sat in the empty seat next to Carla and proceeded to open my menu. I felt like pizza, but I didn't think it sounded appealing enough, so I ordered some cannelloni instead.

As we sat in the solarium of the restaurant, the weather took another turn for the worse. I looked outside and noticed that small, delicate snowflakes had started to fall, accumulating slowly on the glass pane.

"What do you mean, you saw a ghost?" asked Carla.

"I didn't say that I saw a ghost. What I said was that we saw a spirit, which is very different," said Jonas.

"That's the same thing," said Carla, rolling her delightful eyes.

"No, it's not," said Jonas. "A ghost is scary while a spirit is not."

"Ah… are you sure it was a spirit?" asked Carla, still not believing him. I was trying to decide if I should intervene and back him up or just stay out of it.

"I'm sure. I'm not making this up, I swear," said Jonas, sounding very confident. "Mark saw it too! We both did."

"It's true, I was there," I said.

We explained what had happened in great detail over our meal.

Carla didn't seem to believe us at first; I didn't blame her, I hardly believed it myself, and I was holding the book Mrs. Barnes had given me.

"She found us this book. She wanted me to read it."

"May I see it?" asked Carla.

"Sure, here. From what I understand, it has to do with leaving your physical body behind while the spirit wanders freely."

Carla took the book and started to flip through it. She then opened her purse, took out a notepad and a pen, and wrote down the author's name and the title of the book.

"I'm reading it next, so you will have to wait, sis," said Jonas.

"All I need to read most books is a computer with Internet connection. In fact, I could probably read that same book tonight when I get home if I wanted to," teased Carla.

"True, but I still prefer paper books."

The restaurant was packed. Everyone from my school seemed present. You had the jock table, the nerd table, and the nobody-cares table, which was our table.

There were lots of couples as well, but they usually spent more time making out than actually eating.

Normally Wendy would have taken forever to take our orders, but not that night.

"What would you like?" said Wendy, chewing bubblegum.

Jonas just sat there, at a loss for words; looking at her mesmerized.

"I'll have the cannelloni," I said, hoping she wouldn't notice Jonas's puppy-dog face.

"And for an appetizer?" said Wendy, doodling on her pad.

"I'll have the bruschetta and a Coke," I said.

"I... I will... have the stuffed mushrooms—" Jonas stuttered.

"I don't think you should have those," Carla interrupted. "Do I need to remind you of the effect they have on you?"

"Shut up..." Jonas said under his breath.

"I'll have the fried calamari instead," said Jonas, changing his mind, probably to upset Carla because she was averse to it, hating even the smell of it.

"And for dinner?" asked Wendy, still doodling and blowing bubbles.

"A large margherita pizza and a Sprite, please," said Jonas, still looking like he was ready to obey Wendy's every command.

"I'll have the minestrone soup and a glass of lemon water, then for dinner the chicken marsala and a Coke," said Carla quickly, probably just to see Wendy struggle as she tried to keep up.

"Your order should be out soon," said Wendy.

As we waited for our orders to arrive, the snow started to accumulate on the solarium roof like an intricate puzzle in the sky.

"I tried to astral project once," said Carla, almost whispering.

"I'd never even heard of it until today," I said casually.

"You guys are officially crazy," said Jonas.

"And you're not, mister 'I saw a spirit'?" replied Carla. We all laughed.

"That was different, she was… actually quite nice," said Jonas, looking like he was in a daydream.

"Listen, astral projection is simple really. Humans have believed that we are made out of matter and spirit for quite some time now, at least a few thousand years, give or take," said Carla.

"So, Mark, you don't think it was a dream?" said Jonas.

"I don't think so. I felt more aware when it happened than I feel now sitting here with you guys. Everything felt more real, as if I belonged there. It was like my real home was over there," I said. "I know it sounds crazy, but if this stuff is for real, then the possibilities are endless. I could…" The emotion swept over me. "I could see… my mom," I said, finally able to express myself.

"Mark, let's not jump to conclusions here," said Carla. "Besides, didn't you say that something threatened you when you left your body?"

"Yes, but there is no way I'll let anything stand in my way when it comes to seeing my mother again," I said.

"Anyone having dessert?" said Jonas, flipping open the sweets menu.

"No, Jonas. We're going to be late for the movie," said Carla, frowning.

"Are you coming, Mark?" asked Jonas.

We had been going out for dinner and a movie on Fridays for as long as I could remember. The fact that Stoneham didn't have a movie theater didn't stop us—the twins' mother usually drove us to the neighboring town of Woburn to Carla's favorite movie theater, all because my father was too afraid I would end up like my mother if he brought me a car.

"I can't tonight, I need to finish the rest of my homework."

I was tempted to go, but I really needed to finish my assignments, and I wanted to read the book about astral projection so I could try to understand what was happening to me and, more importantly, see if I could use astral projection to see my mother again.

"All right then, if you're sure," said Carla. I could hear a bit of disappointment in her sweet voice, and it broke my heart.

"I'll see you later, mate," said Jonas, taking one last bite of his pizza.

"The bill is on me today," I said so they wouldn't be late for the movie. Besides, it was my turn anyway. They paid last time.

"Mom's here, we better hurry," said Jonas, taking yet another bite of his pizza. Every time I heard Jonas say that, I couldn't help feeling a bit envious.

"Thanks, Mark. I'll see you later," said Carla as she put her coat on.

I looked outside and saw Carla's mom waiting in her Volvo, parked in her usual spot. When she saw me, she smiled and waved, and I did the same.

After they left, I had a slice of Jonas's leftover pizza, and then my head started to throb.

I couldn't believe that a whole week had passed since my emergency landing on I-95, yet my forehead still ached from time to time.

On the way home, I took the side streets because it was quieter and I wanted some time to think. It had been an eventful day, a day that had brought hope back into my life.

Within a week, I had almost died a horrible death, met an unknown creature while astral projecting—something I had never heard of before—and met a seemingly friendly spirit, not to mention all the stuff that happened in school and my invisible stalker. As soon as I thought about the stalker, I sensed its presence; it followed me as I walked alone in the cold and dark side streets.

I realized that I had never felt its presence when I was near Carla.

I was still a few blocks from my house when the snow started to pick up, and the delicate flakes suddenly turned into blobs of heavy snow. My feet began to leave imprints in the snowy road.

I placed the book inside my jacket to protect it. That book held all the answers I needed, and I was going to guard it with my life if I had to.

I should have walked down Main Street, also known as Route 38, but it was too noisy, being the only major road in town. Instead I preferred the quiet side streets, where I could walk down the middle of the road if I wished.

I picked up my pace as the sense of someone following me increased. But the truth was that I rather enjoyed the sense of danger. I had been searching for thrills, excitement, and most of all answers ever since my mother's death—so far in vain. That is, until today. It was a mere glimmer of hope, but at this point I took anything I could get.

CHAPTER FIVE
Astral Secret

I arrived at my house much earlier than usual and caught my dad by surprise.

"You're home early," he said.

"Yes, I'm a bit tired, and besides, I still have to finish my homework," I said, running up the stairs and concealing the astral projection book under my jacket. I didn't have the energy or the will to have a long and heated debate about religion. My dad was a self-confessed, devout atheist. If science didn't recognize it as valid, neither did he.

As I got into my room, I took off my jacket and placed the book on top of the bed. My math homework was still on the floor, and I decided right then and there that was exactly where it would stay for the night.

I jumped in bed and started to devour the book. Mrs. Barnes was right; it described what had happened to me in great detail.

Just after ten o'clock I heard my dad approaching my room.

"May I come in?" he said as he entered the room.

"Sure," I replied, quickly swapping the astral projection book for my math homework.

"Are you still doing homework? On a Friday?"

"I'm almost done. I figure I'd get some studying done for my test on Monday. I'll have it finished before I go to sleep," I said, feeling guilty for lying, but for the moment it was necessary.

"Wow! This is unheard of. Is this change permanent?" asked my dad with a hint of suspicion in his voice.

"Maybe it's about time that I became more responsible. After all, I'm sixteen… isn't that what you keep telling me?" I said, hoping our conversation wouldn't last much longer.

I sensed my dad was feeling a bit under the weather, and although I had a pretty good idea what was bothering him, I asked, "Tough day?"

"No, it's just that… life, well, it gets to me sometimes, you know…" He stopped talking and looked straight into my eyes. That's when I realized he was almost crying.

I couldn't resist the urge to get up to give him a heartfelt hug. He patted me on the back firmly and then cleared his throat. "Don't worry, son, everything is fine. We'll be fine, tiger."

I knew my father well, and I also knew the unwritten and unspoken rule of the house: words like "death," "died," and even "destiny" were forbidden. I'd learned to hate those words from a very young age, as though if we didn't say them, it would make it easier to forget. But it didn't.

"Dad. You need to go out with friends sometimes and socialize," I said, even though I knew it was useless.

"No, I'm not interested in going out, thank you very much," he said as he stood up. "I don't need anyone else."

"Dad, I just meant for you go to some friend's house and relax a bit. There is nothing wrong with being a bit social, you know?" I said.

"I'll think about it," he said, but I didn't buy it. "Listen, don't stay up too late. You have your flight test tomorrow." He gave me a slight pat on the shoulder as he passed me on the way out.

"Sure Dad, have a good night," I said, smiling. It felt good to have a heart-to-heart with my dad. Let's just say it was long overdue. I was proud of myself, because I felt that he left my room feeling better than when he came in.

As soon as my dad closed the door, I threw the math workbook down and resumed reading the astral projection book.

One of the first things the book emphasized was that astral projection, also known as astral travel or an out-of-body experience, was as real and as normal as sleep, and anyone could do it.

Normally, I would have discarded everything that a book like this told me, but this book seemed different. Right in the prologue, the author said not to take his word for it, but instead he encouraged readers to validate the experience for themselves.

Apparently once I succeeded at astral projection, a whole new world would open up to me. I would be able to find and visit a dead relative, visit any place in the world or any other world, and pass through solid matter if I wished. But the most intriguing and the one I was most interested in, was finding and visiting dead relatives.

Part of me screamed that all of these claims were nonsense and outright impossible, but I decided to follow the author's advice and try it for myself. I figured it was worth a wild shot, given what was at stake. Besides, *would the author give such bold advice if it weren't real?* I thought.

Time flew and soon the clock read 1:03 a.m. I had to get to bed soon.

Even though I was dead tired, I wanted to stay up reading. I decided against it, but not before skipping to the chapter about "Astral Projection Techniques," which was a step-by-step guide to achieving full body separation.

I memorized what the book said was the most effective technique to astral travel, and then I got ready for bed.

I carefully hid the book under my bed and shut off the light on my nightstand, leaving the room illuminated by a very faint yellow nightlight.

***

I followed the book's instructions carefully. They stated that I should contract and relax every muscle of my body, starting with my feet all the way to my head.

It took a while, but eventually my body began to relax, and just as the book predicted, after a few seconds I felt my feet and legs grow warm and start to tingle.

Relaxing the body didn't prove to be too challenging, but quieting the mind proved to be an almost impossible task—just as the author had warned.

I was feeling very nervous and excited at the same time because tonight could be the night I would see my mother again… but it could also be the night I met that horrible thing.

It didn't matter, though. I would face any number of dangers for even the slightest chance of seeing my dear mother again. It was my chance to feel whole again, and nothing would be able to keep me from trying.

I found out that the mind is a very hard thing to control. Not thinking about anything was torturous, even harder than the book emphasized.

I lay there for over thirty minutes and didn't experience anything other than a mild tingling sensation in my legs. I was about to give up when I began to see lights floating through my closed eyes. Apparently, I had entered a state called the "hypnagogic state," which was simply a "mental phenomenon that occurs at the threshold of consciousness, when a person is in a between-state, half awake and half asleep."

Although I wasn't sure what it all meant, I knew that I was seeing lights floating in and out my field of view even though my eyelids were closed, which the book had warned me about so I wouldn't be distracted by them.

Sleep was approaching quickly. I struggled not to give in to it completely; I needed to hold onto a small thread of awareness if I was to succeed.

Some people took years to learn astral projection, but I didn't have that kind of time. I wanted to see my mother, and the sooner the better. After all, I'd waited almost ten excruciating years already.

Suddenly, a wave of energy passed through me; it was like being hit by a 240-volt electric shock.

It was the same painless shock that I had felt earlier in the day. It was as though every cell of my body was vibrating at an incredible speed.

The lights behind my closed eyelids turned into a strange, bluish-green hazy image. It took me a few seconds to realize I was seeing my darkened bedroom, even though my eyes were closed.

I could see everything clearly. *How is that possible?* I wondered. *There's no way*, I thought. It was impossible. If I had to guess, I would say I was no longer seeing the world through physical eyes.

Before I could get lost in the perplexity of things, I remembered the book's warning against becoming too excited, or my spirit wouldn't be able to leave my physical body. So I tried my best to contain my excitement, confusion, and the questions that crowded my mind.

I was now in somewhat familiar territory. I knew what should be coming next, and it brought me solace.

I expected to feel my spirit lift up slowly as it separated from the physical body, so I wasn't too surprised when it actually happened.

I'd been expecting that. What I wasn't expecting was the feeling of someone pressing hard against my chest and the sudden and severe difficulty in breathing. I also didn't expect my heart rate to increase tenfold, nor did I know that I was going to be gasping desperately for air.

I was breathless and scared, my heart pounding hard. I wanted to cry, but the tears refused to fall. I wanted to beg for air, but my mouth refused to open.

I wanted to scream from the top of my lungs, but the air refused to vibrate out of me.

I wanted to get help, but my muscles wouldn't respond.

I needed to do all those things at once, but all I could do was lie there: breathless, motionless, in deafening silence, gasping, desperate for the breath of life, a glimpse of hope.

All I managed to get were short and insufficient gasps of air.

I felt that my life was in imminent danger and regretted all those times when I felt depressed and secretly wished my life would end. I was ashamed of my own weakness.

I remembered the dire warning from earlier, the warning I had ignored. In a way, I felt almost glad I hadn't listened. After all, one way or the other, I would see my mother again. Even if I wished a different fate, a different destiny, it was too late. I was about to die. I was sure of it.

I'd given up all hope when I heard a mysterious and seemingly benevolent voice.

"Don't worry, everything will be all right," said the sweet voice. "No, you're not dead or dying!" It answered my question even before I had a chance to ask.

"Help! I can't breathe," I thought, because that was the only thing I could still do.

"Just breathe normally. The sensation you're feeling is your own doing," said the voice calmly. "Your heart is fine, and so is your breathing. You need to control your emotions, and everything will be fine again," the voice continued. The voice reminded me of an angel. Although I didn't recognize it, it sounded familiar and even friendly.

Just moments after hearing that, I was able to breathe a little easier and my heart rate returned to near-normal levels.

Slowly, the pressure in my chest was replaced with a gratifying sense of freedom, a gentle floating. I couldn't have felt lighter if I were floating in space.

I looked around the room, but something felt strangely out of place, almost as if the room had maintained its essence but some of its details were wrong, including the location of my door and windows.

I focused my thought on my window, and suddenly I began to float toward it.

Did I move here by thought alone?

I decided to test this new theory, so I thought about the misplaced door, and sure enough, I found myself gliding gently toward it. It wasn't long before I was standing next to it. Then I tried to think of the closet, and again I started to move toward it automatically, as though thought was the only required fuel. On the way, I thought about going up, and almost immediately I started to float up toward the ceiling.

I rather like this method of transportation, I thought as I kept going to different areas of my room, allowing myself to enjoy the floating sensation. I even tried to do some somersaults, back flips, and other acrobatic moves that seemed impossible in the physical realm.

I enjoyed it so much that I forgot about the voice that had helped me just minutes before.

Soon I was spinning and rolling midair, turning around several times and loving my newfound freedom.

I looked down at my body in bed.

Nothing could have prepared me for seeing my own body lying there, seemingly lifeless. It was a surreal sight, and yet I didn't care about my physical body. It was as if I were looking at a used piece of clothing.

I realized I wasn't my body. I was so much more. The real me was there looking at my old physical and useless self.

I still possessed all my memories. In fact, they were clearer than ever before—memories that were once a blur were now crystal clear. I possessed all my personality traits. All my fears, all my faults, all my shortcomings, and all my virtues were intact.

Instinctively, I knew my astral self was in fact real. I wasn't that motionless body in the bed below. That was only a shell, a machine. Granted, it was a very precise machine. But my true self was this much lighter and fluid body. It was this body that allowed me to float around my bedroom, pushing the boundaries of physics.

Suddenly, I remembered the possibility of seeing my mother again.

***

As soon as the thought of my mother crossed my mind, I remembered my earlier experience. I remembered that raspy voice warning me to stay away from this realm—as if he were some sort of God, as though the undead world belonged to him. The scenery suddenly changed from the familiar surroundings of my bedroom to the musty and fetid cave of my nightmares.

I felt myself covered in mud and becoming stuck in a huge pit of sewage. Trapped and scared, I shivered uncontrollably.

I heard desperate screams in the distance, anguished pleas mixed with strange noises. The sounds seemed to be coming from all directions, making it hard to pinpoint their exact origin.

A dense grey fog permeated the mud pit, making it almost impossible to find anything no matter how hard I looked. With much effort, I was able to move around the room a little, but I still couldn't find the source of those desperate pleas.

I looked for an exit, but I couldn't find one anywhere. I was about to give up when I decided to look above me, and that's when I found the source of the screams. The moment I saw those poor beings, I wished I hadn't.

Hanging in the air just a few feet above my head were very small and cramped cages dangling by old rusty metal chains. The cages housed different beings and animals; most were too big even to fit in their cages, so much bigger in fact that the limbs of the biggest creatures dangled outside their cages. The situation was truly deplorable. In all my life, I had never heard of anything like it.

The smaller creatures seemed to be more vocal, as though their wills hadn't yet been broken. The cries for help came from them. On average, they ranged from two feet to about four and a half feet tall. They were bald and skinny with eyes that seemed too big for their faces. The worst was their skin, which was covered with lesions, scars and bruises. They didn't look humanoid, but there was a faint resemblance. They were all covered with rags. Their voices were faint, yet with some effort I was able to understand some of what they were saying.

"Run while you can!" said a tiny, skinny creature in a weak voice.

"There's nobody here," I replied. "And I can't run in here."

"He's coming!" the creature said, shivering.

As soon as I heard those words, I felt a devastating dread, almost as if death itself was near.

"Who's coming?" I asked.

"HELP!" said a three-foot-tall creature sobbing in its cage as the neighboring creature stretched his long fingers trying to console it.

58

I was determined to find a way to help these poor beings.

I gathered all my strength and climbed out of the mud pit and onto a nearby dirt bank. I lay there, out of breath for a few seconds, and then I remembered that I probably didn't have much time left. I would have to hurry if I wanted to rescue anyone, including myself.

I bent down on the ground and started to look for anything that I could use to defend myself and set those poor creatures free.

Mostly blinded by the fog, I moved my hands in front of me, skimming the ground for anything remotely useful. After an excruciating frantic search, I felt something sharp and cold touch my fingers and pulled it closer. It seemed to be a long tool or weapon, like a spear. As for its use, I could only assume it was a torture device, mainly because it had what seemed to be dried blood on its metal tip.

I picked up the device as I tried to figure out a way to use it to free the prisoners.

The chains clanged as I rammed the long spear against the cages' locks several times.

After some effort, I was able to free three creatures. However, much to my surprise they didn't try to leave. They simply stood inside their cages.

It wasn't until I heard the sound of someone or something approaching that I understood. I must have made too much noise. Whatever it was, it wasn't good.

Next thing I knew, I was hit by a glowing red orb of energy and thrown violently against the furthest wall of the cave.

When I fell to the ground, I was still holding the upper half of the spear in my left hand. It must have split in two on impact.

It was a few seconds before I was able to get up.

"I warned you!" said the strange yet familiar voice in a tone that sent chills down my spine.

"I… I'm sorry. I just ended up here; I didn't mean to," I said, shivering and looking around for what hit me. "What is this place? And what am I doing here?" I managed to ask.

"You have many questions. But what makes you think that I will answer them?" the voice asked.

"How do you know—"

"I can read your thoughts," said the voice.

"Listen, I just want to find my mother—"

"Enough, I know what you want better than yourself," said the voice.

After a short silence, he added, "You undead people never learn."

"Please… sir," I pleaded nervously. I urgently needed some answers.

"And what even makes you think your mother wants to see you?" said the voice, growing more upset.

His words had a profound effect on my mental state. I tried to disguise my fear, but each word made my insides rattle.

"You can't hide anything from me. I know everything there is to know, even your innermost thoughts and emotions."

"Who… are you?" I asked.

"It doesn't matter who I am. All that matters is that you're going to regret not heeding my warnings. You'll pay for your trespassing."

I was lost and didn't know what to do next. If what the creature told me was true, all my fears would be freely accessible to him, and there was no hiding from that sort of thing.

"Do you have a name?" I ventured out of desperation.

"Doesn't everything?"

"What is it? Your name, I mean," I asked, trembling.

"I'm known as Phasma Val-Fraux, and I'm the Guardian of Threshold, but you undead have called me many things over the ages," replied Phasma.

"Doesn't Phasma mean ghos—" I started to ask, but I stopped abruptly, realizing that I might not like his answer.

"Yes, you're right. I'm the sole guardian of the astral realm. In this realm, I'm all there is, no one is above me," said Phasma, not wasting the slightest opportunity to make me even more terrified.

"What's this place?" I managed to ask even as the hairs on my neck stood up and chills coursed through my body.

"You invaded my world, my realm, and you don't even know?" asked Phasma, sounding intrigued.

"I don't. I just read a book that told me what to do. I was just trying to find my… deceased mother."

"She's not here, this is my realm!" yelled Phasma.

"I'm truly sorry. I didn't mean to bother you," I said.

"Too late for that. Every time you venture into my realm, you bother me," said Phasma. He then added, "This world is mine and mine alone. It belongs to me. I'm its guardian. I exist to prevent you undead from crossing into the Threshold," said Phasma.

"What's Threshold?"

"Enough! You don't have any business being here. You must know that every violation will be severely punished," said Phasma, sounding much closer than before.

I looked up and saw a black shadowy figure moving just above the fog. It seemed very large, and yet it moved fairly fast.

Up to that point, I had no idea who I had been talking to. Had I seen him before, I doubt that I would have carried on a conversation with him.

Without warning, I felt a great force push me back down into the mud pit. I suffocated as I was held under the mud. I struggled and tossed, trying desperately to free myself.

After a lot of fighting, I was finally able to move my head just above the mud line. As I caught my breath, I could see that the shadowy figure had returned to circle over me. Partially hidden by the dense fog, it zigzagged in and out of the fog so fast that I couldn't see much of it except its large silhouette.

The dark figure charged me from the fog, grabbing my shoulders as it dragged me across the cave.

I was so terrified that I barely felt any pain until my arm hit a rock wall.

What I'd seen would forever haunt me. It was part animal, part monster, with red curly horns on its head and dark red skin covered by a black hazy silk garment. Its body was covered with seemingly human bones, but the most prominent part of it, was its wide, bat-like wings.

Phasma Val-Fraux stood there pushing me hard against the rocks while my shoulders seared in pain with his touch.

I let out a painful scream and my knees lost the strength to hold me up. Phasma quickly dragged me up and then dropped me a good four feet onto the damp ground.

When I fell, I felt my wrist burn. I lay on the floor, suffering as I never had before. Then I looked up, only to see Phasma charging at me yet again.

I didn't have much time to react, but somehow I managed to roll to my left side as quickly as I could just when he was about to hit me, forcing him to narrowly miss me.

Figuring that I had only a few seconds before Phasma recovered and charged at me once more, I got up as fast as I could and took off running while being careful to avoid the mud pits.

I had no idea where I was going. The cave was huge and full of dead ends, twists, and turns. I just kept pushing on as fast as I could. I ran for what seemed like ages, but it couldn't possibly have been more than five minutes.

I allowed myself a quick look back to see if Phasma was still behind me. The second I turned my head back, I became distracted and tripped on a huge rock protruding from the ground.

I fell helplessly to the ground. I was unable to contain a sharp scream of pain.

The pain was most intense at first, and then it seemed to quickly subside. After a few seconds, all that remained was the memory of the pain. It was as if the pain was simply a reflection of physical pain, a mere fraction of what pain normally felt like. Yet the pain in my shoulder persisted; it was as though the pain caused by Phasma lingered.

I tried to get up and run, but I couldn't even stand, let alone run.

I could feel Phasma approaching. It wasn't long before I heard his evil laughter in the distance as I sat on the floor, helplessly looking for a corner to hide in.

As I crawled toward a dark corner, I felt the air moving around me as Phasma landed just a few yards from me.

As he slowly made his way toward me, grinning, with his wings still outstretched—which only made him seem bigger and more menacing—I saw his features in greater detail, from his big, sharp and terrifying fangs to his long, honed claws.

As his demonic face got closer to mine, I froze. There wasn't much I could do; I was once again facing imminent death.

I closed my eyes as I waited in agony for my last few seconds to tick away.

Even through my closed eyes, I could sense his face near mine. I could even smell his rotten breath. Then I felt a strong wind as Phasma flapped his wings.

A few seconds passed, so I opened my eyes to see what was happening, only to regret it as I saw Phasma lift up his claws in preparation for the fatal strike as though he wanted me to see my demise.

I closed my eyes quickly so I wouldn't see what would happen next, but then suddenly it felt as though the ground opened up, as if the floor tiles were being removed one by one from right under my feet.

When I opened my eyes again to see if it was death welcoming me, I saw that I was falling through a seemingly endless black tunnel, plagued by a darkness not even Phasma seemed willing to brave.

The ground below filled my field of vision at once.

Not knowing what else to do, I let out a scream of madness or desperation… I didn't know which.

Just when I was about to hit the ground, I felt myself bouncing on my bed as though I'd fallen from a tremendous height.

The air thickened, and my breathing became more labored and physical. The dense grey fog that had filled the air just seconds before turned into a light brown haze before disappearing completely.

That's when I felt sweat starting to form on my forehead. I opened my eyes and saw that I was back in my physical body, much to my surprise and relief.

CHAPTER SIX
The Sky is the Limit

When I woke up, I remembered that today marked eleven years since my mother passed away. I tried telling myself that my experience had just been a dream, yet the pain I felt told me otherwise; my arms hurt to the touch, and my shoulder felt sore, along with my toes, which ached like never before.

I wasn't sure of anything anymore, especially considering how real the whole experience had seemed—but everything had happened just as the book said it would. *Was it just a mere coincidence?* I wondered.

I was still debating whether it had been a dream or not when I remembered seeing a small dusty model airplane on the top of my bookshelf while floating above it. Try as I might, I couldn't see it from any other angle. If I found that model plane, there was a good chance that the whole experience was real.

I grabbed the first chair I saw and climbed. Even standing on top of the chair, I couldn't see anything so I fumbled around a bit with my hand. That was when I felt my fingers touch something small. I pinched it with my index and middle fingers and brought it into my reach. It was the same model airplane—God, I must have been six years old when I got it. So it really *had* happened; it wasn't a dream after all.

In retrospect, I'd had a great time flying around in my room—the sense of freedom and peace was nothing like I'd ever experienced before; not even flying in an airplane gave me such a rush. To be honest, I didn't think anything in this world could ever surpass that exhilaration.

What about that creature? I thought.

What did he say his name was? I tried hard to remember; I seemed to be forgetting the details of the event as the seconds ticked away.

I concentrated until I finally remembered... his name was Phasma Val-Fraux.

I quickly searched for a piece of paper so I could write his name down. The only thing I was certain about was that he stood between my mother and me.

I was still in a daze when the alarm clock announced that it was 7:30 a.m., and I had to hurry if I wanted to make my flight test.

I quickly made my way downstairs, doing my best to avoid the photographs on the wall. Much to my surprise, I found my dad already up and waiting to take me to Hanscom Field Airport.

"Good morning, big day today," he said, smiling and taking a sip of his morning coffee.

"Morning Dad. Yes, hopefully I'll find the runway this time," I said.

"Don't worry, you'll do fine. I've already checked the weather, and it's gorgeous out... cold but absolutely gorgeous," he said enthusiastically.

"Dad, do you think they will let me take the test today?" I asked.

"That's up to the FAA, but I certainly hope so," he said.

The FAA was investigating not only me, but my instructor as well. As a result, I was only going to find out if I was allowed to retake my flight test when I got there.

I grabbed a travel coffee mug and filled it with black coffee, followed by three spoons of sugar. I wanted to make damn sure I was awake for my 8:00 a.m. test.

As we rode there, I mentally went through the flying procedures. I had even memorized various checklists.

After a brief and quiet ride, we arrived a few minutes early.

"Good morning, Mark," said Guiles as soon as I entered the building.

"Morning, what's the news?" I asked.

"See that guy over there getting coffee? That's Steve, he's with the FAA, and he will be accompanying you today in your flight," said Guiles.

I was happy to be allowed to retake my flight test, but I was also a bit confused because my flight test was supposed to be a solo flight.

"Mark, I know this is a bit unorthodox. Unfortunately, that was the only way the FAA would allow you to retake your test. Just go with the flow."

"Oh, okay," I said, not knowing what else to say.

"Steve, allow me to introduce you to Mark Anthony," Guiles said as Steve approached with a hot cup of coffee in hand.

"Nice to finally meet you," Steve said.

"Same."

"So, are you ready for your test?" he asked.

"I certainly hope so."

"This is how it's going to work. I will be flying with you; however, I'm not going to talk to you unless you make a very serious mistake. Then I'll verbalize your mistake for safety reasons, at which point you probably will have failed the test. Any questions?"

"No, sir," I replied as my hands already started to sweat.

We were heading outside to where the airplanes were parked, when I realized that I had forgotten to check with the front desk to get an airplane assigned and pick up its keys. I excused myself and rushed back inside.

After getting the keys, I checked the airplane's tail numbers to find it in the parking lot. I was assigned a Cessna 172SP G-1000, which was both good and bad. Good because I wouldn't get lost while in the air and embarrass myself since it had a very powerful navigation system. At the same time, it was bad because I had never operated an aircraft with the G-1000 system; hopefully, it wouldn't be too bad since my flight was Visual Flight Rules, or VFR, which meant that I wouldn't need to rely on instruments or program different frequencies into the onboard computer.

After doing the inspection of the airplane and its various systems, I entered the cockpit and began working on my start-up procedure as the FAA inspector took his seat beside me and put his headset on, then opened his notebook and carefully started to take notes, which made me even more nervous.

Once the engine was up and running, I contacted ground control and obtained proper clearance and taxi instructions. I was once again assigned runway eleven for takeoff.

Steve looked worried as the plane zigzagged in the taxiway centerline as it normally did for a few seconds until I got used to the rudder controls. I was going to tell him not to worry, but I figured that wasn't in my best interest.

"Mark, try not to go over fifteen-hundred RPMs," Steve said as he continued to take notes.

I almost pushed hard on the brakes, but then I remembered that all I had to do was pull back on the throttle control, and the airplane would gradually slow down.

I was sure I had already messed up and became very nervous. My hands wouldn't stop sweating; I had to keep wiping them off on my jeans.

"Strictly off the record, I think you performed a mighty awesome emergency landing last week. However, I also think that you shouldn't have flown at all given the weather conditions at the time, but that's a different matter altogether. Personally, I think your instructor and the tower controller were at fault," said Steve casually, as though he had noticed how nervous I was and was trying to make me feel more confident.

I wouldn't blame him if he changed his mind and decided not to fly with me. It was my first time back inside a cockpit since last week's accident, and I felt anxious.

"Try to relax and go with the flow," said Steve, opening his notebook again and resuming taking notes.

Steve's words of encouragement must have worked because I felt a bit more at ease. My hands even stopped sweating, and I was able to breathe easier.

After receiving proper authorization from tower control, we took off, heading toward downtown Boston as I climbed to eight thousand feet.

This time I kept constant watch on the weather radar screen as well as the G-1000 anti-collision system, so much so that I almost forgot to keep looking for other aircraft through the windshield, as I was supposed to.

As we approached Boston, I contacted Boston air traffic control to ask for permission to fly in their airspace. Because I was planning on flying over Logan International Airport, I had to climb to a required minimum altitude of ten thousand feet.

Everything was going smoothly, when suddenly on the way back to Hanscom Field the radio panel started to smoke, quickly filling the cockpit with a stinky and blinding white smoke. Breathing became extremely difficult. The burning smell was overpowering.

Without thinking twice, I opened the side cockpit window to vent the smoke. I next reached for the fire extinguisher just in case there was a fire, but thankfully there wasn't.

The smoke cleared as quickly as it had started; the combination of speed and high altitude made clean air rush inside the cockpit, forcing the toxic smoke out.

I must have taken the appropriate actions because Steve seemed to be celebrating.

"Good job, Mark. Here, I'll keep an eye on the radio in case it catches on fire while you fly us back," said Steve, taking the fire extinguisher from my hands, seemingly glad to still be safe and alive.

"Thanks. I think it's broken," I said, wondering what was the proper procedure in our case.

"In a situation like this, we just have to land without asking permission. It's not like we have any other choice. Fun, isn't it?" replied Steve. Before adding, "Don't worry, they will probably figure out that our radio is busted once they see us on approach. I'll keep an eye open to make sure there isn't any other traffic around when we are landing."

If it had been any other day, I would have had my cell in my pocket, but because the inspector had accompanied me in my test, I had given it to my dad to hold. I guess Steve didn't have his cell either because he didn't say anything.

As we approached the airport, I aligned the airplane with runway eleven, hoping that no other aircraft would be crossing it, landing on it, or taking off from it.

I applied full flaps and lined up perfectly with the runway—thanks to the great visibility—so perfectly in fact that I hoped Guiles and my dad were watching.

Aside from causing some small airplanes to stop on the taxiway, the unauthorized landing was successful, even uneventful.

I carefully taxied back to the flight school parking lot and parked in the closest parking location I could find. Before I had even shut down the engine, both my dad and Guiles stood outside the airplane with puzzled looks.

"What happened?" asked Guiles, knocking on the cockpit side window.

"The radio blew up in smoke," I said, pointing at it.

"Luckily you guys made it back safely," said Guiles as he opened Steve's door.

"Wow, that was weird, I've never seen that happen before," said Steve, "but the good news is that you've passed. Congratulations."

"Just like that?" I asked, surprised.

"Well, as far as I'm concerned, yes, that's it. By the way, outstanding job, my friend. That was a fantastic performance. I have no doubt you'll make a great pilot," said Steve, shaking my hand firmly.

"Well done," said Guiles, also shaking my hand.

On the way home, we stopped to get some breakfast. I had French toast sticks and soda while my dad opted for another cup of coffee.

"Son, I may go to Phil's house for a bit today, if that's okay. You want to come? He invited us to go over and shoot some pool," my dad said as he drove down on I-95.

"Cool, Dad, but I think I'll pass, I have some reading to catch up on," I replied.

"I shouldn't come home too late, we're just going to cook some food and maybe play some online games, if we have time."

"Sounds fun," I said, already regretting the fact that he would probably be taking his laptop with him. It was the only computer in our house that didn't have Internet monitoring software installed.

By the time my dad dropped me off at our house, it was almost ten in the morning.

"Here, take this so you can buy some lunch and dinner," said my dad, handing me a fifty-dollar bill. "If you need anything, just call my cell. I should be home around eight o'clock, tops."

"Don't worry, Dad. I'll check with the guys to see if they want to come over and have a pizza or something," I said as I closed the car door.

"Sounds good."

My dad took off toward Phil's. I went straight to Jonas and Carla's house.

***

I knocked at the twins' door and waited patiently as I heard soft footsteps coming down the stairs, closely followed by a much faster and louder footstep, which I assumed was Jonas running down the stairs. If I didn't know better, I would have thought he was falling down the stairs.

Figuring Carla would probably answer the door as she normally did, I spent a few seconds caring for my cracked lips and fixing my dirty blond hair. Unfortunately, I wasn't quick enough. Carla opened the door and caught me by surprise.

"Good morning," she said, smiling.

"Hey, buddy!" said Jonas as he shoved Carla aside.

"Good morning, I did it! I finally passed my test," I replied.

"So you're officially a pilot now?" Jonas asked.

"Not quite officially yet. I still need to be seventeen to get my license."

"Great news, I'm proud of you," said Carla, beaming.

"Do you guys want to go to the library with me?"

"Hum… no, it's Saturday, I can think of a million other ways to spend my Saturday," said Jonas. "Besides, I don't think I'll ever set foot in there again."

"I'll go," said Carla, much to my surprise.

"Great, I'll buy lunch. How's Felicia's?" I replied.

"On second thought, I like how that sounds. I'll come too and if that… ghost shows up again, I'll have some questions for her," said Jonas. We all knew Jonas couldn't pass up an eating-out opportunity, especially a free one.

"Okay then, let's go," I said.

"I have to get dressed first, I can't go in these," said Jonas, pointing to his borderline-ridiculous flannel pajama pants.

"Okay, I'll go get my stuff and meet you guys outside in like ten minutes, if that's okay," I said. I needed to run to my house to get the astral projection book.

"Awesome, that will give me time to finish my breakfast," said Carla, looking enchanting and gorgeous even though she had apparently just woken up.

I rushed over to my room and picked up the astral projection book from under my bed. Every time I passed through the Sorrows Hallway, I struggled. My mother's memories haunted me.

There had to be better days ahead; I felt it in my bones, or maybe it was just life's way of getting my hopes up, so it could disappoint me yet again.

I couldn't take it anymore; I had to do something about that picture of us swinging happily under the blossoming shade. The tree, which had been in our backyard, was long gone—a snowstorm took care of that problem years ago. In retrospect, that was when I first strayed from my atheist upbringing. That was when I first thought God might have heard my silent prayers.

Something had to be done about that photo. If I was getting ready to fight a thousand demons or the mightiest of armies single-handed, I would probably have felt better than I did then. My heart was congested with its own beating, my blood burned with sorrow, and my pores felt dirty, as if clogged by shame. My throat couldn't swallow the guilt I felt. Yet I pressed on. I had my target sighted, and even though it hurt to look at it, I bravely pushed forward. When I was within reach, I almost turned around, giving in to regret. In the end, my perseverance won.

I yanked the photograph of my mother off the wall, opened the nearest closet door, and buried it in the midst of some flowery bed sheets that I recognized as being her favorites. It seemed appropriate that her picture should rest among them.

As I walked past the hallway, only a hint that a picture had hung there remained. Nothing more than a mere outline on the old and yellowing wallpaper.

Relieved, I headed outside to wait for Jonas and Carla. I didn't feel like staying in the house alone because I still felt, or rather sensed, a presence following me. For lack of a better word, I felt haunted.

I sat on the steps of our poorly maintained porch and started reading my book, paying particular attention to any mentions of the monster I'd seen earlier.

Not even five minutes passed before Carla and Jonas came out dressed for a winter storm. Which was probably wise, since heavy clouds were starting to overtake the New England sky.

"Ready?" asked Jonas as he crossed the street.

"Sure am," I replied while I put a small indentation on top of the page I was reading and closed the book.

"Aren't you cold?" asked Carla, looking concerned.

"Not really," I replied, trying to sound strong. The truth was that I was a little cold, but I was too embarrassed to admit it. Besides, the library wasn't far, and I was wearing a jacket, just not a very heavy one.

"The weather is turning nasty again," said Jonas, looking up.

"I know, they're saying we could get eight to ten inches of snow and possibly some ice," I said.

Eight to ten inches of snow for us Bostonians wasn't a big deal. Up here, we were used to that and much more, but it was the first snowstorm of the season, and for some unknown reason, people always seemed to forget how to drive in the snow. People also had the tendency to stay indoors for the snowstorm. When snow was forecasted, everyone seemed to expect the end of the world. Certainly by now the store shelves are bare. People rush to buy anything remotely useful. Milk, bread, water, and batteries were always the first items to vanish.

"So, tell me, how was your test?" asked Carla.

"It was good for the most part. Can you believe the radio burned out and filled the cockpit with smoke? Luckily I was able to think fast and solve the problem," I said trying not to sound like a jerk.

"Oh my God, I'm glad you're okay," replied Carla.

"Talk about bad luck. You shouldn't walk too close to me… I have enough bad luck as it is," replied Jonas, distancing himself trying to be funny.

"What are we going to do at the library, anyway?" asked Carla.

"I managed to astral travel last night," I said casually.

"So the book was right? It's really possible?" asked Jonas.

"So far, everything I read happened," I said as we crossed the street.

"Have you seen her… your mom?" asked Carla.

"Not yet, but I met someone or something," I said.

"Who?" asked Jonas.

"I wrote down his name when I got up. I didn't want to forget it," I said as I reached for the piece of paper in my pocket. Good thing I wrote it down, I'd forgotten his name again.

"Here it is. He said his name was Phasma… Phasma Val-Fraux," I said after struggling to read my own morning calligraphy.

"Is that why you want to go to the library on a Saturday?" said Carla.

"Yes, I need to find out more information about him and the astral realm," I said as we reached a stop sign.

"Have you heard of this amazing invention that's called the Internet?" said Jonas.

"Very funny. You know my dad monitors my Internet access in the house. I don't want him finding out about this. At least not yet."

"I sure would like to see you try to explain to an atheist that you're searching for someone that's, you know… dead," said Jonas.

"That's a conversation I'm not looking forward to," I replied.

"Have you told him you believe in God yet?" asked Jonas.

"No, and I'm not even sure that I do," I said. My friends looked confused, and I didn't blame them. I felt confused.

"What I believe is that all this, everything, couldn't have come from nothing. Basically, I don't believe that nothing could've created something so wonderful and complex as everything," I said, trying to be as clear as possible.

"Explaining that you believe in God should be easier than explaining to your dad that you believe in ghosts. I would start with that, if I were you," Carla suggested.

"Wait a minute! I recall telling you that spirits existed and you distinctly telling me they didn't," Jonas said. "So now you admit that you believe in spirits? Just like that? Whatever happened to you must have been very persuasive to change your mind that fast."

"After last night, I can say for sure that I know spirits do exist. I can't prove it, but I know they exist, and it's all thanks to this book and Mrs. Barnes," I said, pointing at the book.

"That would explain why you're in such a good mood this morning," said Carla as we approached the library.

***

Much to my surprise, the library was buzzing with people carrying books back and forth. I must confess that I'd never been to the library on a Saturday morning before—and I never thought I would.

"Here we are," said Jonas, pointing out the obvious.

"Let's see if this ghost story of yours is really true," said Carla as we climbed the steps in front of the library.

"Not ghost, spirit," whispered Jonas. "Besides, I doubt she'll manifest. There are way too many people around."

"Good morning," said Carla as she approached the librarian's desk.

"Good morning, how may I help—" said Jane Olstein, stopping short when she noticed Jonas and me standing next to Carla. She started to tremble and looked extremely nervous.

"May we use the computers for some research?" Carla asked politely.

"What? Sure, just sign in here," replied Jane, pointing with her trembling finger at the sign-up sheet next to her desk.

"Thank you very much," replied Carla as she added our names to the empty sign-up sheet.

"What has gotten into her?" asked Carla as we walked to the computer room.

"Mrs. Barnes's spirit, that's what!" Jonas replied.

"I guess seeing us again must have reminded her of last night," I said.

"Did she see it too?" Carla asked.

"No, but she realized that we saw old Mrs. Barnes's gho... spirit when we described her. She said it was impossible because Mrs. Barnes was dead," I replied.

"She even asked us to wait until she closed the library because she didn't want to be here alone," added Jonas.

When we got to the computer room, I picked the one in the corner next to the big windows. Jonas chose the one next to mine, and Carla sat across from us.

One of the first things I did was search for "Phasma Val-Fraux," but I didn't find anything. Then I remembered he told me he was known as the "The Guardian of Threshold" so I searched that, and surprisingly I obtained just over five million results.

The first was a Wikipedia page. I even found a song from Van Morrison titled "Dweller on the Threshold." Surprisingly, the song had everything to do with what had happened to me, so I wondered if others had gone through the same experience, perhaps even Van Morrison had experienced it before. After all, he described Phasma so well.

As I listened to the Van Morrison song, I clicked on the Wikipedia link, which read: "The **Guardian of the Threshold** is a menacing figure that is described by a number of leading esoteric teachers. The term Guardian of the Threshold, often called 'Dweller on the Threshold,' indicates a spectral image that is supposed to manifest itself as soon as the student of the spirit ascends upon the path into the higher worlds of knowledge."

There was no doubt in my mind that I had found him. *It should be just a matter of time before I can defeat him and see my mother again*, I thought.

I read the entire article twice, soaking in all the available information about my enemy.

"I found him!" I said after reading the article yet again.

"Let me see," said Jonas, hunching over to look at my monitor.

"This is a Wikipedia article about him," I said, pointing at the screen.

"What, no picture?" said Jonas, disappointed.

"I'll see if I can find one," said Carla as she typed on the computer.

"Here's something," said Carla after a while.

I quickly slid the office chair over to Carla's side. I must have pushed the chair too hard with my feet because I ended up closer to Carla than I'd intended, causing a second of awkwardness between us.

"Wow, he looks like the devil," said Jonas when he saw one the drawings of Phasma. It was a drawing of a small, devilish creature.

"That drawing doesn't do Phasma any justice at all. He's way more horrifying than that," I said.

"That one!" I said, pointing frantically to the screen. It was a black-and-white drawing of Phasma flying in a cloudy night sky before a huge full moon. That silhouette gave me chills. I remembered him flying above me just like that, half hidden in the fog. It was a perfect match.

"He doesn't look so bad on that one," Jonas offered.

"Wait until you meet him," I said.

"Meet him? What do you mean?" asked Jonas, looking worried. "I have no plans to meet him, thank you very much."

"You never know, if it happened to me, it can happen to you," I said.

"I wouldn't mind if it happened to me," said Carla. "It might be kind of fun, being able to fly around and stuff."

"Not me, I don't need any devilish creature chasing me—besides you, that is," said Jonas, teasing Carla.

With five million results, I had my research work cut out for me; it would be a long day at the library.

"Good luck with that," said Jonas as he looked over my screen.

Carla was intrigued enough that she was doing her own independent research.

Jonas was the only one not doing anything useful; he spent his time hopping between social networks, music, and video sites.

We had learned a lot after a couple of hours.

"We should break for lunch soon. That way we can discuss what we have learned," said Carla, looking a bit tired.

"Sounds good. I'm so hungry," said Jonas, sliding his chair back.

"Is Felicia's all right with everyone?" I asked. I had chosen Felicia's mainly because it was just a half-block away from the library. I wanted us to get there fast and get back even faster.

"That's fine, they supposedly have the best homemade meatballs in town."

"I think I'll have a nice toasted sub," said Carla.

"Okay, let's go," I said, getting up and folding my notes before I placed them in my back pocket.

***

Getting to Felicia's restaurant didn't take more than five minutes. We walked at a brisk pace, not just because we were in a hurry, but also because we were cold.

A waitress named Margaret greeted us and guided us to a booth overlooking Main Street. The restaurant was very quiet on that particular Saturday. As soon as I'd walked in, I felt like I was an extra on the set of *The Sopranos*. They had old-school décor, complete with wall murals and pictures of celebrities who had eaten there.

"I've never been here before," said Carla, looking around the restaurant.

"Neither have I," added Jonas.

"Look! Is that Senator Kennedy?" said Jonas, pointing toward a signed photo of Kennedy on the wall just as the waitress showed up to take our orders and drop off a basket of breadsticks.

"These are really good," said Jonas, eating one.

"There's nothing better than warm bread on a cold day like today," I said, looking out the window. Not many people seemed willing to venture out in the cold, and the few who did were bundled up in oversized winter outfits, seemingly regretting their decision to go out.

"How can you live without eating meat?" asked Jonas, as though being a vegetarian was a crime against the most basic human instinct.

"Let's not start this discussion again. You guys start talking about food and you always end up talking about philosophy and religion," said Carla.

"Do you guys want to come over to my house tonight? My dad went to Phil's and should be back late tonight," I asked.

"Sure, we can rent a movie," said Jonas, looking impatient.

"What's wrong?" asked Carla.

"I'm hungry, that's what's wrong. Where's our food?" Jonas asked as he played with his napkin and silverware.

"I'm sure it's coming soon, besides, it's only been like ten minutes," said Carla as she fixed her hair.

Margaret brought us our sodas and more breadsticks, which Jonas readily attacked.

"So, what movie do you guys feel like watching?" I asked, trying to change the subject back.

"Something scary," said Jonas.

"I think I've had enough scares to last me a lifetime," I replied.

"What about a comedy then?" asked Carla.

"I don't really care what we watch as long as it's new and fresh," I answered.

"And not scary," added Jonas, laughing perhaps a bit louder than necessary.

Margaret came by and dropped off our meals.

"This is really good," Jonas said, taking a bite of his sub. "You don't know what you're missing."

"Good is relative," I replied, hoping I could avoid that conversation. After all, I had more important things to worry about, including Phasma.

"So does that mean that bad is relative as well?" asked Jonas.

"Depends on your definition of good and bad, but as a general rule I believe good and bad are relative," I replied, even though I knew better. "In fact, I find it very hard to believe that anything in the world is absolute."

"So what about God?" asked Carla.

"God is an absolutely confusing matter to me," replied Jonas jokingly as he wiped tomato sauce off his mouth.

"I think even God is relative… relative to the perceiver's point of view at least," I replied after some thought. Then I added, "Only an absolute being could perceive and understand God as an absolute being."

"Now I'm really confused," said Jonas, which wasn't very surprising because I was starting to get confused myself.

"That's what you two get for trying to play philosopher," said Carla, laughing.

"Funny," said Jonas.

"So where does this Guardian of Threshold live? Do you know?" asked Jonas.

"According to what I read, he lives in another dimension. The astral realm," said Carla.

"So that's where I went in spirit," I said.

"If I understood it correctly, you were in between dimensions, in the Threshold if you will," said Carla.

"Wouldn't my mother be there as well?" I asked, unable to disguise my disappointment.

"I don't know. Threshold is a place that exists between our realm and the astral realm. I can't say for sure if your mother would be there or not," Carla said.

"There's only one way to find out," I said.

"You're actually going to confront this Phasma dude?" Jonas asked, looking worried.

"I have to. Apparently, he's the only thing standing between me and my mother, so yes, I'll do whatever I need to do," I said, probably sounding more convinced than I felt.

"Let me see if I got this right… this astral place is where we go to when we die? And you're planning to go back there?" asked Jonas.

"Yes, according to several articles on the subject, the astral realm is what we would refer to as heaven and hell," said Carla, enlightening both Jonas and me.

"So does that mean Threshold is hell?" Jonas asked.

"I don't think so, I think it's just a realm between the two extremes," replied Carla.

"Either way, I don't want to go there any sooner than I have to," said Jonas warily.

"When we sleep, our astral body, or spirit if you prefer to call it that, separates from our physical body so we can move freely between our physical realm, Threshold, and the astral realm," I explained. "It's supposed to be completely safe to visit, at least that's what the book says."

"It certainly doesn't sound very safe from your description of this Phasma," said Jonas.

"I have to agree with Jonas on this one," said Carla.

"What else did you find out about the astral world?" I asked.

"The astral realm is where all the different thought forms exist. Threshold is supposed to be the entrance into the astral realm. It's a place where the physical ceases to exist and the spiritual flourishes. Apparently, it is where we came from and where we'll all ultimately go when we die, or so it's believed by various religions and philosophical doctrines throughout history."

"Sorry but I have to ask, is the Guardian of Threshold the devil?" Jonas asked.

"The Guardian of Threshold is perceived by each one of us differently. He's often seen as a diabolical figure because he's supposed to be the sum of our collective fears, hate, and negative emotions. However, he also serves a purpose, like everything else in the astral," explained Carla, demonstrating her photographic memory.

"Yep, I most definitely don't want to meet him," said Jonas.

"Mark, why do you hold on to the past? Why not move on and let things just be the way they are?" Carla asked.

Carla might not have known it, but there wasn't anything she could do or say to change my mind. I was dead set on accomplishing the unthinkable. I was going to see my mother again, whatever the cost or consequences.

"I don't know how to explain it, but I feel that this is something that I'm meant to do, almost like it's my dest—" I paused, reconsidering my word choice.

"Destiny," completed Carla.

"Yes, that's the only word I can think of," I said, even though I detested that word. I'd stopped believing in destiny after my mother's accident.

"Guys, we should get back to the library. We still have lots of research to do," I said, getting up to pay the bill because I didn't feel like waiting for Margaret to bring the check and return with the change.

On the way back to the library, Carla kept rubbing her arm and shoulder on mine as we walked side by side, sending jolts of electricity coursing through my body. They weren't much different from the ones I experienced during my astral projection.

***

As we walked back to the library, big snow clumps started to fall heavily from the sky, quickly turning the sidewalk snow into slippery mush.

It was unbelievable that the weather could have changed so much in the past half-hour.

Jonas and Carla were still trying to decide what movie to watch that night while I walked quietly beside Carla. Not even her arm rubbing against mine could divert my attention from something she'd said during lunch: "Threshold is where we came from and where we'll all ultimately go when we die, or so it's believed by various religions and philosophical doctrines throughout history."

I'd given up on religion a long time ago, but it brought me comfort knowing that various religions believed that we all go to the astral realm when we die.

I was brought back to reality when Jonas ran in front of me and stomped on a puddle of slush, sending it flying all over, including onto the bottom of my jeans, which got all damp and smudged.

As we approached the library, I couldn't help feeling that I'd opened a door that couldn't be closed. Not that I wanted it to close.

Jonas and I raced to the computer room. We both wanted the library's newest addition—a top-of-the-line Intel Quad-Core processing workhorse—but it didn't matter because in the end, all that processing power would go to waste. All we would be doing was browsing the web, checking our emails, and visiting the occasional music and social networking site. These days, a toaster could handle that job just as well.

"God, thanks for making me a girl," Carla said when she caught up to us.

Again Carla sat at the computer facing Jonas and me, while Jonas settled for the computer next to mine.

I guess our talk during lunch had spiked Jonas's curiosity because when I peeked at his computer screen, he seemed to be actually reading articles about astral travel, more specifically about astral sex, which apparently was so far-fetched that the library's Internet blocking software failed to flag it as inappropriate.

"Look who's doing actual research for a change," I said sarcastically.

"I don't know, man, this stuff is really out there. I mean, have you heard us talk lately? Other realms, astral realm, guardian…" said Jonas, frowning.

"You forgot to mention ghosts, spirits, and devilish creatures," added Carla.

"Trust me, I know how it sounds, but like it or not, things are happening," I said.

"I want to trust you, mate, but it's hard," said Jonas.

"Why don't you try to astral travel too? In fact, why don't you both try?" I said.

"No way!" said Jonas, looking shocked.

Almost at the same time, Carla replied, "Sure, I'll try almost anything once."

"What? Are you serious? Are you actually going to try this?" asked Jonas. "What if that… thing chases you too?"

"Then I'm sure that I'll figure out a way to get rid of him," replied Carla.

"Jonas is right, it may be dangerous," I said, trying to discourage Carla. The last thing I wanted was to put Carla in any kind of danger.

"Oh well, you didn't listen to me. So now I don't have to listen to you. Besides, I've already made my decision," said Carla. Once she said that, the decision was set in stone. She was determined, much like me. It was one of the things I loved about her.

Jonas was the complete opposite. I could get him to change his mind as many times as I wanted to. All I had to do was to show him a new point of view, and his opinions would shift quicker than the wind.

"I guess I'll try it as well. After all, who's going to protect you guys when you get into trouble?" said Jonas.

"And who says that we're going to get into trouble?"

"Mark, I've known you long enough to know that it's only a matter of time," said Jonas, laughing.

"I second that. As a matter of fact, you already did," said Carla.

"Well, it's settled then, we'll try to astral travel tonight," I said. "After all, we stand a much better chance of defeating the Guardian of Threshold together."

From that point on, Jonas seemed to take our research more seriously. He even kept his jokes to a minimum, which rarely happened.

***

The weather outside continued to get worse. It was dark much earlier than normal because of the low, overcharged clouds surrounding Stoneham.

Around 3:10 p.m., I started to get tired. There was something about watching the snowflakes drifting to the ground that seemed to relax me.

I was sitting back on my chair with my feet up on the window-sill, watching the sky get darker by the minute as the winter night loomed. Although it was dark, none of us felt like getting up to flip the light switch on.

I just sat there relaxed, alternating between reading the astral projection book and watching the snow outside. Suddenly, I felt as if the back of the chair gave away, and I fell. My first thought was that Jonas had pulled my chair back, but then I realized that I hadn't fallen. I was once again floating freely. Everything was covered by a faint, dark green tinge. To my right, I saw Jonas focused on his computer screen, while Carla had immersed herself in a book. They were both so busy that they didn't seem to notice me.

That's when it occurred to me that I must have fallen asleep and astral projected. To make sure, I decided to take a look at my own body. My body was still there, peacefully dozing with the astral projection book resting on top of my chest.

When my peripheral vision caught a glimpse of the big window, I jumped back in shock. Standing outside the window was Phasma. He wore a dark hood that completely covered his face, as though he was trying to protect himself from the little daylight still left.

As soon as he saw me, he charged through the glass, pushing me straight into the wall just like before. It hurt when I first hit the wall, but soon the pain gave way to fear.

I screamed for help, but my friends didn't pay any attention. Apparently they couldn't hear me. I was all alone.

"What do you want from me?" I screamed as he stood there.

"Your dreams, your desires, your hopes and wishes," he replied.

"Leave me alone!" I screamed and then turned around and ran toward the library hall, zigzagging through the bookshelves in a futile attempt to delay him.

I ran past people and noticed that many seemed to have a certain energy emanating from them. They all had auras of different colors; some were dark green, others dark blue, while others were purple or different shades of grey. Regardless of their auras, they all had shadowy creatures following them wherever they went. Yet they didn't seem to notice. It was almost as if they were one.

After reaching a dead end, I stopped to catch my breath. Unfortunately, I didn't have a chance. As soon as I looked behind me, I saw Phasma flying straight through the library's bookshelves. He stopped just a few yards away from me. Then he slowly walked toward me, passing through anyone who stood in the way.

I was still debating whether I should continue to run or face him when I heard a female voice say, "STOP!"

I couldn't quite make out where it was coming from, but it seemed it was coming from all around.

Suddenly, Mrs. Barnes materialized in front of me. Her skin shone a soft, light-blue color and her hair floated in midair as if she were underwater. A powerful yet comforting energy emanated from her, an energy that seemed to stop Phasma dead in his tracks.

"Get back, Phasma," said Mrs. Barnes.

He didn't obey, but he didn't charge either. He stayed still as if considering his options.

"This is your last warning!" said Mrs. Barnes as books started to rattle in place. Some even floated off their shelves as if getting ready to be thrown at Phasma. They all emanated a bright and powerful glow.

"This isn't over. I'll be back," said Phasma; then he slowly turned around and vanished into the ground.

I had many questions for Mrs. Barnes, but I felt as if a giant magnet was pulling me. I tried in vain to hold on to something. I was immediately pulled back into my body at great speed, passing through bookshelves, walls, people, and whatever else stood between my physical body and me.

I opened my eyes, startled to find Jonas shaking me so hard that the astral projection book I had been holding fell onto the ground, landing with a loud thud.

"Sorry, mate, you were snoozing," said Jonas.

"Not to mention snoring loudly," added Carla, to my embarrassment.

"It happened again," I said. "He was here." I looked all around to make sure he was gone. "He was right there," I said, pointing toward the window. "He pushed me against that wall. My back still hurts."

"The way you were sitting, no wonder your back hurts," said Jonas.

"No, it's from when he pushed me," I insisted.

"Come on, let's see it," said Jonas. "Something like that is bound to leave a mark."

I lifted the back of my shirt so Jonas could check, but I didn't think he would find anything.

"Holy cow! That's huge," said Jonas.

"What is it?" said Carla as she got up.

"Wow, it *is* huge," confirmed Carla as she lightly touched my back. Her hands and skin were like an instant anesthetic.

"I want to see it... can someone please take a picture?" I asked.

"One second," said Jonas, reaching for his phone.

"Here, see, it's not that bad," said Jonas, not sounding very reassuring.

Jonas handed me his phone, and I was shocked at what I saw: my shoulder blade was covered with different shades of purple, and my back was swollen.

"No wonder it hurts like hell," I said. The pain actually appeared to be increasing in intensity.

"How did this happen?" asked Carla.

"I told you, Phasma pushed me from here to that wall over there and I banged my back on the wall. Yesterday he hurt my shoulder," I explained.

"Are you all right? Do you want to go to the hospital?" asked Carla.

"Nah, I'm fine, just a bit sore," I replied.

"Those are some nasty bruises," Jonas added.

"I don't understand, the book said that astral travel is completely safe."

"Not safe at all, at least not for you, I would say by the looks of it," said Jonas.

"Everything I read on the subject so far says that nothing in the astral realm affects the physical realm," said Carla, looking confused. "Something else must be going on here."

"I'll tell you what's going on, you're being haunted by a ghost," said Jonas, scared.

"Ah, look who is saying ghost now," said Carla.

"I already told you a ghost is mean while a spirit isn't," said Jonas.

We continued the rest of our research in silence.

At precisely 5:45 p.m., Jane Olstein walked into the computer room to announce that the library would be closing in less than fifteen minutes and to suggest that we should wrap up everything as quickly as possible. If you asked me, I would have said that Jane was too scared to stay at the library a minute longer than she had to.

Because the afternoon flew by, we were all scrambling to print as much reading material as we could.

"I'll be right back," said Carla, getting up and heading toward the library hall.

"Where are you going?" asked Jonas.

"I'll be right back," Carla replied, not looking back.

"I wonder where she's going," said Jonas, getting off his chair.

"I don't know, probably to the restroom," I said, shrugging.

Ten minutes passed before Carla returned to the computer room carrying a thick, old book with her.

"What's that?" asked Jonas.

"It's a book."

"I know that. What kind?" replied Jonas.

"*The Art and Practice of Astral Travel*," Carla responded softly.

"Not you too," said Jonas, cringing.

"If I'm going to try this, I want to make sure that I'm at least a bit prepared for what I may encounter," replied Carla as she threw some paper scraps in the trash.

"Guys, the snow is getting really thick out there, maybe we should go," I suggested.

"Wow, that's got to be way over six inches of snow already," said Jonas, looking through the window.

"Just give me a few seconds, I have to email myself something," said Carla as she sat back at her computer.

"Hurry up, I'm getting hungry," said Jonas.

"Why, are you afraid of Mrs. Barnes's ghost?" I asked to mess with him.

"I'm not afraid. I'm just tired, we've been here all day," said Jonas.

"I've seen her, you know?" I said.

"First of all, she's a spirit and not a ghost, and second of all, I'm not scared of anything," said Jonas, trying to sound brave, but his reputation and track record showed otherwise.

"Thanks, my dear, how kind of you to defend us spirits," said Mrs. Barnes as she floated out of the wall, gliding gently toward us just a few inches above the ground.

"Ah… uh… no problem," said Jonas, stuttering. He looked like someone who had seen a ghost, but at least he was able to talk, which was an improvement over the previous night.

"Ah… did I forget to tell you that Mrs. Barnes recommended this book to me?" said Carla, smiling and apparently enjoying the panicked look on Jonas's face.

"So you know each other?" I asked, puzzled.

"We just met outside when I went to find a book about the astral realm. Mrs. Barnes was very helpful," said Carla, still smiling.

"Don't be scared, Jonas." Then Mrs. Barnes turned to me. "Mark, remember to be yourself, your true self, especially when you astral project."

"Is Phasma gone?" I asked.

"For now, but he's sure to come back," replied Mrs. Barnes.

"By the way, thanks for intervening today," I said.

"No problem, just know that I won't always be there to protect you. You have a rather unusual connection with him that is affecting your physical body, as you found out today. So it's imperative that you exercise extreme caution, because if you get hurt enough in the astral realm your physical body can perish as a result," explained Mrs. Barnes.

"Will that happen to us as well?" asked Jonas, finally regaining the ability to speak.

"I don't think so, but only time will tell. Mark's bond with Phasma is too strong. It's not quite how things are supposed to work. Just know that I'm trying to figure out how to help you three. I'll let you know as soon as I know more. Oh, and don't forget to be there for each other when the time comes," finished Mrs. Barnes just before she dissolved into thin air.

"Where did she go?" asked Jonas, perplexed.

"I don't know," I said. "Perhaps she went back to the astral realm."

Unfortunately, Jane Olstein walked in just as we looked at each other in shock.

"Not again," said Jane. "Whatever it is, I don't want to know. Come on, let's go."

I shut off the computers as we all exited the room. I figured it was the least I could do; besides, I had a feeling that if I didn't, Jane was going to ask me to anyway.

"The hairs on the back of my neck are still up," whispered Jonas as we walked to the front of the library.

"Mine too," added Carla. "But remember, it wasn't a ghost, it was a spirit."

"You guys haven't seen anything yet," I said, trying to prepare them.

"She doesn't scare me," said Carla. "She strikes me as a sweet old lady."

"How do we know that she's on our side?" asked Jonas.

"I guess we don't, we'll just have to find out," Carla whispered.

We all walked to the front door, including Jane. At first I thought she was escorting us out since it wasn't six o'clock yet, but apparently she wasn't about to stay the last few minutes alone inside the library because she walked out with us, her key on hand ready to lock the door.

"Have a good weekend," said Jane as she slipped and almost fell on the snow-covered sidewalk.

Once she got to her car, she opened the door and hopped inside, closing and locking the door quickly. I wondered how she was going to see the road with her windshield covered in snow.

She must have realized it also, because she timidly came out of the car, opened the trunk, took out a snow and ice scraper, and began frantically cleaning the snow off the windshield.

"I think she's lost it," said Jonas quietly. I was thinking the same thing.

"She could at least turn her car and heater on to help melt the snow," I said as we started to walk back.

As we walked, we had fun kicking snow at each other, although I suspected that Jonas and Carla were having slightly more fun than I was because they were better dressed for the extreme weather conditions. Besides, my shoulder and back still hurt.

It wasn't long before the twins decided they wanted to throw snowballs at each other. Even though I expressed my disinterest in the idea, the second snowball rushed toward me without mercy.

I felt like swearing loudly as the snowball hit me, but I opted for revenge instead. So I reached for the ground and packed the most massive snowball I had ever made, then I put all my strength into throwing it at Jonas's head.

Much to my dismay, I hit Carla. But in my defense, she walked into it.

Embarrassed and ashamed, I rushed over to help her, but as soon as I got close enough, I saw her bright smile, a smile so warm that I was surprised the snow around her didn't melt.

I realized her trick too late, as she jumped on top of me and pushed my head against the snowy sidewalk and proceeded to throw snow all over my face.

"Okay… you win," I said, frozen but unable to hide my happiness. Although I still hurt, I wasn't about to say anything. I wanted the moment to last as long as possible.

After a few seconds, we got up. I looked at Jonas and saw him staring at us.

"Are we renting a movie tonight?" I asked to change the subject and lighten the mood.

"I'm not going to the video store, it's too cold. Besides, video stores are so old school. Let's just order something online," said Carla.

"That works for me, I even have enough money left to order us dinner. How does pizza sound?" I said as we continued down the now-deserted Main Street.

"Sounds good to me, as long as we order something meaty," replied Jonas.

"Sure, I'll get two pizzas, one cheese and one pepperoni," I offered.

"Yep, hot pizza sounds really good, especially on a day like this," said Carla, shivering.

"What do you guys say we meet around 7:30 p.m.?" I asked as I moved my arms to relieve my shoulder pain.

"That sounds good, that'll give me enough time to take a hot bath," said Carla as I immediately imagined her in the bathtub.

"Just don't make it a half-hour ordeal," said Jonas, sounding bossy and bringing me back to reality.

"Where did Mom and Dad go?" asked Carla when she noticed that their car wasn't in the driveway.

"I think they went to Aunt Flores's house, at least that's what I heard them talking about," replied Jonas.

"See you soon, Mark," said Carla as she smiled at me and went inside her house.

"I'm counting on you, mate, to help me choose a good movie for tonight," said Jonas before he went inside.

"Depends on what you call good," I said as I made my way to the side door of my house. After all, I didn't trust our crooked porch when it snowed as much as it had. One of these days that porch was going to fall down, of that I was sure.

CHAPTER SEVEN
The Plan

When I reached the side door, I twiddled with the house keys, trying to find the keyhole in complete darkness. Since we rarely used this entrance, the lights were off. When I was finally able to open the door, I reached for the light switch and flicked it up and down several times, but nothing happened.

The power was out, but the old, faithful oil heater was still going strong.

I walked into the dark house, closing the door behind me. There wasn't a soul in sight, yet I knew I wasn't alone.

I could once again feel *his* presence. It was as if he were beside me, purposefully waiting for the right opportunity to strike again.

I felt unnerved and all alone in our old two-story house. Then it occurred to me that I didn't have to stumble in the dark. Since I had my cell with me, I turned it on and used it as a temporary flashlight. It would have to do for now, but if I wanted to have power left for emergencies, I would have to go get the real flashlight from the basement—even though I really didn't feel like venturing down there, not because it was dark or because I was all alone, but simply because the basement was filled with my mother's old stuff.

My dad couldn't bring himself to throw out anything that belonged to my mother, so everything she had ever owned was stored in our basement. I would rather take a trip to hell than go into the basement. In fact, it had been years since I last went down there, but if the power didn't return soon I wouldn't have a choice.

After waiting about fifteen minutes, I decided to get it over with.

I carefully tiptoed down the basement stairs, trying very hard not to fall, which only served to increase my sense of dread. I kept trying to convince myself there was nothing to fear.

Once in the basement, I managed to find the fuse box, which housed the flashlight, with relative ease. I was grateful that it was dark so I couldn't see my mother's things.

Although I had the flashlight in my hand, I didn't dare turn it on yet. I preferred to make my way upstairs in the dark rather than see my mother's old stuff.

"Ouch!" I screamed, scaring myself as my big toe hit something.

I let out a scream of panic and pain and looked down to realize that I'd just kicked an old battery-operated fire truck from my younger and happier days.

I wasn't normally this thin-skinned, but the past few days had made me anxious and nervous. Something within me compelled me to understand what was going on.

I'd always been like this: if something scared me, I needed to understand it before I could get over it. The more scared I felt, the greater was the need to overcome it. I had to conquer my fears until they either vanished completely or became an integral part of me.

Such had been the case when my father took me for my first flying lesson. I was thirteen years old. At the time I'd agreed, thinking it would be just like flying in a commercial airliner, but I quickly found out that I couldn't have been more wrong. When the pilot turned on the small four-seater Piper Arrow airplane, the whole console started to shake and rattle, and my first thought was that we wouldn't survive the flight.

As soon as the airplane took off, I felt ill and turned all shades of green. That's when the pilot asked me if I was all right and if I wanted to go back. Although I was scared, I didn't want to accept his offer. He even tried to have me fly the airplane as a last-minute effort to make me feel better, but it didn't work.

Not sure of what else he could do, the pilot contacted the tower and asked permission to land, worrying the controller on duty because we had just taken off.

It wasn't long before he received clearance to land. However, he was instructed to perform the maneuver quickly because a jet was landing right behind us. Little did I know that quick maneuvers in airplanes meant fast and sharp-angled turns.

After a few excruciating minutes, we finally landed safely, but not without damage—my ego and pride had been badly bruised, especially when I had to walk back to the flight school building not even fifteen minutes after we'd taken off for what was supposed to be an hour-long lesson.

Everyone in the flight school asked us what had happened. I shyly replied that I had gotten scared and asked the instructor to land.

However, even before I'd landed, I had made up my mind that I was going to overcome the fear. That I was going to be victorious, no matter the cost. So I wasn't surprised when I walked to the appointment desk and asked for an appointment for the very next morning. Everyone else looked puzzled and surprised, including my dad.

I had decided that I would get back in the air as many times as I needed to overcome my fear of heights. And for that week and the week after, I attended flight school every single day and flew for at least one hour, sometimes two.

In the end, I'd accumulated almost twenty hours of flying, and my dad was broke after having to pay one hundred dollars per hour for two weeks. It was worth it because I'd learned to love flying and the weightless sensation, but most importantly, I overcame my fear.

Although my toe hurt, I ran up the basement stairs. When I reached the top, I closed the door and locked it behind me, as if that would prevent my mother's memories from oozing out into the rest of the house.

With the flashlight in hand, I grabbed my book from the top of the table and went upstairs to get into some dry and perhaps warmer clothes.

Just as I was passing through the Sorrows Hallway, the power came back on and I sped up so I wouldn't have to look at any of the other pictures.

After I got in my room, I felt relieved. At least now I would be able to take a warm shower and relax by the TV while I waited for Carla and Jonas to show up for dinner.

I wasn't even ten minutes into my shower when I heard the doorbell ring. It had to be Jonas. I hated his bad habit of showing up for things way too early—he tended to do that every time he was bored.

***

Since I was still in the shower and nowhere near being done, I reached for my cell and sent Jonas a text saying I was still getting ready and that he should come in. I also advised him to use the side door as a precaution; I didn't trust our porch when it snowed. Honestly, I don't know why I even bothered; I knew he was going to ignore me.

As usual when it came to doing anything with Carla, I couldn't decide on what to wear. After much deliberation, I decided to go with a careless look, which was funny, considering that the careless look took more planning than if I was getting dressed up for a black-tie event.

"Hurry up!" Jonas screamed from downstairs.

"I'm coming," I replied as I pulled my shirt over my head.

"Can you believe that my parents aren't back yet?" I heard him complaining.

"My dad isn't back yet, either," I said as I walked past the Sorrows Hallway.

"How much snow is on the ground?" I asked once I got downstairs.

"To be honest, I don't know. I'll check the Weather Channel," said Jonas, looking for the TV remote.

"Seems like we're in for a heck of a storm. Currently, we are looking at about ten inches of snow by the time this is over—and that's on top of the six to eight inches we already got thus far. Stay safe and stay tuned for up-to-the-minute information," said the weatherman.

"That's a lot of snow," I said.

I had barely finished the sentence when my cell rang. The caller ID said it was my dad.

"Hey, Dad, I was thinking about calling you," I said.

"How is everything at home?"

"Everything is fine," I replied, rolling my eyes and wishing he would get straight to the point.

"Son, I don't think I'll be able to drive home today—there's just too much snow on the ground—I should have some more money in my room if you need to order dinner," my dad said, sounding worried. "Why don't you go over to Jonas's house and asked the Webers if you can stay there tonight?"

He was concerned about leaving me home alone during a snowstorm.

"Sure, Dad, I'll do that, don't worry about a thing. I'll be fine," I lied. After all, I had no plans on sleeping over at Jonas's house.

The truth was that I knew the wheels were in motion for something extraordinary to happen that night.

"I'll be home first thing in the morning. If you need anything just call my cell. Oh, Mark, I…" My dad paused.

"I know, Dad, don't worry," I replied to relieve the awkwardness.

"Okay then, call me if you need anything at all," he said again before he hung up.

I wondered if he was going to be able to get any sleep. It would be the first time he had slept away from home since my mother had passed away.

"Your dad isn't coming home?" asked Jonas.

"Nope, he's snowed-in at Phil's house," I replied, tossing my cell on the coffee table.

"I should call my parents… maybe they're snowed-in too," said Jonas hopefully.

"Mom, where are you guys at?" Jonas asked into his phone.

After a few seconds, he replied, "Oh, don't worry Mom, we'll ask Mr. Ryser if we can sleep in their guest bedroom for the night." He smiled, then continued, "Sure, Mom, we'll be fine. If we need anything, we'll call, I promise."

He hung up and said, "Parent-free night, we should throw a party."

"Nah, all we need is to choose a nice movie and get some dinner," I said as I reached for the tablet device on the living-room coffee table.

"Where's Carla?" I asked, unable to contain my curiosity.

"Oh, she's taking a bath," replied Jonas, not giving it a second thought while I secretly daydreamed about her.

"Where should we order from?" I asked.

"I don't know, wherever we order from, it will be a while before they can get here with all this snow," said Jonas.

I was browsing the Internet for a nearby pizza place when the doorbell rang.

"That has to be Carla," said Jonas as he got up to open the door. "It's about time!" he said, carelessly opening the front door wider than necessary. He insisted on using the front door even though he knew I didn't want people near the porch when it snowed.

"It's not my fault, you hogged the bathroom, doing God knows what," said Carla, not looking at either one of us. "Did you guys order dinner yet?"

"Not yet, I'm on it now," I said, looking into her beautiful eyes and seeing her soul.

"Just a plain cheese pie is fine with me," said Carla, shaking the snow off her coat, head, and boots.

"I want a pepperoni pizza," said Jonas, voicing his preference for a meaty diet, which he boasted was superior.

"Yep, I'm ordering two pizzas and some mozzarella sticks," I said as I pushed the Return button on the computer to complete the order.

"Sis, I have something to tell you," said Jonas.

"What?" she asked, looking at us.

"Mom and Dad aren't coming home today."

"Really? Why?"

"They're stranded at Aunt Flores's, so we're supposed to sleep over here tonight," said Jonas, excited.

"And I'm supposed to sleep over at your house," I added, apparently confusing her.

"Mom and Dad asked us to ask Mr. Ryser if we could sleep here. But Mr. Ryser is also snowed-in and asked Mark to ask Mom and Dad to sleep at our house," explained Jonas.

"That will work out just fine. That way, we can all be under the same roof when we try to astral travel," replied Carla, much to my surprise.

"You know, they won't be happy once they find out," I said, feeling guilty.

"Well, it isn't completely our fault," said Jonas.

"That's true," I agreed.

"I wonder when the pizza will get here, I'm so hungry," said Jonas, rubbing his belly.

"It will take them a while to get here. Heck, I'm surprised they are even open on a day like today," I said.

"I hope not, because I had a rather light lunch," said Jonas.

"Sure you did, Mr. Two-appetizers, plus a meal and soda," replied Carla, laughing and rolling her eyes.

"You're paying for the pizza, right?" I asked Jonas, joking.

"No, I'm not. I'm completely broke, and besides, we are the ones babysitting you, so you really should be buying us dinner," Jonas said, laughing.

We all laughed and then sat down to watch some TV while we waited for dinner.

Three minutes later, Carla got up, apparently bored with the reality TV show Jonas insisted on watching. She went over to my computer desk.

After another fifteen minutes—which I'm sure felt more like hours to Jonas—the doorbell finally rang.

"It must be the pizza guy," said Jonas.

"Where did you order from? Ah, never mind. I'll find out soon enough," said Jonas as I got up to open the door.

I opened the door expecting a delivery guy but instead found a pretty delivery girl dressed in red and yellow.

I got the pizzas and closed the door but not before noticing that the bright red sky promised even more snow throughout the night.

I headed to the kitchen to get some plates and silverware. I was glad that the dishes were done, a rarity since neither my father nor I liked doing them. Luckily, we had been eating off disposable dishes for the past few days.

I returned to the living room carrying three plates, forks, and knives for all of us, while Carla got some glasses and the soda from the fridge.

Jonas was already eating a slice of his pepperoni pizza with his hands by the time we got there.

Carla placed the chilled soda bottle on the table and grabbed herself some mozzarella sticks—which I happened to know were one of her favorite appetizers—and sat back in front of the computer.

After dinner, Jonas and I opted to rent a movie online, while Carla preferred to read her book on the computer desk.

***

Once the movie finished, we put on the local channel to watch some of Jonas's favorite Saturday night programming.

Just after 10:00 p.m., the Emergency Alert System interrupted the regular programming to announce that a severe weather alert was in effect for greater Boston. The storm system was about to drop buckets of snow, and temperatures were expected to drop drastically.

"Oh goody-goody," said Jonas. "Where's your laptop?"

"It's in my dad's office. He was fixing it for me. I'm not sure if it's done."

Jonas got up and headed to my dad's office. I immediately regretted telling him where the laptop was. Jonas wasn't exactly the most careful person in the world. I might even say that he was cursed with very careless hands.

"Don't make a mess in his office, or I'll have to answer for it," I warned as he walked away, but I didn't think he even heard me.

I took the opportunity to secretly admire Carla as she read peacefully.

"What?" she asked smiling.

For a second, I considered telling her how beautiful she was, but in the end shyness won.

"Nothing," I replied after a few seconds of awkward silence.

A few moments later, I heard heavy footsteps and a peculiar dragging sound, so I looked up and saw Jonas carrying my outdated twenty-one inch laptop, which weighed almost the same as a desktop. Jonas was almost tripping on the power cord as it dragged on the floor.

"Watch out, you almost tripped," I said, pointing out his mistake, even though I knew it was useless. It wasn't the first time he did that, and it wouldn't be the last.

"Sorry," Jonas replied, smiling. It never ceased to amaze me how pretty much everything seemed funny to him.

"What are you going to do with that?" I asked.

"I want to check on something," Jonas said.

"What?"

"Well, you know how we aren't sure if this astral projection is real or not? I think there is a way we can find out for sure," said Jonas as he browsed the Internet.

"Don't search for stuff like that. That computer is monitored," I said.

"Relax, you can just tell him that it was me. Besides, sooner or later, you'll have to tell him what you've been up to anyway," replied Jonas. "Ah, forget this, I'll devise my own experiment," said Jonas, pushing the computer away. "Here's what we'll do. We'll each write a word on a piece of paper and lock them in different rooms of the house. Then we'll go to sleep and try to astral project. Once out of our bodies we'll each go to all the rooms and read the words on the papers," he explained. "That way, in the morning when we get up, we'll write down what we saw in each room and compare the results. If they match, it was real, and if they don't, then it wasn't."

It seemed like a clever idea—a true rarity when it comes from Jonas.

"But that will only work if nobody cheats," said Carla, looking at Jonas.

"Even then, we would all have to cheat for the experiment to fail. Say I cheated, then only my results would be correct. But if all of our results match, then we'll know it was real… unless of course we all cheated, but why would we do that if we're trying to find out the truth?" I explained.

"Let's do it then," said Carla. "Mark, you can place your note in the basement—"

"I don't want to do the basement, Jonas can have it," I said.

"Why? Are you scared of the basement?" asked Jonas without realizing at first that my mother's belongings were in there.

"Oops, never mind, mate, I got it."

"Okay, then, so Jonas can place his note in the basement, lock the door and keep the key. I'll do the same but in the guest room, and you can have your dad's office. That way, we will know for a fact in the morning if we actually left our physical bodies or not," Carla said.

"Why am I the one that gets stuck with the basement?" asked Jonas.

"It doesn't matter who gets the basement. I can do the basement if you're too scared," replied Carla impatiently.

"No, it is fine, I was just kidding," replied Jonas, probably lying.

"Are you guys sure you want to do this?" I asked, feeling guilty for involving my best friends in a dangerous situation. After all, I had a feeling I was in way over my head.

"I have actually learned a good bit about astral travel so I want to try it. Besides, I'm curious to meet this Phasma guy. I'm interested to know what exactly he's guarding, so like it or not, I'm doing this," said Carla, reminding me again why I loved her.

"Isn't this 'Guardian of Threshold' supposed to look different to each person?" asked Jonas.

"According to what I read, yes, he's supposed to be the sum of all our fears and negative emotions. He'll probably look something like Casper to me because I'm so nice," replied Carla, joking and laughing.

"For the record, I'm against this. Just promise me that you'll both be careful, please," I said.

"Houston, we have a problem," cried Jonas.

"What's the problem?" asked Carla.

"Where are we going to sleep?" asked Jonas.

"Good question," I said, limiting myself to just those words as I pretended to be truly concerned while I secretly hoped someone else would come up with the only sensible solution, which was to sleep in my room because all the other rooms in the house were being used for the experiment. However, I wasn't about to come out and say that.

"Why don't we all sleep in Mark's room?" suggested Carla. I was sure she remembered that my bed had another bed stored underneath. After all, the three of us had used it as a trampoline so many times in the past.

"I guess we don't have a choice, but Mom and Dad can't find out about this, otherwise I'll be hearing about it for the rest of my life," said Jonas.

We seemed determined to explore the astral realm, although I suspected each of us had our own reasons: I wanted to see my deceased mother again; I could only guess why Jonas was interested, it probably had something to do with astral sex; and as far as what drove Carla? Probably her sense of adventure and natural curiosity—perhaps it was her willingness to help a friend in need.

"Why are you interested in astral traveling?" I asked Carla.

"I always wanted to visit the world, especially Egypt, and the thought of being able to go wherever I want every night appeals to me very much," said Carla.

"Really? We can go anywhere we want?" asked Jonas with renewed interest.

"According to what I read, we can go anywhere we want as long as we can think of it. The astral is a realm of thought," said Carla.

"Do you mean to say that our thoughts can become a reality there?" asked Jonas, looking skeptical.

"That's how it's supposed to work, but I guess we'll find out. If we're successful, that is," said Carla as she got up to look for something.

"Where are you going?" asked Jonas.

"I'll be back," she simply replied.

"I don't think she likes to tell you what she's going to do," I said sarcastically.

"I know she doesn't, but she asks me all the time," replied Jonas.

The last couple of days had been the worst and best days of my life. I had a real chance of seeing my mother again. I also had an equal chance of running across Phasma. Just knowing with certainty that spirits existed beyond physicality brought me hope. Although part of me still couldn't believe that I had spoken to a real spirit.

Carla returned a few minutes later and handed me a piece of blank paper and a permanent marker. "Here is yours. Make sure you use big letters and write where nobody will see you." She held up the key to the guest bedroom and boasted, "I already did mine."

"Where's mine?" cried Jonas, holding his empty hands in the air.

"If you actually stopped playing with the computer, you would see that it's right there," said Carla, pointing to the computer desk.

"Okay, I'll go first… I guess, since I have to go all the way down to the basement. You guys wait here," said Jonas.

"Place it somewhere it can be easily seen, and don't forget to use big letters," said Carla.

Jonas walked away without giving his sister any hint that he heard her.

"I guess I should go do my experiment now that Jonas is busy, so he won't peek," I said, getting up.

"And what makes you so sure that I won't peek?" said Carla as her bright smile lit up the room.

"I know you won't, I trust you," I said.

"Don't forget—"

"I know, big letters and an obvious place," I said, smiling.

I entered my dad's office. The smell of leather from his chair and sofa was overpowering. The room was dark and gloomy, totally devoid of color, life, and style. Even turning on the light didn't help.

It still was bland. Although I was somewhat used to the plainness of his office, I noticed the heaviness in the air every time I entered it. I even gave him a plant once to bring some life into his office, but it died within a couple of weeks. I suspected it had something to do with lack of water. Last time I checked, plants didn't do so well on leftover coffee.

I sat at his desk determined to write as big as I could to please Carla, but I ran into a problem when it dawned on me that I didn't know what to write. Naturally, I looked around my dad's office for clues. That was when I noticed some brochures on his desk about houses and apartment buildings.

What's going on? I wondered. *Was my dad planning a move?* I'd been trying to persuade him to move for a long time, but he always refused. He even got mad about it. Was he seriously considering moving now? All these questions and more flooded my mind at once. But I didn't expect to feel the way I felt; suddenly, I realized that I didn't want to move. I didn't want to be anywhere else but in that old house. It was comforting to know that Carla was just across the street.

I liked our house… well, with the exception of maybe our porch, which needed urgent and serious repairs, and the walls could use some paint. But it was nothing that couldn't be fixed.

Since I was still lost as what to write, I decided to write the only thing that came to mind. I held the permanent marker and wrote, "MOM."

I noticed then that something else was different about my dad's room: it no longer contained my mother's pictures. The spot on his desk that was usually reserved for my mother's wedding ring was bare.

Did he forget my mother? Did it finally get easier for him to deal with her passing?

I had mixed feelings. On one hand, it was good that he could move on; but on the other, I didn't want him to forget about her. I wanted to talk to him about all of these things.

As hard as it was, I had to put all these worries behind me, because the book said that in order to astral project, my mind had to be free of worries and as empty as possible. It was okay, however, to concentrate on a single thought to help keep myself focused, and I'd already chosen to think about my mother.

I placed my note right in the center of my dad's desk and headed to the door, pausing for a moment as I tried to decide whether I should leave the light on or shut it off. I finally decided to leave it on, thinking that it would be easier to read from the astral realm.

I locked the door behind me and placed the key in my pocket as I walked back to the living room, only to find Jonas standing against the basement door gasping for air.

"What happened?" I asked.

"I felt… something… no, someone," Jonas said, breathing hard. "It was a presence, more like a feeling of being observed, and then suddenly I felt something touch my arm, and I ran upstairs as fast as I could and locked the door." Jonas looked like he was about to pass out from fear, hyperventilation, or exhaustion.

But Carla couldn't contain her laughter.

"It's not funny. Astral sex had better be worth it for all this trouble," said Jonas, revealing more than he probably should have. Although it wasn't a secret, he was going through late puberty.

"Take it easy, Astral Casanova, I'm sure it was nothing," said Carla.

"Nothing? You say that because it wasn't you that… thing, whatever it was, tried to grab," replied Jonas.

The basement wasn't as bad as I made it out to be. It was actually pretty nice. After all, it was a finished basement with a home theater system and a pool table that was rarely used—the surrounding wall-length mirrors always made me feel uneasy and spooked instead of making the room look bigger as they were supposed to do.

Jonas described how he went down the stairs and how the steps creaked as his heart raced out of control, all because of an unknown creature that was hunting him down. Normally, I discarded 90 percent of his stories, but this was different. I knew exactly what he meant; I'd gone through it earlier.

"I don't know, man, I'm having second thoughts about this," said Jonas.

"It's fine. If you don't want to do this, you don't have to," I said.

"Nope, you need my help," said Jonas, trying to look determined, but his body language and worried look betrayed him.

"Where did you put your note?" asked Carla.

"It's on top…" He paused for split second. "Am I supposed to tell you that?"

"Duh… how else are we going to find it when we're astral traveling?" replied Carla, shaking her head.

"Oh… you're right. I put it on top of the pool table, smack in the middle," said Jonas proudly, as if that made him brave. "Why don't you guys believe me? I'm telling you, I saw something down there."

"Lately, I have seen a lot of stuff that I wouldn't believe under normal circumstances," I said. "So yes, I do believe you."

"I was looking for the sleeping bag when I saw a shadow in the mirror. Naturally, I froze for a second, but I knew that I had to get that sleeping bag. Otherwise, I would probably have to go back down there, since my note is there and all," said Jonas. "I saw the green and the blue sleeping bags. I reached down to grab either one when I saw it looking straight at me from the darkest corner of the room."

"Don't overthink it," recommended Carla. She had always been wiser than Jonas and me combined.

Although they were twins, they were very different. While Carla survived on determination and wisdom, Jonas's strongest suits were his pride, loyalty, and even his blunt honesty. Carla was selfless and caring, while Jonas was selfish, careless, and stubborn. They were the perfect evidence that traits weren't biological in nature.

I'd learned throughout the years not to take sides, because if I did they would both end up mad at me. There were times I couldn't believe how smart they were—granted, this happened more often with Carla—and there were times I couldn't believe how childish they could be.

"Sis, you're taking all of this very casually… how come?" asked Jonas.

"That's because I've done it before," said Carla, as though she didn't want to elaborate further.

"Really? You never mentioned it," said Jonas.

"Well, I didn't know what you guys were going to think about it. Besides, it only happened a couple of times before, and that was when I was overtired. I didn't mean for it to happen, it just did," said Carla as she headed toward the front door.

"Where are you going now?" Jonas asked.

"Not that it's any of your business, but I'm going home to grab some pajamas and stuff," said Carla, opening the door.

"Not that way," I said. "Use the side door, it's safer."

"I'm not going all the way around in this snow. Besides, it'll be fine," said Carla, closing the door behind her as I felt a wave of cold air invade my personal space and the floor rumble from the door as the wind blew it shut.

"Get my stuff too!" yelled Jonas from inside. "I hope she heard me."

"I'm sure she did, and so did the neighbors," I joked.

"Has everyone except me experienced this astral stuff before?" inquired Jonas while I was busy wondering if I should use this opportunity to talk to Jonas about Carla or not. I decided against it since we were supposed to be having a sleepover and all. It might make things awkward.

"Maybe tonight is the night," I replied, trying to get his hopes up because positive thinking was a very important factor in astral projection.

"Who do you suppose this Phasma really is?" asked Jonas.

"I don't have a clue... whoever he is, he's out to get me, and I'm going to find out why."

"I wonder if I'll see him too? Maybe my ghost will be a hot chick," said Jonas.

"In your dreams," I said.

"Exactly, we'll be dreaming so there's hope."

After about five minutes, the door reopened and the cold wind once again rushed inside, and so did Carla, carrying a bright pink duffel bag.

"About time," said Jonas, giving Carla a mean look.

"How's the weather?" I asked.

"Believe it or not, it's even colder now. I had to jump over a huge snow bank to get to my house," said Carla, displaying snow marks all the way up to her knees.

"Did you remember to bring my stuff?" asked Jonas.

"Don't worry, I got your ugly stuff," said Carla as she opened her pink duffel bag and tossed a set of hideous pajamas and a worn-out toothbrush his way.

"What do you say?" asked Carla after a few seconds.

"Huh? Oh… thanks," said Jonas, making a funny face by twitching his nose.

"Can I use the restroom?" asked Carla.

"Sure," I replied.

"You guys are already going to bed?" asked Jonas in disbelief.

"Ah, yes, it's almost 11:30 p.m.," replied Carla, looking at her watch.

"So? Tomorrow is Sunday. We can sleep in late," replied Jonas.

"Actually, we can't. As soon as the roads are clear, Mom and Dad will be coming home, which means that we'll have to wake up early and head back home way before they are back. That's if we don't want to get in a load of trouble for not telling them," said Carla.

"Bummer, I better get ready for bed then," said Jonas, closing the laptop screen.

Before we went upstairs, I made sure that all the doors were locked, including my dad's office, the basement, and the guest room.

***

"Well, here goes nothing," I said as I shut off the lights in the living room but left the foyer light on as a night light.

I followed Carla and Jonas up the stairs, and since Carla was in front of me, I chose to focus all my attention on her as we walked past the Sorrows Hallway.

Jonas slowly walked by the cursed hallway, doing exactly what I couldn't. He stared attentively at each and every picture on the wall. I didn't blame him because they did tell a story; unfortunately, it was a story missing a happy ending.

I was so focused on Carla and trying not to pay attention to the pictures that I didn't even notice that Jonas had my laptop in one hand and his hideous pajamas, toothbrush, and the blue sleeping bag in the other hand. Jonas must have tripped on the power cord, which caused him to wobble; he struggled to maintain his balance. I reached over just in time to catch the laptop before it fell on the floor with Jonas.

"Are you okay?" I asked.

"Ouch, that hurts," he replied, rubbing his knees.

"Nice catch," said Carla, opening my bedroom door.

"I'm fine, thanks, Sis," replied Jonas.

"Well, who told you to do stupid things?" said Carla.

"Let's go inside," I said, ignoring what I'd learned over the years about getting in the middle, because I was in a hurry to get out of the hallway.

"Sorry about the laptop," said Jonas as he got up and tossed the sleeping bag inside my room.

"No problem, no harm done, bud," I said.

We walked inside my room. I had a very unusual room for a teenager. It was rather large; originally it had been two separate rooms that were combined into one by the previous owners.

I picked up Jonas's sleeping bag from the floor and placed it on the brown couch inside my room.

Carla headed straight to the bathroom—I'd hoped she would use the one in the hallway so she wouldn't see the mess in my bathroom.

I quickly rearranged things in my room while Carla was in the bathroom, careful not to raise any suspicions from Jonas.

"Where am I going to sleep?" asked Jonas as I hid some dirty laundry deep inside my closet.

"Well, there's the couch, the pullout bed under mine, and the sleeping bag. So it's your choice," I said as I looked for a pair of stylish pajamas. The only problem was that I didn't have any stylish pajamas; I'm not even sure they made stylish pajamas. I would have to settle for something less attractive. My camo pajamas would have to do the trick.

As I waited for Carla to come out of the bathroom, I pulled the bed out and made sure it had clean sheets and pillows—I knew Carla liked to sleep with two pillows, so that's how many I put on the bed, hoping she would pick the bed next to mine instead of the couch or the sleeping bag.

Just as I was about to open my astral projection book, Carla came out of the bathroom looking as gorgeous as ever. She wore bright pink satin pajamas. She had her hair down, and her eyes were shining like glorious beacons of light in the night sky.

I placed the astral projection book on the nightstand next to my bed, grabbed my camo pajamas, and went to the bathroom to change and get ready for bed.

I was brushing my teeth when, suddenly, I heard a huge thud against the bathroom window. I carefully got closer so I could hear better when another loud thud hit the window and sent me fleeing to the other side of the bathroom.

What's that? I wondered. I quickly finished brushing my teeth. I finished so quick, in fact, that I think I even forgot to rinse.

"Did you guys hear that?" I asked after I opened the bathroom door.

"I think the weather is definitely not in a playing mood tonight," said Jonas.

"First snow and now ice? I don't know how much more that porch can take," I said.

"Why do you worry about it so much? I'm sure it'll be fine," said Carla.

"I just don't want anyone to get hurt. The darn thing just seems ready to fall apart at any moment, it's even crooked," I said.

"I wonder when your dad is going to fix it," said Jonas bluntly.

"Probably after it falls down," I said.

It brought me comfort to know that I might be only moments away from seeing my mother. I hoped that by the time the night was over, I would at least know for sure if everything had been a dream, simply wishful thinking, or if it was a real possibility.

"Are you guys scared? What if this thing really works and we leave our bodies?" asked Jonas.

"Not really scared, more anxious than anything," I said truthfully. "I have a lot riding on this."

"What if I can't wake up from it?" asked Jonas.

"The book says that's impossible. Besides, if I were you, I'd worry about Phasma instead," I said, realizing that I wasn't being very encouraging.

"Actually, you shouldn't worry about anything, or you'll never be able to complete the separation process," said Carla from across the room where she had prepared her bed for the night.

"I'm a bit scared, but I'm sure it'll turn out to be just a dream, if anything at all. You know our minds are incredible machines," replied Jonas, almost like he was trying to convince himself that everything was going to be okay.

"What do you guys say we start? I'm getting tired," said Carla, yawning.

"Don't forget, my note is on top of the pool table," offered Jonas.

"Mine is on top of the desk," said Carla.

"And mine is on top of my dad's desk," I replied, feeling in sync with Carla as though we belonged together.

"Why did you bring the laptop, Jonas?" I asked.

"Just in case we need it for research or something," replied Jonas, looking like he was hiding something.

"I don't buy it," said Carla from the pullout bed.

"Neither do I," I added.

"Come on, what's the real reason?" asked Carla.

"Okay fine, I'll tell you, but don't laugh," replied Jonas. "I don't like to be in the dark, so if the power goes out in the middle of the night, it works great as a night light. Besides, I figure it would be best to set an alarm on the computer in case we have any difficulties waking up."

"That makes sense," I said as I looked at Carla, and we both laughed discreetly behind his back.

"Sure, make fun of me now. You'll both thank me later," mumbled Jonas, lying on the couch and covering himself with a sheet, comforter, and the sleeping bag.

We wished each other good night and covered ourselves, which was the best thing to do, according to the book.

The room grew quiet. After a while, all I could hear was the relentless ice hitting the roof and windows of the house and the occasional snore from Jonas.

CHAPTER EIGHT
Beyond Physicality

I think I was the second to fall asleep. Lately, I could sleep anywhere; it was like my body had been programmed to sleep, perhaps because I hadn't had a good night's sleep in a while.

Just when I was about to fall completely asleep, I saw formless shadows moving randomly. I had the same symptoms as before, which I quickly recognized as the beginning of the astral travel process.

Behind my closed eyelids, I enjoyed a colorful light show. Suddenly, my body started to feel like it had been filled with liquid lead. The sight of my room quickly replaced the lights, although it had a greenish tint, as if I were wearing glasses with dark-green lenses.

I seemed more alert than in previous experiences, more alert than I'd ever been in my life. I paid meticulous attention to all the details of my surroundings, taking full advantage of my increased focus.

I was busy looking around the room when I noticed an exquisite light being cast on the wall and ceiling. I traced its source with my eyes. That's when I saw her. She was even more beautiful and charming in the astral realm. Her hair, which was already beautiful, radiated an intense and colorful aura, almost like the sun and its corona, except more vibrant. Her face was diffused and white like snow, making her appear almost angelic and goddess-like. Her eyes captivated me even though she hadn't seen me yet.

One quick look was enough for me to become eternally addicted to her serenity and sweetness. All my worries dissipated in that single look into her soul, a soul so perfect that she seemed like a dream within a dream.

I stood there in amazement as Carla's body floated gently just a couple feet above her physical body. She still seemed unaware of her surroundings. I figured I'd give her some time; after all, her physical body was still tossing and turning in bed.

I decided to look at Jonas and see what was happening to him. He appeared to be slowly lifting out of his body as well. He hovered only a few inches, and then went back down again. He was stuck; his legs and arms didn't move an inch, only his head and torso.

I wanted to help him, but I didn't know how. When I finally decided to try, I grabbed him by his right arm and pulled upward with all my strength. However, I was pulled down as if a giant magnet had been activated.

I started to pull his arm again, and when I seemed to be having some success, I thought: *If I don't have a body, why don't I sink into the ground?*

No sooner had I finished that thought then my feet started to sink into the wooden floor, as though it had turned into quicksand.

It took me only a few seconds to figure out what had happened. My thoughts had influenced my surroundings. I thought about floating up, and almost immediately I stopped sinking and slowly started to move up again. Next I thought about the ground becoming solid, and sure enough, the floor turned solid once more.

Pulling Jonas's astral body out of his physical body proved to be more work and more nerve-racking than I had anticipated. Since I was afraid of doing something wrong, I decided to stop and explore some more.

I wanted to figure out how moving worked in the astral realm, so I devised a little experiment: I thought of my dad's room and suddenly felt myself being pulled into it.

Everything turned into a blur as the scenery sped past. I suddenly found myself in my dad's room, as if I had moved at the speed of light only to come to a full stop less than a split second later.

That was when I first realized that distance only mattered in the physical realm. In the Astral, distance and time seemed inconceivable.

This will take some getting used to, I thought.

Once the shock of ultrafast travel wore off, I noticed that my dad's room had an eerie feel to it, even in the Astral. I'd often felt weird in my father's bedroom, but I thought it was just my imagination. But looking at it in the astral realm, I realized that our emotions created thought-forms that could be detrimental to our living space. The walls of my dad's room were covered in large, still, black larvae, as well as other dark creatures I couldn't even begin to describe.

I didn't know much about the astral realm, but instinctively I knew those things weren't benign. Without wasting any more time, I focused my attention on the guest room. And sure enough, I was again pulled as if by a giant magnet to my destination. However, when my body reached the larva-covered wall, I started to move very slowly. So slowly that I felt every cell of my astral body tingle as they passed through the wall. The worst part was when my head went through it. I could see all the interior details of the larvae and the wall. I saw and felt every nail passing through me. It was a rather disorienting and disconcerting experience, but nothing that I couldn't get used to eventually.

Not only did I move to the room I thought about, but also to the exact location where I wanted to be.

Looking on top of the desk where the note was supposed to be, I didn't find a note at all, but instead I found a yellow rose in an intricate vase I'd never seen before. And that wasn't all. Just by looking at the lonely and singular rose, I could hear Carla's thoughts, as though her thoughts had been impressed into that rose.

I hope he gets the hint, I heard Carla's voice say in my head. At the same time, the image of her sitting down and drawing a yellow rose came to my mind.

That was when I realized that Carla might have feelings for me as well. I could clearly see that she was thinking about me when she drew the yellow rose. Apparently, that same rose manifested itself in the Astral and carried her thoughts.

I was so caught up in the moment that I didn't notice someone approaching from behind. All I felt next to me was a shadow. At first, I thought it could be my mother, but when I turned around,

I found the next best thing. Floating inches above the floor and looking much like an angel stood Carla. I hoped she didn't notice my slight disappointment.

"Not happy to see me, I see," she said without moving her lips. I was hearing her voice in my head. I was feeling utterly connected to her. I was in complete bliss when one of my thoughts caught me off guard. *Since I was able to hear her thoughts, can she hear mine?*

I sure can, replied Carla.

All my thoughts about her being beautiful and angelic vanished with the shock of that realization.

Have you seen Jonas? I asked without using words.

No, I haven't, said Carla.

"When I saw him last, he was stuck in his own physical body. I tried to help him, but it was no use," I said normally.

"We should try again, maybe with the two of us it will be different," said Carla as she headed toward the door.

"You know, we can just teleport there, we don't have to use the door," I said, offering my hand.

"Really? So it's possible to visit far-off places," she said.

"I haven't tried to go anywhere far yet, but short distances haven't been a problem. Here, I'll show you," I said while she grabbed my hand and I held it tight, enjoying her warm and soft touch.

I thought about moving back into my room, and a split second later I felt the now-familiar tugging and the sudden stop that told me it was okay to reopen my eyes.

"Wow, this is amazing," said Carla after she let go of my hand. "How did you do that?"

"I just thought about my room. I just discovered that tonight," I replied.

"That's awesome," she said.

"Look! Jonas's still stuck," I said, pointing at him. We could clearly see him trying to leave as he floated mere inches above his physical body. Apparently, his legs were holding him down.

He looked like he was acting out his dreams. He looked like a drunk after a night at the bar.

I couldn't help but notice how our physical bodies resembled a precise machine more than a person. It was as if I were looking at a used piece of equipment.

"We should try to grab him the next time he floats up," suggested Carla, getting ready to reach him.

"I'll get this side," I said after I floated to his left side.

"Now!" shouted Carla.

I grabbed his left arm while Carla grabbed his right. She counted to three, and then ordered, "Pull harder!"

I pulled as hard as I could. I wanted Jonas to feel the way Carla and I felt. It felt great to be truly free. Only then did I realize that my physical body was actually a sort of prison for the soul.

Without any warning, Jonas came loose and sent us flying through the air.

Jonas was heading straight toward the wall, out of control as he waved his arms and legs frantically in the air. Carla's destination didn't seem much better; she was heading straight toward the wooden floor.

As for me, well, I wasn't in a better predicament, for I was doing uncontrollable somersaults in the air. However, before I hit the wall I realized that all I had to do to stop was to think about standing still. And I immediately stopped.

As Jonas hit the wall, a loud thud was heard, followed by a scream. I could only imagine how much it hurt at first, but I knew the pain would quickly subside. Carla hit the floor but passed right through it, probably to the floor below.

I figured it was best to help Jonas first, because he would probably be scared to death.

As soon as I thought about it, I was pulled toward him. He was stuck upside down with his back inside the wall; only half of his body remained visible.

"Hey, buddy, how are you hanging in there?" I asked.

"Ha ha ha ha, no time for jokes, help me out," said Jonas.

"I'll get you out in a second, just hang in there," I said.

"Very funny… this is great," he said. Then he laughed hysterically.

I couldn't help myself: I started to laugh like crazy at his predicament and my choice of words.

We laughed for several seconds before he finally asked, "How do I get out of here?"

"I guess I'll have to pull you out again," I replied.

"Wow, you're flying," said Jonas, amazed.

"Well, technically I'm floating, not flying," I explained.

"The technical details don't matter. It's cool. Can you please get me out of here? I want to fly too," he demanded.

"All right, hang on," I said, still laughing.

I grabbed his hands, then placed my feet on the wall and pulled, careful not to overdo it again.

This time it was fairly easy to pull him out, and soon we were both floating gently.

"This is freaking awesome," Jonas said as he hovered just inches off the floor. "I must confess that at first I didn't think it was possible, but apparently it is." He floated rhythmically up, down, left, and right.

To be honest, I'm not sure if this is real or not. I certainly hope so, but I guess we'll have to wait until tomorrow to find out for sure, I replied mentally just to mess with him.

"Holy cow... how did you just do that?" Jonas asked while hitting his head as if he was trying to get water out of his ears.

Did what? I asked him mentally.

"That... how are you talking inside my head?" asked Jonas.

"Apparently, here we don't need words to communicate. We can mentally transmit thoughts," I said.

"That feels weird as hell. How do I do it?" Jonas asked.

"All you have to do is put some intent behind your thoughts. Try it, it's easy," I suggested.

Can you... this isn't going to work... can you hear me? Jonas asked mentally.

"Yes, even the 'This isn't going to work' bit," I replied honestly.

"Wow, that'll take some getting used to," said Jonas normally. "Where's Carla?"

"I don't know. She helped me pull you out. The last I saw, she was tumbling through the bedroom floor," I replied.

"We have to find her," said Jonas, looking around.

"I'm sure she's fine," I said. "I must say that I'm surprised to see you adjusting so well to being in the Astral. When I first came here, I freaked out, but then again it wasn't this pleasant," I said. I'd imagined he would be scared and confused, much as I was the first time, but I guess it helped to have a friend around.

"Maybe I'm just braver than you are," Jonas replied.

"Ha ha, very funny," I said.

Jonas hadn't even finished his sentence when I saw a female vampire creature minus the fangs fly swiftly through the floor. It quickly approached Jonas from behind and whispered with a deadly voice, "I have come for you. I've been waiting for a long time." Jonas got so scared that he stopped floating and was about to take off running when the creature began to laugh uncontrollably. The more it laughed, the more it sounded like Carla. Slowly, the vampire changed into Carla.

"I got you two," she said, still laughing like crazy.

"Is that really you?" asked Jonas.

"Yes, over here we can change how we look the same way as we can move about, by thought alone. So you see, Jonas, now there's no reason for you to be so ugly," said Carla.

"Do you think that was funny? I didn't find it funny, not at all. I'll get you back for this, Sis, you'll see," Jonas said.

Carla knew Jonas was absolutely terrified of vampires. He had been ever since he was nine years old and we decided to watch *Bram Stoker's Dracula*.

"So… where do I find myself an astral lover? Do you guys know?" joked Jonas.

"Why don't you wait and see if she finds you attractive first?" Carla replied, laughing.

"Should we check out our notes together?" I asked.

"That sounds like a plan," replied Carla.

"Sure, let's get the boring stuff out of the way first," Jonas agreed.

***

"Okay then, let's all hold hands so we don't get separated," suggested Carla, offering me her left hand while she offered Jonas her right. "On the count of three, think about the basement."

The basement wasn't my favorite place, but it was better to get the worst over and done with. Besides, it was worth it.

We were all transported to the basement as if by magic. By the time I opened my eyes, I saw the pool table's velvet green top.

Right in the middle there was a crumpled piece of paper that read: "9-24-2." It was Jonas's school locker combination—I'd known Jonas's locker combination ever since junior high. Jonas gave it to me when Billy Beu—a fifteen-year-old who was stuck in junior high after repeating two years in a row—locked Jonas inside his own locker.

We were all amazed at how easy it was to travel in the astral realm; everything was so fluid and effortless.

Traveling at a tremendous speed seemed easier than flicking a light switch. Although teleportation was faster and easier than traditional and slower methods of transportation, it didn't allow any time to enjoy the scenery. There was something to be said about flying slowly through the air as the destination calmly materialized in the distant horizon. That alone was a different adventure each and every time.

"Really? You used your locker combination?" asked Carla, amused.

"That's the only thing that came to mind. Well, that and pizza, but I thought pizza would be too easy," replied Jonas.

"Wait a minute, how long have you known my locker combination?"

"I have known that for years. Haven't you learned yet that you can't keep secrets from me? Besides, who do you think put that bag full of horse dung in your locker last year? Of course I didn't touch the stuff, it was gross, but I did open your locker for Billy Beu," said Carla sarcastically.

"You witch. One day you'll pay for it," replied Jonas.

In an effort to avoid an argument, I said, "Guys, we need to remember that Jonas's note is his locker combination." I didn't even know what could happen if they argued in the Astral, but I knew I didn't want to find out.

"I got it. I don't think I can forget my own locker combination," said Jonas, trying to be funny as usual.

"I have a question. If I think about a place I want to go to, I get teleported there. So what happens when I think of a place I don't want to go?" Jonas asked.

"My suggestion would be not to think about such a place, because chances are that you would end up there. In this realm, our thoughts seem to be the only driving force. I suspect that in this realm we're all creators, creating our own realities as well as the realities of others," replied Carla.

"We should keep going. After all, we have no idea how time works here. I looked for a clock, but I can't find one that works anywhere, Even my alarm clock doesn't work. It's just black," I said. I wanted to make sure we had enough time to at least investigate all of our notes. After all, I was eager to validate the whole experience.

***

"Where to next? Guest room?" Jonas asked, but he barely finished his question before he disappeared right in front of us. Until you have seen your best friend vanish in front of you, you'll never know what that feels like. I was lost, stunned, and shocked all at once.

"I bet I know where he went. Quick, think of the guest room," Carla said, grabbing my hand.

In the blink of an eye, we were teleported to the guest room, where we found Jonas, much to our relief.

"Wow, this thought thing works fast, I just barely finished thinking it and I was here already," said Jonas.

"We should be very careful with it," said Carla.

"I can see it being a big problem," I agreed.

"Carla, where's your note?" Jonas asked in a hurry.

"It's right on top of the desk," I said, pointing before Carla had a chance to reply.

"The only thing I see is a flower in a vase," said Jonas, confused.

"It's a rose, and that's my note. Instead of writing a word, I wanted to draw a picture to see what would happen in the Astral, so I drew a yellow rose in that exact vase. That was the picture I had in my mind when I drew it," Carla explained.

"So it just materialized? Just like that?" Jonas asked, still trying to grasp the concept. I didn't blame him; everything was so different in the Astral.

"Yes, the only thing I don't understand is what happened to the paper with my original drawing on it," said Carla.

"I guess it got replaced by the real thing," I suggested.

"Okay, now to my note. First, you must promise me that you guys won't laugh," I said, feeling embarrassed because they would see what I wrote and possibly know what I was thinking about when I wrote it.

"You know I won't," said Carla.

"As usual I can only promise that I'll try not to," Jonas replied. "Can we go there separately? I want to try to fast travel again."

"Sure, I'll meet you guys there," I replied just before I put my mind to work on how to get to my dad's office.

Jonas was the first to vanish, followed by Carla. The twins had astral travel down.

***

Although I was the last one to depart the guest room, I was the first to arrive in my dad's office. Just as I'd expected, my dad's office still looked bland and lifeless, even in the Astral. The only exception was the piece of paper on which I wrote my note. That single piece of paper seemed to glow and illuminate the rest of the room.

I must confess that part of me was hoping I'd see my mother instead of my note, the way it happened with Carla's rose. When I realized that it hadn't happened, I was unable to contain my disappointment and my eyes welled up with tears.

I couldn't let my emotions take control, not now, especially because Carla and Jonas were coming. I quickly wiped my eyes with my hands and started to think about the only thing, rather the only person, who could possibly cheer me up.

"Hey, mate, how is it going?" asked Jonas from behind me as if he had just appeared out of nowhere. "Your dad's office looks even more boring, if that's possible."

"He never had good taste," I replied, relieved to see Jonas. Having company in the astral realm gave me strength and comfort.

"Where's Carla?" I asked.

"She should be—"

Carla appeared right in front of him.

"Speaking of the…" He cut himself short, only to say, "I really wish you wouldn't do that."

"What?" asked Carla.

"Appear out of thin air like a ghost," replied Jonas, now looking around my dad's office.

"You guys missed me?" Carla asked, smiling.

"Nope, not really," replied Jonas.

"Guys, let's finish the experiment. This is extremely important," I said, moving toward the desk, closely followed by Jonas and Carla.

"Is that it?" asked Jonas.

"Yes, I didn't know what else to write," I said, unsure of what else to say.

"Well, at least it will be easy to remember tomorrow," said Carla, smiling as if she was trying to cheer me up.

"Okay then, to recap, my note is the word 'Mom' and Jonas's is his locker combination," I said, still looking at that glowing piece of paper.

"And mine is a yellow rose," Carla added before I even had the time to finish.

"Piece of cake," replied Jonas.

"Right, just like when you thought that building a model rocket was a piece of cake?" asked Carla, referring to the time Jonas blew up his model rocket before the school science fair had even started.

"It would have worked if you hadn't persuaded me to change the design and the size of the motor," Jonas said, not convincing anyone except himself.

"Follow me, I want to try something fun," said Carla.

"Oh boy, here we go again," said Jonas. "I see trouble in our future."

"What do you have in mind?" I asked.

"We should fly outside," suggested Carla.

"Hmm, that might be cool," Jonas said.

Carla had decided that in order to go outside, we should pass through my bedroom wall. Personally, I didn't mind it too much, but for the record I didn't think it was a good idea for Jonas's sake, especially because we were on the second floor and all.

Even though I was used to flying, I had to admit that I was a bit nervous. After all, this would be a much different experience. For starters, I wouldn't have a powerful engine to propel me forward, only my thoughts.

I tried to voice my disagreement, but the twins didn't care to listen.

"Okay, ready?" asked Carla, looking as though she was ready for a rollercoaster.

"Ready as I ever will be," I said, expecting the worst for Jonas.

"Ready, I guess," Jonas said, not sounding as confident. "I hope it isn't too high."

"Okay, on the count of three, think about flying through the wall," ordered Carla.

Carla counted to three, and almost immediately I was propelled forward, quickly heading straight toward the wall. I felt butterflies in my stomach. I hadn't felt this way since my first airplane lesson.

As my speed increased, my heart seemed to be involved in a race of its own. By the time I reached the wall, my heart felt like it was ready to jump out of my throat.

"Oh God!" screamed Jonas, diverting my attention from the imminent collision with the wall.

By the time I looked back, the wall had completely covered my field of vision. Worried but determined, I reinforced my thought and intention of passing through it.

When my body made contact with the wall, I was surprised to meet a rather soft and tingling material instead of solid wall. I slowly started to pass through the molasses-like substance, and as I did, every atom in my body tingled with excitement, as though I was vibrating at a much higher frequency than the actual wall.

In fact, I suspected that was exactly what had happened. Because my astral body vibrated at a much higher frequency than the physical wall, I could pass through it.

Passing through the wall took a bit more time and effort than I would have imagined.

When I finally reached the other side, I was surprised to see how magical everything looked. Each snowflake was charged with powerful energy. The same was true for the trees, bushes, and plants. While normally dried up for the winter in the physical, in the Astral they blossomed with life. Trees had what seemed to be electrically charged leaves, plants glowed, and flowers could be seen emanating light from within.

However, I only saw Carla next to me. Jonas hadn't made it outside.

"Where's Jonas?" asked Carla.

We looked at each other, perplexed.

"I should go back inside and find out," I suggested urgently. Before I thought about going back to my room, I was immediately pulled through the wall. This time, passing through it was a breeze.

Once inside, I found Jonas stuck in the wall again. He was clearly frustrated.

"Again?" I asked, laughing.

"I hate these damn walls. This is what? The third time I got stuck?" Jonas complained.

"You must be doing something wrong," said Carla, emerging from the wall right next to Jonas. "You're the only one having a problem."

"Oh God, please stop popping up like that."

"Perhaps the wall is the astral lover you were looking for," I said, laughing.

"Very funny. Why don't you guys help me out of here?" Jonas asked.

"Fine, but this is the last time I'm helping you," replied Carla. I think she was joking.

"Seriously, though, Carla is right. You must be doing something wrong," I said.

"I don't know, but as I approached the wall, I kept feeling like I was going to crash into it. I was worried it was going to hurt," described Jonas.

"That's your problem right there," said Carla.

"Yes, that would do it," I added.

"What?" Jonas asked. "It's kind of hard to head straight toward a wall and not feel like I'm going to crash into it."

"That's exactly what you need to do. That is, if you want to stop crashing and getting yourself stuck," said Carla matter of factly.

"I'll try," replied Jonas, sounding embarrassed and uncertain.

"This time, why don't you go first?" I suggested. "Try not to think about crashing. In fact, try not to think of anything other than going outside."

Jonas let out a heart-shattering scream. I saw his blur zoom past me, heading toward the wall.

"Holy crap!" I heard him scream from outside.

"I guess he made it," I said as we rushed to his aid.

"Oh, my God!" Jonas was screaming when Carla and I arrived outside.

"What?" Carla asked, unable to contain her laughter.

"This is freaking high," he said loudly.

"You'll get used to it, just try to relax and take a few deep breaths," I said.

"You can look at it this way," said Carla. "If you really want to, you can just fly closer to the ground and never get over your fear. Or you could deal with it and win over your fear. Either way, the fact is that you can will yourself to move closer to the ground anytime you feel the need to."

"Thanks, Sis. I'll try," said Jonas.

As we gently flew through the air, we looked and felt like ghosts of the night. It was hard not to wonder if that was what death felt like. On one hand, it felt like I had died, but on the other, I had never felt more alive in my whole life.

If death was anything like this, then death was more real than being alive. I could smell, feel, sense, and do all those things much better than in the physical realm.

I wasn't sure if what was happening to us was real, but something inside me told me it was. It was as though my physical body was nothing but a piece of used clothing that I needed to move around the physical world; my true self was unrestrained.

In this fluid form, I felt truly free, truly alive. There were no meaningless limitations to hold me back. I could go anywhere and everywhere I wanted to. I could do anything I wanted. Everything felt more vivid, more real than waking life.

Outside, the weather still raged as blobs of snow and ice passed through me, sending shockwaves of energy through my being. Each snowflake glowed with unknown energy, healing and reinvigorating our planet as the ground absorbed its energy.

At that moment, I realized how much I didn't know about how things worked. Before, I had felt as though there was nothing new left to be discovered about my world. I thought I knew it all, when in fact I didn't know anything. The world was still full of wonderment and mysteries yet to be discovered. Behind seemingly insignificant and small things, there was a complex and often hidden greater purpose. I always liked to watch the snow falling—when I was a small child, I used to think snowflakes were magical. Little did I know then that I was right. They were a gift from the Creator himself.

"I can get used to this," said Carla, laughing. I looked around and found Carla flying up and down, making loops around my house.

"The snow feels weird," complained Jonas. I think he was still trying to get used to the height because he hovered just inches from the ground.

"Ah, stop complaining, you'll get used to it," I said.

***

"I have an idea… we should go somewhere really fun," suggested Carla.

"Yes, but where?" I asked. It was amazing how hard it was to decide where to go when the whole world was at your disposal.

"I know! Let's go to the moon," offered Jonas, excited and catching us by surprise.

"What? You're afraid of being fifteen feet in the air and you want to fly to the moon?"

"Fly? Who said anything about flying? I wouldn't mind teleporting there, though. Besides, I'm already getting used to this height thing," replied Jonas.

"I'm not sure…" replied Carla, pausing slightly. "I guess it would be fun to try and see what happens."

"That's just insane," I said.

"How is that any different than what we're doing right now?" said Carla.

"Point taken. But how are we going to get there?"

"Your guess is as good as mine," said Carla. "Probably the same way we got outside."

"I think it may be best to stick together, that way we can't get lost, or in Jonas's case, stuck," replied Carla, looking as beautiful as ever.

I offered my hand to Carla, and we held each other tightly.

I concentrated as hard as I could on the moon. Jonas appeared to be doing the same, although he was trembling slightly. Carla had her eyes closed.

We waited a few seconds, but nothing happened.

"It's not working," said Jonas.

"You don't say, Einstein," replied Carla.

"Are you guys concentrating on the moon?" I asked.

"Maybe we should picture ourselves already on the moon," I suggested.

"Sure, let's try that," Carla agreed, smiling at me.

We held hands again, but this time instead of imagining the moon, I pictured my friends and me standing on the lunar soil. I concentrated so hard I could feel the dry lunar dust under my feet.

After a few seconds, I began to feel even lighter than I already felt. My body started to lift much higher than before. At first, we moved upward slowly, like a hot air balloon. Just when I was getting used to the renewed feeling of weightlessness, our speed increased tenfold. After a few more seconds, our speed increased yet again. Every time I thought we were going as fast as we possibly could, there was another sudden burst of speed.

Jonas screamed the whole way, especially when our speed increased. Carla, on the other hand, just squeezed my hand really tight, radiating a warming feeling from within. She was apparently enjoying the wild ride.

"I don't think this was a good idea," Jonas complained.

"Stop being a baby, we're almost there, see?" said Carla.

The moon was getting bigger—much bigger than I was used to seeing it—doubling in size every few seconds. Even if I wanted to, I couldn't have guessed how fast we were traveling.

At some point, I closed my eyes because of the increasing speed, and the abnormal size of the moon was making me sick to my stomach.

When I opened my eyes, I saw what had to be the most beautiful sight I'd ever seen. Just below my feet, floating peacefully and surrounded by darkness, was our marvelous and beloved blue planet. Upon the realization that I was floating way above Earth's atmosphere, I felt cold but my hands were still warm. I suspected that was because I was still holding Carla's hand.

There was something completely different between knowing the Earth was round and actually seeing its roundness with your own eyes.

As soon as we stopped moving, Jonas stopped screaming.

"Wow, this is beautiful," said Carla, pulling me a bit closer to her.

"What? Are we on the moon?" asked Jonas, still shaking.

"Open your eyes, or you'll regret it the rest of your life," replied Carla.

"Oh my God, this is really high," complained Jonas as he opened a single eye in order to peek.

"Only a privileged few have seen this in person. This is definitely the best night of my life," said Carla.

The view was so gorgeous that even Jonas got over his fear and opened both eyes to take in the sight.

"Where is the moon?" Jonas asked, perplexed.

"Look behind you," replied Carla.

"Wow, that is huge," said Jonas as he turned to see the immense, dark mass behind him.

"Can we land on it?" asked Carla.

"I suppose so," I replied.

As soon as I said that, I felt myself being pulled onto the moon. After a few seconds, my feet touched the cold, dry, and densely packed soil.

For the next minute or so, we just looked around in utter silence.

"Where is the sun?" I asked in awe.

"Wow! It's beautiful, I'd never imagined it to be this amazing," Carla said.

"Holy cow!" was all Jonas managed to say.

"I guess we must have arrived on the dark side of the moon," I said as I took my first barefoot steps on the moon, a feat that not even astronauts could dream of accomplishing. And there I was, walking barefoot on the moon, feeling its frigid dust between my toes. If I were to die at that very moment, I would die a very happy man.

I remembered a story my mother used to tell me about the moon. She used to say that when the moon was full and the sky was clear, she could see the shape of a dragon slayer on top of his white horse, killing his prey with a spear. She used to say that's where Raphael got the idea for his famous painting, "Saint George and the Dragon." I never forgot that old story. Since then, every time I looked into the moon I saw that image.

Memories in the Astral weren't like normal memories. I didn't just remember things. I actually relived the moment, as if I was there in person. I could smell the smells and feel the wind and the coldness of that particular night. I could smell my mother's favorite perfume as I watched her carefully hold five-year-old me on her lap and point to the moon. She then proceeded to tell me that story as a bright and lively smile decorated her face, a smile that showed without words how much she loved me and how much she enjoyed that moment.

"Are you okay?" asked Carla.

"Hum?" was all I could manage to say.

"Are you crying?" said Jonas.

"I was just thinking of my mother… actually, I was reliving a memory of her. It was as if she were there. I saw her, holding me…"

"Seems like there are a lot of new things about this realm we have yet to discover," said Carla with a tender smile.

"I just hope they're all good things," added Jonas.

"What's that?" I asked, pointing toward the horizon.

In the distant horizon, a long sliver of golden light started to grow larger and larger. I took me a few seconds to realize it was the sun peering over the lunar horizon. It was a view none of us could have even dreamed about witnessing.

If someone told me I was going to stand on the moon and watch a lunar sunrise, I would have called them insane. But there we were, standing side by side on the moon watching the most amazing sunrise. Several minutes passed, and none of us dared to say a word, probably afraid that we would wake up.

"It seems alive, doesn't it?" said Carla, finally breaking our awestruck silence.

"I think that it may be. There's so much raw energy in our solar system. What a beautiful thing, so dependable and necessary," I said.

For the first time I could look straight into the sun without having to squint or shield my eyes. I could see the sun in all of its glorious beauty without pain, and it looked even more marvelous than it did from Earth. Its corona spewed life-giving radiation that traveled billions of light years throughout space into eternity.

"We should go back soon," I said, worried that Phasma would find us.

"I'm ready to teleport out of here anytime," said Jonas as he jumped in and out of a small lunar crater.

"Teleport? I don't think it's that simple," said Carla.

"What do you mean?" asked Jonas.

"In case you forgot, we didn't exactly teleport up here. Besides, even if we could teleport back, I wouldn't. There is no way I'm missing the experience of flying back to Earth," replied Carla.

"Hello! I'm afraid of heights, or did you forget?" Jonas said, already looking pale. "I think the lack of oxygen is starting to get to you. And if I remember correctly, objects are supposed to burn up upon re-entering Earth's atmosphere."

"Only if you have a physical body or a space shuttle, and we don't have either," I said, laughing.

"This was your idea. If you don't like it, feel free to stay here," added Carla.

She didn't wait for a response and started to float away.

I waited until Jonas was following her, then I propelled myself off the lunar surface.

Carla and Jonas were far ahead of me, so I sped up a bit. It wasn't long before I was following them closely.

As soon as we began to reenter Earth's atmosphere, all hell broke loose. A wave of dense air hit us, and I immediately felt like hundreds of pounds were added to my body.

We lost control and tumbled toward the ground. Jonas screamed at the top of his lungs. Even Carla let out a couple screams of desperation.

As the ground fast approached, I desperately thought about floating up, going to the moon, and even going to the sun… but nothing worked. I was still falling fast. We all were, some of us with more class and control than others.

"Oh God, this is the end!" screamed Jonas louder than ever before.

I couldn't see anything except a green haze that grew larger and more defined with each passing second. Out of nowhere came a thundering noise. It was the sound of Carla's body hitting the ground. My heart literally stopped beating. My life no longer mattered. A world without Carla didn't make any sense at all. To think everything had been my fault was simply too much to bear.

A couple of seconds later, I heard another thud, followed by complete silence. Even Jonas's screams stopped. The only noise I heard after that was a half-thud. That was the sound my body made as it crashed into bushes and trees and then… nothing… only blackness and utter silence…

I don't know how much time passed before I could open my eyes. I felt my back and legs sear with pain.

Immobilized by the pain, all I could do was move my eyes, and even that was painful. Thankfully, the pain slowly faded. After a few minutes, I could move again. I looked all around, but didn't see anyone.

"Where are you guys? Are you all right?" I asked.

"Ouch! That hurts like a freaking train just ran me over," said Jonas from under a heavy bush, much to my relief.

"I suppose we should be glad that we're still able to talk about this," I said as I let out a painful chuckle.

"It hurts a lot. I don't think I've ever hurt myself this bad before," said Jonas, groaning.

"Stop being such a baby," said Carla, walking toward us dripping wet.

"Easy for you to say, you probably landed in a lake. Wait a minute. Where did the snow go?" Jonas said.

"Actually, it was a river, and I don't think we're anywhere near Boston or North America for that matter," replied Carla. "So what the heck happened?"

"I don't know. We must have lost concentration or something when we entered Earth's atmosphere, but the important thing is that we're all alive and well," I said.

"Alive and well?" asked Jonas indignantly.

"I know that it was painful, but in retrospect, it wasn't as painful as it should have been if we had a physical body," I said to calm him down.

"It wasn't that bad. After all, we are in unknown territory so there's bound to be a few surprises here and there," said Carla as she helped Jonas up.

"Where are we?" I asked when I was finally able to stand up and stretch my arms and legs.

"I don't have a clue," replied Jonas. "One thing is for sure, I have never seen trees this tall before."

Jonas wasn't exaggerating like he normally did. These were in fact the tallest trees I had ever seen. Although it was still nighttime, we could see them clearly, including the lush green grass and colorful flora surrounding them.

Out of nowhere came a group of about eight to ten indigenous tribesmen. They were looking for something nearby.

"Do you think they can see us?" asked Jonas.

"I'm not sure, but it looks like they're looking for something," replied Carla.

"Yes, I think they can. Let's get out of here while we still can," said Jonas, worried.

"What's this place?" I wondered out loud.

"I think we may be somewhere in the Amazon rainforest," said Carla.

"How could you possibly know that?" asked Jonas.

"Contrary to the two of you, I pay attention in school. Besides, there are few places on Earth where indigenous tribes can still be found."

"We should get back to the house before we get into any more trouble," I said as we backed away from the natives while they inched closer.

"I really don't care where we go, as long as we don't stay here and get hit by those spears. They look very sharp and painful," said Jonas.

A spear was thrown our way. Fortunately, it missed my right shoulder by a hair and hit the tree behind me.

"Now would be a good time to go, and I mean right now!" said Carla as the natives charged us.

I concentrated hard on getting out of there, but after what seemed like an eternity, it became clear I wasn't going anywhere.

Carla was the first to vanish; even Jonas didn't take much longer than a couple seconds. Propelled by his fear, Jonas left with a supersonic boom.

Yet I stayed… nothing I tried worked. When everything else failed, I did the only other thing I could think of. I thought of Carla and how much I wanted to be wherever she was. I was immediately teleported to where she was, which was a good thing because an indigenous warrior had just thrown a spear that was destined for my head.

I opened my eyes to find myself on the floor of my bedroom looking at Carla.

"Are you okay?" she asked.

"I'm fine, thanks. I was almost hit by a spear. But other than that, I'm fine. For some unknown reason, it was hard for me to get out of there," I replied.

"You don't suppose it was because *he's* close by?" asked Carla, concerned.

"Who? Ah, I know, it's Phasma, isn't it?" said Jonas.

"I don't know. I did have a feeling of impending doom, but it could have been the fact that a huge spear was rushing toward my head," I explained, still a bit shaken.

"Too many emotions and adventures for one night," said Jonas.

"After what I have gone through in the past few days, this is really nothing," I said, trying to sound braver than I felt.

"Nothing? Let's see if I got this right… over the past few minutes we flew to the moon—and see how crazy this sounds already when I say it out loud? We fell from said moon only to crash in the middle of God knows where, and if that wasn't enough, we were chased away by a group of angry natives who tried to kill us by throwing spears at us, and you say this was nothing?" said Jonas, as his skin turned red and he started to sweat profusely.

"I'm sorry, Jonas, I was just comparing our experiences with the ones I had with Phasma, which was way worse than this," I said.

The ground started to rumble and shake. The walls shook so much that it seemed they were getting ready to crumble right on top of us. I'm not exactly sure how and why it all started, I just know that it did—perhaps the mere mention of Phasma's name was enough to precipitate chaos. Nonetheless, I felt him; I sensed the dread approaching fast.

CHAPTER NINE
A World In Trouble

The closer I felt him get, the stronger the rumbling became. Soon, dust and pieces of construction materials started to fall off the roof and walls. A violent thunderclap pushed us against the wall. The lights in the room flickered and then went off.

"Oh my God, what the hell is happening?" asked Jonas.

"It's him," I replied, looking around. But I searched in vain for he was nowhere to be found.

The rumbling grew louder, and the shaking grew stronger. The noise was deafening. If I didn't know any better, I would have thought I was in the middle of an earthquake.

"I'm not scared of you!" yelled Carla, standing in the middle of the room defying Phasma and the falling debris.

An evil laughter echoed through the house, causing not only my house but also our spirits to shudder.

"I see…" Phasma said, pausing for effect, "you brought friends."

"Yes, and we aren't scared of you," screamed Carla.

"Shh," gestured Jonas, placing his finger in front of his lips.

"Really? We'll see about that," said Phasma.

"Listen, we don't want any trouble," I said, trying to calm the tension in the room.

"Do you really think your friends can help you here?" asked Phasma from somewhere deep in the shadows.

"We'll defeat you, you psycho," Carla said.

Carla seemed to amuse him because he let out another sinister laugh and said, "I don't think that your friend has warned you, so I'll give you two the chance to leave while you still can. Return to your meaningless and worthless lives and forget about my realm. This is your only and final warning."

"Mark, let's get out of here while we still can," said Jonas, looking scared.

"No," screamed Phasma. "That one must stay. He's not allowed to leave."

"What?" Jonas asked.

"You can't do this," said Carla.

"That's where you're wrong," replied Phasma as he appeared in the darkest corner of the room, still surrounded by shadow.

"Listen here, you freak! We're not going anywhere without our friend!" yelled Jonas. I was shocked because Jonas's courage caught me by surprise. Even Phasma seemed at a loss for words for a few seconds.

"Fools, I assure you that I'm dead serious; don't venture out any further. If you're foolish enough to ignore my warnings, then you're foolish enough to deal with the consequences," said Phasma, stepping out of the shadow so we could see him.

Carla couldn't help but let out a screech of horror when she saw his grotesque face and horns. Jonas simply refused to look out from behind the sofa. Not that I blamed him. I felt like hiding myself, but I had to protect Carla.

"We won't leave our friend alone. You can count on that," said Carla, trembling but determined. I knew she meant it because I'd seen that look in her eyes before. It was the look that told me and everyone else who knew her that she wasn't going to change her mind, whatever the cost.

"Then you're fools. You're all fools!" yelled Phasma.

"What are you doing?" I whispered to Carla. I'd hoped to change her mind, although I knew it wasn't going to happen.

"We came here to help you, and that's exactly what we'll do," replied Carla, more determined than ever.

"You there, behind the couch," said Phasma, pointing toward Jonas as the left wall of my room finally caved in and fell to pieces.

"You're coming with me," Phasma added, pointing at the couch. As if obeying his command, the couch moved aside.

I heard Jonas say "Oh God—" then I sprang into action and placed myself between Jonas and Phasma.

"Leave him alone!" I yelled louder than I thought possible.

"Out of my way, undead fool!" said Phasma. He made a flicking gesture with his finger, and I was thrown out of the way.

He pointed to Jonas, and with another flick of his fingers, Jonas's body lifted off the floor as if invisible strings were holding him. Strings that Phasma seemed to be pulling.

I was about to get up and face Phasma again when he suddenly charged straight toward Jonas.

When they collided, they both vanished. The rumbling stopped, and the wall that had fallen rebuilt itself.

"No!" I screamed as tears filled my eyes and guilt crushed my heart so tightly that I could barely breathe.

"Oh my God! Where did they go?" asked Carla.

"I don't know," I replied, ashamed.

"I can't see him," said Carla, looking around the room and still crying.

"Jonas! Jonas!" Carla yelled over and over.

***

"Let's check his physical body," I said.

"Look! He's still fine. He's breathing," I said as I moved closer to Jonas's physical body and found him still sleeping.

"He looks like he's having a nightmare," said Carla, approaching her brother's sleeping body. "Hey, little brother, I promise you I'll do everything in my power to bring you back."

"We'll find him, I promise," I said.

"How?" asked Carla, calmer but still shaken.

"What could that… that thing possibly want with Jonas?" I thought out loud.

141

"I don't know. Maybe if we think about Jonas, we'll be teleported to him," said Carla hopefully.

"I don't know if that's a good idea," I said. "The truth is that I shouldn't have involved you guys in this mess. It's all my fault."

"No, it's not your fault. As long as we stick together and don't give up, we'll be fine," said Carla to comfort me.

"All right. Let's go get Jonas back," I said, determined to fix things.

I offered my hand to Carla. As soon as I felt her hand grabbing mine, I held it tightly and started to concentrate on Jonas. Carla did the same. I felt her squeeze my hand.

After a few seconds of intense concentration, nothing happened. I tried thinking about Jonas and even our childhood together, but still nothing happened.

"It's not working," said Carla.

"It will, trust me," I replied, realizing that simply thinking about Jonas wasn't going to work. I had to connect with either Jonas or Phasma on a much deeper level if I wanted to find him.

I closed my eyes again and thought about Phasma and how angry I felt toward that despicable creature that had kidnapped my best friend. I started to feel the familiar sensation of moving faster than light itself.

The room turned suddenly into a blur and disappeared, giving way to complete darkness. My first impression was that we were once again in space, but there wasn't anything that resembled Earth or the moon; not even the stars were visible as we traveled at an unthinkable speed through the darkness.

I still held Carla's hand, even though I felt my astral body spinning uncontrollably as if the universe was once again conspiring to separate me from what I held dearest—much as it had done when it took my mother away from me.

For a minute, I thought I was going to either tear into pieces or get sick to my stomach—although I didn't even know if that was possible here.

Suddenly, my senses were overwhelmed by vast snowy hills that appeared right in front of us. The air was cold, thin, and crisp. The smell of eucalyptus filled the air and the snow peaks above us reflected the moonlight as though they were made out of crystals. We were above the darkness and gloominess at the base of the mountains.

Dark clouds encircled the mountain almost halfway to the top; below that point, the fog reigned unchallenged. At its peak there was nothing but the frozen, icy, and deserted landscape.

Unsure where to go, I willed myself to land on the highest peak, and almost immediately we started to descend toward a clearing. As we moved closer to the snowy ground, I noticed how each ice flake reflected light from the bright moon above us. Something told me it wasn't the same moon we were used to seeing back on Earth. It was slightly larger, much brighter, and lacked all of the moon's distinguishing features.

"I don't see him anywhere," said Carla. The wind howled in the distance while snow flew in the air, heading toward us.

"He's around here somewhere, I know he is," I assured her.

"How do you know that?" asked Carla.

"I can sense him," I replied.

"You can sense Jonas?" asked Carla, confused.

"No," I replied, pausing for a second, then added in a very soft whisper, "I can sense… Phasma."

"I wonder where we are," said Carla as she approached a lone pine tree and rested against its trunk.

"I don't know. I recall Phasma mentioning something about a place called Threshold," I whispered. I was scared of mentioning his name out loud.

"Whatever this place is, it sure is different," said Carla as she quickly removed her hands from the tree trunk and wiped them on her clothes. "Yikes, that trunk is soft, wet, and cold. It's really gross."

I was walking over to look at it when I realized that my bare feet were freezing. In fact, my whole body was cold. I started to shiver.

"It's freaking cold here," I said, shivering so hard that it was almost impossible to talk.

"Yes, it is," replied Carla, rubbing her hands on her arms to keep herself warm.

"At this rate we'll freeze to death before we have the slightest chance of finding Jonas," I managed to say.

"Quick, think of something warm," suggested Carla, closing her eyes.

I don't know why but white bunny slippers came to mind, and almost immediately, I felt my feet getting warmer.

"Ha ha," Carla laughed and pointed at my feet.

I was surprised to find the actual slippers on my feet. I was definitely not dressed appropriately for the harsh weather conditions of Threshold.

Carla, on the other hand, was wearing a plain white, long-sleeved, V-neck tunic shirt, faded low-rider skinny jeans, and a chocolate-colored hooded cardigan sweater with a faux fur trim accented by a white Norwegian design. Her sweater went down to her small waist. On her feet she had chocolate brown suede boots that matched her sweater perfectly.

Embarrassed and still not properly dressed for the winter, I immediately thought about my regular winter outfit, which consisted of a tight black knit skullcap, a South Pole black ski jacket with matching insulated gloves, and a pair of straight-legged denim jeans with my black army boots. As if by magic, my whole body began to get warm.

"That's better," I said.

From our vantage point, we could almost see the whole continent, which I had named Threshold solely based on assumptions. For miles, there seemed to be nothing but darkness below us. Layers of dark blue, grey, and black clouds covered almost half of the newfound continent.

Far off in the distance, we could barely detect hints of bright and luscious greens and more promising weather conditions.

I ran across the clearing to peek at the other side. I was very curious what mysteries Threshold held. As soon as I reached the other side, I was amazed by what I saw. In the distance, there were signs of a vast sapphire-green ocean just beyond the dark heavy clouds, fog and darkness.

I'd always imagined light to be one of the essential building blocks of the afterlife. Although there were hints of lights in the distance, darkness seemed abundant in Threshold.

"This place is huge. How are we going to find Jonas?" asked Carla.

"There's someone down there," I said as I looked over the ledge and noticed movement below. That's when I realized that the fog was actually smoke that rose from the ground below.

"What is it?" Carla asked.

"I really don't know, maybe a village. There has to be a way to get down there," I said, looking around for a trail.

"Maybe Jonas is down there. We have to get down there," said Carla.

"It's possible, but we really should investigate it further before we just walk down there. After all, this is a new world and we have no idea if they are friendly or not," I said.

"Hey! There's a trail here. Come quick," said Carla, so psyched that she appeared not to be listening to me at all.

Even before I got there, Carla was on her way. I followed her down the small and slippery snowy trail, thinking the whole time that I was going to fall.

Slowly, the eucalyptus smell was replaced by the smell of charred meat and skin. The closer we got, the darker the smoke and the stronger the smell became.

"What a horrible smell, what do you think that is?" asked Carla.

"I don't know, perhaps they are cooking dinner," I suggested. "Shhh," I said, motioning for Carla to stop.

"What is it?" Carla whispered in my ear, causing pleasant chills to run down my spine.

"There," I said, pointing toward a snow bank.

"What do you mean?" asked Carla.

"We can hide there and observe," I explained.

I moved slowly to avoid making noise. I wanted to believe the villagers were friendly, but there was something about the way the place smelled that told otherwise.

We ducked behind the snow bank and listened carefully to the noises coming from the village below, peeking out every once in a while.

"Keep the prisoner alive, at least until Lord Phasma gets back!" someone yelled. Carla let out a gasp. I looked around the snow bank, but I still couldn't see anyone. The smoke was too intense, and the smell was almost unbearable.

"Are they talking about—"

"Quiet, someone's coming," I interrupted Carla, moving slowly behind the snow bank.

"Quick, this way," I said, grabbing her hand as we heard howling in the distance.

We rushed back up the trail and hid behind a rock just a few feet away.

"We should be safe here."

I decided to take a look to see if they were still coming toward us, but thankfully they weren't. Instead, they stood behind the snow bank, talking to each other. There were two of them. They looked human, but the first was covered in mud and animal fur. The other creature was dressed the same, except it was carrying a long and heavy metal axe, also covered in mud and patches of dry blood.

"Who's the undead Lord Phasma brought back?" asked one of them.

"I don't get what the fuss is all about," said the creature carrying the axe.

"Whatever it is, I'm sure it's important," said the other creature as he opened a pack and took out a long, sharp weapon resembling a machete.

"I'm tired of hunting. Nobody else brings any game," said the axe-carrying creature.

"Because that's the only thing that we're good at," answered the other creature as he sharpened his blade.

"I'm good at other things too."

"Yep, like what?" asked the shorter creature.

"I'm the fastest eater in the village," replied the oversized creature. "We better catch something different this time. I'm tired of elk meat," he said, swinging his axe in the air. It was so big that it required both of his large hands to swing it. *My dad with his big hands, wouldn't have a problem finding a job in that village*, I thought.

146

"I know what you mean, I miss a nice roasted mammoth. When was the last time we had that?" asked the machete guy.

"I don't know, feels like many cycles ago. Too many, if you ask me."

"What are those things?" asked Carla, peeking out from behind the rock.

"Sidwick, did you hear that?" asked the axe-carrying creature as he looked in our direction.

"Nah, it's nothing. There's nothing alive up there besides those stupid trees and the crows that live in them," Sidwick replied.

"Come on, Delawi, let's go hunt by the waterfall for a change. Maybe the reason we only find elk is because we always hunt in the same stupid place," said Sidwick.

"I hate that place, but okay. I just hope we catch good game. I'm so hungry, I'm afraid half a mammoth won't be enough," said Delawi.

We stayed quiet as Sidwick and Delawi headed down the trail. I thought it would be wise to wait a couple of minutes before I talked to Carla, just to make sure they wouldn't be able to hear me.

"Oh my God, they smelled awful," said Carla. "Were they talking about Jonas?"

"I think so. I remember Phasma calling me undead before," I replied.

"They didn't look much different than us," said Carla, looking perplexed.

"Yeah, except for the dirt, the smell, and horns," I said as we moved back toward the clearing.

"We need a plan," I said, looking for clues about where Jonas was being held.

"I agree. But besides the fact they have very big and sharp weapons we don't know anything about them," replied Carla.

"If we knew where Jonas was being held, it would make our job so much easier," I said.

"We need to move closer," said Carla, starting to walk down the hillside.

"It's too dangerous," I said, worried about her well-being.

"It will be fine if you follow my lead," said Carla as her outfit changed to the same armor the creatures had on minutes earlier. Although dirty and covered in mud, Carla still looked very pretty... including the horns on top of her head.

The transformation was fantastic and surprisingly fast. I concentrated on having the same look as Carla, and I immediately felt my clothes change to the itchy and smelly animal leathers and fur armor that seemed to come complete with a weapon. In my case, it was a club that was so heavy it made me walk a little off-center. Carla's weapon was a bow, which looked very stylish on her.

As we neared the village, it looked and smelled worse than I could imagine. In the center, a huge bonfire marked the epicenter of trade. A giant column of smoke hovered over the area, covering the small wooden cabins with a dense fog. Roasting on the fire were several animals with their heads still attached.

"I don't know if this is going to work," I said as we passed a couple of locals who stared at us.

"Relax and act natural," said Carla.

We passed a huge wooden gate that had been left open and unguarded. As we entered the village, the smell grew even stronger, if such a thing was possible, but thankfully so did the smoke and fog, providing us with cover. Good thing, too, because I didn't think I was able to disguise the faces I made from the smell.

"He must be over there," I said, pointing toward an opening in the nearby mountain cliff.

"Why do you say that?" asked Carla.

"Because that's the only place they have guards," I replied.

"Quick, follow me," said Carla, heading toward a deserted shed.

"We are going to need a distraction," I said as we looked at the cliff entrance.

"I think I can manage that," offered Carla.

"No, you would attract too much attention, and besides, it's too dangerous," I replied.

"What? Let me remind you that we're in this together. Please stop trying to protect me from everything and everyone. If we're going to succeed in rescuing my brother, you'll need my help," replied Carla.

"You're right. What do you have in mind?" I asked.

"You said yourself that I attract too much attention—I'm going to assume you meant that because of my good looks—do you know of a better way to create a distraction?"

"Good point," I said. "But how are you going to get away afterward?"

"It's really simple. Once you have Jonas, you both make your way up the mountain, and I'll meet you there," replied Carla as she started to walk toward the guards.

"Carla!" I said, but it was too late. She left the shed with a look of determination on her face.

I felt like biting my nails with every step Carla took toward the guards. *How was she going to distract them?* I wondered.

I had to think of something, so I walked outside and picked up a few boxes full of old, rusted weapons that were sitting outside the shed. I started to walk toward Carla and the guards.

From a distance, I could see Carla approaching the guards.

"I'm new here and ashamed to say that I'm a bit lost," said Carla.

"Where do you need to go?" Asked the tallest of the guards.

For a second, Carla seemed at a loss for words, but then she replied, "I'm going to the forge, I have to pick up some arrows there for training."

She must have seen that the box I was carrying was full of old, broken, and blood-soaked weapons and figured out I was heading for the forge. In truth, I didn't even know if they had a forge, but it seemed like a reasonable assumption, judging from the smoke rising from inside.

"I have never seen you here before," said the other creature, who was slightly shorter and much heavier than the other guard.

"As I said, I'm new," replied Carla, getting visibly angry.

"You're a feisty one: so young and yet so bad. You must have arrived with the latest batch of recruits," said the tallest guard. I think he had a crush on her.

"Let me guess, you need to go to the forge too?" the chubby guard asked me without paying too much attention.

"Yep, I need to bring this junk to smelt. We seem to be running out of ore," I replied coldly.

"Go ahead," he said, gesturing me forward.

I wanted to wait for Carla, but there wasn't much I could do. If I lingered any longer, I would attract the attention of well-armed guards, so I had no choice but to trust that Carla was going to figure a way out for herself.

As I headed toward the cliff opening, a putrid cloud of gas rose from deep within. I couldn't help but feel a very familiar sensation as I wandered around the cave's many dead-ends and maze-like tunnels. Phasma had brought me here before. I was sure of it.

As I ventured deeper and lower, I could once again feel the dread growing inside me.

"Wait up!" someone yelled from behind me. I turned around, but I couldn't see anyone, just a cloud of smoke.

"Wait!" I heard again as a couple of locals passed me. I wasn't exactly blending in as I would like to, and Carla wasn't exactly helping by screaming so loudly.

"Shhh, are you trying to get us caught?" I asked nervously.

"It's okay, nobody heard me," Carla whispered.

"Where do you suppose he is?" I asked.

"Your guess is as good as mine."

"Thanks," I said sarcastically. "Right it is then."

Although the smoke cleared, the deeper we moved into the tunnels, the denser the air became.

I grabbed a nearby torch from the wall.

"Good thinking; we may need them," said Carla. She approached the next torch and pulled it out of the wall.

"Where did everyone go?" asked Carla, looking around.

"I don't know, I don't think many people come this far," I replied.

"Either that, or we took a wrong turn somewhere. I didn't see a forge or anything like it," added Carla.

"Should we turn around?" I asked.

"Maybe we should've turned left. Let's go back," said Carla.

We turned around and went back the way we came and turned left at the intersection. After walking for what seemed like just over half a mile, we arrived at a large underground room filled with people going about their business. Right in the middle of the room there was a pool of golden, molten lava.

"This must be the forge," I whispered.

"How are we going to find Jonas?" Carla asked.

"I don't have a clue. We'll figure something out."

Worried, I approached what I assumed was the Forgemaster. He was short, dirty, sweaty, and fat. He had a very dark complexion as though he spent too much time in the sun, or perhaps he just spent too much time standing near the hot lava pool. He carried a huge iron hammer and an assortment of sharp swords and daggers in his belt. They looked so heavy that I thought his pants were going to fall off.

I placed the box of broken weapons on top of his worktable and waited.

"Take that junk away from here. Don't you see that I'm busy? You freaking maggot!" he yelled as everyone around us stopped whatever they were doing to look and laugh at me.

"Sorry, I'm new," I said.

"Why the heck do I always get the new recruits?" he mumbled to himself. "Don't just stand there looking like an anvil. Make yourself useful and throw that junk in the melt pit," he ordered as spit spilled out of his mouth.

"And what do you want?" he said, looking at Carla.

"I just need some more ammo, and I was told you're the guy to see," said Carla, showing off her acting skills.

"Ha ha, nothing is free here, smash-pie. If you want ammo, you'll need to earn it," I heard the Forgemaster say to Carla as I dumped the weapons in the flaming lava pool.

I rushed back, hoping there was something I could do to help her.

"What do you need me to do?" asked Carla as she took off her fur jacket and placed it on the Forgemaster's table. I couldn't tell if she was trying to show him that she was ready to work or if she was trying to charm him.

"Take this cage to the prisoners' chambers," the Forgemaster said as he handed Carla a small metal cage and some chains, both of which appeared to have been recently repaired but not cleaned of the dried blood stains.

"Sure, I'll be back soon," said Carla as she lifted up the metal cage and left.

"And you over there, you take this one," he ordered me, pointing toward a much larger metal cage on the ground.

I bent over and picked up the heavy cage, but I didn't dare look at him. I was afraid that if I looked, he would notice that I was sweating profusely. My shoulder hurt so much that I wanted to scream in pain, but I couldn't show him any weakness. So I held it in.

"I got more for you to deliver after that one," he said, laughing.

By the time I reached the corner, I was exhausted. Once I was out of the Forgemaster's sight, I placed the heavy cage on the floor and sat down to catch my breath.

"Tired already?" asked Carla from behind me, scaring me.

"Very funny, you got the small one," I said, pointing at her cage.

"I guess you're not as good-looking as I am," said Carla.

"It's about time we finally made some progress," I added, stretching my arms and legs.

"Yes, hopefully Jonas will be there," replied Carla.

"I hope so because I can't take this smell for too much longer," I said, smelling my own armpits. "Since the smell is not coming from me, it has to be coming from this stupid armor."

"At least that's what you think," said Carla.

"Anyway, what is this thing made of? It's itchy as hell," I complained.

"If I had to guess, I would say animal hide. Come on, let's go," said Carla, offering me a hand.

I threw the heavy metal chains over my sore shoulders and, after a gasp of pain, started to drag the cage along.

After we had walked for a while, the torches became few and far between. It wasn't much longer before we reached a huge clearing that smelled far worse than I did.

I almost got sick as we entered what could only be the prisoners' chambers.

"Jonas? Are you here?" whispered Carla as we both looked around, perplexed by the sheer size of the place and the deplorable conditions within.

Some of the creatures appeared to be eating their own skin, while others picked at the putrid skin of their cellmates.

We must have walked almost to the end of the chamber looking for Jonas. The creatures in the cages looked like the creatures from the village… that, is until we reached a chamber with a decaying sign that read "UNDEAD HALL" above the entrance.

"Here, he's got to be in there somewhere," I said, pointing at the sign.

"I hope so," replied Carla.

"Jonas!" Carla called a bit too loud.

"I'm here!" came a faint reply from somewhere in the chamber.

"Jonas? Is that really you?" cried Carla, almost in tears. "Quick, I think it's coming from there."

"Jonas, where are you?" asked Carla again as we walked through a maze of cages; some were on the floor while others were suspended in the air.

"I'm in here!" replied Jonas, sounding louder.

We took two sharp left turns and followed the trail. I could swear that some of the people in the cages looked dead, but they weren't. They were humans, although barely recognizable. One thing I was sure of, they certainly weren't treated as human. I'd seen homeless people who looked better cared for. Most just lay in their cages, some still bleeding from what I assumed were their mortal wounds. They lay there as though they didn't have the strength or the will to stand up.

"Oh my God, why are all those people in cages?" asked Carla, crying.

"I'm not sure. They look sick and tortured," I replied, trying to be strong.

Never in my entire life did I think I would find people in these conditions. They didn't have any water or food, not a bathroom in sight.

Although it was freezing outside, inside the heat was almost unbearable. At first, I rather enjoyed the warming sensation, but soon I realized it wasn't a blessing, it was a curse.

When I heard Carla's loud gasp, I quickly made my way to her.

"Oh my God, Jonas, what have they done to you?" asked Carla from a few yards away.

***

I found Jonas covered in dry mud and still in his pajamas, which were muddy.

"Are you all right?" I asked, glad to see him but worried about his well-being.

"That depends on your definition of all right. But I'm happy to see you guys," replied Jonas.

"What happened to you?" asked Carla.

"I'll gladly tell you all about it. Just as soon as you get me out of here and we leave this hell hole behind."

Unfortunately, the cage was locked with a rusty old padlock.

"Where do they keep the key?" I asked.

"I dunno, some short dude carrying a hammer put me in this cage, but I have only seen him a couple of times."

"That's got to be the—"

"The Forgemaster," Carla said. "I'll get the key from him and be back for you soon, little brother."

"I'm not little!" complained Jonas, although I didn't think Carla heard him because she had taken off running toward the forge.

"I'd better go with her to make sure she doesn't get into trouble," I said. I looked him right in the eyes and let him know I was going to be back for him. That no matter what happened, he could count on me to protect his sister and free him, even though I was the person who got them involved in this mess in the first place.

I turned to find Carla, but it was too late. She wasn't around anymore. I was worried about what she would do to get that key from the Forgemaster. Her determination was a virtue, but I could remember more than one instance where it got her into some serious trouble.

I walked briskly after Carla, but I didn't run. After all, I didn't want to arrive at the Forgemaster at the same time as Carla. Besides, I wasn't even sure if she would need my help at all. Not to mention that if the Forgemaster saw me again, there was a good chance he would give me some other random job, and I couldn't let that happen.

I carefully approached the entrance to the forge and found a dark crevice where I could hide and listen undetected.

"Forgemaster, we have a problem," said Carla, looking worried. For a minute, I thought that she forgot her acting skills, but then I realized her plan.

"What is it? I don't like problems, smash-pie. Are you going to be a problem?" he asked.

"No, I just wanted to let you know that one of the prisoners tried to break his lock."

"I don't have time for this. Deal with it, or I'll deal with you," he threatened.

"Sure, I'll punish the little maggot so he learns his lesson. But I'll need the key so I can give him a beating that he'll never forget," said Carla, all gutsy and ruthless.

"Here, and take this lock too in case you need to replace the old one," the Forgemaster replied, tossing another padlock and a bunch of keys toward her.

"Thanks," she said as she turned around and headed out.

"Smash-pie!" he said.

"Yes?"

"Keep this up and you may have a future. Just remember, don't be a problem," he warned.

Carla continued walking away, looking relieved. And to be honest, so was I.

I followed her until she had turned a couple of corners, then I caught up to her.

"So, how did I do?" asked Carla when she saw me approaching.

"Not too bad," I responded.

"And you said theater club was a waste of time," she laughed.

"I admit that I may have been wrong about that. I'm glad it was good for something," I confessed. "Let's hurry before we attract too much attention or worse," I said.

We rushed back toward the prisoners' chambers.

As we entered the deplorable chambers, the fetid smell assaulted my senses again, nearly knocking me out. Our vision wasn't the only sense that was enhanced in the astral realm; all of our other senses, including smell, were extra sharp as well.

"How are we going to get out of here?" I asked.

"I don't know. I haven't thought that far ahead yet," replied Carla, zigzagging through the prisoners' cages and trying her best not to pay too much attention to the other prisoners. I suspected we both knew it was too late for the others, because even if we freed them, it was very unlikely they would have the necessary energy and strength to escape. Most couldn't even get up. Some didn't seem to have the will to blink.

CHAPTER TEN
Friends in Weird Places

A s I approached Jonas's cage, I heard a soft giggling sound, followed by childlike laughter.

Carla and I exchanged a puzzled look as we slowed our pace and approached with caution.

From our vantage point, we could see a creature near Jonas, apparently talking to him. The closer we got, the clearer and more defined the creature and its voice became.

She was about the size of a medium sized bush. Her skin was ashy grey. She had very distinctive long white hair and her face was smooth and childlike.

"What's your name?" Jonas asked her.

"My name is Nyx—Nyxy Serafin, but you can call me Nyx," she replied.

We took advantage of the distraction and looked for a better angle to observe from. We ended up hiding behind a big metal cage in the darkest corner of the room.

From our new point of view, we could see her big green and orange eyes looking concerned.

"Is something wrong?" asked Jonas, looking worried.

"Besides the fact that everyone hates me?" asked Nyx.

"Why do you think that?" asked Jonas.

"I happened different than everyone else, and because of that I have no friends," replied Nyx.

"What do you mean by 'you happened different'? I don't understand," asked Jonas.

"You know, I happened like you did. You happened as well, otherwise you wouldn't be here or even exist," explained Nyx.

Based on Carla's puzzled look, I knew she had no clue what Nyx was talking about either.

"I still don't understand. Do you mean to say that you were born different?" ventured Jonas.

"Born? Is that what you undead people call it when you happen?" asked Nyx.

"Yes, I guess that's what we call it," said Jonas, starting to smile and chuckle.

"I happened like no one else before me, so that's why nobody likes Nyx," she said, almost crying.

"Where I'm from, we're all born different. We have people of many races, with a variety of looks, sizes, shapes, colors, and personalities," Jonas said to cheer her up.

"Oh, here in Threshold we're not supposed to happen different. It's a curse. A curse I'll have to endure for the rest of my life," said Nyx as her shoulders drooped.

"Being different, it's not so bad. Eventually people will accept you for who you are," explained Jonas, surprising me.

"You don't understand," Nyx cried.

She started to sob hard enough that her body lit up with a fierce fire. The room suddenly became much brighter. Jonas took a couple steps back in his cage.

"We have a problem," said Carla. "If she doesn't stop doing whatever it is she's doing, she'll burn him!"

Even from where we stood, we could feel the heat rising from her body.

"Listen, you don't need to get upset. It's okay, what others think doesn't really matter," said Jonas, trying to calm her.

"My people aren't supposed to have a physical body at all, and I have a fiery one," Nyx said, still crying while her body glowed brighter.

"Maybe you need to be with people who appreciate you instead of being with people who put you down and don't accept you for who you really are," offered Jonas, now sweating profusely.

Nyx thought for a second, then backed up against the wall when she finally realized that her body was burning. The water that had been running down the chamber walls moments before turned to steam. The moss turned ash-grey and disintegrated into dust.

"Are you okay?" asked Jonas.

"Yes, but everything around me isn't when this happens," explained Nyx, looking depressed. "I just don't know why I happened so different from everyone else." Her tears seemed to act like an accelerant for her flaming body. The more she cried, the hotter she burned and the deadlier she became.

"Our differences are what make us stronger, and differences are the root of the world's beauty," Jonas said. "Besides, where I come from, we strongly believe in destiny. We choose to believe that there's a hidden purpose to life and a reason why we're the way we are."

"You're not scared of me?" Nyx asked as she wiped away tears from her face.

"Not at all. In fact, I like that you're different. In school, other kids often picked on me. They used to call me names and make fun of me, but not anymore. Now they accept me. Some are even my friends," replied Jonas.

"School? We don't have schools here. I wish I could go to school," said Nyx, looking more at ease.

Much to our surprise, his plan worked. Her fierce glow slowly turned from a bright red into a cool ocean-blue and the blaze retreated. Her skin transitioned from a bright red hue to a cool blue glow before it was returned to a natural and pale tone that was almost human. Stepping away from the wall, she quickly turned to face us, but luckily she didn't see us. That's when I realized she was beautiful. She looked like a princess as her face radiated benevolence, innocence, and goodness. She seemed out of place in the chambers.

"What is it like to be an undead?" asked Nyx.

"Why do you call me undead?" Jonas asked.

"Well, because you are," replied Nyx as she moved closer to Jonas with her big eyes fixed on his face.

"No, I'm not," replied Jonas vehemently.

"Did you die?" asked Nyx.

"Die? No, I haven't, at least I sure hope not," replied Jonas.

"Then you're an undead. If you have a body and you're not dead, then you're an undead. You know, sometimes I feel like an undead myself," Nyx said. "Why do you like to be undead anyway?"

"For starters, it is great to be and feel alive. Not to mention that it's all I know."

"The dead in Threshold also feel great and alive. They just don't have a physical body," said Nyx.

"Why do you call being born a happening? How does it work?" Jonas asked.

"Because the moment you lose your physical body in one of the many physical worlds, you'll wake up here in Threshold. We call that waking up process happening," explained Nyx.

"How do I get out of here?" Jonas asked.

"Why do you want to leave?" asked Nyx, looking worried.

"I was brought here against my will," Jonas said. "What about you? Are you a prisoner too?"

"I am… but not the way you think. I'm a prisoner of my own body," replied Nyx.

"Don't worry, I won't let anything bad happen to you," said Jonas.

"You don't understand—" Nyx started to explain but she was interrupted when the side of the chamber wall opened to reveal a bright moon outside. The snow rushed in, bringing with it cool and refreshingly crisp outside air.

***

I was thinking about making myself known to them when a dark blur flew in through the cave opening.

My heart was suddenly engulfed in pain and my shoulder burned intensely.

"Serafin! What are you doing here?" asked Phasma as he approached from above.

"Sorry… I was just—" Nyx tried to explain, but Jonas cut her short.

"Leave her alone, you dingbat," said Jonas.

"Ha ha, what is this?" laughed Phasma. "You two have met? And are you actually trying to protect her?"

"As a matter of fact, I am."

"I take it you haven't told him," said Phasma, pacing back and forth with his wings tucked away. "You see, this creature you're so set on protecting is probably the only person in this room who doesn't need protection."

"What do you mean?" Jonas asked. As he waited for an answer, he looked from Phasma to Nyx. Nyx looked uncomfortable as her skin started to glow again.

Before Nyx could answer, her body ignited in a flash, sending a blast wave through the air and pushing Jonas back into the wall of his cage.

"How dare you defy me?" Phasma screamed. "From now on, you're not to leave your room. And don't ever talk with the undead again. Do you understand?"

"But, Dad, he understands—"

"Enough!" yelled Phasma, looking upset.

"Dad? You're… his daughter?" asked Jonas.

I wished I could tell Jonas to be quiet because he didn't seem to be helping his situation. Carla also looked ready to charge in. I grabbed her hand to make sure she didn't do anything she would later regret.

"Not by choice," said Nyx, sobbing, although her flames had subsided when Phasma yelled at her.

"Leave us at once," ordered Phasma.

"You'd better not hurt him, Dad," cried Nyx before she left the room.

Phasma didn't acknowledge or reply.

"So you have been chatting with my daughter, I see. It doesn't matter. It won't change a thing," said Phasma. The whole time, Jonas looked scared.

"I don't know what you want, but I know you won't succeed," said Jonas, shaking. "My friend will fin—" said Jonas, but then he cut himself short.

"I sure hope so," Phasma said. "In fact, I am counting on it."

"I'm sure he's not scared of you. You don't even scare me," shouted Jonas.

"Really, is that so?" said Phasma. He approached Jonas, bringing his face to just inches away from Jonas's face. Even standing a good distance away, I noticed details I had missed before. His face had many almost indescribable traits. His teeth were yellow, sharp, and pointy like the fangs of a deadly vampire. His eyes were the deepest icicle-blue color I had ever seen. I had never seen eyes that cold before. They lacked a soul or even a single drop of goodwill. His breath smelled like a week old road kill. His skin was rough and uneven, and his hair seemed to have been ripped right out of a mad scientist magazine.

As he moved closer, Jonas tried to step backward, but it was no use. He only had enough space to take one or two steps in each direction.

"We'll finish this later. You're lucky that your friend hasn't gotten here yet," said Phasma as he stepped back and slowly spread his immense wings. He took off with a forceful thrust, leaving dust in his wake. Just like before, the cave wall opened as he flew through it.

I could still hear Phasma's last words. They frightened me.

After we made sure Phasma was really gone, we approached Jonas's cage.

"Guys, you're not going to believe what happened," said Jonas, still shaking.

"We know, we were hiding over there," replied Carla. "After all, someone needed to make sure you didn't get yourself killed. What the hell were you thinking, arguing with him like that?"

When Jonas didn't answer, Carla inserted the oversized metal key into the rusty old padlock, and it popped open and fell to the ground.

"What about Nyx?" asked Jonas as he stepped outside the cage.

"Are you kidding me? That's Phasma's daughter. Whose side do you think she's on?" I said.

"She didn't strike me as a bad person," replied Jonas.

"She's not a person, she's not even human, remember?" said Carla.

"I don't want to leave without at least trying to help her or saying good-bye," said Jonas. Unfortunately for us, he had a determined look much like Carla's on his face. This was a first for Jonas because he had never been determined about anything in his life.

I stood in the spot where Nyx had been earlier and noticed that the place was bare and dry, thanks to Nyx's fiery outbursts.

"Not to mention that she could kill us all in one of her fiery fits," I said.

"I'll make you a deal. We'll get out of here and find some help, and then we can return to find Nyx," said Carla, looking eager to get away.

"No way!" Jonas said, determined.

"Listen, we can't stay here much longer. Eventually, he'll be back, you know?" added Carla.

"You guys can go if you want to, but I'm going to stay and look for her," said Jonas. Then he took off running.

***

"Jonas! Don't do this," screamed Carla, waking up some of the people who slept restlessly in the chamber.

"Help… me," one of them whispered.

I couldn't ignore a plea for help, so I reached for the keys and unlocked the door. The stranger tried to move, but he was too weak to even reach the open door.

"Thank… you," he said as he closed his eyes and gave up with a long sigh.

"We'd better go after Jonas, before he gets himself hurt or worse," said Carla.

I felt guilty for leaving that poor person behind, but I needed to find Jonas.

We both took off after Jonas, but out of the corner of my eye, I saw a blue-white flash light up the chamber. At first I thought Nyx had returned, but just when we were about to turn the corner I stopped and looked back. I saw several light beings holding the stranger I had just freed. They placed him on some sort of stretcher and vanished into thin air.

"He's gone… someone must've helped him," I said to Carla. She nodded, but she seemed more worried about Jonas than anything else.

"Why do I have to have such a stubborn brother?" said Carla as she picked up the pace.

"You do know that you're just like him, right?" I asked, smiling.

"I'm not stubborn. I'm determined, and that's different," she replied.

I knew better than to try to convince her otherwise.

We had no clue where he was heading. Jonas ran so fast that he was gone from our sight. The many twists and turns of the cave made our job that much harder.

We were about to turn around when we saw a soft orange glow in the distance.

"There!" I said.

"Quick, let's go," said Carla as she sped toward the end of the tunnel.

As we got closer, we heard a faint female sob. We approached carefully. Curious and unsure if Jonas was there, I peeked inside the room. It was a simple room with a canopy bed. Although the bed was grey and had a black metal motif on the support pillars, it wasn't unattractive.

Nyx was sitting near the bed. She was crying and glowed with a soft orange hue. But there was no sign of Jonas.

"He's not here!" said Carla a bit too loud. Nyx heard her and turned around.

"Who? What do you want?" asked Nyx, wiping her tears away.

I decided it would be best to step out from behind the wall and explain.

"Sorry, we mean you no harm," I said as politely as I could.

"Who are you?" said Nyx.

"I'm a friend," I replied as I moved a bit closer. As I did, her glow intensified.

"Please believe me when I say that I mean you no harm," I said as the room temperature rose.

"Stay away," Nyx warned. "One more step, and I'll burn you."

"Okay, take it easy. I was looking for my friend. He went to look for you and disappeared. When I saw this room glowing, I thought he might have found you," I said as I backed away.

"Are you friends with the undead?" asked Nyx as the flame diminished a little.

"Yes. We're undead as well," I confessed. "We're here to help him."

"Jonas is my brother, have you seen him?" Carla said, stepping forward cautiously.

"I saw him earlier, but not since my father came back," said Nyx. She looked us straight in the eyes, and it was as though she could see our very souls. "If you want to find him, you're going to need my help."

"But what about your father?" I asked.

"He won't be back until later," she replied.

"Where should we start?" asked Carla.

"First things first, I'll help you on one condition," added Nyx.

"And what's that?" I asked.

"My condition is that you get me out of here too," she said as tears started to fill her eyes.

I thought about it for a second.

"Agreed," I said, wondering if I had made the right decision. However, looking at Carla I knew I had. Her approving smile said it all.

"Okay then, but if anyone asks, you're helping me find a prisoner who escaped," said Nyx as she stood up and approached Carla and me.

"Since you aren't Night Dwellers, I take it you don't really look like that?" asked Nyx.

"Nope, we look like humans, much like my friend and the others being held in the undead prisoners' chamber," I replied.

"Why are they being held there? What could they have done so wrong to deserve such harsh punishment?" asked Carla.

"Over here, they haven't done anything wrong yet, they haven't had the chance to," explained Nyx.

"What do you mean?" I asked.

"Those you saw chained up are the violent and relentless souls of the physical realm. Once they die, they come here and usually stay until they are either rescued or they join the Night Dwellers," explained Nyx.

"So are they what people call bad spirits?" I asked.

"Yes, but I wouldn't exactly call them bad. I think of them as beings who happened to make some bad choices while in the physical realm," said Nyx.

"Who rescues them?" I asked.

"Nobody knows. I have seen them only a handful of times. They usually come when no one is around. Many Night Dwellers don't believe the rescuers even exist because very few have ever seen them," Nyx continued to explain. "I suspect that somewhere someone cares enough to help their forgotten criminal souls."

"Are they very luminous beings, almost whitish?" I asked.

"Do you know them?" asked Nyx.

"No, but I think we just saw them rescue someone," I added.

"They are beautiful. I want to meet them. In fact, that's where I need you to take me once we find your friend," replied Nyx.

"But we don't know anything about them or this world," complained Carla.

"Neither do I. My whole life, I have been stuck here in Nightside," said Nyx, looking sad.

"Nightside?" asked Carla.

"Ah, I keep forgetting you aren't from around here. Threshold is made of different regions. We're in Nightside, where darkness rules. Then there is Twilight, which only a privileged few have had the fortune to visit. And lastly, there is Dayside. Dayside is still a mystery to most of us. We hear stories about it, rumors really. The main one being that nobody has ever come back from there."

"Why is this place called Nightside?" I asked.

"It's always night in Nightside. We have never seen daylight. Rumor has it that Dayside has never seen a single star in the sky. I personally have only seen Nightside and some of Twilight," replied Nyx.

Some of the things Nyx told us were amazing, while others were downright unbelievable. We had a lot to discover about Threshold. I just hoped we would live long enough to do it.

I couldn't help but wonder if my mother would be at one of the places Nyx mentioned. I was about to ask her about it when we spotted two guards on patrol coming our way.

"Follow my lead," Nyx whispered.

"What are you doing here?" asked a toothless guard.

"Following orders, exactly what you should be doing. These are the new recruits who are going to take over this route. Didn't anyone tell you that you two have been placed onto Phasma's private guard?" asked Nyx.

"Oh, what? Yes, thank you, we're very… happy for the promotion, Scion," replied the toothless guard.

"Well, head out then. Your training begins immediately. I'll personally train these recruits on this route," Nyx ordered.

"Yes, Scion, right away," the other guard said as he walked past us, sarcastically mumbling under his breath: "Oh great, more work… just what I wanted."

"Shhh, the Scion will hear you," ordered the toothless guard.

"Well done," said Carla after they were gone.

"Thanks. This leads straight into the Core. The area is off limits, so we won't have to worry about the guards. I have been here a few times, usually when I want to be left alone," explained Nyx.

"Core? What's that?" I asked.

"The Core is Threshold's energy source. The lava inside the forge, for example, comes from the Core," said Nyx as she started to glow again. Carla and I backed up discreetly.

"Are you guys scared of me too?" asked Nyx, looking hurt.

"No, it's just that everything here is so different," I said.

"Your friend Jonas isn't scared of me, he told me so," said Nyx proudly.

"Neither are we. Just give us a warning before lighting up," said Carla to ease the tension.

"Okay, I'll try. Don't worry, the reason I started to glow is because from here on out, it will get fairly dark. And there aren't any torches because nobody comes down here."

"Where are you guys going?" said Jonas from right behind us.

"Jonas?" asked Carla.

"Where have you been? We've been looking for you," I said when I saw him.

"I was right there, hiding behind that rock. I was looking for Nyx when I saw those two guards approach, so I hid. Unfortunately, they didn't leave, they kept talking and pacing back and forth, and then you guys showed up," explained Jonas.

"I'm glad you're okay. We were worried sick. Don't you dare do that again," said Carla.

"How are we going to get out of here?" asked Jonas.

"Don't worry, I have a plan," said Nyx.

"Are you're helping us?" asked Jonas.

"Yes, we made a deal with Nyx. She'll help us free you, and in return we'll help her escape," explained Carla.

***

"So, what's your plan?" I asked Nyx while Carla hugged Jonas.

"There's an old boat down at the Core that can take us out of here. It hasn't been used in a long time, but it should still be able to get us out, assuming it's still there. When I was small, I used to play in there," said Nyx.

"Great, that way we don't have to deal with those nasty guards," replied Carla.

"I can't take this armor anymore. Do you think we'll see anyone else down here?" I asked, dying to remove the itchy armor.

"I don't think so. From here on, it will be deserted, the area hasn't been used in a long time," replied Nyx as she watched Jonas and Carla hold hands. I sensed a hint of jealousy in her eyes.

Nyx continued to lead the way; her glow grew stronger as the tunnels got darker.

"Nyx, I have a question. How come we can't fly in here?" I asked.

"There's a protective barrier in and around the Cave of Sorrows. Only Phasma can fly here," she replied.

"Cave of Sorrows? Is that where we are?" I asked.

"Yes, the Cave of Sorrows is a complex of caves spanning the whole base of Night Peaks," explained Nyx.

Tired of feeling itchy, I willed my appearance and outfit to change. Almost immediately, my regular winter outfit replaced the disgusting animal-hide armor. Feeling my face change was more disturbing than I'd imagined, but it was a relief to touch my head and discover that the horns were gone.

"Here we are," said Nyx as we turned the corner to find a vast, deserted, and precarious dock connected to an immense underground river. Spider webs covered most of the dock, but as Nyx walked forward, they burnt away. The place didn't look safe.

"This place is falling apart," said Jonas bluntly.

"It's our best chance of escaping. It'll be fine. I used it myself a few years back when I first tried to escape—" said Nyx before cutting herself short.

I wanted to ask what had happened, but I thought it was best to leave it alone.

"There she is!" said Nyx, pointing toward a medium-size wooden boat at the end of the dock that rocked violently with the current. The boat seemed to be in somewhat good shape, except for a couple of rotten wooden boards on its side and the missing glass from the windows.

"Are we supposed to travel on that?" asked Jonas, looking worried.

"You can swim if you like," Carla said sarcastically.

The water rushed past the dock with violence. It was hard to imagine such an old ship being able to withstand the ride. To make matters worse, steam rose from the water. I wanted to find out how hot it was, so I bent down to touch it. As soon as my fingers touched the sapphire water, I screamed in pain. It was scalding hot.

"You don't want to do that," warned Nyx.

"I just figured that out," I replied with a chuckle.

"Are you sure this is a good idea?" asked Carla doubtfully.

"It will be fine, besides we can fly once we're out of the protective barrier of the Cave of Sorrows," said Nyx as she led us toward the boat and her skin returned to normal. Luckily, the raging sapphire waters glowed to provide us with enough light to see where we were going.

As I stepped onto the dock, it creaked. Worried, I placed my other foot onto the next wooden board, and that one creaked as well. The last thing I wanted was to find out how scalding water would feel all over my body.

I paid close attention to where Nyx stepped and tried to follow the same pattern. I figured she knew best. Carla and Jonas followed right behind.

When we got to the boat, I didn't find it any more promising than when I first saw it. From up close, it looked much less appealing and much less capable of withstanding the violent waters than I first thought.

"For the record, I still don't think this is a good idea," said Jonas, probably saying what we were all thinking except for Nyx. She seemed confident about the ship's capabilities.

"Don't worry so much. We don't have to go very far," said Nyx as she stepped inside the boat.

"How do we even move this thing? It doesn't have an engine, or even a sail," asked Carla as she got on board.

"We'll just have to push it and the current will do the rest," I guessed.

"I'm not pushing it. I'm still recovering from my ordeal," Jonas said quickly.

"There! There they are!" yelled a guard in the distance. "They are trying to get away, and they have the Scion!"

"STOP, UNDEAD!" yelled the Forgemaster as he touched his belt as though he was choosing the most appropriate and deadly weapon.

"Maggots! Don't let them get away or it will be your heads!" the Forgemaster ordered.

"I changed my mind, I'll push," said Jonas.

"Guys? We need to go now!" ordered Carla.

"I'll help Jonas," I offered.

"Here, you'll need this," said Nyx as she hurled a dull sword my way.

I stepped off the boat, and the dock creaked louder. I could feel the wood rattle and vibrate as the guards ran toward us. It wasn't long before I found the rope that held the boat in place. I took several swings at it, but it didn't budge.

As the vibration of the dock increased, I could hear pieces of wood falling in the river.

"Come on, try again," yelled Jonas.

"Get on the boat! I'll be right behind you," I ordered.

I took another swing at the rope. This time, the rope broke, and the ship started to move away from the failing dock. I ran as fast as I could. But by the time I reached the boat, it had already left the dock. In a leap of faith, I jumped and grabbed the side of the boat as it sped away from the dock. The weight of the guards must have been too much for the old dock, because it plunged into the scalding river.

"Nice job, mate," said Jonas as he offered me his hand and pulled me into the boat.

"I think you guys need to grab on to something…" Carla started to say as the boat entered a pitch-black tunnel and increased in speed.

We figured we would be better protected inside the boat's wood cabin, even though most of the window frames were splintered and broken and the door hung on its hinges.

"Nyx, can't you light the way?" asked Jonas once we were inside the cabin.

"Sure I could, if you don't mind a flaming boat," said Nyx.

"Oh God!" yelled Jonas.

As the boat rushed through the dark tunnel, we heard all sorts of creaking noises, and to make matters worse, water was filling the back of the boat.

And if that wasn't enough reason to worry, we seemed to be heading straight for a boulder that stood right in the middle of the river.

"Hang on!" I yelled as we smashed into the huge boulder. Our boat cracked and almost turned on its side.

"The rudders are gone," said Nyx, surprisingly calm.

"Are we almost there?" asked Jonas.

"We'd better be, because this boat won't hold together for much longer," replied Carla.

As scalding water rushed inside, we were soon surrounded. We moved to the other side of the boat, but we were running out of places to hide. It seemed our only way out was to jump off the boat.

"When I say go, think about flying," ordered Nyx as a light at the end of the tunnel became bigger and brighter.

"What?" asked Jonas as the boat began to fall off the edge of a waterfall, heading toward the rocky bottom.

"Now!" yelled Nyx.

I immediately thought about floating, and much to my surprise it worked without delay. We were so high above the river that I felt a little scared, but I was also relieved.

Fortunately, we all hovered above the water and watched as the boat crashed into the rocks below, shattering into a thousand pieces.

"We made it! Oh God, this is freaking high," Jonas said, holding on to Carla for dear life.

"We actually did it," I added with a sigh of relief.

***

"Where do we go now?" I asked.

Nobody answered. To be honest, I didn't think any of us knew where we should go.

Below us a fairly wide river made its way downhill with tremendous force.

We moved just over the riverbank and Nyx burst into a flame just bright enough to illuminate the ground below us.

"Well, you are free as promised, but you shouldn't hang around here too long because Phasma will be back soon. Besides, it won't be long before a search party is formed and they come looking for us," Nyx explained, concerned.

"We're not done yet. We made a promise, and we intend to keep it. We aren't going anywhere until we find you a safe place to stay," I said, looking straight into her big and exquisite green and orange eyes.

"Thank you, I'll be forever in your debt," said Nyx as her expression changed from sadness to excitement.

"So, which way should we go?" asked Carla, looking at the boat wreckage below.

"We'll move by land. They will no doubt have scouts on top of the Night Peaks looking for us," said Nyx.

Almost immediately, we started to descend toward a dirt path below in complete synchrony.

"For the record, my vote is for flying wherever we're going, and fast," I said.

I was starting to get the hang of transporting myself by thought.

"Wow, the sky is so dark and the stars seem so distant," said Jonas, looking up.

"It will be better where we're going, I promise," said Nyx, almost embarrassed.

"What's the name of your people?" Jonas asked.

"My father is the Guardian of Threshold, and the creatures you saw back there are the Night Dwellers," explained Nyx.

"You guys don't look related," Jonas said.

"Nope, we're not related at all. Long ago, my father made a deal with the Night Dwellers. They were allowed to rule the village at the base of the Night Mountain, and my father would rule the underworld. They are completely loyal to him," said Nyx as she put her flames out and got off the path, which cut through the middle of a forest.

"Why are we going this way?" asked Carla, puzzled.

"We need to avoid the Bog, they aren't very friendly toward strangers," she replied quietly.

"That doesn't sound very good," said Jonas.

"Why can't we just will ourselves to our destination?" I asked.

"It's a question of vibration. You see, everything is a matter of vibration. Your physical world and body vibrate at a much slower rate than Threshold. That's why you can't come here in your physical body. The same happens with being transported by thought; if you are trying to reach a place that has a higher vibrational state than your own astral body, it won't work. Besides, the more we stick with traditional methods of transportation, the better our chances of remaining undetected—"

She stopped abruptly.

"Get down," Nyx whispered, slowly backing away.

I did as I was told and lay on the ground, almost completely covered by the tall grass.

As my chest touched the ground, I felt the ground rumbling and vibrating rhythmically.

I looked up, careful not to expose myself too much, but I couldn't see anything due to the tall grass. So I carefully spread the grass open with my hands to see what was happening.

I almost couldn't contain my shock when I spotted the creature walking toward us. He was a tall wood being. He appeared to be walking straight toward us with huge strides. With each step he took, the ground vibrated. We couldn't move out of his way without attracting his attention. His hands seemed to be made of branches. He had very broad shoulders, a small mouth, and deep black eyes that seemed too small for his body.

We anxiously waited until he was almost over us. Then, when he lifted his giant foot and was about to step on us, we rolled away in different directions, making a lot of noise in the process.

He stopped and looked around. Luckily, after a few seconds, he resumed his strides. Had we rolled in the same direction, he would have found us.

I didn't dare to move until I was absolutely sure he wouldn't hear me.

"What in the world was that thing?" asked Jonas.

"That was a Bog soldier," replied Nyx.

"I take it he's not on our side," I said as I got up and dusted myself off.

"The Bogs aren't on anyone's side except their own," said Nyx.

"Oh, great," said Jonas. "I'm making tons of friends tonight. I kind of hope all of this is nothing more than a terrible nightmare."

"Does this Bog thing live around here?" I asked.

"No, they live further down. Earth Elementals don't get along very well with, well anyone really, so they prefer to stay isolated. I have only been to their city a couple of times in the past when I was much younger," explained Nyx.

We continued to push forward as the sky gradually turned a tad brighter. Although it was still night, I could begin to see our surroundings more clearly.

The ground and foliage were also changing from predominantly snow white to mostly slushy yellow. The grass was frost-burned, with a few green patches here and there. We approached what seemed to be a raised wood boardwalk that led straight into the heart of the marsh. The trees here were mostly dried birch trees.

"This place almost looks pretty," said Carla.

"I should warn you that I have only been outside a couple of times, so I don't know that many places, but I do know this place. Just don't expect a warm welcome, at least not at first," replied Nyx.

"Awesome, an adventure," I said.

"I think I've had enough adventures to last me a lifetime," replied Jonas, smiling.

As we followed the narrow white boardwalk, it stretched for miles as it curved in the distance.

The once-luscious scenery slowly turned harsh. The deeper we ventured into the marsh, the worse it became.

I was distracted when, out of nowhere, water came rushing toward us. That was when I learned the reason for such a high boardwalk.

"Where did all this water come from?" I asked.

"The Bog must have opened the dam. They flood the area at least a couple of times a day, sometimes more. It's their way to keep anyone in their right mind from settling too close to them," explained Nyx.

"It seems to me that these creatures go to great lengths to be left alone, and yet that's where we're heading," said Carla.

"I don't have a choice. I don't have anywhere else to go," replied Nyx, stepping on a rotten wooden plank. Nyx almost fell in the water, but thanks to Jonas she didn't.

"Thanks," said Nyx, smiling. I could be wrong, yet I could have sworn she liked Jonas. But I wasn't exactly an expert in the subject.

***

"We're getting closer," she said, almost whispering.

"I think I'll wait for you guys by this tree over here," said Jonas, stopping near an old tree and resting his back on its trunk.

"Jonas!" said Carla.

I turned too.

"What? You guys look like you just saw a ghost," Jonas said confused.

I watched as Jonas looked at his feet and then realized that the tree roots resembled feet.

As soon as his hands touched the tree bark, he screamed.

"Holy crap! What's this—" Jonas tried to jump away but fell to the ground.

"Oh no, I think you made it mad," said Carla as we both watched the huge tree lift Jonas by the ankles.

"Why did you disturb me?" said the tree.

"I'm… really so sorry," said Jonas as his face turned red from all the blood rushing to his head. He dangled upside down.

"Who are you?" asked the tree.

Nyx approached and ordered.

"Put him down, Elder! They're with me."

"Nyxy? Is that you, is that really you?" asked Elder.

"Holy arboretum, I haven't seen you since you threatened to burn me when you were just a little sapling," Elder said, gently placing Jonas back onto the narrow boardwalk.

"Elder, it is wonderful to see you again. What are you doing here?" Nyx asked.

"Well, don't tell anyone, but things weren't going so great at the Living Forest. So I crossed the Twilight River and settled here," explained Elder as he shook his branches. Some dried leaves fell on us.

"But what about the Bogs? Don't they bother you?" asked Nyx.

"They don't even know I'm here. You see, I'm getting old, and I need constant water to keep my leaves healthy. This is the perfect place for me since they're constantly releasing fresh water. They think they're scaring others away, when in fact they are actually making my life pretty easy," explained Elder.

"But don't you get lonely?" asked Nyx.

"Oh, I'm not here alone. There's a huge group of us. We chose to spread out a bit in order not to be so obvious."

"Do you think they'll let us in?" asked Jonas.

"I honestly don't know, they aren't exactly the fuzziest creatures in Threshold, but I choose to believe they aren't all bad either, perhaps they're just overprotective of their own kind," explained Elder.

"I have no choice. I just have to trust they will accept me," said Nyx, sounding discouraged.

"What's going on?" asked Elder, raising his wooden eyebrows.

"I've left Phasma, but this time I'm not going back," said Nyx. Her skin started to change, and her orange and green eyes dilated and turned reddish orange, a warning she was about to burst into flames again.

"He'll find you eventually, but I hope I'm wrong," said Elder. The hairs on my arms and neck stood up just thinking about that possibility.

"Elder, I may need your help," said Nyx. "I mean, *we* may need your help."

"I don't know how much help I can offer, but I'll do what I can. I'll pass the word to the others just in case, but I can't promise anything from them. I'm here for whatever you need," offered Elder, smiling compassionately.

"Thank you, Elder. You're a good friend. Right now, I just need to talk to Oldroot… I hope that I'll be able to see him," replied Nyx.

"Be careful. He's still stubborn and even older than you remember. He's getting crankier every season. I haven't seen him in a while," said Elder, pausing for a moment. "If at all possible, please don't mention that we are here."

"Don't worry, we won't," I replied quickly.

"It was very good seeing you again, Elder," Nyx said as she approached the old tree creature and gave him a gentle hug.

"Take care, young sapling. Don't forget to be careful. I sense that the winds are about to change," replied Elder, backing away from the boardwalk and blending with the other trees in the marsh.

"I have to admit, I didn't like him at first, but he actually turned out to be pretty nice," Jonas said.

"We shouldn't expect too much from Oldroot," said Nyx as we pushed on.

CHAPTER ELEVEN

Watertown

After walking for a few minutes, I started to see the hazy shape of a gate in the distance. As we got closer, I noticed it was a big wooden gate with a guard on each side.

"They don't seem very friendly," Carla said as we approached slowly and heard one of the guards grunt and ready his weapon.

"We're here to see Oldroot!" called Nyx.

They looked at each other and then marched toward us.

"We mean you no harm. Please get Oldroot," said Nyx as they continued to march toward us.

"Get back!" warned Nyx as her skin and eyes changed rather quickly.

Soon a ravaging fire ignited from within Nyx's body. Even though I was few yards away, I could feel the shockwave passing through me.

"Get me Oldroot before it's too late!" yelled Nyx as flames burst from her body.

For a minute, I thought the worst was about to happen, when suddenly we heard an old voice coming from the other side of the gate.

"Nyxy? Is that you?" the voice asked.

"Oldroot, I need your help," Nyx said as the flames on her body diminished.

"Calm down, Nyxy. Come on in, and we'll talk," Oldroot said as the guards backed up slowly but kept their weapons at the ready.

"I guess he's not that unreasonable," said Jonas from way in the back.

Nyx seemed to calm down, and her flames extinguished.

The wooden gate creaked as it opened, and Nyx walked forward.

Carla and I followed Nyx from a safe distance, just in case Oldroot changed his mind. Jonas seemed to be doing the same, except that he was well behind us. I guess Jonas realized we would be safer in a group because he came running toward us, crashing into Carla.

"Watch where you're going," complained Carla.

"Sorry, but this place gives me the creeps," Jonas replied.

"I need your help," Nyx said even before the wooden gate was fully opened.

We couldn't see anyone inside because of the thick grey fog. The only exception was a tall and rather large outline of a person in the fog.

Suddenly the outline became darker, and a hole in the fog formed to reveal Oldroot as he walked toward us with gigantic strides. His eyes glowed green. He looked like an old, but fairly large baby, except that he was composed of yellowish roots and a variety of fungi that seemed to grow wildly all over his body, particularly around his face, stomach, and feet. He didn't just look cranky, you could see it in his attitude and in the way he walked.

Jonas stopped in his tracks. Carla was much braver and continued to inch forward with Nyx and me.

"Oldroot, I need a place to hide for a while," Nyx said. "These are my new friends. They must not be harmed. They'll be on their way as soon as they know that I'm all right."

"Certainly, Nyxy. You have grown a lot since I last saw you," replied Oldroot.

"It was many cycles ago since I last saw you. I'm sorry for intruding like this, but this is the only place I know of," said Nyx.

I sensed something was bothering her.

"Can we trust him?" Jonas whispered to us.

"I don't think we have much of a choice at the moment," replied Carla.

As soon as we walked into the town I understood why the place was called Watertown. The whole town floated on top of long and complex boardwalks illuminated by torches. Next to the main boardwalk there were several dock-style shops, shacks and houses.

Everything was made out of wood. Yet instinctively I knew it wasn't regular wood from trees but wood from creatures just like Oldroot. The whole place felt morbid and sinister.

The boardwalk wobbled. I'd never had a weak stomach, but the swaying motion was starting to make me queasy. Apparently I wasn't the only one.

"I think that I'm going to get sick," Jonas said as we followed Oldroot deeper into the town.

"Don't you dare," said Carla.

"Here we are," Oldroot said; fungus spores flew from his mouth as he spoke.

I noticed that some spores landed on my right arm and shoulder, but I didn't dare remove them. After all, I couldn't risk offending him.

Jonas, however, quickly dusted himself off and wiped his hands on his pants, drawing concerned looks from Oldroot, Nyx, Carla, and me.

"Please rest. I'll have someone come and get you once you've had a chance to rest," said Oldroot, looking wary of Jonas.

"Thank you, I don't know how I can ever repay you," replied Nyx.

"Don't worry, Nyxy, I'm sure you'll find a way," Oldroot said, finally looking away from Jonas as he started to walk away.

Oldroot left us outside an old wooden shed.

"I think we're supposed to rest inside," said Carla.

"This doesn't look like the sort of place where one can rest," Jonas replied.

I opened the door slowly. It creaked as moonlight entered the shed and illuminated the dirty wooden floor. One of the first things I noticed were the dust particles reflecting the moonlight... next came the horrid smell. It smelled like old, rotten wet wood. Not only could I smell but I could also see the mold and mildew on the floor and walls. It wasn't a very nice place. In fact, the Cave of Sorrows seemed much more hospitable.

"This isn't my idea of a nice place to stay," said Jonas as we entered the shed.

"This will do just fine," said Nyx.

"Are you sure you're going to be okay here?" Carla asked, concerned.

"I'll be fine," replied Nyx.

***

Despite Nyx's confidence, something didn't seem right. I could feel it in my bones. As hard as I tried, I just couldn't quite figure out what was bothering me.

"Something is not right," I said.

"Everything is fine, don't worry," Nyx assured me.

"No, Mark is right. Something is wrong," said Carla. She had been quiet for a while, so I knew something was bothering her too.

"I agree. I don't like this one bit," added Jonas. "I had a bad feeling about this since the beginning."

"I don't know, I think everything is fine," said Nyx, pacing back and forth.

"Think about it, isn't Oldroot supposed to be cranky?" I asked.

"Yes, he was when I met him before, but I guess things change," replied Nyx.

"According to Elder, he's supposed to be crankier than ever," I said as I went to the door to peek outside.

"What do you see?" Jonas asked.

"Trouble," I whispered.

"What do you mean?" asked Carla, coming closer to peek out as well.

"Two armed guards outside our shed kind of trouble," I replied.

"We need to figure out a way out of here," said Carla, looking at Nyx and me for suggestions.

Carla wasn't sure what to do next, and Nyx wasn't yet completely convinced we were in trouble.

"Nyx, I know we haven't known each other for a very long time, but where we come from people are very deceptive. So I know the telltale signs when someone is trying to be deceitful," I said.

"Maybe Oldroot placed the guards there to protect us from Phasma," Nyx replied, sounding almost desperate.

"If they're truly there to protect us, then they shouldn't mind if we try to walk around," suggested Carla.

"Okay, here's what we're going to do. They do have stores here, right?" I asked.

"Yes, they trade all sorts of goods," replied Nyx. Jonas seemed mesmerized by her; he was looking straight into her big green and orange eyes.

"What's the closest store?" I asked.

"Well, there are some in the center of town, but I suppose the closest one would be the Kunkanly Store. I don't like that place, though," replied Nyx.

"Kunkanly? What is that?" Carla asked.

"Kunkanly is where they sell and exploit harmless creatures for a profit. Manuk runs the place," explained Nyx.

"So it is like a pet store?" said Jonas.

"Nyx doesn't know what a pet store is. She has no point of reference," added Carla.

"Actually, I do. I've visited Earth many times," replied Nyx, surprising us all.

"Okay then, we'll tell the guards that we're going to the town center, and we'll see if they'll let us go. If they don't, then I guess we'll just have to make a run for it," I said.

"Nyx, you go first, and we'll follow you," suggested Carla.

Nyx opened the door slowly and carefully so as not to startle the Bog guards.

As soon as they noticed her, they blocked her way with their spears.

"We're going to the town center to look at some of the stores," said Nyx as the guards exchanged confused looks.

"Very well, don't be long," one replied.

I followed Nyx outside. The water level seemed to have risen, as did the rotten smell. If I had to guess, I would have said they opened the dam again, almost flooding Watertown and flooding the swamplands surrounding it.

As we walked toward the town center on the narrow boardwalk, I looked back and noticed that the guards weren't standing guard at our shed anymore. They were discreetly following us.

"Guys, don't look back. We're being followed," I warned.

Much to my dismay, Jonas turned around and looked back several times before I pulled him by the arm.

"I said don't look back!"

"You can't tell someone not to look back and expect them not to. If you didn't want me to look back, you shouldn't have said anything," replied Jonas.

"Here we are," Nyx said.

I looked around and found everyone looking at us.

***

The store was a large wooden building with windows that resembled glass and a sign that read "Kunkanly Store, Since 6932 WC."

"What's WC?" I asked.

"It stands for wind cycles. We don't count time as you do on Earth. Time here exists exclusively for organizational purposes. One of your years on earth is three WC here in Threshold," Nyx explained.

"Welcome, dear strangers. What brings your kind to my humble store? Would it be this precious and rare gold dragon?" asked the creature behind the counter.

He couldn't have been more than four feet tall. He stood on top of a wooden platform that made him look taller.

He reached behind the counter and waved at a translucent cage, which promptly opened to reveal a small dragon. The dragon took flight and flew around the store several times, as if it had been trained. He must have been worth a small fortune for he looked gorgeous and menacing. I had never seen anything like it before.

"We're not here to shop. We are simply looking around," replied Nyx.

"How do you like living here with the Bogs?" asked Carla, moving closer to Manuk.

"Huh, I can't complain," said Manuk, avoiding any eye contact.

"Can't as in they won't let you, or can't as in it's not that bad?" Jonas asked.

Manuk looked a bit upset but was quick to compose himself. "Are you sure I can't interest you in a companion?" asked Manuk, gesturing to show me his merchandise. Everything was alive and trapped in the same translucent cages.

On his command, the dragon that had been flying around the store returned to his cage, looking depressed. I got the sense it really enjoyed those few minutes of freedom. Worse yet, that would probably be all the exercise it would get unless another customer showed up.

"No, thank you. I'm just looking," I replied.

That's when I noticed him. He was the smallest dragon in the store. He was green and blue, almost the size of a mini-poodle. He had very small wings that blended well with his back. He had big claws and sharp teeth. He cowered in the back of his cage as two slightly larger dragons hissed and charged at the glass divider that separated them from the smaller dragon. I instantly felt sorry for the little fella.

I was staring at the poor creature, wondering what his name was, when I heard a voice inside my head say "Spark." At the time I didn't think much of it.

"What is wrong with them?" I said, pointing at the two angry dragons as they charged and hissed at the smaller green and blue dragon.

"With them, nothing; but with that little scared guy over there, everything. He's useless… I've been trying to sell him for over three long wind cycles without success. I can't blame the customers, though. Who would want a scared guard dragon? I certainly wouldn't," said Manuk.

"Guard dragon? But they're so small," I said as my friends made their way outside to find a way out.

"They're small now, thanks to the nature spirits. Can you imagine if I had to fit ten or twenty fully grown dragons in my store? Never mind trying to feed them all. Nope, I prefer them like this, small and manageable," said Manuk. "My apologies, I keep forgetting that not everyone in Threshold is a native. You see, as long as they don't drink water from the Everwell, they'll age but not grow."

"I see," I replied.

"Oh, this cursed dragon is ruining my business, not to mention my reputation. My customers are starting to talk. They are saying that Manuk sells only wimpy guard dragons," Manuk said as he approached the small cage and knocked on it hard, which only made the dragon inside even more scared.

"Then why don't you set it free?" I asked.

"Are you insane? If I set it free, the first thing it will do is drink water from the Everwell—they're drawn to it—and then we'll have another massacre on our hands. It would be like 1576 WC all over again," replied Manuk, dumbfounded.

"What happened in 1576 WC?" I asked.

"In 1576 WC, Althaer, the greatest warrior ever, thought he could control his dragon companion. So he let him drink water from the Everwell so he could grow to his normal size. His dragon Sparkus grew to his full size and potential," Manuk said, pausing briefly to scratch his almost-bald head.

"Because of Althaer's poor judgment, thousands were harmed. Whole towns and villages were burned to the ground. The Living Forest and its residents were almost completely obliterated. It took Threshold hundreds, if not thousands of wind cycles to recover. A lucky few were spared, but not many, and it was all thanks to Phasma. If you ask Manuk, we don't give Lord Val-Fraux the credit he deserves," he said, frowning.

Since the others weren't back yet, I stayed there and looked around for a bit. However, I couldn't get that poor creature out of my mind.

"Fight, you impostor of a dragon!" Manuk yelled at the little dragon. "I'm done with you. I might as well sacrifice you. In fact, I should've done it a long time ago. After all the financial damages you have caused me. Manuk should never have said the truth about you."

The dragon trembled at his words.

"What truth are you talking about?" I asked.

"Sparkus was a brave dragon, too brave, but that hatchling over there is a coward. Nobody believes me when I tell them that he's Sparkus's direct descendent. They laugh at Manuk, because Manuk tells the truth for once. That dragon is bad for business. Everyone wants a brave guard dragon, not a wimpy one," Manuk said.

***

"If he's so bad for business, why don't you just give him away?" I suggested.

"That's not a bad idea, I just need to find the foo… I mean someone who wants him," Manuk said.

"If you like, I could find him a nice home," I offered.

"Uh, a human? With a dragon? Manuk is not sure if that's such a good idea." He paused. "Well, if it was any other dragon, it probably wouldn't be, but this coward dragon shouldn't even legally be called a dragon. I guess it could work. Yes, it could work," he repeated.

"So what do you say? Do we have a deal?" I asked, trying not to look too hopeful.

"Yes, but first you must sign an agreement," said Manuk as he stepped down from the wooden platform to open a drawer, looking for the correct paperwork.

I tried to control myself. I felt it was important to hide how excited I was. Otherwise, Manuk might change his mind and try to make a profit.

I had no idea how to take care of a dragon or what to do with him once I returned to Earth, but anywhere was better than this store for that poor dragon.

"Ah, here it is," said Manuk when he finally found the paperwork. "Please fill this part out and sign here, here, and here. Or you could just put your thumbprint here and a strand of hair here," said Manuk as he pointed to the different areas on the long agreement riddled with fine print.

"Strand of hair? What for?" I asked.

"Standard procedure, just in case we need to find you," Manuk replied.

I filled out the form as quickly as I could. Something told me I was doing the right thing—maybe it was just a gut feeling, but I trusted it completely.

When I finished completing the form as Manuk had instructed, I handed him the agreement and I had to stifle a smile.

Manuk glowed with happiness.

He waved his hands in front of the translucent cage that held the small dragon, pulled him out of the cage by his tail, and handed it over to me.

I extended my arms to welcome the scared creature when something remarkable happened. As soon as I held it, the dragon almost immediately stopped shaking. It was as though he finally felt safe.

He became so serene that I placed him on my shoulder while Manuk looked at us, dumbfounded. The dragon moved from one shoulder to the other, his tail wagged from side to side.

"Remember, do not let him go near the Everwell. Are you sure you don't want to purchase a cage?" Manuk asked.

"Thanks, but no. He'll be just fine," I replied before I walked out of the store to look for my friends.

I looked around but didn't see them, so I figured they went looking for answers and that it would be best to stand in front of the store and wait.

I took the time to observe the strange town. I was so distracted that I barely heard the footsteps approaching me from behind.

"We found an… whoa! What's that?" Jonas asked. He seemed to freeze in place, as though he expected the worst from the small, purring dragon.

"I got him from Manuk," I explained, petting the dragon.

"What's Manuk thinking? Giving an undead a dragon… you don't even live in Threshold. We should return him at once," Nyx said, walking toward the store.

"Wait! We can't do that," I replied. "He'll sacrifice him, and I can't let that happen."

"He's cute. What's his name?" Carla asked as she approached.

"I don't know. When I first saw him, I kind of sensed that his name was Spark. Yep, his name is Spark," I replied.

"Spark? No, it can't be," said Nyx, looking really worried.

"Why?" Jonas asked.

"It happened so long ago that I thought his lineage was lost," Nyx said.

"I'm lost, can someone please explain it to me?" Jonas asked.

"A very long time ago, there was a dragon called Sparkus that almost destroyed Threshold, my fath… Phasma fought it and supposedly saved Threshold. At least that was the story he used to tell me when I was young. Supposedly all of Sparkus's eggs were destroyed," explained Nyx.

"Mark, who is going to take care of him when we go home?" asked Carla.

"I don't know, I didn't think that far ahead. Maybe Nyx could," I replied.

"No, I don't think so. I don't get along with pets. Besides, I have this little problem with fire, remember?" replied Nyx.

"That's why it will be perfect. He's a dragon, so I'm sure fire won't be a problem for him," said Carla.

"Listen, I know I haven't thought this through, but I couldn't just leave him there to be killed. I can't explain it, but we're connected somehow. I can feel it," I said, looking at Spark.

"The story goes that Sparkus could communicate with Althaer, so if Spark is really a descendant of Sparkus, it's possible he can communicate with you," explained Nyx. "However, if he really is the offspring of Sparkus, we could have a huge problem on our hands."

"I'll take good care of him and I won't let him near the Everwell. I just know he won't be a problem, I promise," I said.

"All right, but we must find him a suitable and permanent home," said Nyx. "In the meantime, we have to get him a collar."

"Collar? Where do I go to get one?" I asked.

"Follow me," said Nyx as she opened the door to Manuk's store and entered the building.

I followed her. As I entered the building, I felt Spark's claws clench my shoulders.

"Ah, you have returned. Is something wrong?" Manuk asked, almost smirking. When he noticed that I wasn't alone, he tried to disguise it. Whenever he spoke, Spark dug his sharp claws onto my shoulders as though he was trying to hang on for dear life.

"No, nothing is wrong," I replied.

"Manuk, we need a collar for this dragon," said Nyx.

"Sure, we have many."

"Why would you sell or give away a dragon without the proper containment collar, as is required by common rule and the Kunkan Protection Society?"

"Manuk is sorry. Here, pick a collar, any collar," Manuk replied. "Free of charge."

I chose the first collar I saw.

"Good, now choose a ring," Manuk replied.

"But I don't need a ring," I protested.

"They aren't just regular rings. They are collar rings that will bond your soul with Spark's," Nyx explained.

"Sort of like a marriage?" asked Jonas, trying to be funny.

"That one," I said, pointing toward a small blue ring on the counter.

Manuk handed me the small ring, and Nyx motioned for me to follow her outside when the other dragons in the store started to get upset. Some even attempted to break free to get Spark, while one spit fire inside his cage, causing it to fill with black and grey smoke, which dissipated through several holes on top of the cage.

"What do I do with this?" I asked Nyx as I followed her outside.

"By common rule, a dragon needs to be bound to its owner… in our case, you. Please place the ring on your finger and then pet Spark so he will be bound to you," said Nyx, concerned.

"Okay, here goes nothing," I said as I placed the blue ring on my finger. At first, the ring seemed too big, but almost immediately it adjusted itself to the exact dimensions of my finger. Then I proceeded to pet Spark, and the ring glowed brightly as my finger and hand became hot.

"It's done. This will prevent Spark from straying too far from you. As long as you wear this ring, he will always be near," said Nyx.

"Great; now you're married to a dragon," Jonas joked.

"Actually, that's almost exactly what happens. You see, you and Spark now share a spiritual link; whatever you feel affects him and vice versa. You must learn to control your emotions, because if you don't you can hurt Spark, and trust me, if that happens he will hurt you back," said Nyx.

"I understand," I replied, although I was worried that I wouldn't be able to control my emotions.

***

I sensed Phasma nearby. At first I thought I was mistaken, but it was no mistake. The feeling was too familiar. He was on his way, I was sure of it, and he was coming to get us.

"Guys, we need to go," I whispered so the guards wouldn't hear.

"What do you mean?" Carla asked.

"Phasma is coming and fast," I replied as my hands started to sweat profusely.

"Okay then, we need to go," said Carla.

"Agreed, we need to leave right now," I added.

"I can't. I don't have anywhere else to go to," objected Nyx.

"You can't stay here. Come with us. I promise you we'll figure something out," I replied.

"Oldroot must have betrayed us," said Nyx as she started to get upset and her skin changed color.

"Nyx, you have to control yourself, we can't afford that kind of attention right now," I said.

"Come with us, Nyx. It will be okay," Carla said to calm her down.

"Okay, I'll go. Hopefully, I won't cause you any more trouble."

"Follow me! I saw an exit when we were walking around," Carla said as she grabbed Nyx by the arm and moved at a brisk pace.

We followed Carla behind a wooden building when nobody was looking.

"Quick, this way," Carla said as she stepped into the swampy waters. Our only hope of escaping was to take the path less traveled, and that meant the swamp behind the camp.

"I knew there was something odd about Oldroot's behavior. He seemed too… friendly," I said as Spark clenched his nails into my shoulder.

"I knew it all along," Jonas added.

We didn't get very far before we ran into an improvised fence. It was made out of branches and dried vines, yet it was very strong; no matter how hard we tried, we couldn't move it.

"We're officially screwed," said Jonas.

"You worry too much," Carla replied calmly.

"Ah yes, in case you didn't notice, we're stuck with nowhere else to go," Jonas replied.

"It's all part of the plan. Nyx, now we need you to do your part," Carla said.

"I can't, it doesn't work like that," replied Nyx as we looked at her in concern.

"You have to. If you don't, he will find us. He'll find you," Carla said.

"Nyx, please concentrate," said Jonas.

"I can't! It's not working," replied Nyx.

If Carla's plan was to get Nyx upset, then I guess it worked, because next thing I knew, Nyx broke down and started to cry. We backed away without saying a word, barely in time to avoid the flaming shockwave that left her body, burning everything within a ten-yard radius.

Even Spark jumped off my shoulder when he felt the heat wave hit.

"You did it!" screamed Jonas.

Although her flames didn't completely destroy the fence, we could kick it and make a hole big enough to get through.

"Thanks, Nyx. I knew you could do it," I said as I dusted myself off on the other side of the fence.

The water was very murky; it was impossible to see the bottom.

"I don't like this," complained Jonas. "I hate not being able to see what I'm stepping on."

The sense of dread and emptiness increased as we moved away from Watertown as fast as possible; the water and the mud made the journey difficult.

"So where do we go now?" Jonas asked as he carefully planned each step.

"I don't know," Nyx replied, sounding sad.

"I can't believe that Oldroot fooled us. I should've seen that coming," Carla said more to herself than to anyone else.

"Don't beat yourself up. It wouldn't have done us any good, and we would still be in the same boat," I said.

"I wish we had a boat, that would make things much easier, not to mention faster," Jonas said while he attempted to pet Spark. Spark didn't seem to appreciate it and let out a screeching sound and moved to my other shoulder.

"I think we should continue to move east," I suggested, pointing toward what I thought was east.

"East? What's that?" Nyx asked to my surprise.

"You know, north, south, east, and west," I replied, pointing to each one of them as I said it.

"Oh, over here we have a different name for that," Nyx explained.

"What do you mean?" Jonas asked.

"Here in Threshold, we use Nightside, Upside, Dayside, and Downside, that's how we refer to different geographical directions," Nyx said as the swamp became a little less murky.

"So that way is… Nightside?" I asked as I pointed west.

"Correct, and that way is Upside," replied Nyx as she pointed north.

"Then we should continue toward Dayside," I said.

"I don't know, from here on it's all new to me," replied Nyx.

"Welcome to the club," said Jonas, smiling.

"Quick, this way!" called a female voice from the middle of the woods.

We looked around to see where the voice was coming from. I was the first to notice a tree moving as if its branches were waving us over.

"Come quick!" the tree said.

"Guys, over here!" I said.

"What is it?" asked Carla and Jonas simultaneously.

"You don't have much time. Come this way. We can protect you," said the creature as I approached it hesitantly.

I was almost face to face with the creature when I noticed Carla right behind me.

"Don't worry, Elder sent me. Please go straight through," said the tree-like creature.

We all passed through the female tree branches and wandered deeper into the forest. After we were through the opening, dozens of trees moved to conceal the entrance and our trail.

After a few very stressful minutes, we stopped near a boulder to rest, mainly because Jonas kept complaining that he was too tired to continue.

"Quiet, he is still nearby," said another tree-like creature.

"Who are you?" asked Carla.

"I'm Broto. Listen, your only chance to escape Phasma is to head straight to Nightwell. Once there, you can take the aerobus to the City of Lights. You should be safe there. I'm pretty sure he won't dare to follow you there," Broto explained, looking truly concerned for our well-being.

"Aerobus? What's that?" I asked.

"Sounds like some sort of subway," Jonas said as he rested. We were all tired since we had been running.

"It kind of is, but it would take too long to explain, besides you can't miss it," replied Broto as he motioned us to press on.

We did as we were told. We didn't have another option. We walked and sometimes we ran. Most of the time, Jonas sounded like he was about to pass out.

Soon I saw a tall wooden structure in the distance. At first I didn't know what it was, but as we got closer I noticed that it looked like an improvised dam.

"How are we supposed to get past that?" Jonas asked as the current became stronger the closer we got to the structure.

"I'm sure we'll find a way," replied Carla.

"It's not that steep," I said as I moved closer to the dam.

"I just hope it's not deep," Jonas responded.

Apparently Jonas wasn't the only one who didn't like all that murky water, because Spark still clutched my shoulder. I must confess that my shoulders were sore from carrying him around. Even though he wasn't very heavy—a few pounds at most—it was tiring.

I wanted to put him down, but I didn't want to risk it. After all, there was a lot of water around, and I didn't know what an Everwell was exactly.

We all decided we should just climb the wooden dam. As we climbed it, I tried to decide which way to go. I noticed there was a little path by the riverbank and decided to follow it.

Slowly, as we followed the riverbank path, the swamp became a luscious green forest. On this side of the dam, the vegetation thrived.

As we moved toward Dayside, as Nyx would say, the sky became increasingly lighter, and its colors more varied and vivid.

CHAPTER TWELVE
City of Lights

"What's that?" Jonas asked, pointing into the distance. But nobody replied. To be fair, I don't think any of us knew the answer.

We had arrived at our destination, a sprawling riverside city.

When we got closer, I saw a long, shiny object floating almost in the center of the river.

"Is that the aerobus Broto told us about?" I asked, perplexed.

"I guess so," replied Jonas.

"It's huge. I didn't picture it being that big," I said as we picked up the pace.

"I suppose that's Nightwell," said Nyx, following me closely.

Contrary to every place we had been so far, Nightwell was a stunning and modern riverside town. Towering spires and glass structures lit up the sky.

But Nightwell was more than a town; it had all the characteristics of a metropolis. The river divided the city into two distinct areas. Throughout, translucent bridges connected both sides of Nightwell.

Another remarkable feature of Nightwell was the modern structures, which were intertwined with vines and foliage. If someone on Earth decided to build a megacity right in the middle of the Amazon forest, I imagined it would look a lot like Nightwell.

As we got closer, the path gradually widened. It wasn't long before we reached the entrance archway, which read in big, bold, and reflective letters, "Nightwell."

"I guess we're here," said Jonas.

"Good job, you know how to read," joked Carla.

 I looked around and noticed that most of the locals looked a lot like Manuk, except they seemed better cared for.

Up close, the city looked even more spectacular. Long, translucent, brightly lit spires covered in green vines and a variety of plants occupied the sky. After everything I'd encountered in Threshold, Nightwell was by far the hardest thing to describe. It was a perfect marriage between technology and nature.

"Wow, this place is freaking huge!" said Jonas.

The people moving around the city were also different. They didn't look anything like the Night Dwellers or the Bog. And even though their features were similar to Manuk's, their attitudes were completely different.

All of them had very fair skin and slightly pointed ears. They had well-proportioned faces and slightly rounded green eyes that looked almost friendly, if it weren't for the puzzled looks I got from some of them.

"Why are they looking at us like that?" Nyx asked.

"I don't know. I'd imagine we look like an interesting bunch," I replied. "We should find the aerobus before Phasma finds us."

And that's when I saw him. He would have gone unnoticed, if it wasn't for his clumsy style that made him stand out as he struggled to balance his own weight and the weight of several books and scrolls he held in his hands and arms—perhaps he had misjudged how much he could carry. I wished I had noticed him just a second earlier. That way, I could have warned Carla, and she never would have crashed into the poor thing, sending his books and scrolls flying everywhere.

Nyx let out a gasp when she saw him. The exquisite Night Dweller elder had several eye-catching features. His feline eyes were better suited for the dark. They were remarkable, even though they sent chills down my spine. His dark garments defined his personality and served as a warning to anyone who intended to mess with him.

His black hair seemed alive and changed shapes in unimaginable patterns.

My immediate concern was with Carla's well-being. Once I made sure that she was fine, I tended to the elder.

"Oh my… I'm so very sorry," he said, sounding sincere. His voice was the complete opposite of his appearance.

"Are you all right?" I asked.

"I'm fine. I'm so disastrous… it was completely my fault. I hope your friend isn't hurt," he replied. "But where are my manners? My name is Dr. Thomas Rainer, it's a pleasure to meet you all." Dr. Rainer sounded genuinely pleased to meet us as he looked around to see where his books and scrolls had landed.

"Nice to meet you too," I replied as Nyx looked at him in fear.

I'd spotted a couple of his books, so I went to get them. As I bent to get the books, I caught a glimpse of their titles:

Dweller on the Threshold
The Constant Struggle Between Light and Darkness
By Simon Sin

Kunkan Endangered Species
What Tomorrow May Hold
By Charles Whithin

I carefully grabbed the fallen books and handed them to the doctor. He gave me a warm smile that didn't seem to fit his looks.

"Ah, what a fine dragon specimen you have. Let me guess. He's a *Draconoides Volan Ventralis*. How intriguing. These markings… I've seen them before," Dr. Rainer said as he opened the book titled *Kunkan Endangered Species* and flipped through its pages.

"Is something wrong?" I asked, seeing the concerned look on his face.

"I knew I had seen those markings before. This dragon is a direct descendant of Sparkus, isn't he? What's his name?"

"His name is Spark. But don't worry, he's harmless," I said.

"Oh my boy, he is many things, but harmless is not one of them," Dr. Rainer replied, surprising me. After all, Spark just seemed like a docile and scared if not scarred creature.

"Spark? Hum… seems fitting. He's remarkable, I wish I could examine him further," Dr. Rainer said. Spark seemed to understand him, because when Dr. Rainer said that, Spark cowered. I felt his nails digging into my collarbone. I could swear that Spark's claws felt stronger, longer, and sharper than before.

"Dr. Rainer, can I ask you a question?" I ventured.

"Sure."

"You see, we have this creature chasing us. His name is Phasma, and I was wondering if you knew where we could go to get away from him," I said hopefully. I didn't know why but I felt like I could trust him even though his appearance looked menacing.

"Well, if I were in your shoes I would go seek help at the City of Lights," suggest the old doctor.

"Excuse me, but aren't you a Night Dweller? How is it that you can roam freely in these parts?" Nyx asked, finally breaking her silence.

"I am indeed. I'll explain. When I was much younger, I tried to escape the confines of the Night Peaks, but I would always end up getting recaptured. Unsure of what to do, I did the only thing I could do. I studied and researched everyone and everything carefully. After many years, I came to the most stupendous realization of my life. I realized that the key to being free wasn't in others. It was inside me all along. All that I needed to change was my way of thinking. So that's what I did. After that, things just fell right into place," explained Dr. Rainer, then asked, "Nyxy? Don't you remember me?"

"Do I know you?" Nyx asked.

"Well, yes and no. You probably don't remember me. You were too young," said Dr. Rainer as he approached and gently grabbed her hand. His eyes welled up with tears.

"What do you mean?" Nyx asked, unsure of how to react.

"I took care of you during your first wind cycles," replied Dr. Rainer.

"Then maybe you can explain why I seem to ignite whenever I get upset and why I'm the only one that this happens to," said Nyx.

200

"Calm down, dear, first things first. You're not the only one, but you're very special. You see, that's why he chose you," explained Dr. Rainer.

"What do you mean? Please tell me more, I need to know everything," Nyx said.

"Nyxy, before you can understand your past, there's someone we need to see first," said Dr. Rainer. "As a matter of fact, I'm going that way right now. Care to follow me?"

"Can we please have a moment to discuss it?" I asked politely, based on the skeptical look on Carla's face.

We moved a few yards away and gathered in a small circle.

"Don't tell me we're trusting this guy," said Jonas as he looked suspiciously at Dr. Rainer.

"Why not?" Carla asked.

"Are you kidding me? Look at him, he looks evil," Jonas replied.

"Jonas, you can't judge anyone based on how they look," I intervened. "Besides, I have a good feeling about him."

"I want to trust him, but I don't know if I should. Sounds like he can give me some answers, though," Nyx said.

"If you want to follow him, we'll go with you just to be safe," added Carla to make Nyx's decision easier.

"Okay, I don't trust him yet, but I do trust you three. If you come, I'll follow him," Nyx replied.

"I can't believe we're doing this again. Remember what I said about Oldroot and nobody listened? You guys saw what happened," complained Jonas.

"Shh, nobody asked you, Jonas," said Carla.

I walked over to Dr. Rainer and explained that Nyx had decided to follow him and that we wanted to come too as a precaution.

"Great, follow me. The aerobus station is just around the corner," said Dr. Rainer. "Would you mind helping me with these books since we're going to the same place?"

"Not at all," I replied as he handed me two big and fairly heavy volumes.

"If you don't mind my asking, what kind of doctor are you?" I asked.

"I'm not the kind you're probably thinking of. I'm a philosopher. I know you must be thinking, what is a Night Dweller doing as a philosopher? Well, there isn't anything else in the world I would rather do even if some people think that I'm crazy."

"I don't think you're crazy," said Carla. "On earth, we're all taught to follow our dreams."

"Unfortunately, that isn't the case for Threshold, but things are slowly changing," explained Dr. Rainer.

We started to walk through the amazing city. I followed Dr. Rainer closely and looked all around.

***

"Here we are," said Dr. Rainer after a while.

We came to a stop near a translucent covered bridge. The bridge stretched over the light green river waters, leading to a long, strange vehicle that resembled a bullet train.

We followed Dr. Rainer as he entered the vehicle. He sat down and apparently left the window seat open for me.

"Relax, my boy. This aerobus will take us where we need to go. Just relax and enjoy the ride," said Dr. Rainer as he opened one of his books and started to read.

I took Spark off my shoulder and placed him on my lap while I petted him to calm him down. He seemed a bit stressed.

"Hum, very strange, it's not common for a *Draconoides Volan Ventralis* to be this friendly… or this scared, as a matter of fact," Dr. Rainer said.

"He's just a bit shy, that's all. I'm sure he'll make a great guard dragon one day," I said.

"Of course he will, I have no doubt. He's still too young and has much to learn. Let's just hope he'll have a different destiny than his predecessors. But I'm sure he will. You seem to be a good trainer," said Dr. Rainer.

"I'm not a trainer. I don't even live in Threshold, I couldn't possibly train him," I said, realizing that Spark and I would have to part ways eventually.

"Hasn't anyone told you yet? Once you put on that ring collar, you and Spark are one. He's your sole responsibility, and you're his trainer. That's how it has been, that's how it is, and that's how it should be," explained Dr. Rainer. "Besides, even if you were to return to Earth, it wouldn't prevent you from being his trainer. For one thing, dragons are inter-dimensional beings, and two, you still need sleep in the physical world, which gives you roughly about eight Earth hours to spend here in Threshold."

"So I can return here whenever I want?" I asked.

"Sure, if that's what you want and with enough practice," replied Dr. Rainer.

"Doctor, I have a question that I think you may be able to answer. I've been looking for my mother, but I can't seem to find her," I asked, figuring it couldn't hurt to ask.

"So you think your mother is in Threshold?" Dr. Rainer asked as he closed his book and placed it on the pile with the rest.

"I'm not sure. But I hope she is," I replied as my heart started to beat faster.

"Oh, dear boy, I'm afraid I may have some bad news," Dr. Rainer replied. I stopped petting Spark in anticipation.

"Your mother may or may not be in Threshold. While it is true that everyone comes to Threshold at some point once they pass away from the physical realm, not everyone stays in Threshold. The universe is a pretty big place, and Threshold is just one of its many realms," Dr. Rainer said, looking straight into my eyes.

"So you're telling me that I may be searching for her in the wrong place?" I asked.

"It's possible. Humans do come to Threshold after their physical bodies are no longer suitable to sustain physical life—the reasons that happens can vary tremendously, for example if a person led a life of crime, their vibrational rate would be so low that the only place they could survive is on the Night Peaks. And chances are that person would turn into a Night Dweller—"

"But you're a Night Dweller. I mean, you don't strike me as a bad person," I said.

As I waited for Dr. Rainer to reply, I looked around and noticed that my friends were looking at me, which I must confess made me feel a bit awkward and self-conscious.

Suddenly, a gentle warning tone filled the air as the aerobus door closed and formed an airtight seal.

"Indeed, I'm a Night Dweller, but before I was a Night Dweller I was…" Dr. Rainer paused, before continuing in a much lower tone, "I was human. I led a life of vanity, leisure, crime, and cruelty. I woke up to find myself here almost as though I was being punished for my crimes. I can honestly say that I thought I'd woken up in hell."

I wasn't sure what to say. I didn't want to risk being insensitive to his ordeal, so I just asked another question.

"So only the criminal and cruel come to Threshold?" I asked.

"No, not at all. Threshold is not a place in itself. It's just one more region of the vast astral realm. Good people are known to come to Threshold as well. Everything in nature is perfectly balanced. For example, where there is bad, there must be an greater amount of good. The universe is not poised to fail, as many seem to think. On the contrary, the universe is destined to succeed. Threshold is not a place of punishment. It's a place of change. Sometimes drastic change is required, as in my case," Dr. Rainer explained, as the aerobus began to move.

I was mesmerized. I didn't know if I should look out the window and take in the wondrous sights before me, or if I should concentrate on the information Dr. Rainer was giving me. Unable to decide, I tried to do both.

"But to answer your question more clearly, no, there are also a lot of good souls in Threshold. Lots of them are humans much like you and me. You'll understand it better once we arrive at our destination," Dr. Rainer said as the aerobus started to hover.

"Ah, guys, I thought this was a train and not a plane," said Jonas, making his disappointment very clear.

"Since you have never been here before, I figured it would be best to take the scenic route," said Dr. Rainer. "Nyxy, I suspect that our trip will be very interesting for you as well."

"Please, Doctor, call me Nyx," she replied.

For a few minutes, all I heard was the gentle humming noise the aerobus made as it glided effortlessly through the air.

As I looked outside the window, questions filled my mind. A large glowing bridge caught my attention, as did the emerald-green river that flowed east.

"Wow, that's beautiful," I said in awe.

"That's Night River, it's a sight to behold," replied Dr. Rainer.

"I don't understand something. When we got here, we could fly. Why do we need to take this aerobus if we can fly?" asked Carla.

"Well, flying is only possible if your vibrational state is higher than the location where you are trying to fly to. I'll give you an example. The reason you were able to fly around Night Peaks is because your vibrational state was higher than the Night Peaks. However, once you moved to a place with a higher vibrational rate like Nightwell, it became practically impossible for you to fly. The reason is that your vibrational rate is not high enough yet," Dr. Rainer said. He then paused for a second. "Also, don't forget that in Threshold we have creatures of various vibrational states. Therefore, there was the need to create a method of transportation that everyone could use."

The aerobus seemed to be following Night River as the minutes passed slowly. I noticed that the sky seemed to be getting lighter the further we moved to the east.

"This is Twilight. Beautiful, isn't it?" Dr. Rainer said, smiling. It truly was the most beautiful twilight sky I had ever seen.

"So we were in Nightside and now we're in Twilight?" I asked.

"That's right. Threshold doesn't alternate between night and day like Earth does. Over here we have Nightside, Twilight, and Dayside, and they are always constant," Dr. Rainer explained.

The aerobus seemed to pick up speed, and the subtle humming grew louder as we flew faster above another river, perhaps three or four hundred feet in the air.

"Wow, I think I'd better sit down," said Jonas after looking out the window.

"Dr. Rainer, do you know why I happened different from everyone else?" Nyx asked.

"Nyx, we're all different. Some of us are very different, while others are just a little different. We're all unique, with many qualities and virtues," Dr. Rainer said. "For now, don't worry. All your questions will be answered once we arrive at our destination."

"Where are we going, anyway?" Jonas asked.

"Our destination is the City of Lights. That's where the answers lie," replied the old doctor.

On both sides of the wide river, fields stretched for miles. It was some sort of plantation that I had never seen before, but we were going too fast for me to be able to properly identify the plants.

"Why do you look like a Night Dweller if you're human?" Jonas asked.

"Every Night Dweller is human, or was human at one point. Our appearances were changed by the crimes and injustices we committed. The more heinous the crime, the worse we look here. But don't get me wrong, not every Night Dweller is a bad person. Trust me, most aren't. But they're in debt to nature and its natural laws. We were created for greatness and goodness. We're all destined for success, just like the universe," Dr. Rainer explained as he handed me the book I had picked up from the floor earlier.

"Thanks, but I can't accept it," I replied.

"You must, because all of you are meant to do great things. The future of Threshold depends on it. You're meant to do things that I can't speak of, things that you must figure out for yourselves. But know this; you're not here by mere chance. There is a reason for everything, there's always a reason," said Dr. Rainer, still offering me the book titled *Dweller on the Threshold: The Constant Struggle Between Light and Darkness.*

"Thank you very much," I replied, accepting the book. "However, I don't know how I can take this with me once I return to Earth."

"My boy, you have much to learn. Chances are there's an exact copy of this book on Earth. Most things that exist on Earth had to be created here first. The astral realm is not a copy of Earth as so many assume, but the Earth is in fact a crude copy of the Astral," Dr. Rainer explained.

"Are you saying that we can find a copy of this aerobus on Earth?" Jonas asked.

"Not yet, but eventually this design will migrate to the physical realm. The same is true with the advanced materials you see here. Just remember that nature is never wrong," Dr. Rainer replied.

Suddenly, the aerobus reduced its speed. The only reason I noticed was because the subtle humming returned, and I could once again clearly see the scenery outside.

The aerobus slowed more, which allowed me to take in all of the marvelous scenery. I could see the grassy wetlands, which had only a few trees spread randomly. Leafy greens floated on the water, coloring its reflection. Occasionally a bubble or two would burst and disrupt the perfect reflection of the surface with long ripples. Surely the bubbles were a sign that something thrived under the water's surface.

***

"Look!" said Jonas loudly.

"Wow!" That was the only word that came out of Carla's and Nyx's mouths.

Curious, I quickly looked outside the window and saw a beaming city of light. It had two very high central towers that seemed to stretch into infinity, toward an eerie twilight. The sky was a mix of orange, red, and purple hues that served as a canvas for clouds of various colors.

"Welcome to the City of Lights," Dr. Rainer said.

"This place is huge and so bright," Carla said in awe.

Excited, I stood up and carefully placed Spark on my empty seat so I could move to the other side to take in all the amazing features of the brightly lit city.

We flew past huge and spacious parks with comfortable benches and bountiful flowers that seemed to emanate a light of their own. Trees filled the landscape, which was complete with small lakes and crystal clear fountains.

A few minutes later, we passed whole communities: houses and stores, all in perfect shape, with coordinated colors that seemed to perfectly complement each other.

After the houses, there were smaller parks and more buildings. They all reminded me of the buildings back on Earth, except that they seemed to be made of a different material.

"Do you see those towers ahead? That's our stop," Dr. Rainer said as he pointed toward a spiral tower in the distance. I looked closely and saw that other aerobuses were coming and going from what seemed to be a very busy central transportation terminal.

As strange as it may sound, I felt as though I belonged there. It felt like I was home. I don't know how to explain it, but deep inside I felt like I had been there before, even lived there.

I thought about what Dr. Rainer had said about my mother. While there was only a chance I could find her, I would search high and low. I would search until there was no place left to look. Seeing the City of Lights gave me renewed hope, and for that I was thankful.

When we came to a complete stop at the top of the spiral tower, the doors slowly opened. I woke up Spark; he was sleeping peacefully in my seat.

"You know, he'll be fine on his own," Dr. Rainer said as he gathered his books and scrolls.

"You want me to leave him here?" I asked.

"No, I simply mean you don't have to carry him from place to place. Wherever you go, Spark will follow. You now share a bond that not even death can break," the good doctor explained.

"Give it a try. If he runs, we can chase him," said Carla as she got up to leave the aerobus.

"I wouldn't worry about it. I'm pretty sure he won't," said Dr. Rainer.

"This place is awesome," said Jonas.

"Extraordinary, isn't it?" asked Dr. Rainer.

"Who are we here to see?" asked Nyx, looking concerned.

I saw that Nyx still didn't completely trust Dr. Rainer. She seemed cautious, which wasn't necessarily a bad thing considering that we had just barely escaped from a trap.

"We're here to see someone who can help us plan the next steps," answered Dr. Rainer.

I placed Spark on the ground, and he followed me through the crowd. At first I kept looking down at him to make sure he was following me, but after a few minutes I was convinced he would follow me wherever I went, so I stopped worrying.

***

"Welcome back, Dr. Rainer," said a familiar voice from behind us.

"I have brought visitors," replied the doctor as I turned to see Mrs. Barnes standing behind me with her benevolent smile.

"Nice to see you again," I said, surprised and yet relieved to see a familiar face.

"The pleasure is all mine," Mrs. Barnes replied. "Please follow me. We have much to discuss."

We followed Mrs. Barnes as she made her way through the crowd. All the while, I couldn't decide which way to look because there were new things to be seen in every direction.

"What exactly is this place?" Carla asked as she caught up with Mrs. Barnes.

"This is where every soul should come, once they finish their time in the physical realm, but that's not always the case," said Mrs. Barnes.

"Do you mean to say this is heaven?" asked Jonas.

"No, dear, I didn't mean to imply that. This is simply another stop in the eternal journey of evolution," said Mrs. Barnes.

"Can you help me?" asked Nyx anxiously.

"I believe we can, my dear," Mrs. Barnes replied.

"Here we are," the sweet old lady said as we came to a stop in front of another tall spiral tower.

I looked around, but I didn't see Spark. I was about to say something when he came running toward me and sat by my feet.

"I know that you have many questions and I promise that they'll be answered shortly. Please come in, don't be shy now," Mrs. Barnes said as she pulled out a mysterious glass key from one of her robe pockets and waved the big sapphire-blue crystal in front of the door, which immediately vanished.

"What is this place?" I asked, unable to contain a subtle hint of suspicion in my voice.

"This is the Hall of the Records and Knowledge, also known on Earth as the Akashic records. These walls hold all the answers that humanity desperately seeks in the fields of science, theology, psychology, medicine, and technology. These walls house every knowledge and event that has ever happened, and those that have yet to come," Mrs. Barnes replied.

"Technology? There's technology in astral realms?" I asked.

"Of course, dear. Everything, and I mean everything, had to exist in the astral realm before it could make its way into the physical realm and Earth. For example, all of Mozart's symphonies were composed here in the Astral by none other than himself while he slept. After perfecting them here, he tried to replicate them back on Earth. Believe it or not, they are much more beautiful here," explained Mrs. Barnes.

"So what is going on? Why exactly are we here?" I asked.

"Mark, I know you had a very hard childhood. You grew up to be a fine young man, but you're not without your own faults and fair share of trouble. It wasn't by chance that your quest to find your mother has led you to Threshold. There's something you must do," said Mrs. Barnes as she led the way through the various hallways, which were embellished with works of art I had never seen before—at least until we reached the end of the hallway. On the wall right in front of us was the 1506 painting of "Saint George and the Dragon" by Raphael. Although the "original" painting on Earth was fairly small, this one filled the whole wall. The "original" on Earth paled in comparison.

"Until you accomplish the task you have set out to do, you won't be able to return to Earth. In fact, none of you can. You all share the same fate—"

"What you mean, we can't return?" asked Jonas.

"I'm sorry, but there isn't much I can do. Phasma has gained too much strength, and until the link between Mark and Phasma is broken, you're stuck here," Mrs. Barnes said as we continued walking.

***

In the distance, something caught my attention. A glowing set of eyes seemed to be staring directly at us. The bright blue glow startled me. I'd never seen eyes quite that bright before. I wanted to turn around and run, but Mrs. Barnes reassured us with her soothing voice.

"Don't worry, my dears, that's Eva Mayflower. She's our record keeper, much as Jane Olstein is your librarian back on Earth," Mrs. Barnes said as she waved her keys at another closed door.

"What happens if morning comes on Earth, and we're still here?" Carla asked, looking rather worried.

"Time is a tricky thing in Threshold. Let's just say that until the bond is broken, morning will never come for you," Mrs. Barnes said as the door vanished. "Come on in. There's someone I want you to meet."

We followed Mrs. Barnes into the room. All the while, the record keeper kept heading our way.

"Welcome, dear friends, good to see you again," Eva said as she entered the room, which resembled our libraries on Earth. They would be almost identical if it weren't for the fact that this library seemed to be more technologically advanced, especially judging by the transparent computer-like screens that had been carefully placed on top of each desk.

I was startled when Spark jumped on my shoulder without any warning. I still wasn't used to his claws, not to mention the fact that he seemed to be gaining weight and strength.

"Excuse me, but did you say good to see you again? I have never seen you before," Jonas said.

"But you have, it's just that you don't remember. As a matter of fact, we sat at that desk over there last time, and you adamantly insisted that you wouldn't forget our conversation," explained Eva.

Eva's eyes glowed a soft blue; she had a small frame and chestnut hair, not what you would expect a librarian to look like. She didn't seem to be a day over thirty years old.

"You do seem familiar," said Carla, looking at Eva closely.

"You see, someone remembers me," Eva said jokingly as she approached another desk and picked up a transparent tablet.

"Phasma's power seems to be increasing as more and more people transition from their physical bodies into Nightside. The world is so full of anger and hatred that very few people are able to overcome such overwhelming feelings," said Eva while Mrs. Barnes went to one of the bookshelves and started to look for a particular volume.

"What's my role in all of this?" Nyx asked.

"Nyx, you're one of the most important pieces of the puzzle. You alone hold the power to defeat Phasma and rid Threshold of his tyranny. However, for it to happen, you must want it and you can't do it alone. You'll need help from your new friends," Eva said. She activated the tablet and a three-dimensional map filled the room. It appeared to be a map of Threshold.

I could clearly see the Night Peaks where we first arrived and the entrance to the Cave of Sorrows, as well as the river where we made our escape. I saw the swamp-infested highlands and Watertown, complete with its stores and nearby dam. Every step we had taken in Threshold was highlighted, as if Eva had been closely monitoring our progress ever since our arrival.

"We are here," Eva said, pointing toward a brightly lit city almost in the middle of the southern continent, which was called Downside.

I saw a dotted red line heading north.

"Is this where we need to go?" I asked, pointing toward a small island in the middle of the map.

"No, that was the original plan, but Phasma is getting too close. We feel that it's best if you take the underground aerobus. Since it's the longer route, we don't think Phasma expects you to do that," Eva said. She looked at Mrs. Barnes as if she sought her support or confirmation. Mrs. Barnes simply nodded and continued to read.

"Do you mean to say that you can't protect us from that thing?" Jonas asked. I had to hand it to him; he had the guts to ask the hardest questions.

"No, but we can help," Eva replied as she touched the three-dimensional map and moved the red dotted line to show us the route we needed to take.

"Nyx, this is Living Forest. Your true home," Mrs. Barnes said, putting her book down. "Phasma kidnapped you from here when you were much younger. He knew you were different from the others and that one day you would seek to put a stop to his reign of fear. He tried several times to teach you his cruel ways and failed. You held strong to your beliefs, and we need you to be even stronger now, for the moment of truth draws near."

We were supposed to take the aerobus from the City of Lights and cross half a world's worth of ocean to arrive in the northern continent where the Living Forest was.

"From here on, you'll have to follow your instincts," Eva said as she touched the tablet device and the map disappeared.

"Why don't you deal with Phasma?" Carla asked. It was a good question; I had been wondering the same thing, but I didn't have the courage to ask.

"Phasma is not from this world, so unfortunately there isn't much we can do," Mrs. Barnes explained.

"What do you mean?" I asked.

"Mark, Phasma is only the Guardian of Threshold, but he's not from Threshold. His powers were always very limited in the past, however he's been getting stronger… I'm afraid you have been making him stronger, Mark. You see, your rage fuels his rage," Mrs. Barnes said.

"I have done no such thing! You're wrong!" I accused her, scaring Spark as I abruptly stood up.

"Calm down, my friend," Dr. Rainer said as he placed his book on the nearby counter.

"Dear Mark, I'm sorry to bring you this news, but it's true. Look, even Spark feels your rage, and it's not all your fault. All the rage in the world quenches his thirst and makes him stronger," Eva said as she approached Spark. He resisted with a mad hissing sound.

"It's okay, Spark, come," Eva insisted, and Spark immediately seemed to calm down. Eva picked him up and started to pet him gently, soothing his fit of rage.

"I'm…" I began, but guilt overtook me.

"It's all right, we know," Mrs. Barnes said as she took my hand and sat me down at the closest desk. Her gentle touch soothed my heart and calmed my nerves.

"Mark, as long as you follow your heart, everything will work out just fine. You can't let Phasma control you. You're a good person, and you need to believe that. Your mother is very proud," said Mrs. Barnes gently.

"My mom… is she here?" I asked as my eyes filled with tears.

"Oh, my dear, she's in the astral realm. From time to time, when the need arises she comes to Threshold. So believe me when I tell you that I know she's very proud of you," Eva said as she handed me a fancy handkerchief.

"Can I see her?" I asked, completely overwhelmed by the thought of seeing her again.

"All in due time, my dear friend," Eva said, patting me on the back.

Although I felt very happy with the prospect of seeing my mother again, not even that prevented the sudden dread that possessed me.

"Oh no, he's close," I said urgently. "I can feel him."

"Unfortunately, we must hurry," said Mrs. Barnes.

"Dr. Rainer, since you know what needs to done, can you help them?" Mrs. Barnes asked as she handed him a scroll, which I presumed contained the map of where we needed to go.

"Sure. It will be my pleasure," replied Dr. Rainer, taking the scroll and folding it quickly but carefully and placing it in one of his pockets.

"It was lovely seeing all of you again," Eva said as she shook our hands.

As we started to leave the room, I made sure Spark was following us.

"I don't know why, but Spark keeps running in front of me," I said in hopes that someone would know what he wanted.

"Maybe he's hungry," suggested Carla as we made our way back through the building.

"I don't even know what kind of food he eats," I replied, realizing that he hadn't had anything to drink or eat. Just thinking about it made my stomach grumble.

"Great, now I'm hungry, if that's even possible," I said, smiling.

Mrs. Barnes followed us out. After several minutes of walking and several sharp turns, we finally arrived outside.

"Don't forget your roots," Mrs. Barnes said as she gently guided us back onto the street. "It was good to see you again. I'll contact you again once you reach your destination. Good luck."

I could tell she wished she could come with us.

I got the sense Mrs. Barnes had to do something very important before we could leave Threshold. There was something familiar about the way she spoke, but I dismissed it, thinking I must have retained some recollection of my previous visit to Threshold.

Everyone seemed to be worried because we weren't talking very much and Jonas had stopped joking.

"Guys, we'll be fine," I said in an attempt to put my friends at ease.

"I know," Nyx said.

"I'm just hungry," said Jonas, obviously lying.

CHAPTER THIRTEEN

The Dawn of Fear

I couldn't blame Jonas. It was very strange and surreal to have your whole belief system turned upside down in a matter of days.

"There's a place just around the corner where we can get something to eat," Dr. Rainer said, pointing straight ahead.

"We can eat in the astral realm?" Jonas asked, looking happier.

"Certainly, we still have a body in the astral realm. Granted, a more rarefied and subtle body, but it's still a body that needs vitamins and nutrients in order to function properly," explained Dr. Rainer.

The streets were very narrow, with stores on both sides. Every few feet, a sign floated freely in the air. Some were made of polished wood while others were more high-tech. The signs seemed to be grouped around the center of the city. I tried not to stare at them, but I couldn't help it because there were all sorts of strange things on display. One advertised Aetherios power cores—whatever that was—while another showed a highly advanced and transparent tablet-like computer.

"What do you use for money here?" Carla asked.

"We don't have any need for money," explained Dr. Rainer.

"So everything is free?" Jonas asked.

"Not quite. We use what we think is a much better economic system. Here in Threshold, everyone works for the common well-being and gets paid in what we call bonus-hours. One hour of work equals one bonus-hour. See those signs by that store there?" Dr. Rainer asked, pointing toward a sign that read:

> ### Twingler Sale Everything for ^1 or less.

"That sign means that everything in that store costs just one bonus-hour, rarely less," explained Dr. Rainer.

"There's work here?" Jonas asked, looking disappointed.

"Of course. Life would be boring with nothing to do. Work is good for the soul, there's nothing better than to work while helping someone in need," Dr. Rainer explained. "It took me a great while to figure that out."

"I don't know about this, I always thought that after my time on Earth was done, I would be able to rest," replied Jonas.

"Well, you can, but I guarantee you it will be a very boring experience. Besides, time doesn't really exist here, although we use it sparingly as an organizational tool simply to help us plan for events… a concept that was created here and later exported to Earth, by the way," said Dr. Rainer as he walked toward a quaint little store.

We followed him inside, and I paid close attention to all the movement going on around me. People of different races came and went, some walked alone, seemingly contemplating the beautiful scenery of the plaza, while others were too involved in conversations to even notice me.

"All I know is that we're going back to Earth one day…" I overheard an exquisite couple saying as their voices trailed off in the distance.

They wore white robes with gold trimming around the sleeves that matched their sandals. The outfit seemed to be the norm. The robes looked like they had been sewn by a tailoring grandmaster. My eyes were drawn to the intricate gold weaving.

"Wow, this place is so vibrant and full. I don't think I have ever seen so many different people in one place," said Nyx as we entered a store that resembled a coffee house back on Earth.

There were some similarities to the stores on Earth, but there were differences as well. To begin with, the counter was made of some unknown material. There were food plates on display, with small holographic signs hovering above each one:

```
DAILY SPECIALS:
Volan Fresh Baked Bread          ^.27
Twingler's Twilight Souffle      ^.18
Elven Energy Rice Spools         ^.35
```

"We have people from many races living and working in Threshold," replied Dr. Rainer as he headed in the shopkeeper's direction.

"Welcome to the Greasy Spoon. How may I help you?" asked a friendly, small-framed lady on the other side of the counter.

Upon noticing our puzzled looks, she continued, "I highly recommend the Volan fresh baked bread with the elven rice. Would you like to try it?" she asked, smiling.

"Sure, I'll give it a try." I figured that any food with that name couldn't be all that bad.

"I'll have two of whatever that is," Jonas said, pushing me aside.

"Wait! There's nothing weird on that, is there?" Jonas asked, apparently having second thoughts.

"No dear, unless you don't like vegetables, that is," replied the lady behind the counter. Jonas face said it all, but I think he was really hungry because he didn't reply.

"That sounds good. Can I try one as well?" Carla asked from behind me.

"Sure, dear," the shopkeeper replied.

"Unfortunately, we'll have to eat as we go," Dr. Rainer said as he handed the storekeeper a translucent card.

"Thank you, Doctor," the shopkeeper said, smiling as she handed Dr. Rainer his card back after scanning it. I got the feeling they knew each other well.

"Thank you," replied Dr. Rainer. As he headed outside, we followed him with our food in hand. I must admit it was awkward to eat and power-walk at the same time, but somehow we all managed. The food was better than anything I'd had before, full of flavor. Apparently, tastes also were heightened in the Astral. The bread was by far my favorite, sweet and salty at the same time. It tasted and smelled just like the bread my mother used to make.

***

We followed Dr. Rainer as he headed toward the outskirts of the city. At first I thought we were going outside the city, but as we neared the front gates, Dr. Rainer turned left into what appeared to be an underground transportation system.

After walking for about three minutes, we arrived at a hall with floating signs that read:

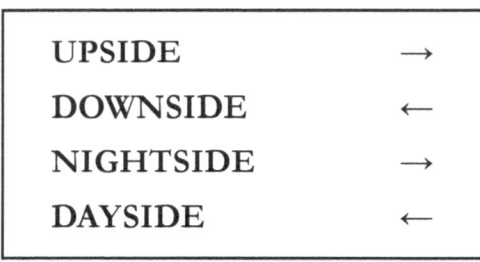

UPSIDE	→
DOWNSIDE	←
NIGHTSIDE	→
DAYSIDE	←

We followed the sign for Upside, until he turned left at another sign that read "**LIVING FOREST.**"

It wasn't long before we arrived at what seemed to be a train platform.

"Come and sit. The aerobus shouldn't take too long," Dr. Rainer said after he spotted a few empty seats nearby.

I sat next to Nyx while Spark found a dark hiding spot under my chair. To my left was Dr. Rainer, and next to him sat Carla, looking lovely as usual. Jonas decided to stand.

Although we weren't the only ones waiting, there weren't too many people around. Suddenly, a subtle humming filled the air and everyone stood up.

"Right on time," said Dr. Rainer, looking at an intriguing watch he had taken from his robe pocket.

In the distance, I could see a long aerobus approaching. It was longer than the previous one we had taken; it seemed made to travel long distances. I couldn't help but stare in awe as it approached slowly, floating just inches above the ground. Once it had come to a complete stop, its doors opened.

We waited patiently as passengers made their way out of the aerobus. That's when I noticed that most of them looked human.

"You look surprised," said Dr. Rainer.

"I didn't expect to find so many humans here," I replied.

"Every being in Threshold was a human at some point. Although they may not always choose to show themselves as so, that doesn't make it less true," Dr. Rainer said.

I timidly took a step forward and approached the aerobus. My posture and facial expression must have reflected my state of mind, because when I looked back at Carla, she gave me a beautiful and much-needed reassuring smile.

I stepped into the aerobus, which was still hovering an inch or so above the ground. I sat by the first free window seat that I saw, in hopes that Carla would sit next to me. But I'd never had much luck in the past, and apparently that wasn't about to change. Ultimately, Dr. Rainer sat next to me. Carla had opted to sit next to Nyx, while Jonas seemed happy to sit by himself with Spark as his only companion.

"He's a cool dragon," Jonas said as Spark slowly warmed up to him.

"Be careful not to be too pushy," I warned as I turned around to see if everything was fine.

"Don't be silly, he won't do anything to me," Jonas replied. Still playing with Spark, he asked, "You're a good boy, aren't you?" As soon as the aerobus closed its doors and started to move, I heard a prerecorded message that said, "Welcome to the Rapid Transit. Wherever your destination, we'll proudly take you there. Please stay seated and enjoy your trip."

If I had to guess, I would have said the trip was going to last much longer than our previous one. Even the seats were more comfortable, like those on a commercial airliner back on Earth, minus the cramped leg space and suffocating aisles.

"Phasma won't stop, will he?" Nyx asked, looking at Dr. Rainer.

"I'm sorry. I'd wish I could tell you something different but I can't," Dr. Rainer replied.

"Do we have a fighting chance?" Jonas asked.

"Of course, there's always a chance. Don't let Phasma, or anyone else for that matter, consume your hopes. That's exactly how he gets his strength," Dr. Rainer said as he opened a book and started to read.

"Don't worry, Jonas, I'll get us home safely. I promise," I said, even though deep down I had no clue how I was going to do that.

Out of the corner of my eye, I could see that Carla and Nyx were deeply involved in a conversation.

As soon as we were about to leave the city, the aerobus picked up speed.

I looked up at the sky and saw that it was getting brighter. In fact, the light resembled the early morning hours on Earth.

I was still contemplating the sky when I looked at the ground and saw a gorgeous forest covered in fall colors. A variety of trees populated the scenery below, while crystal-clear springs and small rivers added the master touch to nature's artwork. The scene was complete with rocks and local wildlife. Strange creatures moved in and out of the bushes. I wished we weren't going so fast so I could see them better.

We passed through amazing valleys, crossing beautiful fields and luscious farms.

"Wow, that's gorgeous!" Carla said.

"That's the Dawn Forest. Beautiful, isn't it?" Dr. Rainer asked.

Although the trip wasn't short, I was never bored. And even though some of the trip was underground and I couldn't see much during extended stretches of dense fog, I always managed to find something interesting to observe, if not outside then inside the aerobus.

In one of the longest underground stretches, I thought that I saw an underground volcano spilling lava. However, I had no way of knowing for sure, because the windows had become foggy with condensation.

When I wasn't looking outside, I was paying attention to the inside of the aerobus and noting how everyone seemed to be happier than people on Earth. Ever since I was little, I tended to notice how sad people were in general. They usually went about their business looking sad and depressed, but that wasn't the case here.

Apparently Dr. Rainer was somewhat famous. Everyone on the aerobus seemed to know him.

"This ride is making me tired. I wonder if I can sleep… oh, I almost forgot that I'm already sleeping," Jonas joked and then let out a very loud yawn.

"I'm sure you can still rest, I know I will," Nyx replied, smiling gently.

On that note, I closed my eyes and let my mind wander.

***

As usually happened when my mind ran wild, I got entangled in thoughts about my mother. I started thinking of how much I missed her all these years, and then I thought about the events of that fateful morning—the morning I lost all hope and faith, the morning destiny betrayed me.

I remembered when I was five years old. It was a day that started like any other, except that the loud roar of a heavy truck engine woke me up. I still felt guilty for fighting with my mom. When I looked outside the window, I saw a bright yellow moving truck pulling up to the empty house across the street. Little did I know then how much my life was about to change.

The rest of that morning was uneventful, except for the chilling air that invaded my soul every time I went outside to look at the commotion on the other side of the street. I remember being curious about our new neighbors; I wondered if there would be any children for me to play with. After all, there was a shortage of kids in my street. I was the only one on the whole block.

Things began to get really strange right after lunchtime. The phone rang and my dad answered, but I recall that he didn't do much talking and he looked weird in a serious sort of way… at least until he noticed that I was paying attention. Once he saw me, he just sat down with his mouth frozen in a half-open position. He was fortunate to be standing near the couch because he didn't even look behind him before dropping onto it. I didn't think anything of it, but for some reason the whole scene got stuck in my head.

After the phone call, he rushed upstairs, pulling me behind him. He got dressed in a hurry, then said, "Son, today you're going to spend some time with Grandpa and Grandma."

Then he hugged me tighter than ever before—I remember because it hurt.

From that point on, the phone didn't stop ringing.

Soon, a flood of people came to the house. My Boston grandparents were the first to arrive, but they didn't sport their usual happy faces. When they saw me, they both rushed over and hugged me tight. I thought it was strange because they usually took turns, and I couldn't help but notice that though their eyes were red and swollen, they smiled at me. Next came my aunts, uncles, and cousins. I remember thinking how strange it was to have all those people showing up at our front door at the same time and on a weekday. Maybe I suspected something was wrong, but I was too young to understand.

The day got weirder as more family members showed up. Some people brought food and looked sad; I remember receiving a lot of attention that day, and a lot of candy too.

I started to wonder why everyone looked so sad. Some people were even crying silently but pretended they weren't. Even at that early age, I could tell they were trying to hide their sadness, because every time they saw me looking at them, they gave me a strained smile and turned their faces away.

In the midst of all the confusion, the doorbell rang again.

My grandfather stood up and opened the door. That's when I saw them for the first time. The boy looked skinny and fragile, while the girl looked beautiful in her white dress with a bright yellow ribbon around her waist. They were my age.

We were introduced, and on that crazy day, I had fun playing with Jonas and Carla. After we got acquainted, they invited me over to their new home. We spent the rest of the day playing in their almost empty house. We ran up and down the stairs, and we chased each other in the yard and played hide-and-seek with empty moving boxes. For those few hours that we played together, everything seemed perfect. I'd finally made new friends, and best of all, they lived just across the street.

Had I known how terrible and unforgettable that day truly was, I wouldn't have had so much fun.

I only started to realize something was terribly wrong when nighttime came and my mother hadn't yet returned from work. It was strange to see the house full of family members. Everyone seemed to be there except the one person I'd been looking forward to seeing all day. I badly needed to say that I was sorry.

I remember asking my grandmother when my mother would be coming home and not receiving a response. Instead, she rushed out of the room, covering her face with her hands. I thought that I had done something wrong to make her sad.

Shortly after that, instead of having my nighttime routine with my mother, I was stuck taking a bath in front of my grandfather while my dad was nowhere to be found.

I remembered asking my grandfather about my dad's where-abouts, and all he would say was that my dad was taking care of some very important things and that he shouldn't be much longer.

I lay in bed, and my grandmother sat next to me to read me a bedtime story. She wasn't as good a storyteller as my mom was. She would often stop reading and just stare silently into the air, but eventually I feel asleep.

That night, strange dreams haunted me. I woke up in the middle of the night with my forehead covered in cold sweat and shaking uncontrollably. I was very cold. I'd been dreaming about being stuck on a frozen wasteland all alone, crying for my mother as the cold snow fell heavily around me. I was soon covered in so much snow that it was impossible to move.

That was the first time in my life that I had a nightmare. From that point on, they would plague me. It was rare the occasion that I could sleep peacefully without having some sort of night terror or nightmare.

I was only able to fall back asleep that night after my father rushed into my room. Apparently I had let out a terrified scream, but my father was able to put my mind at ease, and once my tears dried up, I fell asleep again.

The next morning, I woke up to the sweet smell of homemade apple pie in the air. In my innocence, I immediately assumed my mother had returned in the middle of the night and cooked my favorite dessert to make it up to me. Nothing could have prepared me for the deception I was about to encounter.

I rushed down the stairs still in my pajamas. I was disappointed and surprised to discover that some family members were still around.

I entered the kitchen and found that it was filled with even more people than the day before. Everyone but my mother seemed to be there. Even cousins I didn't know.

Both sets of grandparents were sitting at the table, having breakfast together, which was a sight I had never seen before. I was used to seeing only one pair of them at a time because my mother's parents lived in Florida and were too old to travel—at least that was what she used to tell me.

As I walked into the kitchen, everyone stopped whatever they were doing to stare at me. The kitchen became suddenly quiet. Grandpa Billy got up and came over to talk to me.

"Mark, how about you spend the day playing with your new friends? What're their names again? Jonas and Carla, isn't it?" Grandpa Billy asked as he lifted me up. "Come, let's go get dressed, then I'll take you there."

While we headed back upstairs, I looked back and waved to all my cousins.

After I was dressed, Grandpa Billy led me across the street to the Webers' house, where I found the boy named Jonas and his beautiful sister Carla ready, willing, and waiting to play with me.

On the Webers' living room floor, there was a maze of empty moving boxes waiting for us, boxes that in our skilled hands and minds turned into castles, fortresses, and spaceships. And for the second strangest day of my life we built houses, stores, robots, and whole planets, and we had a ball doing it. But in the back of my mind, I felt anxious. Something was troubling me; something lurked in the shadows. At one point, I even thought I saw something hiding in the darkest corner. But, Jonas and Carla did a great job keeping me busy for most of the time. They too seemed eager to have a new friend to play with.

Since we were having so much fun, time flew. And soon it was lunchtime. We ate inside a rather large and empty box that we proudly named the Great Boxy Inn. The special of the day was homemade mac 'n' cheese, which had been carefully prepared by Mrs. Weber.

We spent the rest of the afternoon playing, but every once in a while I felt sad for no apparent reason.

It wasn't long before it was dinnertime. Dinner was also served at the Great Boxy Inn, but our meal was less than satisfactory because the only item on the menu that night was a yucky minestrone soup. Jonas threw a tantrum and asked for something else. After much complaining, he was finally able to persuade Mrs. Weber to serve us peanut-butter-and-jelly sandwiches.

It was getting late when the phone rang at the Webers' house. After a short conversation, Mrs. Weber told me I would be spending the night with Jonas and Carla. Apparently, my dad was still taking care of some important stuff. Although I didn't exactly understand why my father was absent. I was happy to spend more time with my two new friends.

That evening, the Great Boxy Inn was moved upstairs, and I slept comfortably inside it. Mrs. Weber made sure I had a very comfortable sleeping bag and plenty of fluffy comforters. I didn't know it at the time, but that night would be the last night I would sleep peacefully.

I woke up the following morning feeling fully rested. I remember having very pleasant dreams in which I was flying and holding on to my mother's hand. As hard as I tried, I couldn't remember her exact words. It was something like, "Don't worry. Everything will be okay as long as you follow your heart." She seemed to be saying good-bye. Her forehead glowed, and I thought it was the sun hitting her face, but I quickly realized the light was coming from within her.

While we were having breakfast, the doorbell rang, and I ran as quickly as I could to the living room window to see who it was. I hoped it was my mother, but deep down I knew it wasn't. It was my dad, dressed in a black suit and overcoat. He had a big black umbrella in his large hands. The weather outside was rainy and foggy, and judging by how cold the glass was, it was very cold outside.

"Good morning," said my dad as he came over and hugged me. "I've got you something to wear," he said as he handed me a bag.

I grabbed the bag and quickly emptied its contents onto the carpet. Inside there was a small suit and a tie. I remember not liking that present at all.

"Son, you need to get dressed. I don't want us to be late," he said.

"But, Dad, I want to stay and play," I replied.

"You can't. We have to be somewhere," my dad said as he picked up my clothes from the carpet.

"Mark, you won't be alone. Jonas and Carla will be there too. As a matter of fact, kids, go upstairs and get dressed. I laid out some clothes on top of your beds," Mrs. Weber said, clapping her hands in a futile attempt to speed us up.

"Mom, I'm not done with my breakfast yet," Jonas complained with his mouth full.

"Now, Jonas. We don't have much time."

"Mark, come. I'll help you get dressed," my dad said as he grabbed my hand before I could complain.

He took me to the Webers' guest room and dressed me in those stiff clothes. I hated the way they felt, but I was told that I had to wear them, and the worst of it was that they were cold. Thankfully, my dad had brought my black winter jacket, because I was already freezing.

When we came out of the guest room, I was embarrassed at having to wear those clothes, but my dad assured me it was fancy to wear a suit and that I shouldn't be embarrassed.

"But why do I have to dress like this? It's very uncomfortable," I complained, stomping my foot.

"I'm sorry, but you have to dress like this. It's just for today," my dad said. "Thank you so much for watching him," my dad said to Mrs. Weber almost in tears.

"No problem. We're running a bit late, but we'll be right behind you," Mrs. Weber replied. "If you need anything, anything at all, please just let us know."

My dad opened his umbrella and held me close as we walked toward a long black car that waited for us.

"Are we going in this car? It's huge!" I said.

"Yes," my dad replied as the driver opened the door for us.

I was the first to enter the black limousine. Both sets of my grandparents were already waiting inside. Everyone seemed really sad, with red and puffy eyes. My grandmother looked pale and sick.

I remember being concerned for her, so I got up and held her hand and said, "Grandma, don't worry, everything is going to be okay."

Then I knelt and looked through the foggy back window of the limo, trying to see Jonas and Carla. I could see just enough to spot Carla and Jonas getting into their parents' car, also dressed in fancy, uptight clothes. It was a very cold and stormy New England morning.

We weren't the only car on the street. In fact, behind our limo, there was a long line of cars. Leading the way was a box-shaped black limousine.

After a short ride, we arrived at Saint Patrick's Church. I'd been there a few times before with my mom, but never with my dad. She used to tell me that it was her favorite church. Looking back, I recall wondering why we were going there without her.

A small part of me hoped my mother would be waiting for us inside, even though something told me otherwise.

We drove past a huge white statue of Jesus by the entrance; his outstretched arms welcomed us to the grounds.

The church was painted white like snow and was covered by a light-grey roof. A long stairway led the way to a couple of tall wooden doors.

As we climbed the stairs, I looked up as I usually did when I went there with my mother and saw the magnificent steeple, which was connected to a huge bell tower. Every time I looked up at that bell tower, a dizzy spell came over me, causing me to miss a step. Luckily, I was holding onto my father's hand. Otherwise I would have fallen.

As we walked into the church, another man, also dressed in a black suit, handed my dad a piece of paper. All the family members followed right behind us.

Once inside, my father stopped, pulled me aside to an empty room near the entrance hall and said, "Son, I need you to be strong and brave…" He stopped for a second, as though he needed to catch his breath.

"Okay, Dad," I said as my heart sped up.

"I'm sorry… to have to tell you this, son, but there isn't any other way… Mommy has passed away," my dad said as our eyes started to fill up with tears.

At that precise moment, my world collapsed. Sadness took control of my being. I experienced a mix of emotions so intense I thought I was going to pass out.

"Son, we have to be strong for each other."

"Did she go to heaven, Daddy?" I asked, crying. My dad looked at me, puzzled and at a loss for words. It felt like an eternity passed before he finally replied.

"Yes, Mommy is in heaven," he said, giving me another very tight hug. We cried on each other's shoulders for a while.

"Don't worry, Daddy. Mommy is with God. He'll take good care of her," I said, trying to help.

Come to think of it, I truly believed God would look after my mother, but somewhere along the road, I forgot that innate belief. It didn't help that my father was an atheist. I think eventually I acquired some of his skepticism and doubts.

"Come. It is time to say good-bye to Mommy," my dad said, offering me his hand. I held it as tightly as I could. At that moment, that large hand was my only anchor to safety. I felt sad and guilty for every time I had told my mother no or not listened to her, but most of all I was sad because I was going to miss her love, her caring touch, her soft voice, her kisses and sweet smile.

I was even going miss her yelling at me for doing something wrong.

Once we started to walk to our seats, there was no way of avoiding the disappointment that took hold of my heart. The silence in the church was heart-shattering and disturbing, and the loneliness was depressing.

As we walked, I felt every eye in the room focused on my father and me. The church was filled to capacity. There were lots of friends and family all around, and yet I had never felt so lonely.

The most disturbing sight was that strange and surreal black wooden box that was fitted with gold handles on top of the altar and knowing that my mother's body was inside. Something told me I would have much to endure from that point forward.

We walked all the way to the front of the church and took our seats. Suddenly I felt my mother's presence. I felt her love radiating toward me, giving me a warming and calming sensation even though it was cold inside the church.

Right in front of us, a bit to the right, there was a large picture of my mother giving us a comforting and cozy smile.

"Is Mommy inside there?" I asked my dad.

"Yes, she is," he replied and held me tighter.

"Am I ever going to see her again?" I asked, almost crying.

"Yes, you certainly will. Every night when you go to sleep, you'll dream of her. You may not remember, but you'll be with her every single night," my dad replied.

We watched as the priest came to the front of the altar and started the morning service. I knew from my previous visits to the church that priests required complete silence and utmost concentration. Anything remotely fun and exciting, such as running wildly through the pews in the echoing church, was strictly forbidden—but on that day, I didn't feel like doing any of those things. All I wanted was to do everything that my mother had taught me.

After a few minutes, my grandfather came to sit next to me while my father got up and took a piece of paper from his suit pocket. He walked to the front of the church and started to talk.

"Dear friends and family, Clara's accident has left us with a hole in our hearts, but she didn't leave us. Her memories, and the joys that she brought into our lives will live within every single one of us. I'm especially thankful to my loving wife for giving me the greatest gift of my life: our son, Mark Anthony. It is with a heavy heart that I come here in front of you today and ask that you do not let her memory fade. Always remember her as she wanted to be remembered: as a good person, a wonderful wife, and above all, a great mother," my father said tearfully.

Once my dad was finished, Uncle Robert went up to the altar and helped him back to his seat.

"Hang in there, champ," Uncle Robert said, patting my back.

After sitting perfectly still for about forty-five minutes and listening to the priest and family members talk about my mother, I got up and followed my father as we left the church, following the strange wooden box with my mother's remains.

We got back inside the limousine and rode for about a half-hour in a single file of cars until we reached a grassy field decorated with some sparse trees and benches.

"Daddy, what are we doing here?" I asked.

"This is where your mother's remains will be buried," my dad replied.

The weather was so treacherous that I was surprised my dad let me get out of the limo. Heavy, cold raindrops filled the scene, and even though we were under a big umbrella, I still got wet and cold.

As the wooden box was being lowered into the ground, I ran over and threw a rose on top of the box. All the while, I heard not only my own sobs but also the desperate cries of my grandmother and the rest of the family.

I wouldn't fully understand what had happened that day until several years later.

Ironically, those were the days I met my best friends. They were there for me every step of the way during those hard times. And in return, I had promised myself that I would be there for them until the end, be that what it may.

In retrospect, I'm still not sure if I understood the horrible events of that fateful day. There was something inside of me that revolted whenever I thought about it. And think about it I did, more often than I would have liked. Perhaps more often than was considered normal.

"Are you all right?" Dr. Rainer asked, worried.

"Huh? Yes, I'm fine," I replied.

"I know you love your mother dearly. I'm sure she knows it, and she's very proud of you," Dr. Rainer said, patting me on the back.

"I'd hoped I would find her here," I said.

"I know, but don't give up hope, for hope is the light of tomorrow, the heartbeat of the universe," Dr. Rainer said with such conviction that his words brought me encouragement.

I was about to ask if he knew something about my mother when Carla called my attention to the window.

***

Curious, I looked through the aerobus side windows and noticed we were going through an underwater canyon with a huge opening in the flat below where hot air seemed to be expelled from the ground. I touched the window and found it hot.

"Beautiful, isn't it?" asked Dr. Rainer.

"What is this place?" Carla asked.

"That's the Core. If it wasn't for the Core, Threshold would most certainly not exist," Dr. Rainer explained.

The aerobus started to move in a steep upward angle, which was strange because I didn't think we were that far underwater.

It wasn't long before we were above the water level, but nothing could have prepared me for the sight before me.

Giant white birds flew along with the aerobus. Their wingspans were easily eight feet, and they had very long beaks. They seemed to be hunting some sort of marine life.

"Larus albus is a graceful and intriguing species," Dr. Rainer explained. "Wildlife is one of my interests, sort of like a hobby."

"Are they dangerous?" asked Jonas.

"Not unless you're a fish," Dr. Rainer replied, smiling.

"Ah, Dr. Rainer, that doesn't look good," Jonas yelled from the backseat.

As I looked where Jonas was desperately pointing, I noticed that the ocean seemed to come to an abrupt end.

"Oh, that's… that's Mammoth Falls. We need to ride past them to get to Living Forest. Actually, we should consider ourselves lucky. Normally, the weather isn't this nice. It's said that if you happened to get lost here, you wouldn't notice the deadly falls until it was too late," Dr. Rainer explained.

Jonas held on to his seat for dear life.

"I suppose it's too late to tell you that I'm scared of heights," Jonas said, shaking.

"No, it's not, but there isn't anything I can do about it. You know what they say… what goes up must eventually and inevitably come down," Dr. Rainer said, laughing. We laughed for a bit, but deep down we were all more than a little worried about the impending drop. I knew I was.

As the drop loomed closer, I held tight to my seat. Little did I know that my worries were completely unfounded.

The aerobus simply slowed to a crawl. Up close, the falls looked even more menacing, but instead of the fast drop we were expecting, the aerobus proceeded to descend slowly down the immense waterfall.

"Is that it?" Jonas asked with his eyes still closed.

"Pretty much. We'll continue to descend at this rate," Dr. Rainer replied as he pointed out the various wildlife species we saw on the way down.

An ocean of water falling fifteen hundred feet into the ground right before my eyes was a sight to behold. Never had I seen a more amazing and seemingly impossible thing, not even at the movie theater. The spray that was created when the water hit the rocks below was simply magical. The result was colorful rainbows that decorated the mist.

"There," said Dr. Rainer, pointing outside the window. "Those are the creatures the early explorers of Threshold first sighted when they arrived here. They are the reason why it was decided to call this place Mammoth Falls. Huge, aren't they?"

In fact, they were immense. Some were brown with huge tusks, while others were young and white. The smallest of them was about the size of a truck. They cooled themselves by the water.

"The whole ocean just drops into that abyss?" Nyx asked, looking down into the rupture in the ground.

"Yes, it does. The heat evaporates some of the water while the rest flows underground, distributing heat, nutrients and minerals throughout Threshold. Each continent has its own well. We have the Nightwell—where we met—then there is the Daywell, and the biggest of them is the Everwell," Dr. Rainer said.

Just past the Core there was a shallow pool of water about a quarter of a mile in length. The large pool was formed from the falling mist as the water crashed violently into the Core. Even more amazing, it stretched all the way to the beach.

Incredible wildlife thrived here. Most of the animals seemed to be passive and even, dare I say, friendly. Medium dog-sized birds populated the skies as they flew in and out of the misty spray, while larger animals roamed around bathing and playing in the big wading pool.

The sky was a peculiar mix of bright yellow, blue, and red. A few carefully placed clouds decorated the sky, while the warm yellow sun hung high in the background.

"Welcome to Dayside," Dr. Rainer said, beaming with happiness.

I must confess that it felt good to see the sun once again—I was told that the sun never ceased to shine here. But inside I felt the darkness looming.

With the exception of a few ports and small villages, the area appeared to be untouched by civilization. Its wild beaches would beat any vacation resort back on Earth. We seemed to be the only visitors.

"That's a gorgeous beach," said Carla as we glided gently above the crystal sands.

"That is Daybeach, and if you think that it is pretty from up here, you should see it up close. If you were standing on the beach, you would hear a mix of surreal and majestic songs filling the air. The wind is the maestro and the rocks are the instruments. On any given day, it's possible to hear up to five distinct melodies emanating from various hollow points on the rocks. This soothing music is constantly played as the wind passes through. Those natural songs are an awe-inspiring outlet for nature's creativity, not to mention that they are considered one of the ten wonders of Threshold, followed closely by Daycliffs," Dr. Rainer said.

The further we moved inland, the more agitated Spark became in the seat with Jonas.

"Come, Spark," I said, tapping my leg after I'd noticed how worked up he was.

Spark jumped from the seat behind me, and I saw his small, outstretched wings. That was odd because I had almost forgotten he had wings. Instead of resting near me, Spark decided to hide under my seat. I called him, but he refused to come.

"Spark is acting strange," I said, hoping Dr. Rainer would know why.

"Actually, he's been acting strange ever since we got here," Jonas replied.

"He's bound to feel a little agitated around the Everwell," Dr. Rainer explained as he started to put his books away.

I took another look outside and noticed that we were flying above an odd and rather large forest. The sun had all but disappeared, and we were back in twilight. Living Forest extended beyond twilight, with almost half of it crossing on to Nightside. But Living Forest wasn't any normal forest, for normal forests don't have trees that move freely about. At last I understood why it was called Living Forest.

Trees moved in all directions. Initially, I thought they moved randomly, creating congestion points that spread throughout the forest.

"What's that down there?" Nyx asked, looking outside.

"That is the Living Forest; don't be surprised if the place looks familiar to you," said Dr. Rainer.

"Why is that? I feel like I know this place," Nyx asked, puzzled.

"Because it's your home… Phasma ordered you taken from here when you were very young, too young to remember," explained Dr. Rainer.

Nyx looked at a loss for words.

"That's my home? But, it's so pretty. I'd never imagined that my home could be such a pretty place," Nyx replied.

"Nyx, I've been waiting for a long time for this opportunity, and finally the time has come for me to correct a wrong that has been haunting me for many wind cycles," Dr. Rainer said tearfully. Jonas, Carla, and I just stood there, surprised.

"What do you mean?" Nyx inquired, worried.

"I'll tell you everything, but first I must ask you all a favor… Please keep an open mind and know that I'm ready to make reparations for my past mistakes. Also, please remember that this all happened a long time ago. I was a very different person then. I've changed much since the event in question," Dr. Rainer said, visibly shaken and embarrassed.

After a quick nod of understanding from everyone, Dr. Rainer proceeded.

"Nyx, I was the one who took you from your people… Phasma ordered me to take you. I'm so very sorry. Back then, I had no choice but to serve Phasma. Please understand that I was lost." Dr. Rainer paused as though he was thinking about how to continue.

"Believe it or not, the minute I took you from your sisters, that was when I started to change. I couldn't bear watching you. You see, I was responsible for you when you were very young. But I finally had enough. So one day when nobody was around, I took you in my arms and fled to the only place I could think of at that time… Oh, I wish you knew how much I regretted taking you to

Watertown. I needed Oldroot's help, but all I got, all we got, was deception. Needless to say, Phasma found us in no time."

"So I'm not Phasma's daughter?" Nyx asked.

"No, you're not. He took you back to Cave of Sorrows and threw me in the dungeon. He wanted to see me suffer, he said. So, for many wind cycles I stayed there, chained and believing that I deserved to suffer. While I suffered, I watched everyone around suffer as well, and a seed of compassion grew inside me. One day I decided to take control of my life and did some serious introspection," Dr. Rainer explained, crying.

Nyx started to get upset. Everyone but Dr. Rainer backed away as we thought she was going to burst into flames, but it didn't happen. She was learning to control her emotions.

"Nyx, I tried to go back and rescue you, but I was told it would be impossible and that when the right time came, I would be given the opportunity to help you."

"So when we bumped into you, it wasn't an accident?"

"No, it wasn't. I was there waiting for you to arrive. I wanted to help you however I could," Dr. Rainer replied emotionally. "Please forgive me, Nyx. I should never have helped Phasma take you away from your people."

"My people? Who are my people?" asked Nyx.

"Nyx, you're a Twingler, and Living Forest is, always was, and forever will be your home. There you'll find not only others just like you, but your family members and relatives," Dr. Rainer said in a soft voice.

"But what about Phasma? Won't he come and get me again?" asked Nyx.

"He can't. Nobody knows why, but there is something in the heart of Living Forest that keeps him away. You see, that's why he had to use me to do it for him back then. Besides, now that you're all grown up and you know the truth, it wouldn't do him any good to take you away again," said Dr. Rainer.

Nyx started to cry, but she kept her cool. She didn't even get red.

"Dr. Rainer, I forgive you, and I'm very grateful for all your help and guidance. It's funny. I don't even know these people, but

I've missed them so much. I can't thank you all enough for helping me out. You have shown me that there is a decent life, and for that I'm forever in your debt," Nyx replied, still sobbing.

CHAPTER FOURTEEN
The Dawn of a New Day

Soon we spotted the station, which was located next to a giant tree. The tension had been building up for hours. The closer we were to our destination, the more stressed Nyx became. All the while, Spark continued to act oddly, moving from one end of the aerobus to the other.

My spirits weren't exactly high. I still missed my mother, and I was starting to miss the physical world I'd left behind when our adventure started. The only person who didn't seem bothered by the whole situation was Carla. Unlike Jonas, she was confident of a successful outcome.

Down on the ground, the scenery was nothing like Nyx's old home. Flags waved in the wind. Dozens upon dozens of people gathered at what appeared to be the town center, cheering. From my vantage point inside the aerobus, they looked short, but they stood tall and proud. The first thing I noticed about Living Forest was its buildings, which resembled tree houses, most were built on top of giant moving, living, and breathing trees.

Most of the largest trees had several buildings on top of them. The structures seemed to grow from the tree itself. It was an amazing sight. Whenever they were near each other, a dynamic wood-and-vine bridge appeared to connect them. They stayed connected for a few minutes until the organic bridge retracted, and they lumbered on to connect to other trees in the vicinity.

"What's going on down there?" Jonas asked.

"That, my dear boy, is a celebration, a welcome party of sorts," Dr. Rainer replied with a timid smile.

"What are they celebrating?" Jonas asked.

"They're celebrating our arrival, more specifically, Nyx's return. Your people missed you very much," Dr. Rainer said, looking at Nyx. She simply looked at him, displaying nothing but a tender and compassionate smile. At last, Nyx had arrived back home.

As soon as the aerobus stopped, I got up. Carla, Dr. Rainer, and Nyx were already up and waiting for the doors to open, while Jonas was still glued to the window.

Much to my surprise, the inside the station was nearly empty. An expansive high celling hall seemed to have been roped off just for Nyx's arrival. Waiting for us outside was a few city officials and two short girls. They looked ready to jump for joy.

"Nyx, I have some people I want you to meet," said Dr. Rainer offering his hand. "This is Twil, and this is Teil. They're your sisters and my best friends. They have been waiting to see you for a long time," Dr. Rainer said before Nyx's sisters interrupted him as they ran to hug her. I must confess the scene brought tears to my eyes and placed a knot in my throat.

We hung back to give them some space, but it wasn't long before Nyx came running toward us, thrilled.

"Come. I want to introduce you to my sisters," Nyx said. It was the happiest I had seen her.

"Come, come," repeated Nyx as she dragged Jonas along.

"These are my friends. They helped me escape the Cave of Sorrows," Nyx told Twil and Teil.

"Thank you very much. Our kind is forever in your debt," Twil said. She appeared to be the older sister. She was petite with long, highlighted hair that she kept braided. Her eyes were almost like Nyx's except for the color, which was bright blue.

"You don't need to thank us. And besides, we helped each other out. If it wasn't for your sister, it's possible we would still be Phasma's prisoners," Carla replied.

"Are you staying with us?" Teil asked. She appeared to be Nyx's much younger sister. If I had to guess, I would have said that she looked to be about twelve years old.

"I'm sorry, but we can't. We have to go back to our physical bodies," Carla replied.

"Yeah, as soon as we figure out how," I quickly added.

"I'm sorry to rush, but we must keep moving. Phasma shouldn't be too far behind," Dr. Rainer said.

"He'll come here?" Nyx asked, worried.

"Don't worry, he won't. Once we're gone, he won't dare," Dr. Rainer replied, looking around as though he was getting his bearings.

"Well then, I guess this is good-bye," Jonas said, looking heart-broken.

"We'll still see each other," Nyx replied, nearly crying.

"It was nice meeting you, Nyx. I hope our paths cross again," Carla said as she gave Nyx a hug.

"I'm sure they will," Nyx replied.

"Thanks for everything," I said when it was my turn to say good-bye.

"I hope you find what you've been looking for," replied Nyx.

"I'll see you soon, Nyx," said Dr. Rainer as we started to walk away from Nyx and her sisters.

"Where to now?" Jonas asked.

"Now, we go to Everwell. Unfortunately, this is the closest aerobus station. We must be prepared as we move forward. He's not too far behind," Dr. Rainer said. I noticed he kept looking back to see if Nyx was all right.

"You know, she will be fine," Carla said.

"I know. I'm very grateful that she forgave me, but I don't know if I can forgive myself. After all, I've caused so much pain and suffering to that poor girl," Dr. Rainer said.

"Don't beat yourself up," Jonas said, patting Dr. Rainer on the shoulder.

We zigzagged in and out of the crowd and tried not to lose sight of each other. We weren't the same group as before. Without Nyx, we walked with heavy hearts and shoulders. Although there wasn't much in my future to look forward to, I tried as best as I could to keep my spirits high.

"Wait up!" said a faint voice from behind.

Was that Nyx? I thought as my heart skipped a beat.

"Wait for me."

I turned around and realized I wasn't the only one who had heard the calling. Our moods changed quickly.

"Is that you, Nyx?" Jonas asked.

I was happily surprised to see Nyx moving frantically through the crowd, yelling for us.

"Here!" screamed Carla, waving frantically.

"What is she doing?" Dr. Rainer wondered out loud.

"Good, I found you. I was worried I wouldn't be able to... I'm coming with you," said Nyx when she finally caught up to us.

"But Nyx, you're home now, and what about your sisters?" I asked.

"Oh, they're coming too. They're right behind me, somewhere," Nyx replied, still trying to catch her breath. Jonas looked especially happy.

Nyx's sisters soon caught up with us.

"You know, you don't have to do this," Dr. Rainer said as he continued to walk.

"We know, but we want to help. Besides, we have a score to settle with Phasma," Twil replied.

***

While we walked, my finger started to burn. At first I tried not to pay much attention to it, but I gave up after a few minutes when the pain started to really bother me. I looked down at my finger and saw that Spark's collar ring was glowing.

"Something is going on with Spark," I said.

"It's the Everwell. It tends to have that effect. It should pass soon," Dr. Rainer said.

We seemed to be moving away from the city, even though it was hard to tell for sure because we were so high up. We crossed from one big tree to the next. The only hint that we were moving away from the city was the decreasing number of people and buildings we encountered.

Soon we were crossing trees with no buildings or houses, just a rough platform. The further we ventured the more precarious the connecting bridges became. To make matters worse, we were running out of trees. They grew few and far between, and the bridges that connected them became narrower, longer and less stable.

"We're almost there. Hang on tight," advised Dr. Rainer, leading the way.

"I don't like this, it's too high," complained Jonas.

"You're doing fine," I said.

"I'm not crossing that! No way, no how," Jonas yelled as we came to the longest and most unstable wooden bridge of our journey. The thin bridge had several planks missing and many more rotting away.

"You have to," Carla replied, offering her hand.

"I can't," Jonas replied, but he grabbed his sister's hand nonetheless.

Jonas hesitated for a few seconds. Just when I thought he was going to turn around and run, he made the sign of the cross over his body and slowly started to make his way across the long, windy bridge.

I carefully followed Jonas and Carla as they inched forward.

When Jonas was about halfway through, he stopped dead in his tracks and said, "I can't go on. I really can't."

"Don't look down, just keep walking forward," Carla replied.

But Jonas wouldn't move.

"Everyone looks down when they hear that. Besides, the secret to getting used to heights is to take a long, detailed look down. If you do that, the fear will slowly disappear. It worked for me," I replied as I looked down and enjoyed the sight of strange wild animals running in all directions.

"It doesn't work. I can't move or feel my legs," Jonas replied, looking like he was about to have a panic attack.

Once Nyx saw that Jonas had stopped in the middle of the bridge, she came back toward us.

"Jonas, I know you can do it. We're almost there. You have to do this. Besides, it's not like you have anywhere else to go. We're right in the middle of this bridge, and there are only two ways we can go, back or forward, and since they're both the exact same distance, we might as well go forward. Here, hold my hand," Nyx said.

Jonas started moving forward slowly, aided by Nyx. I followed right behind with Carla to make sure he wouldn't stop again or turn around and run back. From our vantage point, we could see that a bridge didn't connect the next gap at all.

"Oh God, no," said Jonas when he saw there wasn't a bridge ahead. "We are stuck."

"Nope, but I'm afraid you won't like our descent very much," replied Dr. Rainer.

I didn't have a clue how we were going to get down. We were fifteen hundred feet or so from the ground.

"I wonder why this tree isn't moving," Carla said as she touched the old tree.

"They are very old. This one has been around for well over a millennium. Although it spent more than half of that time living and breathing, they too need a change of scenery every now and then. So her spirit has moved on but left this empty shell behind. Good thing too, because it's still useful to us," Dr. Rainer explained.

It took a while, but we arrived at the next wooden platform. I was about to ask how we were going to get down, when I saw a long cable at the end of the platform. It looked like a zip line, except that it seemed to go on forever.

"The only advice I have to give is this: whatever you do, do not let go, because it's a long way down," Dr. Rainer said, smiling as he picked up Spark. He held Spark in one arm, grabbed a handle from a wooden box next to the zip line, placed it on the line, and jumped off the ledge. I couldn't help noticing the confused look on Spark's face as he zoomed down.

"Something tells me that Dr. Rainer is enjoying this," Nyx said. Before she got hold of the zip line handle and thrust herself forward, looking Jonas straight in the eye and saying, "I'll be waiting for you."

It wasn't long before they both disappeared into the distance.

"Your turn," Carla said to Jonas.

"No, I'll go after you," Jonas replied. "This isn't that bad."

"Well then, I'll see you guys down there, wherever that is," Carla replied as she took another handle, placed it on the zip line, and jumped. I had to confess that I was a little worried for her. She looked tense.

Jonas had been quiet for some time, which usually meant trouble. I could count on my fingers the number of times Jonas had been completely quiet.

Even though I was used to heights, I was apprehensive too—but I sensed that Jonas's problem was deeper than that, so I pulled him aside and asked, "What's wrong?"

"I don't know for sure. I'm scared, but it's more than that, I…" Jonas paused.

"What is it?" I said. "You can tell me."

"Well, I guess I have mixed feelings. I mean, I like it here, but at the same time I miss home. I miss my mom and dad, but at the same time, I don't want to leave here and be away from everyone we've met," Jonas replied. For a second, I thought he was going to cry, but he quickly composed himself.

"Ah, I know what this is about. This is about Nyx, isn't it?" I asked.

"Promise me you won't tell her anything."

"I promise. I won't say a word."

"Okay, I'm trusting you. I think I like her. What should I do?" Jonas asked.

"I know how you feel," I said as I considered telling him about my feelings for Carla. But I quickly decided against it. It didn't seem like the right time. There might never be a good time.

"You know, there's no easy answer for that question, but I wouldn't worry too much if I were you. After all, if we get home, we can still astral travel again and come for a visit," I said to put his mind at ease.

"You're right. Now if I could just figure out how to get out of going down this zip line," Jonas half-joked, which was a very good sign.

"Listen, buddy, I want to tell you something. We will get home, that much I can promise you," I said, patting my friend on the back.

"So do you want to jump next?" Jonas asked, looking down.

"I would, but I'm afraid that if I did, you would be stuck here all by yourself for God knows how long," I replied.

"You're probably right. So how do I do this?" asked Jonas with a nervous smile.

"I guess there isn't much to it. Just grab the handle, and like Dr. Rainer said, don't let go," I replied as I started to worry about it myself.

Surprisingly, Jonas gripped the handle firmly. He seemed ready to go but then paused for a few seconds.

"Don't make me push you," I said, laughing and trying to motivate him.

"Here goes nothing!" Jonas yelled as he clumsily almost fell off the ledge. Luckily he was holding on tight to the handle. I think he screamed the whole way down, but I couldn't say for sure because after a while I was unable to hear him.

So there I was. Standing all alone, looking over the massive drop before me and the wilderness below when I started to wonder *what in the world was I doing? What have I been doing all these years?* For a split second, I thought that if I fell, everything would be over and I would finally be able to see my mother again. No delays, no fuss… but deep down inside I knew it wasn't an option. I was sure there would be excruciating consequences for anyone who tried to take the easy way out. From what I had seen so far, I knew enough to know that I didn't know anything, except that there was no easy way out. There was simply the way it had to be.

Worried, I paced back and forth, contemplating all that had happened to me.

Suddenly, my right shoulder blade started to burn. I didn't even have time to blink before I felt him approaching. As the pain grew, so did my rage.

In a moment of clarity, I realized that I was extremely angry: I was angry for having to grow up without a mother. I was angry for having to jump without knowing where I would land. And most of all, I was angry for being in Threshold for so long and not seeing any signs of my mother.

My heart rate increased with my anger. As the sense of dread filled my veins, I knew I was running out of time.

I had a decision to make. If I was to slide down the zip line, I would be involving everyone I cared about in my fight against Phasma. If I stayed on that platform, my friends would probably be safe… yet something told me I shouldn't face Phasma alone. I weighed the pros and cons of each scenario for a few minutes before I realized that no matter how much I tried to protect my friends, they were already involved. I had no right to make the decision for them. So I decided to trust my gut feeling and share my burden with the only friends I had. If I was going to face to Phasma, at least I would have the best friends I could have asked for by my side.

***

I was reaching for the box of handles when I heard Phasma's raspy voice coming from behind. He couldn't have been more than five feet away.

"Where do you think you're going?" Phasma asked.

I cringed as I tried to decide whether or not I should turn around, but in the end it was inevitable. So I turned around to face the figure who had been haunting me ever since my mother passed away. It was as though her passing had opened the floodgates of hell.

I knew instinctively that I wasn't fighting just Phasma. I was battling fear, rage, struggling against a stew of negative feelings and emotions that had dominated my very being for a long time.

"You know what? It's time for us to settle this," I said.

"As you wish," Phasma replied. "You'll pay for your trespassing."

"I won't let you push me or anyone else around anymore," I said as Phasma stood there staring at me with his cold eyes.

"It's about time you stopped running from your destiny," Phasma finally replied.

"Don't worry. I'm not running anymore. I'll make a deal with you. Whatever happens, you leave my friends and family alone," I said.

"They don't matter," Phasma replied.

"I beg to differ. They matter much more than you could ever imagine," I replied, looking around for anything I could use to defend myself.

"We're more alike than you know," Phasma replied.

"I'm nothing like you!" I yelled.

"You're in denial, but it doesn't matter," said Phasma.

There was nothing I could use to defend myself.

In a way, I felt like simply giving up. But in the end, I decided that if I was going to die, I would die fighting. Even if I had to do it with my bare hands.

"You're a fool if you think there is any hope left," Phasma continued.

"That's the only thing I have left, and not you or anyone else can take it away from me," I replied.

"Hope is nothing but an illusion. Just something to keep fools afloat until the last second, until the end," Phasma replied with a horrifying laugh.

"Then I guess I'll die a fool. Speaking of which, why haven't you killed me yet?" I said.

"The moment had to be right," replied Phasma.

Cornered, I did the only thing I could: I ran as fast as my legs would take me, figuring that with any luck I would get to the zip line before Phasma had a chance to stop me.

As I turned around and started my desperate run, I felt his claws hit my back and push me to the ground. My face slid across the wooden platform and I felt each splinter as they punctured me. There was little I could do besides scream. My face burned, and my skin felt like it was being ripped off.

My body came to a stop several yards away, but I still felt as though his claws were digging deep inside my back. The pain made me nauseated and weak. When I tried to get up, the pain only intensified.

When I finally managed to get up, Phasma pushed me back onto the ground.

"Get off me!" I screamed with all the strength I had left.

I was wheezing, and the pain was almost intolerable. I became convinced that Phasma was probably right after all: the end was near. A part of me said I should just stop fighting the inevitable, because it would make the permanent transition to the world of the dead easier. I knew then that death was unavoidable, and most of all, that death wasn't real. There *was* life on the other side, I had seen it, touched it, felt it, and most important of all, lived it. Death was simply a transition, an inevitable change that everyone would have to endure sooner or later. The other part of me argued that I shouldn't give up. That I should never give up, even when everything seemed lost and hopeless.

At that moment, I remembered what my mother used to tell me when I was a child. In fact, I heard her voice saying, "Mark, as long as you follow your heart, everything will work out just fine. Don't let anyone tell you otherwise. You're a good person, but you need to truly believe that."

Suddenly the pain didn't bother me anymore. I was busy trying to figure out where I had heard that recently. *No... it couldn't have been her,* I thought. But I wasn't mistaken. It had to be her. Had she been right under my nose all this time? Had I been too busy to see her?

I was sure of it. I had spoken with my mother on several occasions; I just hadn't realized it was her. She looked so different yet familiar. I'd finally figured out where my feeling of knowing Mrs. Barnes came from. She was... I paused for a second. She was my mother. I could hardly believe I actually found her. How could I not have realized this sooner? My mother always told me she wanted to be a librarian when she was growing up.

"Let me go! I have to see my mother. She's here," I yelled at Phasma. As I struggled, the pain became unbearable.

"It's too late for you," said Phasma as he forced his claws deeper into my back.

"No, you're wrong! It's never too late. And hope is never an illusion. I know that now. Get off me!" I demanded.

For years, I had hoped to see my mother again, and now that I'd finally realized I had, I was bound to the floor without anything to defend myself with. I clung to life by a single thread of hope. At least my friends were safe.

"Get off him!" said a fast-approaching voice.

I tried to see who it was, but I couldn't.

"I said get the hell off him now!" Jonas said, sounding much closer.

The voice was definitely Jonas's, but I had never heard him sound so courageous or determined.

Suddenly, I felt Phasma's claws being pulled out of my back. I turned around and noticed that Phasma was no longer on the platform with me.

Puzzled, I looked around, only to find the platform deserted. I hadn't realized at first that help had come from above, at least not until I saw Spark's gigantic shadow. As he flew over my head, the bright and sunny day turned into darkness.

Jonas, Carla, and Nyx were riding Spark. His wingspan was insanely large. The only resemblance to that little scared dragon I'd seen just moments before was the color of his scales and his face.

"Oh my God!" I screamed as they took another pass over me. They flew so low that the wind from Spark's wings kept me grounded. But Spark wasn't just flying around for show: Phasma was dangling unconscious from his claws. Apparently, Spark had grabbed Phasma and taken him into the air. The impact must have knocked Phasma out.

Unfortunately, the effect was temporary. I noticed that Phasma was coming to his senses.

Scared, I did the only thing I could think of: I ran and grabbed a zip line handle and threw my body forward with all the strength I had left, aiming for the narrow zip line. It was the scariest thing I had ever done in my life. I almost regretted jumping once I was in the air and it looked like I would miss the line. I was relieved when I finally heard the clicking noise the handle made as it connected to the zip line. The fact that I made it to the zip line was a miracle; I had jumped from several feet away.

I looked back and found Phasma flying right behind me. As he flew, his body left behind a dusty, thick, and black trail. Wherever he flew, darkness took over. Dayside was turning into Nightside.

I was sliding so fast and the ride down was so bumpy that I had trouble holding on to the handle bar with my left hand. The pain in my back came back. Phasma must have left a wide hole in my back that affected my ability to hold the handle bar.

I glanced back again. Phasma was much closer than I'd hoped. Right behind him were my friends, holding onto Spark's back for dear life. *Whose idea was this? Certainly not Jonas's.*

Suddenly, I felt a searing pain on my left side. Phasma had shot me with some sort of dark energy beam.

I was about to get hit by another beam when Spark flew in front of Phasma's line of sight and took the hit on his right wing. He screeched with pain and tumbled through the air. I saw my friends' faces change to complete desperation.

It hurt too much to continue to hold with both hands, so I let my left hand go and hoped that I could keep holding on with my right.

Phasma was preparing to shoot a potentially fatal energy beam.

I was faced with a choice. I was either going to get hit and fall to the ground, or I could simply let go and hope to find a soft landing spot. I didn't dare to look below me to find out how far away the ground was.

I needed to follow my heart and just trust that everything would work out the way it was supposed to. For someone who didn't believe in destiny, I found myself trusting it with my life.

I waited as long as I could; I waited until his energy beam was coming toward me, and then I just let go.

All my fears and doubts came to the surface as soon as I felt my fingers let go of the handle bar. I had expected the whole thing to be quick. But it wasn't. At first my heart seemed to stop beating, and then I began to fall. As the adrenaline rushed through my body, my heart felt like a tremendous jolt of electricity had jump-started it.

Deep down I knew that one way or another, my life would be changed forever. I hoped I would survive the fall and that I would be able to get back to my normal life, knowing that my mother was well and not lost forever in the unknown, or worse, into nothingness.

I surrendered to my destiny. I'd put my trust not only on what my mother had taught me but also in her.

Even though I didn't dare to look down as I fell, I knew that the ground was approaching fast. So I closed my eyes in a futile attempt to shield myself from the shock. As I did, memories started playing behind my closed eyelids, and again my life flashed by. I saw every smile I'd had since I was a child, every dream, every hope and wish. But they flew by too fast for me to fully appreciate them. I stared as all my childhood illusions, aspirations, and delusions were presented to me without any censor or filter.

I saw my own birth, my first steps, my first day of school, my first kiss—which happened sort of by accident with Carla when I was eight; how could I have forgotten that? All in all, it had been a good life, even though I had wasted most of it blaming everyone and myself for my mother's death. I'd blamed God, the cosmos, my dad, her job, and myself—but at last I realized that I was wrong.

Call it what you will: God, creator, unconsciousness, evolution, or whatever else you can think of, "It" knows exactly what we need in our lives. The path we are given is the best path we can hope to walk. I knew that now; it all made perfect sense. As I fell to my death, all the pieces were falling into place.

It wasn't that I had given up on life. I had finally given up fighting for a *different* life, the life I believed I deserved.

At last, I made peace with destiny. Destiny and I were finally and fatally in sync. I surrendered to the feeling of weightlessness feeling, to my destiny. I was ready to take the next step.

When everything seemed lost, and all I had left were seconds, I felt a warm and soothing arm grab me and carefully slow my fall. My back touched the grass gently.

I opened my eyes and saw the most amazing sight. It must have been an angel sent to receive me into the steps of heaven. It had to be.

"I know what you're thinking, son, but you're wrong. It's not yet your time," said Mrs. Barnes as she gradually became younger.

"You're… my mother. Why didn't you say anything before?" I asked, crying tears of joy. I felt relieved, happy, and betrayed all at the same time.

"I couldn't, son. You needed to free yourself before you could see things clearly," my mother said as she tended to my wounds. The pain ceased almost immediately as the light emitting from her hands quickly healed my broken body.

"My friends: are they okay?" I asked as I tried to get up, but I couldn't.

"I'm not done with you!" said Phasma loudly from above us.

"Phasma, it is over! I'm not going to let you create any more havoc," my mother said.

"You can't stop me. One way or another, I'll win," Phasma said as he charged toward us. I tried to move again, but it was useless. Even though Phasma was still threatening me, I felt content. I had finally been able to see my mother again, and there was nothing more that I wished for.

"You leave my friends alone!" Nyx yelled as she conjured up a deadly fire bolt from her bare hands and launched it toward Phasma. The fire ignited his cloak and spread quickly. Within a few seconds, he was engulfed in bright red and blue flames.

His rather large body hit the ground with a loud, vibrating thud.

I thought he might be dead, but much to my surprise, Phasma got up slowly and limped toward me while my mother stood between us.

"Phasma, my son, you need to let your rage go; your brother has," my mother said.

"I just want what's rightfully mine," said Phasma as he struggled to breathe.

"What you want is revenge, and that I cannot let you have," my mother said, still standing between us.

"Then you'll pay as well," said Phasma as he accelerated toward my mother and me.

"Enough!" Nyx said as her body burst into flames. Taking the shape of a massive fireball, she flew toward Phasma.

As they collided, a huge thunderclap could be heard. A shockwave of heat rushed past us, along with a deafening scream and a boom.

Jonas had tried to stop Nyx, but she wouldn't listen. He even attempted to hold her back, but Carla held him.

I could see Jonas's desperation as he watched from afar while the girl he loved disappeared in a fierce explosion. I felt responsible.

"It's not your fault, Mark. You need to stop blaming yourself. You don't know how many times I wanted to tell you that. I've been there your whole life, but you couldn't see me. When you did manage to hear me, you would disregard it as being your intuition or your own inner voice. I saw you cry, and I did the only thing I could do, which was cry with you. Son, trust me when I say this. I missed you so much," my mother said as tears filled her eyes.

"I… missed you too," I struggled to say, crying as I had never cried before. Her hug only made me sob louder. I held her tight, tighter than I had ever held anyone before. I didn't want to let go because I was afraid I wouldn't have another opportunity.

"Are you all right?" Carla asked when she saw that Phasma was gone and it was safe for them to approach us.

"I'm fine, but I don't know about Nyx. Have you seen her?" I asked. I still couldn't move around to look at the area.

I heard Nyx's sisters crying and hugging each other in the background, so I figured the news wasn't good.

"I'm so sorry—" I was saying when Carla interrupted.

"Don't you dare apologize. You were right the whole time. You found your mother," Carla said, wiping my tears away.

"Oh, Carla and Jonas, I wanted to thank you for being there for Mark, especially just after my death. It was a very hard time for all of us, and I appreciated your help. I have visited and looked after you as much as I could. You both have a very special place in my heart," my mother said as we all hugged and cried together.

"Jonas, have faith, darling," my mother said.

"Hey! Save some for me, will you?" said Nyx from the other side of the clearing.

"Nyx?" Jonas said, breaking up our group hug.

"Sis! You're well," said Twil as they ran toward each other.

"I'm a bit sore, but otherwise I'm fine," said Nyx as she hugged her sisters first and then gave Jonas a big hug. None of us could have guessed that she was going to give him a kiss. But she did.

"Eeew, that's disgusting," Carla said.

"Oh no, what about Spark?" I said as I tried again to get up, somewhat more successfully.

I saw Spark lying in a large pool of water. I made my way over as fast as I could, which wasn't very fast.

When I got close to Spark, I dropped to my knees.

"How are you doing, big boy?" I asked. I didn't see any reaction on his part, although I could see his chest move up and down slowly.

"What happened? How did he get so big?" I asked Dr. Rainer as he placed some herbs on Spark's wounds.

"When we got down to the Everwell, we waited for you. When you didn't show up, we figured that Phasma must have gotten to you while you were still up there. That left us no choice but to let Spark drink some of the Everwell water. The water contains a certain combination of metals and minerals that allows him to grow extremely fast, which worked a bit too well. Thankfully, he was able to help save you from Phasma. However, now his system is going into shock. There isn't anything else I can do for him," Dr. Rainer said while his eyes filled with tears.

"There is one thing we can try, but we'll need Nyx's help," my mother said.

"Dr. Rainer, may I remove those herbs?" my mother asked.

"Certainly, though I don't know how that would help," replied Dr. Rainer.

My mother proceeded to remove all the herbs from Spark's wound, leaving the basketball-sized hole exposed. She then started to fill the wound with water from the Everwell.

"Nyx, as soon as the wound is completely filled, I need you to heat it up. You need to make it as hot as you can," my mother ordered, waving for us to move back.

When the wound was filled with clear water from the Everwell, Nyx's hands started to glow hot and soon the water began to boil.

"Hotter. Don't worry about me, you can't hurt me," my mother said as Nyx's body glowed red-hot. The heat got so intense that I had no choice but to move back even further. Even standing far away, we started to sweat.

After a few seconds, black steam began to come out of the wound site. Nyx returned to her normal body temperature and color, which allowed us to approach Spark again. Much to our surprise, the wound was completely healed. In place of the huge hole, there was only a scar.

Spark's breathing normalized, and he got up slowly.

"Welcome back, Spark, and thanks for saving my life, buddy. I owe you one," I said, giving him a hug. Well, I meant to hug him, but all that I could do was hug one of his legs.

"That's a remarkable recovery," said Dr. Rainer.

***

"What happened to Phasma?" Jonas asked.

"I… don't know. Once we collided, he just seemed to disintegrate into nothingness. I don't remember anything after that, I only remember waking up a few moments later on the grass," Nyx replied.

"I can't sense him anymore," I said.

"That's because the hate and rage that used to unite you and Phasma is gone. It was broken when you decided to let go of your anger," my mother said.

"Wow, what a ride," Carla said as she hugged Jonas, and then gave me an extra-long hug. She seemed relieved.

"Son, I'll need you to be strong, even stronger than before, because the time has come for you to return to Earth. The connection with your physical bodies is growing weaker. But rest assured that I'll always be watching over you and that you have plenty of people who love and care about you on both sides of life," she said as my eyes filled with tears. I broke down crying on her shoulder. I had known the time for us to part ways would eventually come, but I had no idea it was so soon.

"I don't want to leave you. I just found you," I said. "I wanted to stay in Threshold and live the rest of my life in this amazing world."

"I know, but trust me, it's for the best. One day you will join me here or somewhere else, but for now you have a destiny to fulfill. You still have a lot to learn and a lot more to teach. If you just follow your heart, you'll be fine. Always remember that, my son," my mother said as tears rolled down her face. I could tell she was trying very hard to be strong.

"Mark, my dear. Do you think you can deliver a message to your dad from me?" she asked, smiling as she placed both palms on my face and looked me closely in the eye.

"Anything you need, Mom," I replied.

"Good, then please tell him that it's okay for him to live life and even find someone to keep him company. Tell him that, somehow, I knew that my time with you was going to be short, and that I left him a letter hidden safely behind our wedding picture. Please tell him that besides the day you were born, our wedding day was the best day of my life. Oh, and tell him that I'll be here waiting for him. And that I hope he will have fixed the porch before that time comes," my mother said, smiling as her eyes grew watery and red.

"I'll tell him. I'll miss you, Mom," I said. I looked at my mother first and then around at all the new friends I had made in Threshold. Every one of them would live forever in my memory: Dr. Rainer, Nyx, Teil, and Twil, and Spark.

"What about Spark, is he going to be okay?" I asked.

"I'll take good care of him while you're away. Fortunately he didn't drink too much Everwell water, so he should be back to his normal size in a bit. But if he isn't, I'll send him over to Earth so you can take care of him," Dr. Rainer said, trying to lighten up the mood.

"So how do we get back?" Jonas asked.

"All you have to do is think about your physical bodies lying in bed," my mother said.

As soon as she said that, Jonas vanished from sight.

"He wasted no time," said Carla, laughing.

"Shall we go together?" I asked, afraid that if I was the last to leave, I wouldn't go.

"Sure," Carla replied, offering me her hand.

I couldn't help feeling very sad as I prepared to leave Threshold.

I waved at everyone, and they waved back at us. As soon as I felt Carla's hand, a surge of electricity flowed through my body. The last thing I saw of Threshold was my teary mother waving good-bye to me, and then everything went dark.

***

I opened my eyes and took a deep breath of fresh air. The first thing I saw was Carla lying on the mattress beside my bed. Even though everything was blurry and it was morning, she looked gorgeous.

The sun invaded parts of my room; the sky was deep blue and clear.

I got up slowly and sat at my desk, trying to process everything that had happened to us. I was forgetting details of the experience at an alarming rate, so I started writing about it. I wasn't sure if everything had really happened or if it all had been just a weird dream, but my heart told me it was true.

I had only one way of knowing for sure, but I would have to wait for Jonas and Carla to wake up before we could confirm that we'd had an out-of-body experience and traveled the whole night.

I was typing at the computer for a while when I heard Carla's sweet voice.

"Good morning," Carla said, stretching her arms and twisting her hands in the air.

"Good morning. How did you sleep?" I asked, not wanting to ask her about Threshold directly.

"Like a rock," Carla replied, sending chills down my spine.

What did she mean, like a rock? I wondered. Yet I couldn't bring myself to ask her about it. I wished Jonas was awake because he would definitely ask us what happened during the night. I could always count on Jonas to ask the questions that nobody else seemed to have the courage or will to ask.

"What time is it?" asked Carla, searching for a clock.

"It's 6:46 a.m.," I replied, looking at the computer task-bar clock.

"What are you doing on the computer so early?" Carla asked as she got up to go to the restroom.

"Writing a book," I replied, joking.

"What's it about?" Carla said from the restroom.

Before I could even reply, she continued, "Let me guess, a group of friends proceed to have an out-of-body experience, and together they fight and defeat a nefarious creature named Phasma. Am I right?" Carla smiled as she opened the restroom door.

"Don't look so surprised. I was there, remember?" she said.

"That can mean only one thing. It was real," I said, awestruck and very happy.

"I wonder if Jonas will remember," said Carla.

"I was starting to forget, so I figured it was best to write down what I could remember," I replied, still typing.

"Should I wake Jonas up? My mom and dad should be home soon. The roads are probably clear by now," Carla said as she looked out the window and then headed for the couch to shake Jonas awake.

"Wake up. Mom and Dad will be home soon," Carla said as Jonas mumbled something then turned over on his side and continued to sleep.

"Jonas, come on. It's almost 7 a.m.," Carla said.

"Dad isn't going to drive home this early on a Sunday morning," Jonas mumbled before he closed his eyes again.

"Still, we need to get home. Get up!" yelled Carla, losing her patience.

"Fine, but I'm having breakfast first," said Jonas as he sat up on the couch in his hideous pajamas. "Wow, I haven't slept so well in years, which is surprising, considering that I slept on the couch. You, my friend, have the most comfortable couch in the world. So, what do we have for breakfast?" Jonas yawned.

"Not much, just some cereal and toast. We haven't been to the store in a while," I said.

"Cereal and toast sounds great, actually," Carla replied as she made the bed she had slept on.

We didn't say anything about Threshold until we were all sitting at the kitchen table.

"That was insane. Do you guys remember what happened?" Jonas asked.

"Of course. How could I forget?" I said, beaming.

"I'm so happy you got to see her again," Carla said, squeezing my hand discreetly.

"Well, we don't know for sure if it really happened, or if it's just a shared dream," I said cautiously.

"Nope, but we can find out. What did you guys see in each room?" said Carla as she looked for a pen. "I'll write it down just to make sure we have the correct info."

"Okay, shall we start with the basement?" I asked.

"Sure, sounds good to me," replied Jonas.

"Okay, so what do you two remember about the note in the basement?" asked Carla with pen and paper at hand.

"That one is easy. It was Jonas's locker combination," I replied quickly.

"More specifically, it was 9-24-2, and it was on top of the pool table," added Carla.

"Yep, that's right on the money," replied Jonas.

"Should we go and check?" Carla asked.

"We can, after we write them all down," I replied with my heart about to jump out of my throat.

"The next experiment is mine. What do you remember of the guest room?" Carla asked, ready to write down our answers.

"There was a yellow flower," offered Jonas proudly.

"It was a yellow rose carefully placed in an intricate vase, but instead of the drawing we saw the real flower as you had envisioned at the time of the drawing," I replied.

"Also correct, two down. One more to go," said Carla.

"Well, let's see if you guys remember this next one. Personally, I have no doubt in my mind that it really happened," I said, probably beaming.

"I recall that in your dad's office, we found a piece of paper with the word 'Mom' written on it," replied Carla.

"I recall a boring room with the same note," added Jonas, joking.

"Well, that does it, at least for me. I have personal confirmation that we were all out of our bodies last night," I said proudly. "I did it. I saw my mother again, after all those years of rage, fear, and disbelief. I can't believe it. I feel so much better. I mean, I still miss her, but at least now I know she's fine. It wasn't my fault that she passed away."

"Oh my God, that's amazing. Can you imagine the possibilities? I want to visit Cairo while astral travelling." said Carla.

We quickly finished our breakfast and proceeded to each of the rooms to verify our notes, and sure enough they were exactly as we had seen them the night before, with the only exception being Carla's drawing of a yellow rose, that we had seen as the real rose.

"So, are you going to tell your dad?" Jonas asked.

"I will. I think that it's about time I have a good talk with him."

I shook Jonas's hand and said, "See you later, my friend."

After Jonas left the room, I held Carla's hand and caressed it gently for a second as I tried to decide if I should tell her how much she meant to me. Unfortunately, I didn't have the courage, and instead I just said, "Thank you very much for everything. I couldn't have done it without you. I don't even know if I would be here if it wasn't for you."

That was the closest I'd gotten to telling her that I loved her.

"I'm glad everything worked out great and that you got to see your mother again. See you later?"

"Without a doubt," I replied.

Carla picked up her backpack and left, still in her pajamas. She rushed across the street—just in time too, because not five minutes passed before I heard a car pull into the driveway.

I looked out the window and saw that my dad was home. It was the first time in years that I'd seen my dad up that early on a Sunday morning.

"Good morning," he said, looking surprised to see me up and about that early.

"Morning, Dad. How did you sleep?" I asked, wondering how I was going to tell him everything that had happened.

Since I couldn't decide the best way to tell him, I pulled a Jonas on him.

"Dad, we need to have a serious talk," I said bluntly.

"What's wrong, son? Is it drugs?" he asked.

"No, Dad, as a matter of fact, nothing is really wrong, but I have to tell you something important," I replied.

"What happened?" my dad asked again, still looking worried.

"Dad, I know that you're an atheist and all, and I respect that, but I need you to know that as much as you're my role model, I can't share your disinterest for religions, because I believe… Dad, I guess what I'm trying to say is that I can't be an atheist like you because I believe in life after death. Not only that, I have irrefutable proof that life exists beyond death." I was afraid I would hurt his feelings, and that was the last thing that I wanted to do. But he needed to know the truth.

"What are you saying exactly, Son?" he asked after a minute or so of silence.

"There is no easy way to say this Dad, so I apologize in advance. I saw Mom last night. Not only last night, but for a few days now," I said fearing his reaction.

"Son, it can't be true, your mother is dead. You know she's been dead for many years. You'd better accept that. And it's really unhealthy to think otherwise," he replied.

"Listen, Dad, I know how this whole thing sounds, but regardless of your personal beliefs, are you willing to put them aside for a minute and let me explain? Do you want to know the truth? Do you want to know what happened to me?" I asked.

We exchanged looks for a few seconds before he took a deep breath.

"Son, I want to believe what you're telling me. Trust me, I really do, but it's very hard to accept. It goes against everything that I believe to be the truth. However, I'll listen because you're my son, and what you think matters most to me," he said.

We sat at the kitchen table, and I told him everything that had happened to me in the past few weeks. At times, he seemed like he might storm out of the room, while at other times he looked like he was about to cry. Yet he endured my whole story and sat there bravely, only interrupting me a couple of times to clear up a question or two.

"That's an amazing story, son, but I fail to see how that's anything other than a dream," he replied.

"Dad, I haven't told you the whole story yet. Jonas and Carla were also there. They slept here last night because their parents also got snowed in. They just left a few minutes ago, after we checked the results of an experiment we did. They also remember everything that happened last night in Threshold, and they too saw Mom," I explained.

He sat there, looking serious and thoughtful.

"Dad, I'm sorry if you're mad, I figured it was better to tell you everything," I said.

"Son, I'm not mad. If anything, I'm very proud of you. Your mother has taught you well. She used to say that if she could teach you only one thing, it would be to always follow your heart. I trust you, son. I know that you did what you thought was best in a bad situation, but as far as this out-of-body experience is concerned, perhaps it was only a shared dream," he explained.

"Dad, Mom wanted me to give you a message," I said with a knot in my throat and my eyes filled with tears.

"What message?" he asked as his lips shook. He was almost crying.

"Mom wanted me to tell you that it's okay for you to live your life fully and that you should find someone to keep you company," I said as he started to sob. "She also wanted me to tell you that she had a feeling her time with us would be short, so she wrote us a letter and hid it behind your wedding picture frame. She also said that apart from the day I was born, her wedding was the happiest day of her life. Oh, and before I forget, she told me to ask you to please fix the porch," I said as we looked at each other with tears in our eyes.

"I'm sorry for doubting you, son. I love you so much. You guys were my world. I'm sorry for letting you down after she passed away. I just missed her so much that it hurt," my dad said, sobbing.

"Dad, I love you too, and you don't have anything to be sorry for. Come. Let's go find her letter," I said as we stood in the kitchen, hugging and crying.

After we dried our tears, we went upstairs to find my mother's good-bye letter. We read it together, taking turns and crying some more. So many years had gone by since her passing, and only now we were able to properly mourn her.

I felt deeply blessed by the whole experience. Over the course of the next few weeks, our relationship slowly transformed. I wouldn't go so far as to say that my dad became an ex-atheist, but he tried hard to believe that the human soul is at the very least immortal.

In the meantime, I found solace knowing that my mother was watching over us and that one day we'd be together again.

THE END

The Guardian of Threshold
Coming Soon:

Dweller on the Threshold - YA
(Book Two of the *Threshold Series*)
July 2013
www.TheDwellerOnTheThreshold.com
www.ThresholdSeries.com

&

I Am Goblin - MG
(Book One of *I Am Chronicles*)
2013
www.TheIAmChronicles.com

For more of Book features visit us on:
www.TheGuardianOfThreshold.com

For news on current projects, progress and deadlines visit us on:
www.AAVolts.com

If you enjoyed this book please don't forget to leave a review on Amazon and Goodreads.

Sample Chapter:
Dweller on the Threshold

Threshold Series - Book Two
This is a work in progress and not a finished product.

Chapter One
The Cape

When I was first offered a summer job in my old flight school, I thought I was going to be flying all day long or something cool like that, not answering the phones, scheduling flying lessons for other people, and cleaning up the bathrooms. To top things off, I had a miserable week. Some disgusting kid threw up in the bathroom after a flying lesson. When I think about it, I can still smell the putrid vomit. I glance at the clock and realize that it's almost 1:00 a.m. surprisingly I don't feel tired, but since I have to fly tomorrow I force myself to get ready for bed.

I head toward the bathroom to take care of business for the night. I hold the toothbrush loosely with one hand while I manage to unscrew the toothpaste with the other. I spread a generous amount on it and start to brush my teeth.

After a good minute or so, I open the faucet and dip the toothbrush under the cool stream of water. I cup my hand and let it fill with water and rinse my mouth. When I lift my head to squish the water between my cheeks, for a second my heart stops. In the mirror, the most horrific figure stares at me icily. He's tall with a long neck. His eyes are piercing cold. He has gold hair with white highlights and matching eyebrows and his pale complexion reminds me of death itself.

Toothpaste-spiked water rushes from my nose and mouth, burning as it passes through my nostrils. Foamy water covers every-thing including the sink, the faucet, and the mirror. As the jolt of adrenaline hits my system, it gives me enough courage to clean up the mirror and take another look. Whatever it was, it's gone now. *Maybe it was just my mind playing tricks on me. I must be overtired.*

Shaking uncontrollably, I bolt out of the bathroom, banging the door behind me, and leap to my bed. I make sure to cover my body completely, that helps ease the shaking a bit.

For several minutes I lie there, eyes wide open staring at the closed bathroom door. Waiting for that creature to come after me.

What could he want with me? It wasn't my first encounter with the supernatural, but this is different. I didn't sense him like I had sensed Phasma. I simply saw him as though he was physically there. I saw, felt, and smelled his cold breath on my neck. His presence drained the room of warmth, of life.

Maybe I'm really going bat-shit-crazy as people said in school. It makes sense. Perhaps what I really need is the help of a good shrink. *Yeah, that's it; a good shrink should solve my problem.* The thought that I may be insane comforts me and eventually I feel myself slowly drifting to sleep. But instead of a quiet night's sleep, I'm immediately faced with the same creature, chasing me through the back alleys of the city. I glance back at him, with his long and threatening fangs right behind me.

It doesn't matter how fast I run. He inches closer and closer. I leap on a dumpster and over the wall, but that doesn't detain him.

I climb the fire-escape stairs and rush up toward the roof. Even before I reach the top I realize my mistake. I'm trapped on this roof, so I quickly scan my surroundings in search of an escape.

It doesn't take long for the mysterious creature to catch up to me. In an act of desperation I start running toward the building closest to the one I'm on. When I reach the edge, I leap at the last possible moment, thrusting my body forward. For a moment I feel weightless and think that I may just start flying like I did when I astral projected. But soon gravity takes hold of my feet and pulls me down. When I land on the edge of the other building, I almost fall backward.

I'm hopeful that I've managed to get away, but that doesn't detain him. The gap is no obstacle to him. He leaps in the air several feet higher than me as I desperately follow with my gaze. He lands right in front of me.

He stares me right in the face and thrusts something forward. At first I don't feel anything, then something warm and thick seems to drip from my body towards my hip and thighs. Although I can't see the size of the gash, there's too much blood spilling out. Next, the pain hits like a train. I fall on my knees and they too hurt as the rocks pierce my skin and chip my bones. A shock spreads through my body. I'm certain this is the end as my torso drops on the ground.

In a fit of rage the creature pushes my now limp body over the edge and I fall. Everything quickly fades to black. Suddenly—nothing, no pain, no fear. I still feel the sensation of falling but I'm too lost in my own thoughts to worry about it.

***

As I fall, I remember how much things have changed since I had my last astral projection. To begin with, I no longer seek danger; in fact I now have an unexplained aversion to it. Seven months ago, if anyone told me this would happen, I would have said they had lost their marbles.

Since my return from Threshold, the only thing that mildly interests me is flying, but even that pales in comparison to astral flying.

My life wasn't the only one that changed. Take my dad's life, for instance. He's still an atheist, but at least now he contemplates the possibility that life may exist after death, which is a huge improvement, compared to just a few months ago. Don't get me wrong, I won't be taking him into church anytime soon.

The best example of change is our home—once a pile of rubble on the verge of collapse, now the proud jewel of the neighborhood complete with a relatively fresh coat of paint, a shining new porch, and a new deck to boot. The only thing missing is a pool, something to do with living in New England, which apparently disqualifies me from having one. Arguing that summers in Boston are just as fierce as, say… Florida is useless.

One area of my life that didn't and may never improve is my love life. I'm still hopelessly in love with Carla. By the way, she managed to become even more beautiful, which only made revealing my love for her that much harder. If I ever get out of this predicament, I may ask her to the prom.

After Threshold even Jonas changed, he's more… mature is not really the right word to describe it, and I don't think it will ever be; perhaps the word understanding is better suited, not by much but it's noticeable.

If there's one thing that didn't change, that's high school. Well, except for the fact that everyone now thinks that I'm a short hop from bat-shit-crazy. In my defense, it wasn't my fault. To this day I don't know why Jonas decided to tell Wendy Hartwell about our astral travel into Threshold. I mean, I wasn't the most popular guy in school before but at least I was considered normal. Now even the unpopular crowd shy away from me. I guess it sort of worked in my favor, since I now spend a lot more time with Carla, but unfortunately it also means that I spend more time with Jonas as well.

I haven't seen my mother since my astral travels, not that I didn't try. I tried to astral project for months before I finally gave up.

The thought of my mother made me somehow conscious of the fact that I was asleep. *Wake up, dummy, it's just a nightmare.* I say to myself.

***

After repeating that several times, I finally wake up drenched in sweat.

A host of familiar sensations rushes through my body. My heart pumps in my chest so hard that it forcefully spreads my ribcage. My head pulses as the blood rushes through my neck and veins.

It's morning but the room still feels gloomy. I can hear the rain pounding outside. *I can't believe my nightmares are back, but what does it mean? Is Phasma back? It can't be, I saw Nyx destroy him. Maybe I'm truly insane.*

The adventure continues in Chapter 2. To get the full book visit us at: www.TheDwellerOnTheThreshold.com

www.ThresholdSeries.com

I AM
GOBLIN

A. A. VOLTS
BOOK ONE OF THE I AM CHRONICLES

Sample Chapter:
I Am Goblin
This is a work in progress and not a finished product.

Chapter One
Who Am I?

If you saw me in the streets of Boston, you wouldn't recognize me, of that I bet you 100 gold shiverings. You would never guess what I am and more importantly where I'm from.

You would think that at least my age you could guess, but you would most certainly be wrong. Appearances are a funny thing in my kind.

You see, I'm cursed. My curse is that everyone thinks that I'm ten, but I couldn't be. For, I have not a single tooth left, my hair is grizzly white—nearing baldness and if that weren't enough, the little hairs I have left resemble a Brillo pad. Granted, I'm as tall as a ten-year-old, but doesn't anyone see my battle scars? Or the green tinge of my skin? Surely, my long and pointy ears should be enough to make everyone run as though the world were coming to an end, but no. People just tell me how much I've grown since they last saw me and how cute I am.

At times, I wonder if I'm the one cursed or they are. All those people living their miserable lives, working for Monopoly money. Imagine that, a content life with just a smidgen of gold, sometimes just a trinket or two. How is that possible?

How rude of me, I didn't even introduce myself. I'm Clash. Goldblood is the last name. My family owns this city, well not technically, but in a sense. My mother is the school principal so she bosses everyone around. My father owns the biggest building in the city, you may have heard of it. It's called "The Prudential Building." Okay, okay you got me, he doesn't own it yet, but he manages it. Their jobs are so important that I have lost track of how many shiverings they bring home, and I don't normally lose track of such things. You don't believe me? I'll show you. Since I was born I've collected 6,278 gold shiverings and spent a whopping 37 shiverings.

I know, I splurged, but it was for a good cause. Ember needed my help. What was I supposed to do? Let her cry?

Sigh… I guess you still haven't figured out who I am, well, trust me, it's for the best. Anyway, she had lost her precious trinket and was inconsolable, I don't even know why; it wasn't even made of real gold. How do I know? I know gold when I see it, besides I get this unmistakable itchy feeling on the tip of my nose whenever I'm near it.

So, in a moment of insanity, I opened my super-secret safe and took out the 30 shiverings. It sort of worked. I mean, Ember stopped crying after I gave her another trinket. However, every time I remember that I spent 30 shiverings I feel like crying myself.

I wonder if you are ready to know who I am? First, promise not to tell anyone… Okay, I'll just assume you did.

Come closer… Okay, listen… I'm cursed to look like a regular boy, like any other ten-year-old. But, I'm not. Far from it, I'm really a—I'm a goblin… there, I said it.

My dad is a goblin too, but nobody knows that, not even himself. As far as my mother, well, I couldn't figure that out yet. I can never catch her near a mirror to check.

But, there is more. As if that wasn't enough. My dad's boss, Mr. Moneybags, is also not what he seems. Promise you won't laugh? Okay, don't tell anyone I said it, but he's a leprechaun.

That's right, a freaking leprechaun.

What's worse is that my father doesn't believe me. Imagine that, a goblin working for a leprechaun. That's wrong in so many ways that I can't even begin to describe, but for the sake of argument I'll try.

Everyone knows that goblins love gold—in fact I would even

say there is nothing we like more—and what do leprechauns love to steal? That's right, gold. I can tell you one thing for sure, no sleaze-ball leprechaun is coming anywhere near my shiverings. The reason Mr. Moneybags has so much money is because he stole our family's gold.

How else do you think Mr. Moneybags got that name? Not to mention that building. Even if it's the last thing I do, I'll see to it that the Prudential is returned to my family. Besides, that's the only way I can get this curse broken and assume my true goblin form.

Here is how I figure it happened; my family owned the Prudential for centuries. I assume that we lived on top in the penthouse, but maybe the penthouse was in the basement since it is closer to the super-secret-hidden-underground vault. On a rainy day Mr. Moneybags—well, back then he was called Mr. Nobags—rang the doorbell of 800 Boylston Street. My father's soft spot must have taken control over his actions and he probably offered Mr. Nobags a job. But little did he know that Mr. Nobags had a master plan and in an ultimate act of betrayal Mr. Nobags stole our family super-secret-hidden vault when my father trusted him with its super-secret location.

From that day forward, I suppose Mr. Nobags became Mr. Moneybags and my family was evicted from the Prudential. I can only assume that Mr. Moneybags offered my dad the manager's position so that he could keep a close eye on him and my father probably accepted the offer to do the same to Mr. Slimebal—Mr. Moneybags.

So now it's up to me to fix the mess that Mr. Moneybags caused.

I was finally in a position to execute my first plan of action. I was on my way to my new school.

It was called "Kids are People Elementary School" or something like that, I guess nobody told them that some kids aren't people but goblins. Maybe I should let them know that. Anyway, the reason I chose this particular school was because that's the school Mr. Moneybags's kids attended.

My second plan of action is to discover their names and befriend the little slime-balls. That shouldn't be too hard since I'm bringing my secret weapon, the reflectionator. What's a reflection-ator you asked? Well, to put it in terms your ungoblin mind can understand, let's just say it's… a mirror.

I doubted there would be many leprechauns in that one school. Just thinking the word leprechauns made me feel nauseated. To distract myself I looked outside the bus window, and as luck would have it, we happened to be passing right in front of the Prudential Building. Maybe it was a sign that my family was destined to own that building again.

Since the bus came to a complete stop in front of Dunkin' Donuts, I thought we were getting breakfast or something. But, I was wrong; the school was located just above the store.

As I went up the stairs to the office, Mrs. Buttkins greeted me with the most unnatural morning smile.

"You must be Clash, we've been expecting you."

"Hello," I said, unsure of what else to say.

"You'll love it here. We have music and poetry. Talking about that, here is your journal. We encourage every student to keep a diary. Follow me."

Mrs. Buttkins took me on a tour of the place. She showed me the library, the different classes, media rooms and bathroom. The whole grand tour took less than five minutes.

"Your teacher today will be Miss Robinson."

"Huh, excuse us, Miss Robinson. This is Clash, he'll be start-ing today."

"Oh hi, nice to meet you. Let me see… here you are, Clash Goldblood is it? Wow, what a fancy name. Please come in and have a seat."

I quickly scanned the classroom and among so many ugly human heads I spotted a single familiar face, Ember's… And as luck would have it, next to her was the only free seat in the whole class. It took me ten long steps to get to my seat. I know because I counted them. My face was beet red as everyone stopped doing whatever they were doing to stare at me.

I felt so out of place that I almost tripped on my own feet. Luckily, nobody seemed to notice, at least I hoped they didn't. I looked at Ember and she smiled at me. Somehow her smile was warming and comforting.

Miss Robinson was nice enough, but this school was nothing like my old public school. Everything and everyone seemed more… preppy. Even the subject matter seemed harder, but the teacher was more patient.

I couldn't wait to get started with my nefarious goblin plans. He was here, I could sense it. One of these innocent looking kids was a sleazy, slimy and greedy leprechaun.

Wait a minute… I thought. *All I have to do is look for someone wearing green,* I told myself.

As we were leaving for lunch I stayed behind pretending to arrange my things in my new desk while I looked for the slightest hint of green. Clearly, that wasn't my lucky day because everyone was wearing green, including myself. I couldn't believe my bad luck. *A leprechaun has to be behind all of this,* I thought.

Come to think of it, I remember my mother saying something about that day being a religious holiday of some sort, Saint… What was his name again…? Saint Patriots? No, I think it was… Saint Patrick's Day. Yep, that's what it was.

Well, there goes that plan. I told myself.

It didn't matter, sooner or later I would find the sleaze-ball, and then… well, better not spoil the surprise.

At lunch, I sat alone in the corner of the room. Ember kept looking at me and even gestured for me to sit with her and her friends, but I wasn't about to sit in the middle of a bunch of girls. Besides, I had other plans.

I would use the diary that Mrs. Buttkins gave me to write in detail my master plan. Hopefully, it would be useful to another goblin one day. After all, my family couldn't be the only one that was affected by the curse.

Too many people were staring at me during lunch for me to use the reflectionator properly. I did manage to take a peek or two.

I can tell you that the brunette twins (Margie and Marta) are in fact trolls. No. Not that kind of troll. They're the school bullies. They seemed to terrorize everyone who stood in their way.

But, if it's trolls that you want, trolls you shall have. Taters, the poor clumsy kid no one seemed to care about, was a real troll. Six foot tall and about 300 pounds, to anyone with a reflectionator. But, to everyone else, he looked like a regular kid.

Should I let him know that I know? I wondered. How would that conversation play out? *Hey, I'm Clash your friendly goblin. By the way, I know you're a troll. Do you want to be my friend?* I didn't think that would be wise. Besides, I didn't even know the history between goblins and trolls. We could be mortal enemies for all I knew.

Nah, I wasn't there to make friends or to play nice. I was there for a single reason… to get the Prudential back for my family.

How was I going to accomplish that, you asked? Well, you will see in due time, but know this, once I find the slime-ball, he'll regret having a leprechaun for a father.

"What's that?" Taters asked as he walked toward me.

"What?" I replied.

"That thing you're trying to hide."

"Oh… It is personal," I said closing my backpack.

"It's a toy, isn't it?"

"No, it's not, I assure you."

"Fine, don't show me. I don't care anyway, I have lots of other friends to play with," said Taters.

I must not be a very good goblin because my heart ached seeing Taters's disappointed look.

"Wait!" I said, already regretting it. "You want to see what it is?" I said carefully opening my backpack. "Here, I'll show you."

"Wow, that is cool. What does it do?" Taters asked.

"It's a reflectionator. What I'm about to tell you must stay between us… nobody else must know the truth."

"What is it?"

"I know what you are," I began, and Taters turned all shades of purple.

"I don't know what you're talking about. Oh, look at the time. I must go."

"It's okay, don't worry, I won't tell anyone," I assured him.

"I really don't know what you're talking about," Taters said nervously.

"You're a troll," I said a bit louder than I should have.

"What…?" said Taters looking around. "Snaps, I guess there's no point in denying it. You can't tell anyone ever. Promise?"

"I promise."

"How did you know?"

"I'll show you. Here, look through it."

"No way! Is that a trog?"

"It sure seems like one."

"How many of us are there?" asked Taters.

"From what I have seen, the humans outnumber us by five to one."

"I wish I was one of those five."

"Not me, I can't stand looking human. The ears are too small, and don't even get me started on the nose. Why do you want to be human anyway?"

"I think people can sense that I'm a troll, that's probably the reason I don't have any friends."

The human in me flourished and spoke before I could think things through.

"I'll be your friend." I almost felt like punching myself. *What was I thinking?* I wondered. I don't need friends. All I needed was to get back what was rightfully mine. I needed the Prudential.

Taters's face lit up as he said, "Great, we'll be best friends."

"Oh, look at the time. Class is about to start," I said, glad to have an excuse to leave before things got too… awkward.

The afternoon was uneventful, I almost fell asleep a couple of times. I loved reading but it depended on the subject, and the book of the day wasn't very interesting.

If only I could walk downstairs and get myself a cup of coffee from Dunkin' Donuts. Our classroom was right above it and the fresh brewed coffee smell inundated the class.

In hopes that time would pass more quickly, I stalked the clock. Unfortunately the opposite happened. In a way it was good, because I had time to plan my next move.

If I planned everything just right, I would be able to avoid getting on the bus. That way I could walk to the Prudential, sneak in and do some investigating, all before my parents got home from work.

I wished it didn't have to be that way, but even though my father was the manager, I was still considered *'persona non grata'* (an unwelcome person) as far as the security guards and Mr. Moneybags were concerned. It may have something to do with my grabbing Mr. Moneybags's leg and not letting go, when I was much younger—last year.

The plan was to sneak in by the Prudential service entrance. I just had to be inside long enough to smell where the gold was hidden.

As we were leaving school for the day, I managed to sneak inside the 7-Eleven convenience store.

"Hey, Clash. Aren't you taking the bus?" asked Taters.

"Shh. No, I have some things I need to do."

"If you're sneaking out, I want in," said Taters.

I didn't want to sound mean, especially since he was so happy, but I had to move forward with my plan and Taters wasn't in it.

"Sorry, you can't."

"Why not?"

"Because, I have to follow the plan and you're not in it," I replied.

"Where are you going anyway?"

"I'm sneaking into the Prudential building," I replied.

"Well, that settles it. I'm going that way anyway. Besides, if you don't let me come, I'll tell the Safety Patrol that you're trying to sneak out."

"Fine, but I won't be responsible for you," I replied, as I paid for my bag of chips.

"I can take care of myself," replied Taters.

By the time we left 7-Eleven, the bus was gone and so were the Safety Patrol kids.

"What are we doing there?" Taters asked as we walked at a brisk pace.

"I have to find something. Something that used to be in my family."

"Can you imagine what people would say if they saw us walking in our true form?" Taters asked. "A troll and a goblin, what a combination."

I didn't tell him that if I had my way, that day would come. I thought it was best to keep that from him for the time being.

"I can't even imagine," I said. His question made me think about it. Would they run from us? Accept us? Perhaps they would hunt us.

Only time would tell. Deep down I knew that day would come, I just didn't know when.

"If there was ever a war between the humans and us, what side would you choose?" I asked.

"I don't think I could," replied Taters. There was something strange about Taters. I couldn't put my finger on what exactly, but the way he looked at everything as though he was longing for attention. I had the impression that Taters was a very lonely kid.

"Here, this way," said Taters.

"No, we are going through the service entrance," I replied.

"You'll never make it past security that way."

"I have a plan," I said.

"Unless you can turn invisible, that won't help you. Trust me, I know the way," Taters insisted and started to walk toward the underground parking garage.

I followed close behind him. After a couple hundred feet or so I noticed the security cameras.

"This isn't going to work, security will be all over us."

"Don't worry about it, just follow my lead," said Taters. I was sure that any minute we would be caught and I really wasn't looking forward to being grounded yet again. But it served me right. That's what I get for not following the plan and for listening to my lower human tendencies.

"I'm telling you, we should've followed the plan."

"What's up with you and all this planning business?" asked Taters.

"My dad always tells me that I need to plan for the future, if I want things to work out."

"I don't think that includes planning to sneak into high security buildings," said Taters, laughing.

He was probably right. In any case, it couldn't hurt to be prepared.

"A car is coming. Hide," said Taters as he ran behind an oversized SUV.

Uncertain of where to hide myself, I followed him.

"That was close," I said. "Great, here comes security. How do you suppose we get past them?"

"See that door straight across?" Taters asked.

"That's no use, we need a code to enter it," I replied. My heart raced as security got closer.

The adventure continues in Chapter 2. To get the full book visit us at: www.AAVolts.com/I-am-Goblin.

"I Am Goblin," **is the first book of the new middle-grade series** *"I Am Chronicles,"* **which is scheduled to be released in 2013**.